OUT OF CALABRIA

$\rhd\!\!-\!\!\!\bullet\!\!-\!\!\!\bullet\!\!-\!\!\!\diamond\!\!-\!\!\!\bullet\!\!-\!\!\!\bullet\!\!-\!\!\!\lhd$

By Peter Chiarella

Trafford
PUBLISHING™

Also by Peter Chiarella
Calabrian Tales

Order this book online at www.trafford.com/07-1751
or email orders@trafford.com

Most Trafford titles are also available at major online book retailers.

Note for Librarians: A cataloguing record for this book is available from Library and Archives
Canada at www.collectionscanada.ca/amicus/index-e.html

Printed in Victoria, BC, Canada.

ISBN: 978-1-4251-4218-6

*We at Trafford believe that it is the responsibility of us all, as both individuals and corporations,
to make choices that are environmentally and socially sound. You, in turn, are supporting this
responsible conduct each time you purchase a Trafford book, or make use of our publishing services.
To find out how you are helping, please visit www.trafford.com/responsiblepublishing.html*

*Our mission is to efficiently provide the world's finest, most comprehensive book publishing service,
enabling every author to experience success. To find out how to publish your book, your way, and
have it available worldwide, visit us online at www.trafford.com/10510*

 www.trafford.com

North America & international
toll-free: 1 888 232 4444 (USA & Canada)
phone: 250 383 6864 ♦ fax: 250 383 6804 ♦ email: info@trafford.com

The United Kingdom & Europe
phone: +44 (0)1865 722 113 ♦ local rate: 0845 230 9601
facsimile: +44 (0)1865 722 868 ♦ email: info.uk@trafford.com

10 9 8 7 6 5 4 3 2

Dedication

To my mother, Catherine Zinzi-Chiarella, who was my foremost beacon of inspiration and who, long ago, convinced me that I could accomplish whatever I set out to do.

Acknowledgments

My thanks go once again to my brother, Anthony, and his wife, Marie, who labored to add substance and style to this book and whose editorial work is without parallel in my experience. As in the past, my brother's remembrances of the family stories on which this book is based were invaluable. My sister-in-law continued to add inspiration and critique to my writing and to guide me in the process. I am also grateful to Anthony Kilgallin, an accomplished author who has permitted me to draw endlessly on his experience and talent; and to Dr. Joe Sabella who gave generously of his time and skill to edit. And, I thank my partner in life, Frances Marie, for encouraging me and allowing me the time and space needed to create this book.

Contents

Prologue

There is an abiding quality to the people of Calabria that was perhaps infused into the culture of the region centuries before the birth of Christ. The toe of the Italian peninsula known as Calabria was first settled by the ancient Greeks. Calabria was part of *Magna Graecia* in the fourth, fifth and sixth centuries BC, when it enjoyed the most prosperous times in its history. The Romans conquered the region in the third century BC and for more than two millennia thereafter, the locals were dominated by a succession of conquerors that included the Saracens, the Normans, the Austrians and the Spanish. Unlike the Greeks, these latecomers treated Calabrians as possessions, to be used for their own enrichment. Even the Risorgimento, Italy's war of unification fought between 1860 and 1870, could not break the yoke of domination. The new King considered Calabria a wild and unsettled addendum to an otherwise cultured nation, and had little appetite to develop the region. Even the Holy See entered into the equation of oppression, excommunicating those who fought in the Risorgimento, as Church interests conflicted with the desire of the nation to unify. Civil uprisings flew in the face of the occupying forces, Europe's most powerful influences of the time: Austria, Spain and Holy Mother Church. And, despite the valiant participation by Calabrian men in the ensuing war of liberation, little changed for them afterwards. The result was that most Calabrians held to themselves abidingly and focused on family survival and fundamental spiritual beliefs.

Notwithstanding the huge advances in living standards for Italian Northerners and most other Europeans by the late nineteenth century, the vast majority of Calabrians lived in poverty. Despite the huge bounty that they produced as farm hands, sharecroppers and fishermen, the system was so designed to perpetuate privation among the peasant class, due in no small measure to absentee landlords from the North. Emigrating seemed the only route to advancement. Lovely mountain country, sparkling seas and the warm culture of the ordinary people made Calabria a difficult place to abandon. Yet, huge percentages of the populace emigrated from Calabria between 1860 and 1920, bound mostly for the United States. There, they worked as menial laborers and were often harshly viewed as a plentiful source of cheap labor competing against established locals. Mostly, they desperately missed the old country and many did return, but the most tenacious remained and became part of the landscape of America. From out of Calabria came a rush of immigrants anxious to improve their lot and to provide opportunity for their progeny. In their wake came the stories of difficult separations from family, terrible conditions in the fabled havens of the Americas and, occasionally, success found on a foreign shore.

Out of Calabria is the story of a privileged Calabrian family that emerged from poverty by a circumstance of war and the unswerving fortitude of one man; and of how the young women of his family refused to bend to the mores and traditions of the times, pitting them against their social order and their own father. The doggedness of their pursuits resulted in their decline in social status and their eventual emigration to the United States. It is a story of contradiction, of rebellion by women in a society that presumed their obedience and adherence to tradition. And, it is a story of the enormous love that is possible between a man and a woman, when they forsake everything to be together, flouting tradition in the face of disgrace and family disharmony. It is a story from out of the distant past that is relevant even today.

Chapter 1

Journey

Sharon, Pennsylvania, October 1, 1911

On a cool, drizzly day in the drab Pennsylvania coal country, a scruffy young man boards the Erie Lackawanna Railroad bound for New York. He is tall and lean as a western wrangler, but his foreign accent belies the fact that he is local, that he is American. He is forlorn, as though death has descended on him, and the whites of his piercing blue eyes are streaked with red veins. As the train lurches forward and throws him off balance, he finds a patched, tan wicker seat in a quiet corner of the starkly painted green and maize rail car and sits. He slides the seat-back in front of him forward, creating a space for four passengers, and places his feet on the seat ahead of him. He leans back, closes his eyes and is soon asleep, his gray wool sweater buttoned at the collar against the damp air, his cap turned down over his eyes.

The intermittent tapping of raindrops on the blurred window soon awakens him and his mind sharpens as he emerges from his brief sleep. His first thoughts are of Caterina, the young immigrant wife he left behind in Sharon that morning, the woman who had come from their home town in southern Italy to be with him. They had made love in the early morning hours, and now they knew they would not see one another for several long, lonely days. The day before, he had anxiously cut and split a huge quantity of firewood and stacked it high, blocking the light outside their kitchen door. She had asked, "Why so much wood?" and he had playfully responded that perhaps he was never returning. His sad eyes told the truth, however, that he would miss her enormously and would be back very soon. She had placed her arms around him and held him tightly. He cherished the aroma of her body, the feel of her firm, shapely form and the taste of her lips.

"Te amo," he had said to her.

"No, Raf, speak English," she responded, "you know how important that is here."

He looked impishly into her eyes.

"OK, I love you!"

She then teasingly admonished him to get to his train, the wide smile on her cupid-like face revealing dimples in both cheeks and accentuating the cleft in her chin.

"I love you, too, but you had better get to your train before it leaves without you."

The overcast autumn day adds gloom to Raffaele Brutto's already depressed mood as he watches the grayed hills and russet-colored trees of fall dart by as the train speeds along its route, snorting black smoke from its coal-fired engine. He thinks about Enzo, his brother who has arrived with the human confluence descending on Ellis Island and whom he will greet as he disembarks in the South Ferry receiving area. By now, Enzo would be longing for one last comforting glimpse of Gagliano, the quickly vanishing image of their small village in southern Italy where they were born. Its medieval-era patched concrete and stone structures were drab and unimaginative, and life was stifling for young, ambitious men. But it was home. He knew what was expected of him there and what to expect from others. The days ahead in the new world would be difficult. There would be no family, no old friends; and the language was different and difficult to learn. Raffaele contrasts his own arrival, in 1899, alone and desperate for a start, foolishly accepting of the *bounteous* employment offers made by railroad hawkers strategically positioned at the arrival dock. Enzo will not make that mistake, he vows. It is more than a decade later and a lot has changed.

The irritating drizzle ends as the train approaches its final destination in the industrial hub of Hoboken. Raffaele lifts his tall frame to its full height and stretches his arms and back as the train slows and stops with screeching abruptness, steam bursting out from below the engine's carriage. A thick, black column wafts from the locomotive, as it sits in the terminal, releasing its spent residue of ash. Gathering his small, worn valise containing changes of clothing and a cloth bag with the remnants of the lunch that Caterina had packed for him, he steps down to the platform alongside the train. The mass of thirty passengers, huddled and resembling a posse in pursuit, scurries to the end of the wooden platform and descends a long covered stairway to the landing below, where the Hoboken Ferry anxiously waits to cross the murky Hudson River. A bearded deck hand stands in the passageway taking tickets purchased in advance or receiving cash payment. Raffaele pulls a nickel from his pocket and receives three cents change. He murmurs a question in his broken English, "When do we leave?"

"...in a few moments. We were waiting for your train."

The dense salt aroma invades Raffaele's senses as he steps onto the ferry. He is suddenly dizzied, feeling a sharp pain in his chest that blurs his vision and hinders his breathing. He stumbles and drops his valise. In an instant he recovers his balance and the symptoms are gone. He is grateful that no one has noticed, but wonders what could have caused the sudden illness. Perhaps the lunch that Caterina packed for him, the soppressata salami and provolone cheese, didn't agree with him. He disregards the incident as he climbs the stairs to the passenger deck where the view has captured the focus of the passengers. They are captivated by the gargantuan effigy of freedom standing on a tiny isle in the middle of the river barely visible in the distance, holding her torch high, her sculpted robes seeming to flow with the blustering autumn wind. The Great Lady stands beside Ellis Island, the place whose huge interior resembles a cattle barn, where Raffaele first heard American English spoken and where his brother now gains admittance. It was not a pleasant process for Raffaele when he arrived a decade ago. He was given a rigorous physical examination, immunized on the spot to a variety of diseases and interrogated about his intentions in coming to America.

The other side of the great river is overwhelming in its enormity, the nation's largest and most complex city with its unending skyline of tall gray and brown buildings reflecting the late afternoon sun in their windows and creating the sense of eyes peering pensively to the west. The ferry climbs the river's modest billows and drops gracefully down the other side. Passengers grasp the railings and feel the gentle undulating motion of the river. At the eastern shore, the ferry captain skillfully guides the boat against tide and swell until it slides gently into its slip. The pungent New York City air drifts menacingly up into the faces of the newly arrived as they prepare to disembark. Swirls of black soot appear everywhere, driven by the fall wind.

Raffaele glances across the century-old boat slip, its aged planks and fractured pilings leaning and groaning with the river's swells. Across the wide boulevard he spots a familiar figure, dressed in dark baggy trousers, heavy maroon sweater and black cap. It is Giuseppe Rossi, his friend from Gagliano. The two men had been casual acquaintances in Italy, but here in New York, they are tied in close alliance as they face the common challenge of surviving in the new world. This remarkable new place holds hope and is free of the continuum of war and poverty ravaging the old country; but it demands a huge price for providing a haven from the misery. Here, there is disdain for the humble immigrant who, seemingly, will displace established workmen by accepting low wages and poor working conditions. The Establishment of the great city casts aspersions on the newly arrived, exaggerating their bent for lawlessness and violence and engendering fear of association.

Raffaele smiles generously, his broad teeth flashing as he calls out, "Hey, paisano, how are you? I've just arrived. Do you think Enzo is here yet?"

The surprised man looks up, and replies with a heavy dialect.

"*Ciao*, Raffaele, it's good to see you. No, the launch has not yet arrived, but we had better get down to the dock. It's due in at any moment."

Together, they walk the cobbled streets to South Ferry, where the transport from Ellis Island will soon arrive.

┣━◆━0━◆━┫

The Ellis Island launch seems top heavy as it inches its way to the dock. Its deck is crowded with dozens of anxious new arrivals, their weary faces showing nervousness, even fear. They had imagined pristine streets, and now they are confronted by the dull edge of reality, hoping that the interior is more as they anticipated. Raffaele searches nervously for the sight of Enzo, and finally sees him.

"Enzo! Enzo!" he calls, as the weary traveler reaches the gangway and looks toward his older brother. Despite years of separation, Enzo is easily recognizable, the jut of his jaw, the protrusion of his cheekbones and his Roman nose. He manages a nervous smile and a diminutive wave. He tries to look confident in his best set of clothes, a frayed tweed jacket and an umber cap pulled down over his forehead. As he nears Raffaele, he notices a drawn look on Raffaele's face, as though he is holding back an expression of pain.

"What's wrong, *fratello*?"

Raffaele steps forward and embraces Enzo.

"Welcome to America," he says, ignoring his brother's query, but feeling the tightness in his chest returning. "This is Giuseppe…from Gagliano. You're too young to remember him. He left before you were old enough to walk. You will board with Giuseppe while we find work for you. Now let's walk over to Giuseppe's house."

The three men are foot weary by evening, when they reach the far off Mulberry District, the locus that defines Little Italy in turn-of-the-century New York. They have traversed the streets of New York's financial district and west side, and Enzo had fallen silent as he gazed up at the smoke-stained wooden buildings, many of them five and six stories high. Some have lofts with huge uncovered windows, where people toil into the evening, cutting cloth patterns and sewing garments. There are apartment flats with fire escapes covered with potted plants and vegetables. Heavy-set horses in a dark, fetid stable at the end of one street are eating their supper from canvas satchels slung around their necks. The air is rancid with the smell of wood fires and horse manure, and Enzo finds himself rubbing his itchy eyes. A great many people crowd the streets and seem to be converging from all directions. Some sit out on their fire escapes or on their front steps, smoking cigarettes, cigars and pipes with an array of foreign aromas. They speak and even argue in languages unfamiliar to Enzo, except for Italian and even some Calabrian dialect. To Enzo, this is the American form of the *passeggiata*, the Italian stroll after dinner, except that there are many more people and they are from more parts of the world than he had imagined.

Raffaele breaks the numbing silence as he looks ahead at the number on Giuseppe's house. It strikes him that he hasn't used his private moments with Enzo to re-establish their family connection.

"Enzo, how is Ma doing? How did she take to your leaving?"

Enzo thinks for a long moment, not wanting to equivocate, but also not wanting to offend or cause concern. After all, Raffaele left the family behind in Italy and was not heard from for a year, not even by his young wife.

"Not well, Raf, she misses you and she didn't like my leaving either, but you know how she doesn't complain. She prays daily that we will return to Gagliano and raise families there. She lights candles at the altar in St. Rosalia's, and prays that our brothers will return safely from the war in Libya."

Raffaele is feeling guilty, but he knows this isn't the time to talk about the circumstances of his first miserable year in America. No, Enzo would be alarmed if he knew. There will be time to talk about that later.

"I'm sorry to hear of Ma's sadness, but I won't be returning any time soon. Caterina and I need many more years to save enough for our return to Italy. She works hard to save and to make our life here acceptable, but she longs for her return to Italy. She takes boarders into our house, washes their clothing and cooks for them."

He continues as though Enzo is not aware of the circumstances that all of Gagliano chattered about for years.

"She was a rich man's daughter in Italy, and before she married me, everything was done for her. I don't want her to work so hard, but she's determined to save enough money to buy a property of our own in Italy, that we could farm for ourselves."

Enzo again finds himself in a quandary, not wanting to offend, but wanting to rouse a response.

"What of her father's wealth," he asks, "doesn't she intend to claim her inheritance one day? After all, Vitaliano is a rich man. And he won't live forever."

Raffaele's deportment changes as it becomes obvious that his young brother is aware of the scandalous behavior that gripped the consciousness of the whole village.

"Her father's wealth means nothing to her! Her mother is gone and Vitaliano has remarried. Who knows what will happen? His new wife will want her offspring to inherit his land and there isn't much we can do about that. Besides, Caterina has said that she will never again be beholden to anyone or lose any part of her independence."

Enzo has crossed the line and made his brother angry. He becomes silent. Surely, his brother is more experienced in these matters than he, but what was he talking about? Women aren't supposed to think that way. Independence is for men, and so is earning a living. Had Raffaele gone soft in the head?

"Giuseppe! Raffaele!" Shouts come from two men on front steps of the frayed tenement house. They are Giuseppe and his brother, Alfonso. "We've been waiting for you. Dinner is ready and everyone is here waiting to meet Enzo."

The plaster walls inside the four-story tenement are stark, with a faded green, peeling paint that has been washed far too many times. The stale odor of cooking combines with the smells of aging paint and permeates the hallways. Bags of refuse pose outside the doors of the flats waiting to be brought outdoors for collection. The sour-smelling hallways also house a common toilet on each floor of the building for the tenants to share. Inside Giuseppe's third floor flat, the ambience contrasts greatly with the hallways leading to it. It is freshly painted in soft bland colors and is clean and orderly. The aroma of the cooking is of another place, the south of Italy. The apartment is heated by a wood-burning stove in the large kitchen and down the hall there are two sparse bedrooms separated by an airshaft. A small parlor at the far end is used as a bedroom for boarders. Giuseppe and his wife, Angela, sleep in the first bedroom and their two boys sleep in the room next to the parlor. Two large windows in the kitchen look out onto a small, littered yard far below with a fig tree and a dozen tomato plants yielding the last of the season's crop. They struggle to separate themselves from the rest of the overgrown, weedy turf.

The windows are imbedded with wire twisted in circles to protect them from shattering. The Fall evening has turned unseasonably warm, and the aroma of stale garbage that drifts up from the yard is mostly unnoticed by the residents.

"Hey, Enzo, when have you seen a spread like this?" It is Raffaele, engaging Enzo and at the same time complimenting Giuseppe and Alfonso for the substantial meal placed before them. There is antipasto containing Calabrian salami, wedges of mozzarella and provolone cheeses, an assortment of fragrant olives and fresh fennel. A vessel of spaghetti smothered in tomato sauce sits on the stove releasing a seductive, familiar aroma that fills the room. Roasted capon and rabbit stew are waiting to be served after the appetizers and pasta are eaten. Hours later, desserts of candied canoli and rich wheat pie will make their entrance, along with a huge pot of steaming espresso.

"Raffaele, are you all right? You haven't been eating much." Giuseppe takes his friend aside to express concern.

"I'm fine. I suppose I ate too much on my trip to New York. The food here is wonderful and the thought of our friends coming together like this for Enzo fills me with gratitude."

Raffaele looks around at this group of nearly twenty friends who had come to welcome Enzo to America. Alfonso and his wife, Alba, walked up from their apartment on a lower floor. There is Joe, the butcher (his given name, Giuseppe) who furnished most of the evening's fare. Ernesto, the barber, Gino, the carpenter, and the four boarders are all there, recollecting their own arrival from Italy not long ago. Some of the lesser-known neighbors recently hailed from Calabria, join in as well. All of the wives participate with Angela in cooking and serving the meal.

"Everyone! Let's be seated and start our dinner." Giuseppe is host and it is up to him to signal the others. "Enzo, welcome to *America*." He holds up his glass of homemade red wine and toasts the young man's arrival. "May you live happy and long here in this great country."

The guests hold up their glasses and respond, "*Salute'!*"

Raffaele is seated between Giuseppe and Enzo and quietly forces himself to eat, despite feeling faint and unbalanced. It would be discourteous of him not to partake in the meal. He listens to scattered conversations taking place simultaneously, reminding him of the kinship he left behind when he and Caterina moved to Pennsylvania.

"You must have seen the black and blue on Angelo Catena's face. Rumor has it that he couldn't make his weekly payment to the *Mano Nero* and they punished him with a beating. He better decide what he's going to do before they kill him."

"Did you know? The king offered Garibaldi an important position in the government and he turned it down. Do you blame him? He was not a politician, he was a freedom fighter. Besides, who would want to serve a government that allows its people to be exploited as we were?"

"Have you heard about the new policeman on our street? I hear that he stops the boys from pitching their pennies. Isn't that awful?"

Raffaele listens as attentively as possible, trying to appear normal, despite the distraction caused by his ailment. By now it is beginning to affect his speech and vision. He speaks blurrily to Giuseppe.

"I'll always have a fondness for New York and the friends I have made here. I would have remained, but I earn more in the steel mill in Pennsylvania than I can here as a longshoreman. Besides, living is cheaper there and Caterina is happy with her boarding house. I just wish she didn't work so hard."

Giuseppe turns away as Joe, the butcher, taps his shoulder to get his attention. He turns in the same instant as Raffaele's demeanor changes from a forced geniality to anguish. His eyes are no longer focused. He stares ahead and downward. His lips are apart and his tongue swells and fills his mouth. He wheezes and sweat forms on his brow. He feels excruciating pain in the center of his chest and back. Then, his left arm throbs and becomes the focus of his pain. There is no doubt, he thinks to himself, he is having a heart attack. The fear of death overtakes him.

His thoughts turn fleetingly to his wife of twelve years. Caterina, his beautiful, wonderful Caterina. How unlikely was their marriage, he a field hand, she from a family of wealth. He had aspired to the unthinkable goal of having her as his wife. When it happened, he was astonished. Her love for him was so great that she had given up the dowry her father would otherwise have given her in marriage to a man of appropriate means. Thus, providing for this gem of a woman had become Raffaele's overwhelming purpose. And, how proud he had felt when she would not remain behind in Italy, indulged by her father, while he sought fortune in America. Her urgent need for him caused her to leave her familiar surroundings and share his arduous existence in America. He had moved with her to Sharon, to a Pennsylvania steel mill, adding 500 miles to the distance between her and her beloved Calabria; there, to toil as a servant to boarders so that she could one day return with him to Italy and take a suitable place in Gagliano's social order. What would she do now? They had savored and shared every choice they had made for the last twelve years. How would Caterina make decisions without him? How would she delight in the abundant, simple joys of life? He thinks of the stricture to remain true until death. It doesn't seem possible that he will die after so short a time. They will part and she will be alone. God knows, they were not able to have children. And, except for her younger sister, the rest of her family is far away in Italy. He is tortured by the thought of leaving her alone, defenseless in a treacherous and apathetic world.

His thoughts focus on a time when, as a child in Gagliano, he ran up and down its dusty streets, calling to his mother, eagerly relating how he had seen her earlier in the day at the town center washing clothes at the fountain in the square, its exterior elaborately carved with an image of Neptune rising from the water. She had beamed her toothy, genial smile, the distinctive aquiline features of her face masking the shame she felt for the life she had lived before he was born. He thought of how she would receive the news of his death. He hadn't increased his odds of survival after all by escaping military service in Italy. Ma was always so silent, enduring her grief alone, never imposing her sorrow on others. He recalled his father, Lorenzo, with face bronzed by the many seasons of toil under the Calabrian sun. Lorenzo had spent a lifetime of struggle to feed his family and maintain a sense of personal dignity that was often difficult to sustain. How Raffaele loved these simple people whose lives were integral with his. What had he lost by leaving Italy to seek his fortune in America?

"Oh, God, if only I had another chance," he thinks, "I would never have left. I would have accepted the life with my loving family and not lusted for wealth."

"Raffaele! What is it? What's wrong?" Giuseppe is now gaping in horror at what he sees, a nervous tick fluttering over his right eye. Raffaele's eyes bulge, enlarged reddened orbs that stare blindly. He presses his chest with both hands. He cannot respond to the shrieks of those around him who can by now see that this is a grave situation. Enzo's face twists in fright.

"Raffaele! What's wrong?"

Chapter 2

Emerging Power

Calabria, January 15, 1885

A light winter rain sweeps the lush outdoors as Vitaliano Zinzi peers
out from a window, gazing pensively. From his second floor perch,
he can see the morning horizon to the east, and all that he sees is
his. There are tidy rows of olive trees, laden with ripe, black fruit, stretching
to the end of a narrow valley made verdant by the January torrent. The olives
are ready for harvest, he thinks. To the north, south and west, there are endless rows of lemon bushes, orange trees and grape vines. Vitaliano has come
to own more of Gagliano and the lands around it than any other man between
this tiny hamlet in which he was born and the region's capitol city four miles
away. But it was not always that way. It has been many years since Vitaliano
has allowed himself to think about the catastrophe that blemished his youth
and eventually led to his material triumph. Now, as he waits to meet his eldest
daughter's prospective suitor, his thoughts race back to his formative years and
the horrific Risorgimento that marked him for life.

His fortune had taken root in the terrible conflict that took place in the
adjacent province of Reggio, when his father and two older brothers were
killed by Spanish lancers in the historic fight to reclaim Italy from its foreign
rulers. It was in the summer of 1860 when the rugged farmers of Calabria
were called on to serve the army of the Risorgimento. They responded in

droves, despite even the opposition of Holy Mother Church. Six thousand Calabrian men gathered on a huge, barren beach below the hilltop city of Reggio, looking like an invasion of ants from the tower of the fortress looming above the beach. There, the revolution's leader, Giuseppe Garibaldi, and his cadre of scruffy Red Shirts had arrived, following their victory in Sicily.

When the moment arrived for engaging the enemy, the Calabrian troop advanced and was soon met with brutal resistance by a unit of highly trained Spanish regulars. The Calabrians fought fiercely, forcing the Spaniards to flee back to the city's mountain garrison. As they sprinted into the fortress, the ancient wooden doors of the hilltop stronghold slammed shut. Within moments, they reopened, spewing a mounted detachment of Spanish lancers, a column of death descending on the hapless farmers. The horsemen stormed down the hill to where they were met by the Calabrians. At the head of the Calabrian troop, the three Zinzi men fought within earshot of one another, the younger two straining to hear their father's ferocious beckoning above the clamor.

"Aldo! Franco! Use your rifles! Fire into their faces! Don't try to reload. Make use of your sabers!"

His commands were useless. All three were run through by lances, as were most of the Calabrians unfortunate enough to be in the front line. As the Zinzis lived their final moments, their comrades exacted a huge toll on the Spaniards. Great numbers of lancers were killed, torn suddenly from their earthly existence, the look of pain, terror and disbelief on their young faces. Seeing the inevitability of victory for the attackers, the Spaniards raised a flag of truce and the fighting was ended.

"It's over! The Spaniards are surrendering." The exhausted officer beamed as the Garibaldi forces gathered to take control of the fortress and tally their losses. His enthusiasm was dampened by Count Leone, Calabria's richest and most acknowledged noble. "Yes, we've won, but the toll has been heavy. I saw three men from one family fighting to the death."

"I knew them," the young officer continued, "they're from Gagliano. There's a ten-year-old boy in that family and the rest are women. They're poor tenant farmers."

⊢•◆◦◆•⊣

From the moment she saw the two soldiers striding towards her that afternoon, Amelia Zinzi suspected a terrible tragedy; but she could not fathom the horror of what she was about to hear. Battle weary and grim-faced, their red shirts and pantaloons identified the soldiers as two of the Garibaldi Thousand. Amelia had seen them as she came out her front door and saw one of her neighbors pointing her out to them. The older of the two soldiers approached her, a moment of empathy overwhelming him. It was easier to face the Spaniards than to now reveal to Amelia the death of her sons and husband.

"Signora Zinzi," he began, "it is my duty to inform you of death in your family from the gallant action at Reggio." Amelia was stunned, despite the obvious purpose of the soldiers' presence. After a breathless moment, she looked up at the officer, her head whirling in thought.

"Which one is it?" She held her breath and prayed to her Savior, not daring to hope for the survival of one over the other. She tried to envision the images of her husband and each of her sons, but the agony ahead made it impossible. For a moment, she wished she already knew who it was. The soldier's face stiffened, his eyes narrowed and he hesitated to speak. He realized that Amelia was expecting to hear that one of the men was killed. Finally, he nervously stammered, "All three were killed as they fought on foot against a unit of lancers. They were in the front line and they were side by side when they were brought down by the enemy. The outcome for our side…"

Amelia held up her hand in anger and looked away in a ferocious gaze that demanded silence. A hideous hiss emerged from her throat. The tumultuous jolt had overwhelmed her senses and she was briefly unable to speak. Her eyes opened wide, but she could not see anything. She raged inside. How could this senseless thing happen? What for? The liberation of Italy? Who cares? She shrieked, "To hell with Italy and Garibaldi! I want my husband, my boys…my family!" She fell piteously to her knees, overwhelmed by anguish. She lowered her head to the dusty ground and sobbed.

"No, no, not my boys, not my Mario."

Her body heaved as she wept hysterically, her fists up to her forehead, then beating down against the earth. The soldier motioned to the women in the crowd that had assembled. Two of the older women dressed in mourning black, stepped forward, each taking an arm, and leading Amelia, limp and whimpering, into her house. As she crossed the threshold, she looked around at the familiar objects inside. She began screaming uncontrollably, throwing bowls and plates within her reach, falling into the table that filled half the room, turning it over and cursing in an obscure idiom. Finally, she collapsed and was carried to her bed in the adjoining room, moaning incoherently.

Ten-year-old Vitaliano observed the pitiful commotion from a distance, trying to comprehend what was taking place. He welled with confusion about what he had heard, and felt desperate to cure the ill that had suddenly over-whelmed his mother. He looked for his two older sisters, but they were not there. What did this mean? Would his father and brothers not be coming home from the war? Who would care for the family? Who would be his mentor as he grew to manhood? Who would work the land to which their family was contracted? To whom would their mother look for guidance and support? He decided not to succumb to rage and tears or to dart home seeking the comfort that he knew his mother could not give. He instinctively knew that he was the sole male of the household now, and that he had to behave accordingly. He walked into his home with calm determination, as the crowd watched with pity and awe. He sat on his mother's bed, placing his hand gently on her back, listening quietly as she wailed, concealing the pain he felt. He had never known such anguish.

A week later, the Prefect of Catanzaro province called on Amelia with the deed to an abandoned farm in his hand. The land had been confiscated only a few days preceding, from a cowardly deserter, one Aldo Caristi, who fled the battle at the sight of killing. As Amelia opened the door, the Prefect forced himself to be expressionless, peering into her devastated face. Blackened eye-lids encircled her bloodshot eyes. Her cheeks were wrinkled and drawn. She stooped forward as though she were bowing, and clutched her stomach with one hand. A flatulent odor betrayed the fact that she had not bathed. Her voice was hardly audible.

"Good afternoon, Prefect, what can I do for you?" Her teary gaze revealed the mental torment she had been suffering. He spoke in an almost inaudible whisper.

"Signora Zinzi, the army of the new government has ordered that the Caristi land be given to you in acknowledgment of the heroic service of your husband and sons in the war. We rushed the matter through so that you could get over there and tend the orchard."

Amelia shouted at the bewildered man.

"Are you mad? How can I think of that when I have just lost all of the men in my life?"

The prefect's pronouncement had been enough to send Amelia back into a frenzied grieving. How dare they equate the value of some deserted property with the lives of her family? Who were these terrible men who caused her man and her sons to be killed?

The Prefect held his hands up in a gesture that begged for understanding.

"But, Signora Zinzi, do you realize what this means? Yes, you have lost your husband and sons, and nothing can replace such a loss. But now you have your own property. You and the remaining members of your family can ease the hardships of the past by working your own land. We cannot ever restore the lives of the men that were lost, but this we can do. You must endure your fate and take advantage of this opportunity. Do you understand?"

"Do you understand? I no longer have the men in my family!"

"Don't say that, Ma, I'm here and I'm a man." Vitaliano stood before her, a careworn look on his boyish face. For one incredulous moment, he appeared to have the wisdom of an adult. He continued, "I'll go with you to see the farm. We can decide then what needs to be done and who can do it." The Prefect stood in amazement as he witnessed the scene.

The ten-year-old's considered words oddly calmed Amelia and she experienced her first healing thoughts since receiving the terrible news the previous week. She clenched her teeth determinedly. There were others, she thought, who had lost family members driving the goddamned Spanish out of Calabria. They, who rousted our men, telling them what they could and couldn't do and taking for themselves whatever they wanted. Now, let them roast in hell for what they had done to Italy! She began crying softly and held her handkerchief to her face, "...but they didn't have to take all three of them."

⊢•⊶•○•⊷•⊣

It pains Vitaliano to think of that terrible time almost a generation ago.

His mother never overcame her grief. She mourned endlessly, praying to the Blessed Mother for the souls of her dead men, and visiting their graves daily. She lived on for another five tormented years, becoming weaker each day as she mourned. Vitaliano's boyhood had ended abruptly, and by sheer default, he stepped into his father's role as head of the family.   He would not allow himself to be drawn into Amelia's whirlpool of grief. Instead, he focused on shielding his family from ruin. His sisters were frightened at first by the prospect of being directed by their young brother, but Vitaliano's astonishing leadership soon alleviated their fears. He pressed them hard to work the farm they now owned, and they eventually accepted his direction. He showed a remarkable ability to bargain for his crops with the olive oil producers, the citrus buyers and the wine merchants.   Before his fifteenth birthday, Vitaliano had gained his reputation as a formidable businessman. It was at that young age that he stumbled onto a method for assembling his fortune.

Young Vitaliano walked barefoot through the vineyard, his short pants drooping and the cuffs of his shirt sliding over his wrists. He and his sisters had cultivated the ground and the soft earth felt good under his bare feet. The warm wind blowing against his legs reminded him that spring was just ahead. He thought about the money that he had accumulated from the sale of his wine grapes and olives that previous year, and he was pleased with himself. He had restored the Caristi property and it had yielded a large crop. If only he had a larger property, he thought. He had made the necessary contacts to market the crops he grew; surely he could sell more if he could grow more. Never mind the enormous work it would require. There were plenty of willing farmhands available to work. Or, he could rent out acquired land to sharecroppers and perhaps even market their crops. But how could he acquire more property? Land was expensive and hardly available. His thoughts about expanding depressed him. He would rather dream of the extravagant villa he would one day build in the center of the property he already owned. He would call it *La Stella*, the Star, and rows of vines and trees would reach out in all directions from the house with crops of every kind. Thinking about his future in those terms excited him and his pace quickened with anticipation.

"Hey, Vitaliano!" It was Agabito, a farmer who had emigrated to America, returning to Gagliano for a visit. He walked in from the edge of Vitaliano's property, the sandy earth filling his shoes and slowing his walk as he proceeded in long strides to where Vitaliano stood. Vitaliano greeted the older man.

"How are you, Agabito? How is life in America? Are you returning for good?"

"No, Vitaliano, I'm happy in America. My boys and I have started a coal delivery business and it makes us a good living there. America is a good place to live."

"Do you miss Gagliano?"

"I do, but my children's prosperity has swept away their desire to return. My sons were children when we left and don't have the memories that I have of this sad but wonderful place."

"Well, what can I do for you?"

"Vitaliano, I was wondering if I could interest you in purchasing some of my land next to yours. I could let you have it for a bargain price and you could easily farm it from your own property."

"I would love to own it, but I don't have enough money. I've saved hard, but I haven't enough money to buy property."

"I could let you have it and you could pay me in the future…with interest of course. You could send the money to me in America when you sell the crops."

"I don't know how that works, but I can find out."

"There is little to know. If we can agree on a price, the *avvocato* at the bank will work things out for us."

The two bargained, one a man and the other still just a boy, eventually agreeing on price and terms. They left the field and rode to Catanzaro in a small wagon that Agabito had waiting at the edge of Vitaliano's vineyard. Within a few hours, Vitaliano had tripled the size of his property with only the promise to pay the purchase price with a percentage of the proceeds from the crop coming from the land he had just purchased. It was a mature vineyard and the start of the new growing season was just ahead. Vitaliano had only to arrange for field hands to work the vineyard and, of course, he would pay the land taxes that would be due later in the year. He estimated that the proceeds from the harvest would be more than sufficient to pay expenses with money left over. A profit!

Why hadn't <u>he</u> thought of this? There were scores of emigrants who had savings enough to leave for America because they owned property and could save a portion of the proceeds from their crop sales. In some cases, they retained their property, believing they would be returning in a few years. When they chose not to return and wished to sell their property, they were vulnerable to buyers who would take advantage and pay only a fraction of their property's worth. Vitaliano offered to pay full value if they would accept his promissory note. His reputation as a successful farmer gave them confidence that they would eventually be paid for their land. It had worked for Agabito, why not them? Thus, Vitaliano was able to acquire land with future profits. Over the next ten years, he surrounded his initial property with farms purchased from the Martinos, the Trepassos, the Beccios and others, all of whom had left Italy for America without selling their land. He had found a way to add to his property ownership.

Eventually, Vitaliano accumulated so many of Gagliano's discarded farms that he became the largest landowner in the town. He won over the absentee owners with his fairness and honesty, but was not above responding in kind to contempt. In a rare instance, when a property owner living in America became condescending, demanding that Vitaliano increase his offer price because of the value of the dollar, he furtively arranged for the early harvest of the emigrant's crop that seemed to disappear from sight, leaving the owner to pay for property taxes out of his own pocket and increasing his desire to sell off the property. Vitaliano was becoming worldly.

His dream of constructing a villa in the center of the property he amassed became a reality. Removing orchard and vineyard from the area designated for the dwelling was painful, but he became increasingly comforted by the sight of the stately two-story manor with a large stable and gardens surrounded by six-foot stone walls. He promptly named the property *La Stella*. It was then that his workers began referring to him as Baron Zinzi, though he was never formally elevated to the aristocracy.

Not the least of Vitaliano's accomplishments was marrying Rosaria Caroleo, a young, educated signorina from a generous family that deeded a handsome property to the young couple on their wedding day. In time, Rosaria bore him four children, two boys and two girls, all of whom were afforded a genteel life accessible to few of their countrymen.

⊢—•—○—◦—┤

Now Vitaliano must think of this new phase of his life as he contemplates meeting yet another suitor who would ask for his daughter's hand in marriage. A faint smile takes form as he muses at the prospect of the most eligible of men seeking the dowry that will come with wedding Caterina, the eldest of his four children. Not that she is unattractive, to the contrary, she is quite lovely, but this is an uncommon opportunity for a lucky suitor to supplement his own possessions. The smile quickly leaves Vitaliano's face as he thinks of giving up land in tribute to this derisive custom that causes young men to feel entitled to property in exchange for taking a woman in marriage. What if he refuses? What right does anyone have to lay claim to his property? No! Any man wanting to marry Caterina will have to take her without invoking this foolish custom. Then, he faces the reality that grips the gentry of all of Europe. He cannot become known as a stingy father who leaves his daughter without resource. It would embarrass the family. It might even mean that Caterina, attractive as she might be, could go through life as a spinster. He feels trapped. He must consider deeding property to the newlyweds. But, the man who marries Caterina had better be worthy!

⊢—•—○—◦—┤

Chapter 3

Erstwhile Suitors

From his chair in the outdoor café in Catanzaro, Nunzio Laguzza looks across the small square and studies the young woman's figure with unbridled lust. He has spoken to her several times during the past year and thinks of her often. Her large, chestnut brown eyes are piercing and inviting. She is barely five and a half feet tall, but her long, slim legs make her appear taller. Her faint olive skin is like flawless velvet running down her long, thin neck to a full bosom, a slim waistline and buttocks round as grapefruits. Raven colored hair frames her cupid-like face, a model of Raphael's cherubs. She is surely the most engaging woman in Gagliano, he thinks, and he craves to have her in his bed. Because he is rich, he gives no thought to his own personal bearing, that of a grossly overweight, unsightly man with a bloated ego to match.

Nunzio has inherited considerable wealth from an industrious father who was rumored to have been well paid by Calabria's organized netherworld, the Ndranghetta, for supplying information on the movements of the local police in the capital city of Catanzaro. He had privileged intelligence because of the proximity of his home to the Carabiniere barracks. From the small yard behind his two-story dwelling, he could overhear the murmurs of the troopers tending their horses behind the barracks building. Often, they talked of the latest orders coming from Rome or from the local administrator in Catanzaro. He was handsomely rewarded, it is said, the day that he sounded

the alarm that sent the local thugs scurrying north to Naples while the Carabinieri searched for them in vain. He had been eyeing the gradual massing
of troopers from surrounding units in the countryside. Listening in on their
conversation, he determined that the Carabinieri intended to round up all
of the suspected nethermost brigands and end their grip on the respectable
citizens of Catanzaro once and for all. He was eventually suspected of his
handiwork and, before suspicions turned to inquiry, he leased his home to a
local shopkeeper and relocated to the remote village of Gagliano. There, he
quietly retired to the life of a minor padrone, having been preceded in death
by his wife of forty years. In just a few years, he died peacefully, leaving his
wealth to his young and only child, Nunzio.

Until Nunzio was twenty-five years old, he lived a carefree existence, collecting his rents and managing his landowner's share of crops. He often visited nearby villages where friends and extended family lived and, despite his
unattractive persona, he had no dearth of attention from the opposite sex. His
obvious wealth attracted many of the women he met from his travels as well
as the eligible women of his hometown. Numerous of his romantic conquests
were rumored to have occurred in his lair in Gagliano, none leading to permanence in relationship. But now, as his mindset grizzles along with the hair
on his head, he is ready to marry. The woman will, of course, be beautiful, but
the size of her dowry will preempt all other attributes, since his wealth will
not be wasted on a woman of lesser means. No one, he thinks, can be a more
suitable mate than Caterina Zinzi. She is lovely and her father is wealthy,
more so even than he. His amorous dreams of Caterina are frequently interrupted by the thought of the dowry that will accompany her in marriage. He
sometimes wonders which is more enticing: making love to Caterina or savoring the wealth that will accompany her. Mostly, he dismisses the thought,
but in his most contemplative moments he is not certain. Now, he will see
Vitaliano Zinzi to ask for Caterina's hand in marriage...and bargain for a
choice dowry.

‹——•—◇—•——›

The morning rain slackens as Nunzio Laguzza approaches the Zinzi villa,
his nostrils filling with the aroma of lemon bushes situated outside the walls.

He admires the wide iron gates with metal flowers and angels welded into the black steel. He walks the long stone path to the front door. There are lilies, hyacinths, daisies and roses along the way, defying the season as though insensible to temperature and time. Palm trees on either side of the path reach across, creating a tunnel-like refuge from a light drizzle. It is as though Nunzio has entered a sanctuary on his path to providence. He breathes in deeply, and confidently taps on the door.

"Signor Laguzza? We have been expecting you." It is Rosaria, Caterina's mother, nervously opening the door for her daughter's prospective suitor before her servant can reach the entrance to the house. "Come this way."

Nunzio at once notices the elevated ceilings. He has never seen such affluence in Gagliano. The walls inside are beautifully hung with oil paintings of forested landscapes. Heavy oak side tables contain small urns that might have been claimed from an ancient ruin. The terrazzo floor is partially covered with rugs brought to Calabria from afar, purchased twenty years earlier for Vitaliano and Rosaria as wedding gifts from Rosaria's family. Nunzio silently applauds himself for having chosen a future inheritor of this grand place.

Rosaria opens the door to a large room containing several sofas, stuffed chairs and a desk at one end, covered with plumed pens, papers, blotters and bottles of ink. Behind the desk sits her husband, Vitaliano.

"My dear, this is Nunzio Laguzza. Signor Laguzza, this is my husband."

"I am very pleased to meet you, signor Zinzi. Thank you for making time to see me."

"Yes, well, let's get down to business. As you can see from this mess, I'm a busy man." As the two men meet, Rosaria leaves the room and closes the door. Vitaliano is not in a good mood. He is busy and doesn't relish the notion that this man would lay claim to part of his fortune. He is also attempting to defuse his opponent's aggressiveness in the negotiation.

For the first time in his imaginary pursuit of Caterina, Nunzio's self-assurance wavers. He has finally decided on who he wants as his wife and this is the moment in which to stake his claim. But, in the presence of this powerful man, he hesitates to state his business, lest he err and lose his appeal. His beady eyes are fixed on the older man, and still he fails to speak.

"What is it you want from me, signor Laguzza?" Vitaliano pretends ignorance, but knows well the purpose of the meeting. He has been informed
by Rosaria, who had heard about Nunzio's intentions the previous week from
one of Caterina's friends. Vitaliano wants to keep an open mind, but has a
dire impression of the obviously flawed and unattractive man. His riches are
a consideration, but overall, Nunzio does not make a favorable impression on
Vitaliano.

Beads of sweat appear on Nunzio's large forehead as he considers his approach. When he speaks, his words are slow and deliberate: "Don Vitaliano,
I have always admired you as a man of accomplishment, much like my own
father, may God have mercy on his soul. I know of your heroic father and
brothers, and how they gave their lives for the liberation of our country. I
know, too, of the great sadness that you experienced as your mother agonized,
in her last days, over the terrible loss of such a large part of her family. I have
heard of your impressive rise to material comfort despite the handicap placed
upon you by those past circumstances. I know these things because my father
admired you as much as I do and often spoke well of you."

"Thank you for your admiration, signor, but you must get to the point. I
await the arrival of an important buyer and must prepare for a meeting." The
heaping of praise does not alter Vitaliano's feelings. Nunzio, he thinks, is not
nearly the man to marry into his family.

"All right, I'll get to the point. I am prepared to take Caterina's hand in
marriage and I ask your permission to court her. If we marry, she will become
heir to my fortune. I will ask for very little in return."

Vitaliano is pensive. He is wary of the proposal.

"What do you consider 'very little'?"

Nunzio clears his throat, an intense look on his face. He knows what he
is about to say will run the risk of angering Vitaliano, but his greed conquers
his fear and he speaks his mind.

"I would like to have The Star. Naturally, you would continue to live in the
villa and conduct your family life and business as you have in the past, but I will
own the vineyard and orchard surrounding the house, and I pledge to care for it
as you would. I also ask for the right to inherit the villa upon your death."

So that was it! Very little indeed! Vitaliano musters up all of his composure so as not to reveal his rage. He stares callously at Nunzio, a flurry of thoughts churning in his mind. Moments pass before he speaks.

"Thank you again for the very flattering comments. It is every father's wish to have his daughter married to a man who respects him and who can give her a comfortable life after she leaves his home. However, I must decline your request, and let me tell you why. In asking for her hand, you did not extol her virtue or loveliness. Nor did you speak of the joy she would bring to your life. Instead, you talked of me and the distinction my family earned in the war. Those are not reasons for asking for a woman's hand in marriage."

"Don Vitaliano!" Nunzio coughs and stammers, as though he is choking. "Please don't misunderstand me. Your daughter is beautiful and I would be honored to make her my wife. If I am asking for too much, tell me and I'll reconsider."

"I'm sorry, Signor, but my decision is final. I will have my housemaid show you out." He opens the door and calls, "Angela, our meeting is over. Please show Signor Laguzza out."

Then, Vitaliano turns to Nunzio again, "It was a pleasure meeting you, signor, perhaps we'll meet again."

As he leaves the room, Nunzio looks back, a mask of defeat on his face and a feeling of depression engulfing him. He has been turned down utterly and completely. His dreams of a conjugal life with Caterina are ended. What is worse, he will never own The Star.

⊷—⊶—○—⊷—⊶

Vitaliano is thankful that he did not speak the words he was thinking of while Nunzio was in the room. He was simply another disappointed hopeful of the several prospects that have approached Vitaliano with their wish to marry Caterina and to bargain for a dowry. As he sits back in the chair behind his desk, the door across the room swings open. It is Caterina and she has overheard the brief, stinging conversation between her father and Nunzio Laguzza.

Her feelings about Nunzio are quite different than his feelings about her. She had felt his stare often, and it repulsed her. She thinks of him as a drab court jester with layers of padding to fill out his costume. His portly appearance sickens her and his mindset of superiority is offensive to her. Why would she be interested in such a man? She had had better prospects for sure. "Thank You Pa., I'm glad you sent him away. He's repulsive and he obviously is more interested in which property he could get from you than he is in me."

"And what of Alphonso? Did you decide to accept his proposal? He is a far more attractive man than the others and he, too, has the means to care for you properly."

"No, Pa, I don't want him either. He may be better looking than Nunzio, but he is after the same thing...The Star. I heard him say so."

"And what of the others?"

"I don't want any of those fortune seekers, either."

"Caterina, when will you marry? Every man that asks for your hand in marriage will ask for a dowry. It is expected. It assures your future. What's wrong with that?"

Caterina wonders if this is the time to reveal her secret intent to Vitaliano. Knowing her father's unalterable opinion, she has avoided the subject. Now she looks at her father with beseeching eyes, her brow forming a plea. She decides she will speak her mind.

"...not every man," she says softly.

"What does that mean?" Vitaliano raises his voice.

She shouts back.

"Not every man that comes to you seeking to marry me will ask for a dowry, that's what it means!"

Their voices are suddenly loud with emotion.

"Caterina, what are you trying to tell me?"

"Nothing."

"Caterina, have you found a man you want to marry? Have you?"

"Yes, I have."

"Why haven't you told me? Who is it?"

"I can't tell you."

"What? That's ridiculous. Why can't you tell me? Do I know him?"

"Yes, you know him."

"For God's sake, Caterina, tell me who he is!"

Caterina looks up into Vitaliano's face, her eyes filling with tears. "It's Raffaele Brutto, that's who!"

She runs from the room, shutting the door behind her and leaving Vitaliano stunned and unable to speak. He is facing his worst torment, an anguish that reaches far beyond the prospect for his daughter's marriage.

Rosaria Caroleo-Zinzi has been the bonding force in Vitaliano's immediate family for their twenty-three years of marriage. As the inevitable brush between the forceful Vitaliano and his more pliant and complacent children occurs, it is Rosaria who inevitably heals the breech in understanding and brings harmony back to the family. When his oldest son, Saverio, chooses the priesthood for his life's vocation, Vitaliano is obstinately opposed to his choice. Seeing the importance of the decision to her son's happiness, a sympathetic and thoughtful Rosaria intercedes, convincing Vitaliano that Saverio's calling is an opportunity for Vitaliano to give thanks for the enormous turn of events in his early life. It is a difficult time for Vitaliano, but he eventually views his son's decision as a call from God for his repentance. Saverio went on to the priesthood, eventually returning as pastor of Gagliano's St. Rosalia's church. Rosaria had won the day.

Etruscan by ancestry, the Carloeos trace their lineage to the mass exodus from Etruria during the Roman expansion in the third century B.C., into what are now the Italian regions of Tuscany and Umbria. Along with masses of Etruscans, Rosaria's forbears migrated to Calabria, claiming barren land that was available to those who would convert the harsh soil into farmland. As they had been grape growers in the region they left, they brought vine cuttings with them and planted vineyards in their adopted land. Over the centuries, they found themselves subject to foreign rulers including Rome, Greece, the Normans and Spain. Always, they paid homage to their rulers and always they survived and held claim to their land. As Italy emerged as a nation in the mid nineteenth century, the Caroleos' farms were recorded, so as to formally acknowledge them as owners. Unlike most of their fellow Calabrians, the Caroleos were literate and economically content. It was to this family that Rosaria Caroleo was born and it was to Vitaliano Zinzi that she was betrothed and married at the age of twenty. With her came a dowry that complemented the wealth that Vitaliano had earned in his years of leading the Zinzi family out of desperation. The marriage became idyllic as Vitaliano successfully pursued his destiny and received Rosaria's stalwart encouragement along the way. Now Rosaria would be called upon by her daughter, Caterina, to take her side against Vitaliano in choosing the man she would marry without consideration of wealth and dowry.

A red-faced and wild-eyed Caterina storms into the sitting room where her mother has retreated from the muffled shouts of dissonance coming from Vitaliano's office. She has been refused the right to choose for herself the man she will marry. What's more, her announcement of his name left her father thunderstruck. How much more frustrated can she possibly become? Only her mother can understand her frustration.

"Ma, I don't know how to talk to him. He won't listen to reason. I won't have any of those men who stalk me and come looking to extract a large dowry from Pa for marrying me. You've got to plead with him. I can't do what he wants me to do."

Rosaria draws in a long breath and measures her response.

"I understand your plight, my dear, and I sympathize with you. Very few women from families of means can have a man of their choice. They must consider the consequences of a poor marriage."

"Marriages for wealth are the poor marriages. You know that. Look at the men who find their way to Maria's brothel. They're bored with their marriages because their passion is for money and not for their women. Is that how you want me to end up?"

Caterina is crying. Her mother takes her hand.

"My marriage to your father was arranged and we have been happy and fulfilled. You can have that, too. However, I will speak to your father for you, since that's what you want; but you must understand that it's doubtful that he will allow you to marry a field hand...yes, I know of your interest in that man."

Caterina is amazed. How did her mother know about Raffaele? She smiles into Rosaria's face.

"Thanks, Ma, I'm sure you'll make him understand."

The relationship between the intelligent Rosaria and the intense Vitaliano is atypical of most Calabrian couples. She has grown with him from young entrepreneur to baron of his hamlet, and is far more educated than most Calabrian wives. A *femina moderna*, she has listened in on Vitaliano's business dealings and stated her opinions, frequently adding to his perceptions and occasionally saving the day. At a meeting with a new buyer from Bologna, Rosaria sat innocuously in the corner of the room, listening and observing as the portly, untidy man drove his bargain with Vitaliano for a thousand boxes of sweet oranges, to be delivered to a market in Bazzano, a small but commercially dynamic village near Bologna. Payment for the crop would be made by drafts on Banca Commerciale de Bologna. Half of the total sum would be paid upon delivery and the remainder a month later. Quietly exiting the room while the men sipped their grappa and shook hands over their deal, the suspicious Rosaria rode in her carriage to the telegraph office in Catanzaro and sent an inquiry to her closest friend during her one-year's attendance at the University of Bologna. Within the span of two hours, she had determined that the destination for the fruit did indeed exist, but there was no account at the bank in Bologna in the name of the purchaser. Neither was the name of the buyer known to the local merchants. An irate Vitaliano, learning from Rosaria of the attempted ruse, and accompanied by two Carabinieri, was able to apprehend the perpetrator as he was leaving his hotel the next morning. Vitaliano's partner in life had proven that she was also an important partner in his business.

Somehow disavowed of the notion that two people could fall in love without actually being married for a time, Rosaria approaches the task of clearing the way for her daughter with some reluctance. It is an unconvincing attempt. "Vito, our daughter has found this handsome young man…" He holds up his hand and stops her short. "Please don't ask me to approve of her wish to marry a man without the means to take care of her. I will not be pushed into something I don't believe in and I don't like being prodded by two emotional women."

"Can I try to reason with you?"

"Of course you can, but you need to be realistic. Do you believe that she should consider marrying that man?"

"Yes, Vito, I do. She truly believes that she loves him. Surely you know that she will not have the life that she leads here, but you could make it easier for them by giving them a property of their own. You owned the property that started you off years ago. Why not let them have something as well?

"Absolutely not! You are asking me to reward Caterina for marrying a man whose family cannot contribute to the marriage."

"Then you will let them marry if they don't ask for anything from you?"

She has trapped Vitaliano into revealing his true feelings.

"No!" he shouted, "I do not approve of him under any circumstances."

Rosaria is surprised by the emotion in Vitaliano's voice. She nods, acknowledging his final position.

"I'm sorry that I made you angry, Vito."

She leaves the room believing that she has yielded to Vitaliano's steadfast conviction that dowries need to be agreed upon by both families of betrothed couples before marriage can be permitted. She could not have known how wrong she was, nor could she have imagined the truth.

>+<>-0-<>+<

Chapter 4

Hidden Past

Vitaliano's head is swimming in thought as Caterina flees his office, tears streaming down her cheeks. He sits back in his leather chair and breathes a deep sigh of apprehension and regret. He retches over what he heard a moment ago from Caterina. Raffaele Brutto of all people! With all of the choices, why does she have to choose <u>him</u> to marry? And what made her run off after speaking her intentions? Does she fear Vitaliano's rejection because of Raffaele's standing as a field hand? Or has she somehow learned of the veiled incident that Vitaliano stores guardedly within him? It could not be the latter, he thinks. He has done everything possible to keep such things from her. But now, if indeed she is to marry Raffaele, the truth might surface, causing an onslaught of embarrassment and conflict. He feels a nervous impulse, as though he is facing the loss of credibility with his family. His mind flusters with alternatives for either preserving the secrecy of those events or, in the event they are revealed, appeasing Caterina. Perhaps he could grant her an especially generous dowry to marry another man. After all, he will not give her a dowry in marriage to Raffaele. Raffaele has nothing to offer and giving them property –any property- implies that he is a fortune seeker. Vitaliano doesn't like bribing Caterina, but what else can he do? Perhaps she'll decide to drop Raffaele on her own, in which case he might send her off to vacation in Sicily. That would be the best solution. Then, the characteristic calm that has served Vitaliano well for most of his life returns to him. His hands stop moving nervously and his mind stops racing. The past contains some heady times, he thinks, and though they are disparaging, they had been exhilarating as well. He leans forward and stares into space as he recalls the lurid events of those times.

⸻◦⸻

It had taken the crafty Vitaliano only a decade to develop into a thriving property owner, and during that time, he had remained the product of his parents' upbringing: fair, honorable and deeply moral. He devoted himself to his closest living relatives, his two sisters, who reciprocated by caring for his home and person. He assumed the role of their guardian and sanctioned their marriages, giving them generous dowries. When they left to be married, he hired servants to cook and clean for him. He occupied many of his free moments playing with the nephews and nieces coming into his life and was always available to listen to his family's needs and to offer assistance. Often the subject of attempts to arrange his marriage to a suitable woman, Vitaliano skillfully avoided such encounters with scheming fathers. He was known to ride off alone to faraway villages where he was unknown and could enjoy the company of women without scrutiny and speculation by others.

As the years passed, Vitaliano became so immersed in business that he had less time to himself, opting to circumvent the farmer's *consorzio* and selling directly to produce buyers. It took more of his time, supping with them as they talked business, but it brought higher returns and status to his produce. Eventually, the line between business and his personal life blurred. On Sunday mornings, he found himself in the countryside shooting game birds and other creatures of sport with his new associates. His attention to spiritual life became less important to him and was eventually forgotten. As his fortunes grew in proportion to the time devoted to his new acquaintances, he increased contact with them and redirected his life. In time, he became detached from the simple family existence he had led, and began to live a more worldly life. He often carried a weapon for self-defense from attacks by vagabonds who preyed on the affluent.

"Vitaliano, is it true that you lost your father and two brothers in the Risorgimento?" Carlo, the citrus buyer from Naples, had wanted to hear it directly from Vitaliano, though he had heard the story from others. Now that they were enjoying a late dinner in Catanzaro after a long day of touring the Zinzi citrus groves, he threw aside caution and treaded on Vitaliano's very private past.

"Yes, it's true."

"Can you tell me about it?"

Vitaliano's eyes narrowed and his brow furrowed.

"Carlo, if you don't mind, I don't like talking about those terrible times."

Carlo persisted. "Well, let me tell you, Vitaliano, the Risorgimento was a war worth fighting. We're free from Spain now, no thanks to the Pope."

"What do you mean?" Vitaliano feigned surprise.

"Surely you know that the Pope stood against the liberation of our country from its captors. Not only did we have to fight the Austrians in the north and the Spaniards in the south, but we also had to fight the Pope himself in central Italy. We even had to fight France, in the end, to finally unite the Papal States with the rest of Italy. And surely you know that whoever took part in the war on our side was excommunicated by the Pope."

Vitaliano pretended not to know the historical facts. His brave father and brothers had indeed died as excommunicants because they fought on the side of Italian unity. Their battered bodies had been brought back from the battleground in Reggio and were buried in a distant corner of the church cemetery in Gagliano. They did not receive the customary funeral Mass and gravesite blessings associated with burials of the faithful. Years later, Vitaliano acquired property adjacent to Gagliano's St. Rosalia church, and deeded over a portion of his purchase. This allowed for a much needed extension to the cemetery. He also contributed funds that paid for extensive repairs to the antiquated church buildings. Those acts of charity so moved the church pastor that he petitioned Rome and won the posthumous removal of the excommunications from the Zinzi men. A special post-burial service was later held at their graves.

"That may be, Carlo, but my father and brothers were given a Catholic burial in Gagliano."

"If so, they were the exception. There were many good men who faced their creator without the benefit of last rites or religious burial."

There was a condemning tone in Carlo's voice typifying the negative attitude that many of his peers felt toward their church following the reunification of Italy. While they continued to maintain a belief in a Heavenly Spirit and the Hereafter, they had lost their trust in Holy Mother Church as the conduit to the supernatural. Such was the world to which Vitaliano exposed himself as he fell away from Church and family.

———◦———

The workday ended as the Sun's rays tired and hugged the quiet ground. Dust clouds rising from the soil intruded on the celestial light scouring the dappled fields. As the stillness of evening approached, Vitaliano mounted his horse and rode towards Catanzaro. He was quiet and tense from overseeing the planting of a new vineyard, and looked forward to enjoying a glass of wine with his two buyers from Cosenza. It was now dark and the evening *passeggiata* was over. The streets of the city were quiet and nearly deserted.

"Hey, Vito!" Luigi Forlenza called from the barroom of a local inn as Vitaliano entered. "We've been waiting for you to arrive. There's someone we want you to meet."

Inside at a table in the tavern, the two buyers sat with three women. Vitaliano was quick to understand: Luigi and Pietro were there with three women from Catanzaro and wanted Vitaliano to couple with the third woman, whom he had never before seen. Vitaliano was the only single man of the three.

"How do you do, signora?" Vitaliano felt the need to oblige his friends by sitting next to the woman. He was pleased that she actually appealed to him and leapt into conversation with her."

"What's your name?" The darkly pretty woman peered at him, her penetrating blue eyes and attractive face smiling.

"Michela. Are you Vitaliano Zinzi? Her eyes opened wide with anticipation, having heard of him and his famous legend.

"Yes, I am. Have I seen you before? What's your last name?" Vitaliano was becoming interested in her.

"Just call me Michela."

As the evening progressed, Vito and Luigi's consciousness blurred from consuming an excess of wine, and they finally retired to their rooms, taking their lady friends with them. Vitaliano and Michela, both of whom had avoided overdrinking, were now alone and wanting to continue their evening together. They left the Inn arm in arm and walked the streets of Catanzaro, talking and laughing at the stories they shared. Vitaliano surprised himself at the ease with which he talked about his past, a luxury he rarely permitted himself. He told of his start from a small farm given to his family a decade ago and of how he was able to multiply his property holdings over time.

"I was devastated back then when, suddenly, the three men most important to my life were gone. I don't know where I got the strength to take charge of my family and do what I did."

"Vito, you are so different from any man I have ever known."

"And what of you my dear? Why are you here with these people? And what sort of life do you live?"

Michela drew in a breath. Her otherwise cheery face became dour as she began. "I'm afraid my story is quite wretched. I am here earning a living with those two other women because I have no family and there is no one to support me."

"How is it that you have no family?"

"Well, you seem very interested, Vitaliano, so I'll tell you. My parents were very poor, my father a field laborer and mother cleaning and scrubbing floors at the Capurro villa to earn a few lire. My brothers left for America as soon as they were old enough to work. I was the only child left at home and all I could do was menial work at my age. When I had barely reached puberty, my father took payment from an old friend, a widower from Gimigliano with three small children, who offered to marry me. I agreed to the arrangement because it seemed like a way out of my hardship at the time. He was twenty-two years my elder, and he was kind to me, but less than a year following our marriage, he was accused of being a petty thief, convicted and sent to prison. I was faced with the choice of somehow supporting the children on my own or abandoning them so they would be eligible as orphans and be taken in by the nuns. As I had no means of supporting them, I left the children and went home to my parents. I was astonished that they would not take me back. They were repulsed by my leaving the children, despite the improvement to their lives in the orphanage. I was turned out by my own parents." At this point, tears streamed down Michela's cheeks.

Vitaliano was shocked by what he had just heard, almost wishing he had not prompted her to tell her story. It somewhat reminded him of the difficult choices he was forced to make following the deaths of his father and brothers.

"Where is your husband now?"

"Two years after he was taken to prison, I received a notice from the Carabiniere that he was killed during an attempt to escape from prison."

Vitaliano's head was swimming from all that he had heard. He was filled with feelings of pity and at the same time felt that Michela had perhaps acted selfishly by abandoning the children.

By now it was two o'clock in the morning and the two were alone on the winding, cobbled streets lit only by an occasional oil lamp attached to the side of a building. As they rounded a corner, they were abruptly confronted by four men wearing cloth head wraps that identified them as mountain men from high in the Appenines. Their intentions were soon made obvious.

"Give us your wallet and the woman and we will spare your life." The hoodlum had pulled his head gear down over his brow, making it difficult to see his face. The others brandished knives and stood behind him in the shadows. Michela immediately paled and was trembling.

"I'll give you all of the money in my wallet, but the woman stays with me." Only a quickening of his breathing revealed a trace of nervousness in his voice. He remained motionless and calm, hoping his offer would be accepted.

"Keep your money and give us the woman." The four men roared with laughter.

"Not a chance, signore. You are not being very gracious. Now take the money and get on your way." He held out his wallet in a hopeful gesture.

"What?" The man turned to the others. "This man thinks he is dealing with children. He doesn't believe that he is in danger of losing his life. Perhaps we should show him that we mean business."

One of the men moved quickly out of the shadows toward Vitaliano, while the others encircled the couple. Vitaliano called out to Michela, "Back up against the wall!" With their backs to the stone wall, it was impossible for the men to surround them. As the largest of the assailants reached for Vitaliano, knife in hand, he was greeted by Vitaliano's boot in his groin. He doubled over and fell to the ground. The others, enraged at Vitaliano's action, charged at him.

In an instant, Vitaliano reached into his trouser pocket and produced a small caliber Berretta pistol. He fired a shot above their heads, making a deafening sound that would awaken the entire neighborhood. For a moment, all movement stopped. A shocked and frightened look covered the faces of the four men, who were but moments ago confident of their assault on one man. After a fleeting glance at one another, the uninjured three brought their comrade to his feet and escaped into the shadows. The dead of the night had been shattered by Vitaliano's shot; shutters flew open everywhere and angry cries were heard from those awakened by the commotion. The Carabinieri would soon arrive on the scene. Vitaliano returned the tepid pistol to his pocket and turned to Michela. Still trembling, she fell into Vitaliano's arms, sobbing and thanking him profusely for his heroic actions. For several moments, they held one another. He smelled the rose perfume in her hair and the nervous perspiration on her body. She could sense the moisture that had appeared on his forehead, combined with the leathery aroma of the skin on his face. Their eyes met and held the glance for a long, sensuous moment.

The arrival of two mounted Carabinieri interrupted the reverie. The rapture would have to wait. One of the troopers recognized Vitaliano.

"Signore Zinzi, are you all right?"

"Yes, we're all right now. Thank goodness that I was carrying this gun."

After a short interrogation, Michela and Vitaliano left, walking with arms around one another. Michela looked up into Vitaliano's face. "Will you come home with me? It's one small room, but it's just down the street and you look exhausted."

Vitaliano felt a surge of passion and nodded a quick yes. In a moment, they were climbing the staircase to Michela's room in a stucco structure housing a dozen tenants in the center of the city. The tumult had ended and the neighborhood shutters were latched for the night. Inside Michela's room, Vitaliano wondered how many men she had brought to this room. Then, as she disrobed and he drank in her shapely allure, he could think only of the pleasure that she would bring him.

⊷⊷◇⊷⊶

It was the end of a long day in the field, and Vitaliano came home to his easy chair and a glass of wine. There were two letters on the table in the entry hall, and he took them with him. He quenched his thirst and listened to the muddle of sound in the distance as his supper was being readied in the kitchen. He glanced down at the letters on his lap, noticing one bearing the name Michela on the flap. He immediately sat up and tore the fold open. He had not heard from Michela in some months. The passion of their brief romance following that glorious first night had yielded to the demands of Vitaliano's busy life. He had felt something more than youthful infatuation, he thought, but how could he have allowed her into his life? She was an unfortunate coquette, not to be taken seriously. As he looked at the letter he saw a handwriting that was clearly not that of a woman. Michela had gone to a scribe to write this letter for her. It read:

"My dear Vitaliano:
    As I have not heard from you these past months, I assume that your interest in me has lapsed. I can understand that and I thank you for saving me from those horrible criminals and for seeing me for a time thereafter. However, I feel you should know that I have become pregnant and will leave Catanzaro. I am not in need of money and I will have a respectable pregnancy, as I will be married within a few days to a man who will accept responsibility for the fetus I am carrying. His name is Lorenzo Brutto and he is from Reggio. He has found work in Gagliano, and has been assigned a small house there by his employer. I will do everything I can to ensure that our paths do not cross and that no mention of our connection is ever made.

With affection,
Michela"

Vitaliano's head whirled with conflicting thoughts. Was he being jilted?

How dare she? Had she forgotten his importance? Could this unborn child be his? Should he allow Michela to forever pretend that the child was conceived with another man? Should he simply accept what Michela has told him and not burden his life and reputation with any further inquiry? His housekeeper disrupts his thoughts.

"Signore Zinzi! Your dinner is ready. Please come to the table."

Vitaliano was frozen in his seat and unable to respond. He felt pangs of loss, a jealousy that henceforth another man would be with Michela. A notion consumed him to immediately go to Catanzaro and find Michela. He would demand that she not marry this Brutto fellow, and remain his mistress until he released her. He would provide for her and for her child. Or, maybe he would preempt her plans to marry by taking her as his wife. No, he thought, he was Vitaliano Zinzi and he had an obligation to his family to marry fittingly. He would not allow himself to act in this childish manner.

"Signore! Please! Your dinner will get cold."

He rose from his chair and walked somberly to the dining room, the crumpled letter held firmly in his hand. He would never again think about Michela or her unborn child.

Chapter 5

First Meeting

The distant chatter of field hands grows louder as the early light of dawn expands to fill the cold, dank valley. Their words are blurred, but the sounds are decipherable: complaints of meager wages, the cold morning, the romance of the previous night. Waves of canes reach skyward from the grape vines, needing to be pruned away and burned to ash in stacks. Columns of malodorous smoke proclaim the presence of these men, breathing vapor into the morning chill and cutting at the vines with their small, hooked knives. The swift pace of work does not interfere with their banter.

"I heard that Luigi was replaced because he was suspected of prodding the men to ask for more pay. I guess we'll never get justice as long as the boss can fire anyone who speaks up."

"Lord, it's cold out here this morning. My hands are so stiff that I may not be able to prune my quota for the day. I hope it warms up."

"Who was the *ragazza* I saw you walking with the other evening in the town center? Did her chaperones leave you alone at all? Did you get into her pants?"

"Mind your damn business!"

"I heard the baron's daughter was out walking the vineyard yesterday. Madon', she's a beauty, but why hasn't she married? Doesn't she like boys?" There is a moment of laughter.

"What a catch she is. Not only is she rich, but she's damned pretty and even knows how to read and write."

"Who else but a rich guy would want a wife who could read and write? She'd be telling you how to zip up your pants."

The laughter catches the attention of the foreman.

"All right, you men, keep your mind on what you're doing. You'll go home missing a finger if you aren't careful. We have a new man starting today and I don't want him picking up your bad habits. Hey, Raffaele, you can begin here in this row. Make sure it's done by sundown and don't make any cuts that aren't necessary. We want those vines to produce lots of fruit next season."

The young man looks up. "Sure, boss." His youthful voice and thin muscular body distinguishes him from the older, thicker men. It is evident that he is young and far less experienced than they.

"Hey, you, aren't you Lorenzo's kid? He doesn't work for Baron Zinzi. What are you doing here? Did you take Luigi's job?"

"I don't need to work where my father works. There's work here, and I'm here to earn my living."

More laughter and notice from the foreman. "OK, leave him alone to work. He'll do fine without your questions."

A workman whispers to another: "That's one of Michela Brutto's boys. He might even be the one who came along before she was married, and got her a husband and out of whoring."

"Quiet, you fool; do you want to start trouble? Keep what you think you know to yourself."

"Yeah, well I don't like a boy coming in here and taking work away from Luigi and getting paid the same as we do."

"How do you know what he's being paid?"

"It's the rule with these growers. They don't want us experienced men asking for more money, so they pay us all the same...just enough to keep us coming back."

A bored and edgy Caterina paces the polished wooden floor of her bedroom in bare feet. It is summer and the humid midday air makes the upstairs room unbearable. She opts for the downstairs, finding Vitaliano in his office, busily reading a letter when she enters the room.

"Father, it's so hot and I just don't have anything to do."

"Why don't you assist your mother? You'll need to know how to do woman's work when you marry and have a family."

"I already know all of that. Ma knows I can cook and clean when it's necessary. Why can't I be involved in what you do? Some day you'll wish you had trained me to take charge."

"What are you talking about? Are you mad? You need to marry and have children, not operate a business. That's for men to do. Your brothers will take over as they grow older. If you had only accepted Gennaro as a suitor, he'd be knocking on the front door wanting permission to take you for a walk. Then you wouldn't be so bored."

"He's not interested in me. He wants the dowry he would get for marrying me."

"Caterina, I've told you many times, that's how marriages are arranged. Just because he bargained with me for a dowry doesn't mean he doesn't want you. He wants to ensure your future, that's all."

"Stop it, Pa. You know that without a dowry Gennaro wouldn't be talking to you about me."

"Have it your way, but remember my words when you're an old woman and alone in life."

Seeing that she cannot get Vitaliano's interest, Caterina puts on a small sun hat and walks a long way on the sandy soil that surrounds the vineyard nearest the house. As she walks, she can feel the eyes of the field workers on her. Her shapely, slim body dressed in an ankle length flowered gray dress gives cause to look and admire as she walks past them, fanning herself with a handkerchief and looking at the clusters of grapes. There is a dead silence as she picks an unripe grape and tries to eat it. She promptly spits it out and grimaces.

"You can't eat them yet. They aren't ripe enough." She turns to see the smiling face of a handsome young farm worker. He stands up, stretching his six-foot frame and smiling broadly through large white teeth. His tanned skin and dark, wavy hair accent his aquiline features and stabbing blue eyes. Caterina feels a sexual attraction, but suppresses the thought and blurts out instead, "Should you be talking to me? I'm the baron's daughter and he would be very disturbed if he knew I was talking to you."

"Ah, so you are the Caterina I've heard so much about. Are you?"

"Yes, I am. What is it that you've heard?"

"Only that you are lovely and are also very smart."

"Well, now that you've met me, what do you think?"

"I think you're very attractive, but I can't tell how smart you are."

A voice in the distance called, "Caterina, where are you? It's lunchtime. Please come back to the house." It is her mother's servant, her face a mask of concern.

"I'm coming."

She turns to the young man and asks, "What is your name?"

"I'm Raffaele...Raffaele Brutto." He smiles confidently, feeling that she had shown interest in him. He adds boldly, "Will I see you again?"

Caterina turns back as she strides quickly towards the house. She covers her smile and curtly says, "No." The response belies her true impulse, but she decides it is unwise to reveal her thoughts. After all, he could be an opportunist currying favor, or he might have a wife and five children.

Raffaele's face dulls. He stands gazing at Caterina as she struts toward the house, finally out of sight. He feels the sting of hopeless rejection. She lives in a privileged world, he thinks, and would never become involved with a lowly field worker like him. His heart sinks as he returns to work.

The fall season has finally arrived, and its panorama of red, yellow and maize signal the time for harvest. Chestnuts, olives, oranges and grapes hang copiously from their stems, petitioning for attention. For Vitaliano Zinzi, it is time to harvest grapes and make wine. The other crops can wait, but the wine grapes demand priority. The pace of the workers quickens as the coming of a rain spell requires the completion of the grape harvest. Only one man's attention is deflected from his work, his neck craning now and again to catch a glimpse of the girl who has captured his fancy and who has since taken center stage in his dreams.

The foreman cries out, "Come on, Raffaele, catch up with the others. We need to beat the rain. Work faster!"

"I'll try, boss, I'll try."

Raffaele's knife increases its pace as he slices the rigid stems. Faster, faster. Fill those baskets. Beat the rain. One day left. Catch up to the others. Suddenly, he feels a stinging pain in his hand. He looks down into his basket and sees a stream of blood flooding onto the fruit from a long slash in his left palm and wrist. He feels cramping in his forearm as the stinging pain darts up from his wrist.

"Help!" he calls, "I'm cut and bleeding."

"You damn fool! What do you think you're doing? Now you'll be out of work for days, maybe weeks from the look of that cut." Enrico, the foreman, quickly removes Raffaele's belt and twists it around his forearm, reducing the bleeding to a trickle. Then, he removes Raffaele's neckerchief, rolls it into a large ball and presses it to the cut.

"Hold tightly against the cut and stop the bleeding."

"You asked me to work faster, boss, and I was just trying to catch up to the others."

"We'll need to do something about the bleeding. Let's get up to the house."

Raffaele trails blood as they make their way to the villa. The house appears unattended as they approach the rear, looking for someone to come to the door of the kitchen. Enrico cries out, "Is anyone here? We need help. Hurry!"

A large woman in an apron comes to the door holding a pan fragrant with crushed tomatoes. A look of fright engulfs her face as she sees the two men, Raffaele holding the bloody neckerchief to his wrist, bleeding and wincing with pain.

"Come in. What can we do for him?"

"We need some strong wine…and bring me a needle and thread." Enrico pulls a long bench toward the center of the room. "Lie down," he says to Raffaele, as he positions a chair alongside the bench. He finds a bowl, places it on the chair and stretches Raffaele's arm out over the receptacle. The kitchen will serve as infirmary, the bench as Raffaele's recline.

Raffaele's eyes open wide with apprehension. He knows what's ahead.

His hand will be sewn closed and Enrico will have to do it. The alcohol will sanitize the cut and, if he can drink enough of it to dull his senses, he can endure the pain. The genuine test of Enrico's handiwork will come in a few days time, when the possibility of infection will need to be dealt with. If it isn't, the arm can fester and need to be amputated. The large woman returns to clean the trail of blood into the kitchen. Rosaria enters carrying a sewing basket. Behind her is Caterina, a large bottle of brandy in her arms, gasping at what she sees. Raffaele looks up and sees Caterina. He is weak from the loss of blood, his red-veined eyes drooping and his movements slow and deliberate. For a moment, his pain is gone and he wants to speak, but no words form. He tries to rise from the bench, but loses consciousness and falls back. Caterina brings her hand to her face and gasps, her mind aflutter with conflicting sentiments. Is she feeling an intense sympathy for a man she hardly knows? Is there more to her feelings than empathy? Why does she feel an intense attraction to this man? How can she allow this peasant to invade the sanctity of her mind?

When Raffaele opens his eyes hours later, he is puzzled. The beamed ceiling he looks up at is not in his home, and the floral scent in the room is new to his senses. The stillness is also different. Had he died? Was this heaven? A sharp pain in his wrist and hand sobers his senses and reminds him of where he is. He looks down and sees that his hand is across his chest, bound in a huge white cloth fastened with a pin. Looking around the room, he becomes aware that he is in a corridor of the baron's home. His shoes have been removed and he lies on a cushioned chaise that sits high above the floor. A blanket, silky to the touch, has been draped over him. He thinks about the horrible possibility that his hand will have to be removed. He concentrates on his wrist and hand. The pain is horrific, but he senses no throbbing.

A bespectacled, gray-haired man walks over to Raffaele from across the corridor. "I'm Doctor D'Angelo. I've been waiting for you to awaken. Baron Zinzi summoned me to attend to you. By the time I arrived, your hand had been sewn shut and I decided to leave it alone. There is every indication that the wound will heal well. Try to stand up. Can you?"

Raffaele struggles to his feet, and falls back, unable to stand or walk. His eyes are heavy and barely open, but he is elated at what he has just heard. His hand is likely to heal. The doctor places the palm of his hand against Raffaele's forehead, feels his pulse and checks his eyes. He writes his diagnosis on a slip of paper which he slips into his pocket and says, "You're condition is stable, but you'll have to be helped to get home. Stay off your feet for a few days until you gain back your strength." Without further discussion, he leaves the room. It is then that Raffaele notices that he and the doctor have not been alone. As he looks back, he sees Caterina sitting on a chair directly behind him. He sees the cupid-like face, the heart shaped lips and the chestnut brown eyes. His heart races. What is she doing here? He dares to hope that she has somehow developed an interest in him, unlikely as it seems. He searches his mind for words, but before he can say anything, she speaks.

"I've watched as your hand was stitched and the bleeding stopped. You were fortunate to have Enrico as your surgeon. Untrained as he is, he has saved many a hand or finger. Yours was particularly difficult because the cut was deep and he needed to clean it carefully before he sewed it closed. Thankfully you were unconscious and you lay perfectly still while he worked on you."

Raffaele forces out his words. "Do you always observe these incidents? Are you a medical student?"

"No, I don't like seeing blood and pain. I could never be a doctor."

"Then why did you watch my ordeal?"

"I don't know. I just stayed and watched after bringing the alcohol."

There is a moment of tense silence when neither of them speaks. Caterina again feels an intense attraction that puzzles her and prompts mixed feelings about being near Raffaele. He feels the desperation of his hopeless wish to be close to Caterina and to explore his attraction to her. He looks at her with an unyielding gaze, his large blue eyes beginning to brighten.

"The first time we met, you said that you did not want to see me again. Now you're here and you've watched over me for hours. Is it possible that you really <u>would</u> like to see more of me?" His heart is beating rapidly and his face is flushed. He has placed his ultimate fantasy of courting her flatly in the open and now waits for her response. Please, God, let her grant me my wish.

"I am not allowed to see men who work as laborers and who have no means or promise."

"And have you found a man who qualifies?"

"There have been many such men, but they don't want me, they lust for the land they'll be given to take me as their wife. I will have no part of that, and I will not be married off to the best negotiator."

"Perhaps you don't understand because you have always been in your father's house and have always been cared for."

"I do understand and I know that my father is trying to protect me, but I want a man who appeals to me and who wants me regardless of my father's wealth."

The conversation emboldens Raffaele.

"Caterina, I would like to see you again, when I'm recovered. Is that possible?"

"It would be impossible to get my father's approval."

"That means that you would like to see me." His heart leaps.

"I didn't say that."

"Yes, but that's what you meant. Don't worry, Caterina, I'll get him to agree. He doesn't have to worry about dowries with me. I don't have anything and all I am asking is to be with you."

Caterina is shocked. She has unwittingly revealed to Raffaele that she does indeed wish to see him and received the response she had furtively hoped for. The veil of decorum is lifted and she is able to speak her mind.

"I would like to see you, Raffaele, but I am helpless to get permission."

"I understand that, and I will approach the baron as soon as I am able."

At that moment, Vitaliano enters the house from an entrance door down the hall from Raffaele and Caterina. Dusk has arrived and he is home for the night. At first, he doesn't recognize Caterina, thinking that a house servant is attending Raffaele. When it is clear that it is Caterina, he becomes annoyed and speaks gruffly.

"What are you doing here, Caterina?"

"I'm just seeing to this man's comfort. Dr. D'Angelo has just left and said that someone would have to help him get home. He's had a bad injury."

"Very well, you can leave now." Vitaliano shows his anxiety about separating Caterina from what he perceives to be a compromising circumstance. In his world, single women who are not caregivers do not attend to men even if they were injured. When his young daughter was gone, he sat in a near-by chair, showing concern for Raffaele. "How are you doing? How is your strength?"

"I am still very weak, but if you can arrange for me to have some assistance, I am ready to leave...after we've had a short talk."

"Talk? What is it that you need?"

Raffaele stares at Vitaliano, mustering all of his nerve. His heart pounds and he feels a surge of blood coursing his brain.

"Baron, this is very difficult for me, but please...I want...I wish to...would you..."

"What is it? What do you want?"

Raffaele screws up more daring than he ever believed possible.

"I want permission to court your daughter." There, it was over. He said it and it's over. He is able to breathe again.

Vitaliano is silent. Had he heard correctly? Is this peasant asking to court his precious Caterina? Where could he have gotten the notion that he could ask me that? It's ridiculous. He looks at the poor fellow and asks, "What is your name?"

"I am Raffaele Brutto."

Suddenly, Vitaliano explodes with emotion. His face turns ferocious. He holds on to his chair as he stands up, clenching his teeth, widening his eyes and tightening his fists. He cannot contain himself. Raffaele Brutto, indeed. This is the man who grew from the child that Michela had conceived a generation ago. At best he was the reason that Michela had chosen to discard him for another man. At worst, he could be Vitaliano's own bastard son. He does not resemble Vitaliano, but he looks very much like Michela. For a moment, Vitaliano imagines that he is looking into the face of his own son. All of his emotions roar out of him.

"No! It isn't possible. I will have you booted out on your ass if you go near her."

Raffaele's head is spinning. What could possibly have ignited Vitaliano? "May I ask why?"

"No, you may not!"

Vitaliano calms himself. He is almost breathless as he continues.

"Caterina will be married to a man of substance and promise. Dowries will be given to the couple from both families. Surely you can understand that Caterina wishes to be married properly."

"I know only that I have deep feelings for her that I cannot suppress. I would like to speak with her under supervision of your chaperones to see if she has any interest in me."

"I will speak for her. She has no interest in you. She is to be married to one who has wealth and position. Do not question my authority again."

Raffaele has failed totally in his plea to win approval to court Caterina. In his desperation, he wishes that an infection had developed in his hand had spread to the rest of his body and killed him. The disappointment adds to his weak condition, and he mutters to Vitaliano, "Please get help to take me home. My family will be concerned."

Chapter 6

Love Catches On

It is difficult for Caterina to understand the intensity of her father's decree. She is to avoid seeing or contacting Raffaele at all. He is not of her class and can never be considered a part of her world. There are others to choose from and any one of them would make a superb provider and give her a life of dignity to which she is entitled. Any transgression would mean immediate expulsion for Raffaele and isolation for her. She stares into a window of her bedroom and loses focus to the outside. Instead, the reflection she sees is Raffaele's face: the dark hair, the swarthy aquiline face and the penetrating blue eyes. His warm voice and effortless bodily movements are different than any other man she has known. The men who ask for her hand in marriage are unexciting. Not one of them can compare to this magnificent man. He is tall, muscular and very good-looking. Though they have never touched, she imagines being in his burly arms, their lips touching, their bodies pressed together. She feels a carnal longing coursing her body, wishing he were present to perfect her desire. She decides that she must see him. Surely her father will understand in the end.

⊢⊷⊙⊶⊣

The heavy winter rain pounds the soil, its mission seemingly to tear away the surface of the ground. Sheets of rain sweep across the small valley from west to east, sending a destructive torrent through the orchards. Hollows appear at the base of young trees as the soil is pulled away and swept into the sea of rain forming in a swale below the village of Gagliano. Occasional flashes of lightning illuminate the gray sky, and are followed by claps of thunder. From the warmth of her home, Caterina gazes out at the storm and thinks of Raffaele. She has not seen nor heard of him since the night of his accident two months ago. She wonders how he is coping in the stormy outdoors, now that he is back at work and assigned to a grove far away from La Stella. Raffaele has been true to Vitaliano's demand that he not contact her at the risk of being dismissed. It has been a disappointment to her. The man with whom she is obsessed has not pursued her simply because her father has threatened him. Perhaps he doesn't really desire her as much as she imagines. Is she fantasizing? What is wrong with her? Why doesn't one of the other men appeal to her as Raffaele does? How it would simplify her life. She becomes angry for a moment, imagining the possibility that he has found another woman that he truly cares for. Then, she warms as she again supposes that he is working in the cold, harsh weather longing to be close to her. She damns the culture that is imposed on her, giving her father such power over her that she cannot live her life as she wishes. She wants only to determine whether or not Raffaele is the man she imagines him to be. What would it be like to be alone with him? How would he behave towards her? The imponderable is maddening. She needs to know. She will brave the weather and find him, wherever he is. She will confront him. If he doesn't want her, at least she will know. Ah, but if he feels as she believes he does, the world will be theirs. To hell with dowries and social orders! To be with him would be all she would ever want or need; to cook breakfast for him, to be present as he returns home at the end of the day, to go to bed with him and make love to him, to give him children and to grow old with him. He would be the essence of her entire life.

It is a gray afternoon as Caterina throws a shawl over her head and heads for the small shed behind the house. She shuffles through storm clothing contained in boxes and on wall hooks. There are boots her size. Her bare feet slip in. There is a cloak and rain bonnet that her mother wears, too large for her, but adequate in this time of urgency. She is protected from the severe weather. Now, she must determine Raffaele's whereabouts. She remembers that Enrico is just outside in the vineyard with his crew, keeping the swells of rain from invading the house. She finds him directing his men. They are digging small trenches that direct the streaming water away from the buildings. She walks up to him.

"Enrico, is it you? It's Caterina. I need to talk to you."

"Signorina, what are you doing out in this storm?"

She gets right to the point.

"I need to find Raffaele. Where is he?"

"You must be crazy. Your father would be mad with rage if he knew you were out in the rain looking for Raffaele. Please, go back to the house." He looks guardedly to the right and left as though he might be overheard by the baron.

"Enrico! Tell me where he is. I need to see him. Now!"

Enrico is stunned. He is being ordered to betray his baron by the baron's own daughter. He is confused. What should he do? He is in a most compromising position. Finally, he agrees.

"You must never tell anyone how you learned of Raffaele's whereabouts or I will be dealt with severely."

"I swear it, Enrico, I will never betray you. Please!"

"Do you know where the Beccio ranch is?"

"Yes, I do."

"I believe that Raffaele was assigned there because it is the farthest from the house. But, it is a long way to go in this rain. How will you get there?"

"I'll ride the largest of the donkeys."

Enrico looks at the desperate face that has been pleading with him. He thinks of his own desire for his Angelina two decades ago, and his heart warms. He would have risked death itself to be near his love. Why should it be any different for Caterina?

"Good luck, signorina. And remember, you didn't hear anything from me."

⊢•◦•◦—◦—◦•◦•⊣

It is as though Divine Intervention has chosen to assist her, as Caterina pushes her way south to the Beccio property. She is mounted on Perla, the largest donkey she could find. The wind eases and the rain moderates to a drizzle. The usually stubborn mare obliges. Though they slide precariously in the mud for the entire 2 miles to the edge of the Beccio grove, Perla does not once try to halt or turn back. Caterina is cold, drenched, and muddy, but not for a moment does she regret having ventured out. She can almost feel Raffaele's presence and she is too excited to sense the inclemency of the weather. As she looks ahead, she sees a group of workmen. Raffaele is sure to be there. She will ride up to them and call his name. Then, when she has found him, she will ask the foreman to allow him to step away with her. She begins to formulate the words she will speak as she confronts Raffaele with the notion that, if he cared, he might well have disobeyed her father and pursued her. She speculates as to what he would say and how he would behave, but it is too painful to continue the fantasy. She arrives at the spot where the men are working. They are restoring the eroded soil with their shovels and creating channels for the water to circumvent the trunks of the olive trees. She looks for Raffaele, but the men's caps are down over their brows, making it difficult to identify one from the other. She decides that he is not there and calls to the foreman.

"Can you tell me where I can find Raffaele Brutto? I have an important message for him."

The foreman looks up, his eyes widening. He must know that Caterina is not to see Raffaele. He stammers.

"No, signorina, he is not here and I frankly don't know where he is. Why don't you try another gang just down the hill?"

Sadly, Caterina turns her mount around for yet another half-mile ride to the next group of workers. Once again, he is not there. After the third try fails, she concludes that Vitaliano has indeed instructed his foremen to prevent her from seeing Raffaele. She slumps down and a tear rolls down her cheek. She has braved the storm and risked Vitaliano's wrath for nothing. She turns and begins the long trip home. Suddenly, she hears a whisper.

"Signorina! Look here, on this side. Please try not to be obvious."

An older man is standing in the grove to the other side of the road, away from the rest of the crew. He is signaling Caterina to ride over to him so they can speak. A flood of hope fills her. She leans down from her mount so she can hear him.

"I can tell you where Raffaele is working, but only if you promise never to reveal my assistance."

"Oh, yes, I swear it. I will never tell anyone of our meeting. Please, now tell me where he is."

"There is a barn not one mile from here that contains several horses. The foreman sent Raffaele up there an hour ago to muck the stalls and feed the horses. You can get there by turning up the next road." The look on the old man's face is a combination of fear and beneficence, as he contemplates the punishment that might await him for defying the baron's order and measures it against the happiness his defiance will bring.

"Thank you, I know where it is."

Caterina's heart races as she tugs on the suddenly recalcitrant Perla and heads her in a new direction. She has at last located Raffaele and she will have her moment of confrontation once and for all. If he does not respond as she expects, she will promptly go home and forget him. Her father will never know that she ventured out. But…could she ever forget this man? She is not sure.

The stormy sky lightens and the rain has stopped since just before she spoke with the old man. There is a slight incline in the last hundred yards to the barn, and Perla brays as she struggles upward, sliding in the slick mud, and announcing their arrival. The barn is constructed of natural stone, its wilted, leaking wood roof showing its age. From the loft above the barn entrance, Raffaele looks out. He is curious. He spots the rider and strains as he attempts to determine who it is.

Caterina calls from under her large bonnet, "Raffaele, is it you?"

Her voice is unmistakable. Raffaele shouts down to her.

"Caterina, what are you doing here? Your father will be furious!"

She is devastated. Raffaele has quickly and unquestionably let her know that he isn't willing to wage war with her father to win her hand. He is more concerned about saving his skin than about her. Her anger emerges.

"I've come all this way in the rain and mud and is that what you have to say to me? You son-of–a bitch, to hell with you!"

She turns her mount and urges her on in a homeward direction. Perla will have none of this turnabout. She promptly bucks Caterina off of her back and trots away as quickly as the mud will allow, braying and slipping as she goes, and trailing her reins.

Caterina picks herself up out of the mud and calls out.

"Perla, come back here! Perla!"

A light rain begins to fall, adding misery to her already damaged pride. Perla isn't coming back. Caterina frustrates as she considers what she will do to get home before the storm returns. She is angry with herself for venturing out on this stormy day, only to determine that Raffaele is not terribly interested in her after all.

"Come with me. You must get out of the rain." It is Raffaele, who has dropped down from his perch in the hayloft to assist Caterina. He takes her hand and leads her into the cover of the barn. It is the first time they have ever touched. Her mood brightens as the feel of his hand on hers sends a warm sensation through her body. She does not speak.

"You must dry yourself off. You're soaking wet and muddy."

"How can I do that in this dirty old horse barn?"

"The Beccio house is not far, and though it isn't lived in, there is a useable fireplace. I can build a fire and get some water from the well so that you can wash. Then, when you're ready, I'll saddle a horse for you to get you home."

She is speechless. Raffaele is still urging her to return home, but she senses that this is her opportunity to validate her feelings about him. She must know if she acted hastily in presuming his indifference.

"Take me there. I want to wash and dry my clothing."

Like the barn, the Beccio house is made of natural stone, has a sagging gabled roof and is very old, perhaps as much as five hundred years. Though it has been uninhabited from before Vitaliano purchased the property two decades earlier, the stone construction has protected it from complete deterioration. Inside, there are two cavernous rooms on the first floor, one a large kitchen and living area and the other a bedroom. Most of the furnishings are gone. Raffaele quickly gathers firewood that has escaped the rain and starts a fire, using a flint stone that he finds on the mantel and some straw that is strewn across the dirt floor. As the fire takes hold, he finds an old bench for Caterina to sit on in front of the fireplace. He goes to the well just outside the house and brings back a large bucket of water. He directs her as he would instruct a complete neophyte.

"First, drink some of the water. Then, use it to wash yourself and remove the mud from your clothing. I'll go to the barn and saddle a pony to take you home."

The room warms as the fire glows. Caterina removes her hat and cloak and drapes them over the bench. She cups her hands in the bucket and raises them to her face filled with water. She drinks, then scrubs her face and neck and uses a handkerchief to dry off. She splashes water onto her cloak to wash off the mud and places one end of her bonnet into the water to clean it off. Then, she spreads the cloak and bonnet across the back of the bench to dry. Finally, she removes her boots and heaves the remaining water against the muddy bottoms. She sits in front of the fire and contemplates Raffaele's return. Outside, he ties a saddled pony to a post and enters the house carrying a large horse blanket to line the bench for Caterina.

"It looks as though the rain will start again. When you are ready to begin your trip home, there is a pony outside for you to use. One of the men can come by for him in the morning."

She looks at him gratefully. She is in a playful mood.

"Not so fast. You can't get rid of me that quickly. Now that we're here together, I'd like to get to know you."

"Caterina, I don't want to get you in trouble with your father. Perhaps I should go."

Caterina is again enraged by Raffaele's insistence on her leaving for home.

"Bullshit! You're afraid for yourself, not for me. I want to know. Are you courting a woman?"

"Yes, I am."

Caterina is momentarily wordless, shocked beyond comprehension. She says, sheepishly, "You told me that you wanted to see me. Weren't you truthful?"

"That was months ago. I pleaded with your father, but I was unable to get his permission to see you. When I asked, he raged and demanded that I stay away from you. His words were very harsh and I thought I would never see you again."

"Is this other woman prettier than I am?" Caterina sits straight up in her seat and looks directly at Raffaele, the glare of the fire reflecting off one side of her face.

There is a long pause. Raffaele sits on the far end of the bench. He looks at Caterina, barefoot and disheveled from her trek out into the storm. She is as lovely now with the fire forming her silhouette as when she appears in his dreams. Her face, her form, her very being is mesmerizing. This is the woman he really wants.

"No, Caterina, she isn't. But I am not violating her father's wishes when I see her. Her family welcomes me and respects my interest in her. I would give anything to have that opportunity with you, but there isn't a chance with that father of yours."

Tears stream down Caterina's face. In so many words, he has said that he wants her. Her words are bounded by sobs.

"What kind of man are you? Are you too weak to stand up to my father?"

"Your father is very opposed to me. You should have seen him in his fury. Perhaps he knows something about me that I don't know. There are secrets in my family that even I don't know. "

Caterina's sudden curiosity calms her.

"Tell me about your family."

"My father is from Reggio. He is the only one in his family who survived during a typhoid epidemic. He worked a farm for a despotic landlord who demanded an unfair share of the crop, condemning him to a life of poverty. He eventually left Reggio and went to Catanzaro in hopes of finding employment. He met my mother there and they were married shortly after he secured work in Gagliano."

Raffaele hesitated to talk further. He looked at Caterina pleadingly, hoping that she would say something to keep him from saying more.

"Go on, Raffaele, I need to know the rest."

His voice grew faint as he continued.

"Six months later I was born. No one openly questioned who my father was, but it was quietly hinted that I was a bastard child who my mother conceived before she met my father. What is clear is that my mother was a prostitute for a time when she was desperately poor. I have five siblings and none of them look like me. Though I believe that I am my father's son, it is impossible for me to know for sure. He has always treated me the same as the others and places his trust in me as his oldest son."

A tear stains the side of Raffaele's face and Caterina makes a hand gesture signaling that she has heard enough. She has urged him to tell his story and it has affected him deeply. She takes his hand in hers.

"I'm sorry to have caused you pain. None of what you have told me affects my feelings for you. If my father doesn't approve of you because of that, so be it. If you are interested in me, then you must end your courtship immediately and I will see you in defiance of my father's wishes."

Raffaele's face lights up. He is enormously pleased with what he has heard. Not once in his experience has anyone dared to defy the baron. Now this exquisite woman would risk her own well being to be with him.

"Though I have dreamt of you often, I have seen you only a few times. Yet I feel that I know you well. I have been in love with you since the time I first saw you in your father's vineyard."

She is euphoric. She loses restraint and leaps forward into his arms. They are both surprised by her sudden boldness. The lust that she had felt in merely thinking about him was slight compared to the uncontrollable craving she now feels. She looks up to his face, her lips parting. He brings her up to him in his arms and kisses her deeply. She breathes in the balm of the evergreens surrounding the house and it mixes with the aroma of Raffaele's skin and hair and the feel of his whiskered face. He feels the silk of her face and the softness of her moist lips. He glimpses her long, shadowy eyelashes. He places a hand on her breast. It is soft and full and the nipple is hard. She does not push away. His hand falls to her thigh and he grips it tightly. Still, she does not object. How far should he take this first physical contact with the woman he adores? They are both intensely stirred and are truly alone in this abandoned old house. He looks at her, his eyes burning with desire.

"Caterina, are you sure you want to do this?"

"Yes, my love, I must have you."

Together, they spread the horse blanket on the warm floor in front of the fire and remove their clothes. Then, they clutch one another in a fervent embrace and fall to the floor in a tangle of limbs. They are oblivious to the storm that has returned and is raging outside.

Chapter 7

Shame

Vitaliano and Rosaria lie awake in their bed as the first light of dawn makes its appearance. It is six O'clock and they have not slept. The night's storm is over and the morning sky will soon brighten with a carroty winter sun. They listen for the least bit of sound in the still air, hoping that they will hear Caterina returning from her night's roost. Vitaliano is beside himself with anger, but calms himself to ease Rosaria's worry. A foreman working near the Beccio ranch had stopped Vitaliano as he made his way home the previous evening. The overseer was able to piece together the events of Caterina's feral exploits earlier in the day and recounted them to Vitaliano. His dignity at stake, Vitaliano showed no emotion whatever. Without hesitation, he instructed the dutiful foreman to dismiss the old man who had told Caterina where Raffaele was working. No one was to go near the Beccio house, whose chimney had unexpectedly sprung to life, belching a column of dense smoke; and whose wooden front steps were sporting a pony, saddled and ready to ride. With Caterina having been sighted approaching the house and Raffaele found missing from his post in the barn, the facts were self evident without further thought or investigation. Mortified and enraged, Vitaliano simply retreated home and waited for the licentious Caterina to arrive home. He would deal with her –and Raffaele- on his own turf and in his own timeframe. He did not expect her to remain with Raffaele throughout the night, however. Nor did he expect the dissension that he would confront when Caterina finally arrived home the following morning.

At the first sound of Caterina riding her pony to the stalls at the rear of the house, Vitaliano carefully considers what he will say to her. 'Has she slept with Raffaele?' Of course she has; he had better be more incisive than that. 'Why has she done such a thing?' That is closer to what he feels he should ask. He considers sharing his worst fear with her, the possibility of incest; but he knows that he is not able to discuss such a bizarre subject with her and quickly dismisses it from his mind. Some things are better not revealed or discussed. Above all, he needs to restrain himself and not descend into rage. He has been disobeyed in the worst possible way, and it will not be easy to remain calm. He rises from his bed, gives Rosaria an assuring look, and dresses slowly and deliberately, giving Caterina time enough to enter the house and reach her bedroom. He will meet with her there among the artifacts familiar to her since her childhood: a wooden cross with an alabaster Christ hanging in familiar demise; a Madonna in blue veil, her arms beckoning the faithful to emulate her purity; and a St. Anthony statue with the Christ child on his shoulder, summoning the world to salvation. Surely these objects would assist him in making his point with her. He slips his woolen robe over his nightshirt to warm him from the morning chill, and walks down the hall to Caterina's room.

⪥⪥⪤⪤

Caterina lies on her bed, smiling broadly. She feels the pain in her groin from the previous night's pleasure, but it is a sting of joy. She and Raffaele had at last been able to share their bodies and prove the depth of their physical attraction. They had spent the entire night together, making love repeatedly. There was no quenching of the passion they both felt. He was hers as completely as she was his. She had found her man, her spiritual partner in life, and she had easily surrendered her virginity to him. He had responded beyond her greatest hope, pledging undying love and expressing his willingness to defy Vitaliano so that she might become his woman forever. He had no interest whatever in dowries; he simply wanted her. What more than this could Caterina have hoped for? Now she must make amends with her father for having taken her life so boldly into her own hands and having behaved so shockingly.

There is a loud knock on her door, and in the next instant, Vitaliano is in the room. His eyes are fierce dark orbs glaring odiously at her. His lips are pursed in anger. He closes the door behind him and begins to speak, almost in a fierce whisper, hoping not to be overheard by Rosaria.

"Where have you been? What the hell have you done?"

He has had no difficulty selecting his words after all. Caterina is frightened, but she does not back down.

"I did what I had to do. It's my life and I'm not going to live it with one of those dull men that you want me to marry."

He is shocked. He has never seen Caterina so bold and defiant. An instant sense of pride and admiration for her flashes across his mind, but is instantly consumed by his anger.

"Did you have to protest with such a horrendous act of defiance? Am I that unimportant to you that you defy me publicly and shame me by fornicating with a common field hand?"

It first occurs to Caterina that she and Raffaele had been discovered making love in the Beccio house. She is sickened by the thought that they may have actually been observed. Her face flushes, but she recovers her senses.

"Pa, I'm not going to let you talk about Raffaele that way. He's a decent man and we love each other...and we're going to be married."

Vitaliano looks at his young daughter scornfully. He draws a deep breath and falls wearily into a chair, a look of disgust on his face.

"Love...what do you know about love? And what does your lover know about it? Live for a year in a hovel and scratch for anything and everything you want and need. Then talk to me about love. You think you can be happy because he has good looks and flatters you with attention. Wait...wait until the flush of new love is gone and living is about the food and shelter he can provide for you and the children you will have with him. His skin will dry out from the sun and so will yours. Neither of you will be so pretty for long. Then you will wish you had listened to me and married a man who has position and can provide you with the life you have led up to now. Go on, marry him, but don't look to me for anything. You have humiliated me and scarred your family with your escapade and I do not easily forgive such an inconsiderate act."

Caterina is weeping into her hands. She runs to him and throws herself into his arms, sobbing and begging forgiveness.

"I'm sorry, Pa. I didn't mean to hurt you and Ma and bring shame to the family. I didn't know that anyone had spotted us. Please forgive me."

"It is not only important that you were seen together under compromising circumstances. What you did was against God's law and you will have to beg His forgiveness."

She dismisses the thought of having violated her Christian values. She was a virgin and he is the only man she will ever submit to. Though she desperately wants to marry Raffaele, to her it is merely a formalization of their current relationship that will bind them together in the eyes of the Church and their community.

"Pa, what can I do to get your permission to marry Raffaele?"

"Nothing! You need to forget him."

Caterina rises from the chair to get away from him. She screams at him, "No! No! I won't ever forget him. You must allow me to marry him. I don't want anyone else."

Vitaliano can see that unless he defers to this determined woman in some way, he will lose her. He becomes silent for several moments. His brow creases as he sinks into deep thought.

"There is a way for you to gain my approval. I will need some time to work things out. In the meantime, you must not see Raffaele."

"What is it, Pa, what do we have to do?"

"Just stay away from one another for now."

<hr />

Vitaliano gives a frightened and mortified Rosaria his assurance that the crisis with Caterina will soon be resolved, but does not tell her how. He posts a trusted guard outside the house to assure that Caterina doesn't venture out, giving orders to physically restrain her if necessary. He dispatches a messenger to the home of a mysterious resident of Catanzaro, well known to the gentry, asking for a meeting later that evening. Then, he lies down on a couch and catches up on the night's sleep he has lost.

As nighttime arrives, he hitches his horse to a carriage and forays into the night, the full moon lighting his way. He has neglected his usual day's activity in the orchards, but he is rested and his mind is clear. Within the hour, he will meet the man known only as the Egyptian. Rumored to possess an extraordinary understanding of the human anatomy and the fluids that course the body, the Egyptian is, among other things, embalmer extraordinaire to the elite who wish to keep their deceased family members looking alive and natural for extended periods of time. For the prominent Count Leone, largest landowner in Calabria and companion to the king, the Egyptian kept his beloved wife, Beatrice, looking as though she were merely asleep for two years following her death. The adoring widower then continued to lavish affection on her while she lay in her coffin, in a ghoulish display of his love for her. Most of the Egyptian's work is performed in the homes of his clients, but he maintains a laboratory in his home where he accomplishes his best work for those who can afford his extraordinary price.

On a narrow, snaking road near the center of Catanzaro, an oval brass plaque appears on a heavy wooden entrance door reading simply 'Impresario of the Deceased.' Only a house number appears below the words. No reference is made to the Egyptian as an undertaker. In fact, he does not partake in final observances or the funereal processions afforded the deceased on their way to eternal rest. He merely proffers to perform the ultimate final adornment.

Vitaliano arrives and knocks at the door. Though he has servants to handle every menial task, the Egyptian answers the door himself, knowing that it is Vitaliano calling on him. He is dressed in a maroon brocaded jacket and black trousers and his neck is concealed by a black ascot patterned with gold scroll. There are gem-studded gold rings on his forefingers, thumbs and pinkies. His head is shaven and he is very dark, looking almost as though he is charred from the Calabrian sun. It is more likely that the darkened pigments of his skin are the result of his Egyptian origins. He has a large, hooked nose and facial creases that extend from his cheekbones to his jaw. His eyes are black and peer stealthily through long slits that hint at a trace of Asian ancestry. His speech is distinctly Italian with Arabic affectations. He speaks with a deep, deliberate voice.

"Greetings, baron, please come in."

Vitaliano is escorted directly to the laboratory, where there is a small seating area with four intricately carved wooden chairs surrounding a marble table sitting on a Persian rug. Only a few large candles on floor stands light the area, but Vitaliano can see across the room to what appears to be two open coffins with ashen cadavers awaiting their final beautification. There is a peculiar combination of aromas in the room, one distinguishable as alcohol and another as the strangely sweet smell of decaying flesh. Vitaliano wonders what lurid secrets the Egyptian hides inside the recesses of his mind.

The Egyptian pours them each a glass of anisette without uttering a word to his guest. It is a welcome gesture. Vitaliano sips the drink gratefully, appearing to need the alcohol to calm him.

"What can I do for you, Vitaliano?"

"I have come to seek your help in a very unusual and extremely personal matter that must never be revealed. I know that your work extends beyond that of the embalming for which you are so renowned, and that you are discreet beyond question."

"Our conversation will be known only to the two of us. You have my abiding word on that. Please tell me what I can do for you."

"More than twenty years ago, I was involved with a woman who became pregnant, possibly through our intimacy. Two months after I first met her, she took up with another man and hastily married him. A son was born to them in just a few months. The child's father could be either of us and I must know which of us it is."

"Why do you need to know?"

Vitaliano is irritated. What possible use could that information be to him? He decides that he must respond.

"That child in question is now a man, and that man, who could be my bastard son, wishes to marry my daughter. No one knows of my affair with his mother, and I do not wish to reveal to my family an incident from my impulsive youth."

"I understand."

The Egyptian stands and walks to his laboratory bench. He removes three glass vials from a drawer, each enclosed by a wooden stopper. He numbers each one successively with a piece of coal ash. He fills a fourth vial with alcohol, and brings them all back to where Vitaliano is sitting.

"Yes, I may be able to help you, but you must follow my direction carefully." He hands Vitaliano the glass vials. "Take these with you. You are to fill each one with blood. The vessel numbered 1 is for your blood. The one numbered 2 is for the young man's blood, and number 3 is for your daughter's blood. Use the alcohol to wash the area around the vein before and after the blood is drawn, and bind the wound until it completely heals. You must bring all three bottles to me immediately after the blood is drawn."

Vitaliano marvels at the Egyptian's instruction. Is there anything he doesn't know about the functioning of the human body? He squirms at the thought of what must be done in order to fill the vials he was given, but revels at the magic the Egyptian will invoke to determine Raffaele's lineage. For a moment, he questions whether he really wants to know. How would he tell Caterina if Raffaele is his son after all? It has the potential to ruin her life; but he must know for sure.

⊱───◯───⊰

Chapter 8

Assent

It is a bright winter day and Vitaliano's crews have been busily harvesting the black Ascolano olives that will later be cured and pickled for the tables of the more prosperous residents of the region. The men work on heavy wooden ladders, clubs in hand, beating the branches laden with fruit and dropping the bounty into huge sheets spread out on the ground to facilitate collection. The men sing pastoral songs of Calabria as they work, easing the passage of time. Raffaele works quietly alone, seemingly out of favor with the rest of the crew since his discovery at the Beccio ranch with Caterina. There is uncertainty as to how Vitaliano will deal with him, and the others are careful to disassociate themselves from him and his recent escapade. He is uneasy as a messenger from Vitaliano approaches him.

"The baron asks that you come to his home when your work is completed today."

"Can you tell me why?"

"I know only that you are to be there."

Raffaele nods his assent and the messenger leaves, stopping long enough to instruct the foreman to release Raffaele an hour early. There is a suspenseful quiet in the olive grove as the harvest workers observe the messenger's approach to Raffaele, and wonder what is in store for him. He is noticeably pensive for the balance of the day, mulling over and over in his mind the possibilities that he will face when he meets with Vitaliano that evening. Will

Vitaliano give his approval to a betrothal? Not likely. Will he take personal pleasure in dismissing Raffaele? No, Vitaliano is not vengeful and singling Raffaele out in that way would reveal his innermost feelings to the world. He will not be dismissed, despite the family crisis he has created for Vitaliano. It will have to be something else. But, what? Nowhere in his span of thought is the possibility that he would be called to have two ounces of his blood drawn.

As he enters the Zinzi home that evening, he is quick to notice an overcoat slung across the chaise where he had lain several months ago during his recovery from the stitching performed on his hand by Enrico. Someone besides Vitaliano is present to meet with him. A moment later, Doctor D'Angelo greets him.

"Raffaele, how are you?"

"Fine, thank you." Raffaele is wary.

"Vitaliano has been called away, but he asked me to be here in his place, and to perform a minor procedure on you...with your permission, of course."

"What is it?"

"I would like to draw a small sample of your blood."

"What? What foolishness is this?"

"Please don't be disturbed by my request. It is quite normal for blood to be tested these days. It won't hurt you, I promise." He opens a black case containing a hypodermic needle and two of the bottles that the Egyptian had given to Vitaliano, one containing alcohol and the other an empty vial with the number 2.

"But...why is this being done?"

"I don't really know, but I know it's a simple thing and it won't take long or cause any pain."

"I must have an explanation of this or I won't agree to proceed with it."

A door opens down the hall and Caterina enters the foyer. It is the first time that they have met since their night of intimacy. She appears radiant to him, her cheeks more pink than ever, her cherub face smiling at him. They look at one another longingly for a moment before Caterina speaks.

"Raffaele, I know that you are being asked to provide blood for a test of some sort, and I wish that I could tell you why. I have already submitted to the test myself because I believe it will convince my father to allow us to marry." She holds out her arm, showing a bandage just below the elbow from where the blood was drawn.

"Please, Raffaele, do this for me."

Raffaele's eyes are wide with wonder. He is confused. He cannot understand the need to be bled in order to satisfy Vitaliano in some sordid undertaking. He would like to decline, but he will not refuse Caterina's very first request of him. He turns to the doctor.

"Very well, to please Caterina, I will agree."

⊢⊣⦿⊢⊣

It is late in the day when the Egyptian enters his laboratory with Vitaliano trailing behind. His body is swathed in an intricately patterned jade and gold robe. He wears emerald-studded sandals with interlocking laces reaching to the top of his calves. His fingers and arms are adorned with gleaming gold rings. He locks the door behind him and climbs onto a stool in front of a table containing a large sheet of papyrus that has been drenched in a thick, green fluid and left to dry for several days. It is firm, thick and very porous. He chants in ancient Egyptian as he pours the three vials of blood that Vitaliano has brought onto the paper, each in a different area. For each blood sample, he observes the rate of absorption of the blood into the paper, the color change of the paper and the amount of residue left unabsorbed. The blood taken from Vitaliano and Caterina are virtually identical. The rate of absorption into the paper and the crimson shade created by the blood are alike. There is very little residue on either sample. Raffaele's blood is absorbed much more slowly, produces a russet tint and leaves minute black deposits. The Egyptian stares at the results for several moments, as though in a trance. The practice of ancient Egyptian medicine has served him well. Though there is little basis in scientific fact, he is able to persuade Vitaliano that the blood difference he observes proves that he has no paternal relationship with Raffaele.

A relieved Vitaliano is elated. It was what he wanted to hear. He is forever free of the fear that Raffaele might have been his bastard son. Having that weight removed from his mind leaves him with the solitary problem of how to convince Caterina to marry a more suitable man than Raffaele. But, since Caterina and Raffaele have provided their blood for analysis, their expectation will be that Vitaliano will give quick approval to their betrothal. Vitaliano thinks that perhaps he could contrive an outcome of the blood test. It may well have uncovered a blood deficiency of some sort in Raffaele. Or, perhaps the test was inconclusive. No, Caterina is too clever to accept any such subterfuge. Moreover, she is so intent on proceeding with her betrothal that Vitaliano's effort is certain to fail. He will make one last attempt to discourage her.

———◦———

An unfamiliar aura envelopes La Stella as Vitaliano rides past the flower garden to the horse stalls in the rear of the villa. It is very strange that no one is tending the plant life or otherwise maintaining the villa. Even the stable is left untended, though the animals have been fed and seem content. Vitaliano hastily frees his horse to roam the stable and enters the house from the rear door leading to the kitchen. All is quiet and it appears that no one is present. It is dinnertime and Maria is not there preparing the evening meal; nor is Angelina there to help with serving. There is no aroma of food and there are no family members impatiently anticipating their dinner. Where could Rosaria be? Something has happened and there is no one present to tell him what everyone else seems to know. He calls up to the second floor.

"Rosaria!" No answer. He calls again, this time to his children.

"Caterina!...Saverio!... Vincenzo!...Concetta!" No response. What could possibly have happened?

He strides rapidly through the interior of the house to the front foyer and finds the stout Father Luigi from St. Rosalia's Church sound asleep on the couch, seated in an upright position. The sound of Vitaliano's leather boots on the stone floor awakens him abruptly. He leaps up in one motion, his face flushing with embarrassment. He is a younger man than Vitaliano and is flustered by the baron's sudden appearance. The presence of a priest alone in the house does not bode well. Vitaliano shrieks at him, "What has happened? Where is my family?"

The priest looks timidly at the older man. "I'm sorry to inform you, Don Vitaliano, but Donna Rosaria has had a heart attack. She is receiving treatment from Dr. D'Angelo this very moment at the infirmary. Your family has assembled there, as her condition appears grave."

Fury overcomes Vitaliano as he realizes that he is the last to know of the affliction of his beloved Rosaria. He overlooks the fact that he has been meeting secretly in the private recesses of The Egyptian's laboratory listening elatedly to news he had been praying for. He shouts at the young priest, "Why wasn't I summoned? Why am I the last to know of this tragedy?" Then, before the priest can answer, he turns and hurries to where he had left his horse, not waiting for a response. He leaps onto the startled mare's back and strikes her side, causing her to spring into a full gallop.

Gagliano's infirmary is a converted residence located in the center of the village, containing three rooms: a waiting area, an examination room, and a surgical chamber painted white and outfitted with the most rudimentary of surgical instruments and supplies. There are scalpels, saws, files, stitching equipment, bandages and bottles of ether and alcohol. The regional government has constructed the clinic in response to the King's order that medical clinics be set up in the countryside to deal with the onset of malaria. For the poor in most of Calabria's smallest hamlets, it is their first contact with formalized medicine. It is Dr. D'Angelo's duty to preside over the infirmary on this particular day. Thus, when it becomes clear to the household in mid afternoon that Rosaria Zinzi's condition is grave, she is brought to where he is quartered. He can see from her complexion and breathing that she will not live through the day. He makes her as comfortable as he can, placing a pillow under her head and covering her with a sheet while she lies on his operating table. He summons her family to her side and advises them to say their last words to her. Caterina enters the room, teary and forlorn.

"Mother, I love you and will always honor your memory. Please forgive me for causing you pain and embarrassment by running off with Raffaele. It was thoughtless and disrespectful of me."

Rosaria strains to speak. Her drawn ashen face and long white hair are moist with perspiration and her voice is inaudible. She looks at Caterina with waning eyes and breathes in heavy gasps. Her arm moves slightly and Caterina takes her hand in hers. In a strained and desperate moment, Rosaria is able to speak a few words.

"My dear Caterina…you have had a difficult time accepting your father's way. He is a good man, and is only trying to secure a happy life for you. He does not know what it feels like to be a woman in love."

Her eyelids press together, momentarily revealing her pain. "You must do as you see fit, but also consider your father's feelings, especially now, and you must not hurt him. He must be allowed to grant you permission to marry Raffaele. Do not act without his consent." Rosaria is unable to speak further.

Tears stream down Caterina's face. Her mother has acknowledged her right to assert her independence, but also her obligation to respect her father's wishes. Caterina feels evermore justified in wanting to break from the tradition of marrying for dowry, but she must salve the wound that it will inflict on her father. A nurse leads her away from Rosaria's bedside, to allow others to make their final visit. Vitaliano arrives and brushes brusquely by Caterina as he makes his way in to see Rosaria. He turns quickly and touches Caterina's arm in a gesture of acknowledgment.

"I must see your mother now," he mutters and resumes his pursuit. As he enters, Rosaria holds one arm out to him.

"Vitaliano," she calls. He runs to her side and leans down to embrace her. Her breathing is heavy and her eyes are sunken and moist. She is near death. Vitaliano is overwhelmed with grief.

"My dear Rosaria, I'm so sorry."

"Vito…you must do something for me."

"Anything. What do you wish me to do?"

"You must give Caterina your blessing so that she can marry Raffaele. Promise me."

Vitaliano is stunned by the priority that Rosaria has placed on Caterina's desire to marry Raffaele. He surrenders his last hope. He will not deny his dying wife's last wish.

"I promise, Rosaria, I will allow them to marry."

She looks into his eyes. It is the last time she will see him. She is grateful for his promise, but she is unable to express her thanks. Her eyes become lifeless and remain locked in their final gaze.

Chapter 9

Blissful Times

The evening is cool as the sun sets and night falls on Gagliano, the tiny hamlet two miles long in a valley formed by the hills rising in the east and west. It is the last hour of daylight and shadows lengthen as the sun descends, outlining the crumbling masonry and exposed stone foundations of buildings constructed in the Middle Ages. As the day ends, the cooing of swallows reveals the whereabouts of their perch, and the buzzing of insects fills the air. A lone donkey brays in the distance as the townspeople make their way indoors, lighted candles their sole defense against the darkness. Alive with verdant splendor, Gagliano is nonetheless a place of contradiction. The hillsides thrive with abundant crops despite the sparse soils and irregular drenching from rainfall, a tribute to the hard work and ingenuity of the farm hands. But, despite their demanding labor, the workers' pay is meager and they remain at the edge of privation, resigned to their fate. They will live with their families in small hovels. They will own a spare change of work clothing and a suit to wear on Sunday and in their coffins. Their food will consist mostly of pasta and beans. They will walk the *passeggiata* daily. Most of all, they will dedicate their lives to family and the prospect of spiritual salvation; and their offspring will take their place when they have gone to their reward in heaven.

In an area that houses the poorest of the town's inhabitants, two young hopefuls lie in their conjugal bed, holding one another and wishing for a long life together. They have experienced a courtship that flew in the face of convention, but now they are together at last. Their wedding was a cause for celebration among the peasants of the village, and it attracted large numbers to witness the ceremony in St. Rosalia's church. Strings of white and pink camellias decorated the inside of the starkly appointed church and there were more candles lighting the altar and chandeliers than ever before.

An organist played the Ave Maria as Caterina entered the church, arm in arm with her brother Saverio, the stand-in for her grieving father. Her white beaded and veiled dress was made for her by the groom's mother, encasing her shapely torso and lighting up her cherubic face. As she strode to the spot in front of the altar where she would be joined to Raffaele for the rest of her life, Caterina smiled broadly, visibly elated that the cherished moment had arrived against all odds. Raffaele beamed ecstatically in his dark suit and white shirt as he looked upon the beautiful woman he had dreamt of repeatedly, coming into his life forever. There was no thought of the responsibility he was assuming for her welfare or the reproach he might have felt towards Vitaliano Zinzi for his opposition to the marriage. It was the happiest day of his life.

Still mourning the sudden death of his beloved Rosaria, Vitaliano sat obediently in the pew designated for the family of the bride along with his two other children. He wore the black arm band that signified his grieving. His resentment towards the wedding of his daughter to a man who earned his pittance at the behest of others was well hidden, but he would make no gesture of generosity towards the couple. They would receive no dowry from him and there would be no rescue from the economic uncertainty of the life Caterina had chosen for herself against his urgent pleas. At the very least, he is very grateful that the Egyptian has said that they are not of the same blood.

The wedding reception was, likewise, one of great euphoria. Caterina had demonstrated for all to witness, the rejection of a system organized to benefit the fortunate few who own the land. Every lowly man or woman who worked by the sweat of his or her brow were present to add approval to the schism and to quench their curiosity of this controversial couple. While the break with tradition was daring for a culture that places enormous value on marriage both as a societal function and a holy sacrament, the mood of the moment was festive and forgiving. The concentration was on the gifts of special foods for the wedding celebration, made by many friends and relatives of Raffaele's mother. The fare included Zeppole, candied almonds, sugared wedding cakes and deep fried pastries laced with anchovies. Chairs lined the town square, seating the dozens of well wishers and extended family. The town's uniformed band played into the afternoon and evening. There were French horns, clarinets, trumpets, a drum, a flute and even a tuba. An accordion joined the band as the afternoon wore on, playing the *Tarantella*, *Vicin' O Mare*, and the *Funicular*. The music and drink provided a stimulus for all to dance into the night.

Caterina and Raffaele were the first to leave their wedding reception except for the small children and some of the elders. The party continued on until midnight with most of the townsfolk enjoying the spate of freedom from their usual tedium. The couple's honeymoon in their own bed would last for just one night, as Raffaele would need to be at work the following morning promptly at dawn. The night was a sleepless spell for both of them, as they alternately enjoyed making love and gazing at one another with great anticipation and the satisfaction at having won the right to be together in life. They eventually dropped off to an exhausted slumber as the music finally stopped and quiet blanketed the town.

An unwelcome dawn arrives quickly. Caterina awakens as the sun streams into her bedroom window, poking at her slumber. She looks quickly to the other side of the bed, but Raffaele is gone. Her reaction is anger that he has left her bed so thoughtlessly, without even a word or caress. Then, she warms at the thought that he is now her sole support and eagerly performs his duty by showing up promptly for work. She rolls over, tired from the lack of sleep and, imagining Raffaele's naked body against hers, falls into a deep sleep. She dreams of being trapped in a raging sea, with large black swells rapidly rising and falling in a sort of nautical rhythm. The sky is dark and angry and the wind is canting a prediction of death. There is little hope of being rescued. She begins to drown, tasting the salt water and feeling the cold wet of the sea that is stealing her life away. She sees Raffaele in the distance, stripped to the waist and fighting furiously to keep his small craft, its sail furled, afloat and headed towards her. He calls out to her, but her reply is faint over the howling of the wind and crashing of the sea. He turns toward her and sees her, but his boat is capsized and he falls into the sea too far away for her to reach. She begins choking from swallowing sea water and is now entirely submerged. What will become of them, she thinks? Can their lives be over so soon after being wed? Will they be denied a life of happiness together? She is drawn deeper into the sea by a whirlpool of undercurrent and loses consciousness. She awakens with a start and finds herself gasping for breath in her own bed. The nightmare is over, but she has been sobbing and her breathing has become heavy, as though she has been deprived of air. She jumps up and quickly slips into clothing that she finds among articles she has brought to her new home from the villa. She must go out into the land to find Raffaele.

⊱──────⊰

The oppressive and monotonous summer sun of Calabria beats down on the parched earth. At times it is unmerciful, stamping the countryside with the discomfort that can only be caused by the combined effects of heat and humidity. Large black flies and mosquitoes are everywhere, spreading the dreaded malady of malaria. Once afflicted, there is no physician to diagnose or medicine to cure the infirmity. Field workers wear protective clothing, an unwelcome necessity in the intense heat. Animals are brought indoors, when they are few enough, to avoid contact with the feared vectors.

Raffaele carries buckets of water from a nearby stream to the base of orange trees on the Capurro citrus grove. The oranges will need moisture to keep them from drying up and the trees' roots require water. Sweat rolls down his face and arms, and his shirt is wet with perspiration. The sun breaks through the shade of the high leaves and penetrates his head, despite the protective hat he wears.   Rows of trees in perfect alignment stretch out as far as he can see. All of them must be watered and each tree takes him farther and farther away from the source of the water. He has been working for several hours and his hands ache from the weight of the full buckets. He is saved by the arrival of *pranzo a mezzogiorno*, the meal taken in the middle of the day, accompanied by *siesta*. He will rest and his body will regain the strength he needs to see him through the remainder of the work day.

From behind a hedge at the edge of the creek, Caterina watches as Raffaele labors. She has seen men toil many times before, but this time she observes her groom of only two days. It is a different experience. There is an empathy with the soreness and discomfort he must be feeling and she is relieved when he comes to the stream to wash his hands and face before sitting on the verdant slope to eat. She would like to rush out to where he is sitting and embrace him, but she knows it would embarrass him. She sits back in the intense heat of the day and watches as the other men join him in quiet repose.

"Hey, Raffaele, I heard you were married last week...to the Baron's daughter. Is it true?" Tommaso is not from Gagliano and has heard gossip about the courtship from others.

"Yes, it's true, I am married to Caterina."

"Why do you work here for Count Capurro? Why don't you take a favored place in the orchards of Vitaliano Zinzi?"

"That's none of your business, Tommaso; I am here because I wish to earn my living here," Raffaele snaps defensively, before he realizes he has lost his composure.

Caterina is barely within earshot of the two men, but she is able to decipher the conversation. Angered, she decides to leave for home before she, too, loses control and cries out a defense of Raffaele. It is clear to her now that the rift between her father and her is not behind them. It is not merely up to Vitaliano and her to end the discourse about her variant attitude towards arranged marriage. It will be the subject of conjecture for those who enjoy pondering the lurid facts. Perhaps in time, her past behavior will be forgotten and the wagging tongues will calm.

⊷⊶⊙⊷⊶

The patched masonry dwelling that Caterina and Raffaele rent is a humble, one-story, two room house with a door and window facing the street in front and a door and window overlooking a small back yard area where they grow their vegetables. For several days prior to their wedding, Caterina walked from her home at the villa to the vacant hut to prepare it for their arrival. It had a stale odor of dampness and of animal droppings. Field rodents had been its sole occupants since it was last lived in and animal urine and dried fecal matter littered the dirt floor. Along with expelling the unwelcome creatures with the flash of her broom, Caterina swept and scrubbed the tiny quarters. The clean open windows brought in much needed air to clear out the stench. She lit the fireplace and incinerated old, soiled rags and fragments of broken crates that were strewn about. During one of Vitaliano's trips to Naples, she appropriated an old bed and chest that had been kept in a storage room at the villa. They would occupy the bedroom of her new home. As she looked around at the transformed hut, she marveled at her previously untested ability as a homemaker. It hadn't been difficult at all. Who said that the peasant life had to be hard? Didn't they have money enough to eat and pay for the essentials of life? What else mattered? They had one another and that was all that was necessary.

Now that Caterina and Raffaele are living in their home, Raffaele surveys the modest dwelling that they occupy as man and wife. He has a forlorn look on his face.

"Caterina, what have I done to you by bringing you to this place? You lived in a splendid house with servants and wanted for nothing. Now you live in this humble place and have to clean and care for it yourself. I'm sorry that I didn't see that before we were married."

Caterina is furious.

"What are you talking about? Don't you think I considered the loss of my privileged life before I married you? Giving up that empty existence was no sacrifice at all. I am here because I want to be here. I want to love and take care of you and our home and I never want to go back to my previous life. Don't you see that?"

"I understand, Caterina, but I wish that I were more skilled so that I could earn more and give you a better life."

"I'm not complaining. Don't grumble over what we have."

She leads him by the hand to the bedroom and holds him tight. She kisses him deeply and looks longingly into his eyes. Then, they both shed their clothing and fall onto the bed in a fiery embrace.

"You are all I will ever want," she says.

The months pass and the happy couple pursues a contented existence. There is no further talk about their meager status in life or the hovel in which they live. The fervor of their life together intensifies as they come to know one another intimately. They can sense one another's needs and respond accordingly. Caterina is reassured with how right she had been about her feelings for Raffaele. For the first time in her life she is calm and serene. When Raffaele is at work, she sometimes gathers with the women who remain at home while their men are at work, washing clothes at the fountain in the town center, caring for children and preparing for the evening meal. One such woman, Francesca, approaches Caterina with a frank question.

"How long is it that you and Raffaele are married?"

"About six months. Why do you ask?"

"I'm surprised that you aren't pregnant."

It suddenly occurs to Caterina that she might well have conceived in all these months of sexual intimacy with Raffaele. But she has not. She has been so preoccupied with her new life that she hadn't thought about it. Now the words spoken by Francesca sear her brain. How could she have been so naïve as to think that she has been the consummate wife to Raffaele? He will have wanted her to bear him a son or even a daughter. The shocked look on her face reveals the surprise and disappointment that overtakes her. But her answer is defensive.

"How do you know that I'm not pregnant?"

Francesca responds only with a sneer.

As Raffaele arrives home that evening, he is immediately confronted with Caterina's blunt question.

"Are you disappointed that I'm not pregnant?"

"Caterina, I haven't thought about that. I'm happy with being married to you and when God is ready, he will allow us to become parents. I'm not thinking about it, believe me."

"But why hasn't it happened? It's been six months."

"Don't be concerned. It will happen eventually."

Raffaele does not share his true feelings with Caterina. He has thought about it often in their few months of marriage and been sorely disappointed with each recurrence of Caterina's menstrual cycle. He has even been asked by Michela, his mother, concerned that perhaps her son has wed a barren woman. In Michela's most secretive thoughts is the possibility that Caterina and Raffaele are related by blood and that it may somehow preclude their ever having children. Besides Vitaliano, she is the only one privy to the fact that Raffaele was conceived around the time that she was intimate with Vitaliano. Unaware that the Egyptian has proclaimed that Caterina's and Raffaele's blood were dissimilar in his dubious experiments, she has had deep concerns about the possibility that Raffaele is Vitaliano's son and a half brother to Caterina. She has kept her doubts to herself, hoping and praying that they are unfounded.

Chapter 10

Antonio

At age 57, Anita Ruggiero sometimes labors to rise from her bed. Arthritis causes her no end of pain and, since she has been widowed, there isn't anyone present to hear her complaints. She curses her malady and deflects the thought of her pain by admiring her oil paintings of the landscapes and cities of Calabria, her chairs and tables crafted in Tuscany from alder wood and the lamps fashioned of Venetian glass. There are hand painted plates from Verona in her cupboards and her flower garden is overflowing with golden thistle and blood red poppies. She thinks about how much material wealth surrounds her and has little regret for the twenty-six years that she was married to Giovanni. Their marriage had been arranged by their families and, since they found one another generally appealing, they were both pleased with the result. Giovanni had inherited a substantial land holding and Anita's dowry included a lemon grove in the nearby countryside. Only their inability to produce children disturbed what was an otherwise tranquil union. Still, she is hugely incensed by the posthumous discovery that Giovanni had been unfaithful to her. He had gone to his grave in a fishing boat accident off the straits of Messina, and though he left Anita a prosperous estate with almost one hundred acres of prime producing groves, his final moments in life had been shared with a woman who had proven to be his paramour. Shocked and badly deflated, Anita retreated into a reclusive life.

Two years after Giovanni's death, she met a young man, Antonio Russo, in a grocery store where he was employed as a clerk by the Altamonte family whose only son had perished when he was struck by lightning in an electrical storm. Antonio had been born into the archetypal poor family of Calabria. Their struggle for survival was tolerable only because it equaled that of almost all of the other families in Gagliano. Their son Antonio was extremely fortunate in that he was exceptionally handsome. Tall and muscular, his sandy-colored hair and large chocolate eyes complemented his toothy smile and fair complexion. The youngest of seven siblings and, at age 23, the only unmarried member of his family, the handsome Antonio was considered very desirable among the eligible women of Gagliano. He showed little interest in courting, however, and no one had yet appealed to him as a love interest. Attracted by Anita's wealth, he was quick to serve her whenever she entered his employer's store.

"*Buon Giorno, signora*, may I assist you?

"Yes, of course. Get that salami down for me and show me your cheese rounds."

Slim and well groomed but slightly stooped, Anita was the consummate dowager, using a stippled walking stick to help her negotiate the cobbled streets and uneven sidewalks of Gagliano. The attention of an attractive young man pleased her. She could not help but notice his manners and good looks. For a moment it occurred to her that it would be a telling revenge for her to find a young man like Antonio to marry. It would be licit for sure, but age disparity would give the town gossips their grist and all would agree that Giovanni had earned the affront to his memory. While it would not likely be a marriage based on love, there would be no dearth of candidates that would spring at the prospect of sudden riches, and it would send Giovanni spinning in his grave.

After purchasing a round of cheese, a whole salami, several bottles of wine and two loaves of bread, it was evident that she would need assistance to bring her purchases home. She made payment to a smiling grocer and ordered Antonio to assist her.

"Deliver these items to my home at the end of the day," she told him. He nodded agreement and, in the late afternoon, carried Anita's purchases to her home a mile from the store. Having not been there previously, Antonio was immediately impressed by the luxurious interior of Anita's lavish home. He had made deliveries to other well appointed homes, few as they were, but this was his first look at Anita's home. He could not help but stare.

"Do you like my home?" Anita was quick to redirect Antonio's purpose for being in her home.

"Yes, *signora*, I do."

"Would you like to call me Anita?"

"Anita...You're home is lovely."

"Can I pour you a drink?"

Anita poured him a glass of wine, hoping that her interest would strike him. He was uneasy because of her social status and their age difference, but after a glass of wine, it didn't seem to matter as much. Even his awkward manners seemed less important. When the thought suddenly occurred to him that he was due back at the store, he placed his empty wine glass on the table and headed for the door.

"I'm sorry, Anita, but I need to get back to the store before closing time."

"Come back when you are finished for the day. We'll have dinner here."

Shocked and hardly able to speak, Antonio nodded and left. On his way back to the store, he considered the implications of engaging in a private dinner with Anita. What would people think? Did they have to know? Of course, everyone would know once the gossips learned of it. He thought of how his family would react. Then, he cast aside his doubts and decided to return to Anita's home later that evening. She was, after all, a wealthy woman and he had nothing to lose by granting her an evening of his presence. When he returned, he found that she had sent her housekeeper home and had herself cooked a meal that included octopus, mussels and vegetables that Antonio had never seen. She opened a bottle of her favorite white wine, made especially to her taste in Piedmont. As his senses filled with the ambience that Anita had created, Antonio became receptive to her questioning.

"Do you mind if I ask you some questions about yourself?"

"Not at all. What would you like to know?"

"Do you live with your parents?"

"Yes, I do."

"What do they do?"

"If you mean what does my family do to earn a living, the answer is that we are farm laborers; except for me, of course, I'm an apprentice grocer."

"Do you have someone you court?"

"I'm not betrothed but there is someone that interests me."

Her tone became less gentle.

"And who is that?"

"I am not at liberty to reveal her identity. She's from a wealthy family and is not permitted to see anyone unless her father approves."

"Doesn't he approve of you?"

"He doesn't even know of me."

For the rest of the evening, Anita was quiet, serving her food and drink to Antonio, and allowing the conversation to drift away from any further talk of his love interest. It was evident that Antonio was upset over not having approval to court the woman of his choice and Anita was not going to pursue it.

Antonio had not been completely honest with Anita. Months before, he had met Baron Zinzi's young daughter, Concetta, and was struck by her good looks. Her cupid face and dark brown eyes were like that of her older sister, Caterina. But unlike Caterina, she was tall and very slender, resembling a fawn, with doe-like eyes and delicate bone structure. She had come to his store to purchase groceries and he was beside himself with anticipation to meet her. Her visits to the store became more frequent and, over time, they developed an easy friendship. She would ask for the food items she wanted and he filled her basket with them. He was eventually able to tell her of his infatuation with her and to ask if they could meet away from the store. Her response startled him. She would have easily agreed to meet him, but her father would not permit it, even allowing for an entourage of chaperones. She told him that her marriage would be arranged by her father in concert with the families of eligible hopefuls whom she had never met. When she told of the huge frustration with this ancient custom, Antonio saw the opening he was looking for. He asked her to see him secretly, and after several refusals, Concetta finally consented to meet him in the countryside where they would not be seen together. They chose to meet in a remote lemon grove away from any of the work crews and, after several encounters in which they talked and held hands, became earnestly attached to one another. Concetta was distraught with frustration over her father's determined views towards arranging her marriage and, by now, could discuss them with her new *confidente*, Antonio.

"My father has arranged for yet another suitor to call on me. I think I may have seen him once before but I could never be interested in him."

Frustrated, Antonio could not restrain his anger.

"Concetta, you must tell your father about me. I can't stand the thought that he might actually force you to marry one of those men."

"He didn't get my sister to marry a man of his choice, and I won't allow him to pick my husband either."

It was what Antonio had hoped to hear. He pulled Concetta close to him and looked longingly into her eyes, placing his lips on hers and kissing her deeply. He felt a surge of passion flood his senses as their bodies came together. He could no longer control his savage emotion. He took Concetta's hand and drew her to a thicket. They dropped to the ground in a passionate embrace, parting only long enough to remove their clothing. Within moments, he mounted her with the grace of a yearling and, as they climaxed, he heard her call, *Antonio, Antonio, te amo*!

＞＞◆◇◆＜＜

Maria Russo had done her Christian duty rearing seven children, six of whom were married and on their own. Only her youngest, Antonio, was still at home and he, too, would soon be gone. Some fine young *ragazza* would ensnare him and he would soon be bringing Maria grandchildren to adore. Sure, her family members were poor farm workers who scratched for their daily sustenance and had few material possessions, but they were honest, hard-working people who loved their families and respected their elders. And her husband, Angelo, was a good husband and father. What more could she have wanted? As she thought about her life, it helped to allow that all of her relatives and friends were in a similar economic state and many of them had familial strife to boot. She happily conducted her household duties: cooking, cleaning, washing clothes and shopping for the few foods that did not grow in their own garden. She rarely left the house, and could be counted on being there if she was not otherwise attending to her chores.

The morning was as usual for Maria. She had tidied the house, stoked the fire she used for cooking and hung a pot of *fagioli* on a hook directly over the hearth. It would be ready for the middle of the day when her husband and son would come home for *pranzo* and *siesta*. That done, she began to gather the soiled clothing for her daily trip to the water fountain, but before she could complete the task, she heard a gentle knock at her door. When she opened it, she was startled to see a well dressed, aristocratic-looking woman peering at her and at the inside of her home.

"Can I help you?"

"My name is Anita Ruggiero. I have come with a proposition that will interest you. May I come in?"

Maria looked warily at Anita, wondering what possible connection she could have to this woman of obvious means. Though the two had never met, hearing her name reminded Maria of who she was, the circumstances of her husband's death and the subsequent scandal involving his infidelity.

"Yes, of course, please come in."

Once inside, Anita resumed her inspection of the meager surroundings. The building was tiny, yet a family once as many as nine had once lived here. Where did they all sleep? How did they all fit around the table at dinner time? There were dishes that were obviously made by Maria herself, fashioned from clay of the kind found at the riverbanks. Forks and knives were crudely fashioned from steel scraps. The dirt floor produced columns of dust and had signs of recent spills from the pots and pans that hung over the hearth. Anita could now understand how the man of this household survived on the pay of a farm laborer. It was pitiful, she thought, that people should have to live this way. As she turned to Maria, her regal form an obvious anomaly to this place, she could not help feeling the condescension of the landowners for the very peasants they employed. She was very direct in addressing Maria.

"You are Maria, the mother of Antonio Russo, yes?"

"Yes." Maria was anxious. What was this about?

"Are you aware that your son has been courting a young woman without the consent of her father?"

Oh, my God. Was Antonio in trouble with the law?

"No, I'm not. Who is the girl?"

"I don't know, but her marriage to another man is being arranged by her father, and they will receive dowries from both families."

"Why are you telling me this?"

"Because your son will never end up with that girl and may not realize that he will miss his chance to enrich himself and his family by a proper marriage."

Maria looked astounded. What did this woman know that would make Antonio rich?

"Signora, please come to the point. What are you trying to tell me?"

"I will be very frank. As you may know, my husband was drowned in a boating accident several years ago. I have lived as a widow these past years and am tired of it. I would like to have a man such as Antonio to be my husband. He would, of course, be elevated to a life of abundance and would be able to shower some of his wealth on other members of his family."

Maria was shocked. This elegant middle-aged woman was asking to marry her young son who had nothing but the promise of a life as a grocer's apprentice. What could she possibly be thinking?

"But, signora, Antonio is only twenty three years old. You are much older than that."

Anita clenched her teeth. Her eyes narrowed and her lips pursed. Her words were heated.

"You think like the rest of your impoverished friends! Don't make the mistake that will condemn your son to a life of hardship. Why does my age matter? I can make Antonio happy and he can fulfill my life as well. You and your husband can make the choice for him and perhaps even convince him that he will not regret spending his life with me."

"Does Antonio know of your intentions?"

"Not exactly. We have been together once, but only for supper."

"How would you reward me for agreeing to this marriage?" Maria surprises herself that she is inclined to listen and perhaps even profit from the arrangement that Anita was suggesting.

"We can work that out once you tell me that you and your husband will arrange for me to marry Antonio. But you can be certain that your husband will never again earn a meager pay working for someone else so long as I am married to Antonio."

Maria has experienced the most extraordinary day of her life. Not only had she been exposed to a woman of considerable affluence, but she has surprised herself that the thought of material wealth would mean so much to her that she would consider marrying her son off to this older woman. Who was the young woman that had Antonio's interest? How serious was he about her? Maria could feel her blood racing through her veins as she anticipated the wealth that could be hers and Angelo's. A feeling of greed overwhelmed her. The grinding poverty that dominated their lives could at last be over. She had only to convince Angelo and Antonio and they would all benefit.

><+>-0-<+><

With her husband and son both present at the midday meal, it was all Maria could do to hold back discussing Anita's offer. She needed to think about how to posture the proposition to Antonio and for that she would need to talk privately to Angelo. He would have the right to decline Anita's offer. If he did, Maria would simply let Anita know their decision and Antonio would not be told anything. It was unlikely that Anita would later approach Antonio directly, since her initial judgment had been that he would need family approval to accept an offer from her.

Following *pranzo*, Maria caught Angelo's eye and indicated by a sideways nod of her head that she wished to see him alone. *Siesta* time had arrived and Antonio sat himself down against the heavy trunk of a large fig tree just behind the house. In moments he was asleep. Angelo had followed Maria to the bedroom, wondering what she had on her mind.

"What is it, Maria?" His voice sounded a bit cranky. She was keeping him from his sleep.

"I had a visitor today. *La signora* Ruggiero was here. She told me some things you need to know. They involve Antonio."

"What could Antonio have to do with that woman?" Angelo had a stolid impression of Anita from the onetime hearsay of her husband's death. He imagined her as being matronly and stubbornly discontented with life.

"You might be surprised to learn that your son has been courting a woman against her father's wishes."

Angelo shrugged. "Why is *La Signora* telling you this?"

"Because she wants Antonio for herself." There, she had told him. Now she held her breath awaiting his response. It was several moments before Angelo could speak.

"Why would we want her as a wife for our son? She must be thirty years older than he."

"Because, Angelo, she will make a wealthy man of our Antonio, and you will not have to work as a field hand for that Count who pays you nothing for your skills and the use of your back."

"Have you told Antonio of this?"

"No, of course not. I wouldn't do that without your consent."

"Am I understanding that you want him to marry her?"

"Yes, I think we should tell Antonio that we want him to marry Anita. When he hears what's involved, he'll leap at the chance to become rich."

"Perhaps so. That will depend on how deeply he feels about the woman he's been seeing."

"Then, you are in favor of this arrangement?"

Angelo lapsed into deep thought. This sudden opportunity would be an answer to his prayers, and an opportunity that would certainly never recur. His lifetime struggle to feed his family would be over. He might get by working fewer days in his old age. He could even have meat on his table. The embarrassment of marrying his son off to an elderly woman would wear off and, after a while, his friends would see the wisdom in it and even come to envy him. He turned to Maria with a look of avarice that she had not seen in him before.

"I will agree, but only if it is made clear that we are to profit from doing this."

"Of course. We'll decide on what we want and hold out until La Signora agrees to it. But first we need to talk to Antonio."

It is evening and Maria, Angelo and Antonio sit indoors, where their conversation cannot be overheard by the neighbors. Maria has told Antonio that she and his father need to talk with him.

"Is it true that you have been courting a woman whose father does not approve of you?" Maria's question startles Antonio.

"Where did you hear that?"

"Never mind. Is it true?"

"Yes. But it isn't me he disapproves of, it's anyone who can't provide a large dowry."

"Who is this woman?" Antonio looks to his father hoping to gain reprieve from answering Maria's question. Angelo does not assist him. He must tell them about Concetta.

"She is Concetta, Baron Zinzi's daughter. He is trying to get her to marry some wealthy landowner, but she won't let him push her into doing that. He tried to do the same thing with his older daughter, but she ended up marrying the man she loved."

Maria declares her leaning for arranged marriages, hoping to form Antonio's opinion for espousing the custom.

"Yes, Caterina married Raffaele Brutto, but where is she now? She lives not more than five houses from here, with the rest of us who have nothing. She had a palace to live in and a father who gave her anything she wanted. Now she scrubs clothes at the fountain like the rest of us."

Antonio does not respond. Then, for the first time, Angelo speaks.

"My son, your infatuation for Concetta must be put aside. She will marry a land-rich man and continue her life as a privileged *Donna*. Leaving that life for what we have is not easily done. She would become discontented before long and make your life and hers miserable."

"What do you want me to do, Pa?" Angelo looks at Maria, hoping that she will answer the question. Maria draws in a long breath and speaks.

"*La Signora* has made us an offer. She will lift us out of this life of drudgery once and for all if we agree to arrange your marriage to her."

"What?! When did this thought arise?" Antonio is startled by his mother's statement.

"She came to see me today to tell me about her feelings for you and to ask your father and me to allow her to marry you."

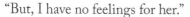

"But, I have no feelings for her."

"Of course not. You hardly know her. But once you are married, you will come to love her."

"How can I love a woman so much older than me?"

"Why not? She has everything any other woman has and is rich besides."

"Ma, I think I love Concetta."

"Don't say that. You are taken with her youth and beauty. But those things don't last. Marrying her —even if that were possible- would bring you nothing but misery."

Angelo holds up his hand, wanting to be heard.

"Antonio, you have lived many fewer years than I and have the disadvantage of seeing the world through young eyes. My eyes are old and I look around at the house we live in, the food we eat and the clothes we wear. We work and sweat and have little to show for it. We are sometimes hungry and our clothes are threadbare. Our very homes are threatened by landlords who come to our doorstep demanding their rents. And the older we get, the less certainty there is that we can continue to toil and survive. Antonio, you must give up Concetta and marry *La Signora*. You will leave this shack and take your place among the privileged landowners. And as *La Signora* has no offspring, you will some day inherit all of her wealth while you are still in the prime of your life. You must do this not merely for yourself, but for our family."

Antonio has thus been told what he must do. The logic was laid out plainly. He has been given an opportunity to step up in the world to high rank and to bestow prosperity on his struggling family. It does not seem as though Angelo is giving him a choice.

"OK, Pa, but don't give your consent yet. I need to see Concetta one last time."

The warm afternoon spawns a gentle breeze that ruffles the white blossoms appearing on the lemon trees. The fragrance of citrus fills the air and the complete absence of sound completes the idyllic moment. It is the grove where

Antonio and Concetta have met many times and where Concetta surrendered her innocence to Antonio. Now she comes to meet with him again, this time to be told that he will be betrothed to Anita Ruggiero. Concetta believes that they are meeting to share their love as they have many times before. As Antonio arrives, he sees that Concetta is already there, anxiously awaiting his arrival. She looks up and sees him. She runs to him and throws her arms around his neck. He is not responsive.

What's wrong, *caro*?

"Concetta, I must tell you something that will hurt you, but please believe me that it isn't my wish to do so."

"What is it? What's wrong?"

Antonio hesitates, but he knows that he must tell her regardless of the hurt.

"My family has told me that I must marry *La Signora* Ruggiero. I know that it is you that I love, but I am not being given a choice."

Concetta's eyes fill and tears roll down her cheeks. She looks down at the ground. Her young mind is confused by her intense feelings for Antonio being cast aside by people she has never met. She is unable to speak. She looks up at Antonio pleadingly, her dark eyes glistening, but doesn't speak.

"My feelings for you haven't changed, but I must do this for my family. They are desperately poor and this is their chance to have something more in their lives."

Concetta becomes angry.

"Why should I care about people I don't even know? What about me? Am I supposed to forget that I ever loved you and surrendered my virginity to you?"

"You have no idea what it's like to live as my parents do. Your father has always given you everything you would ever want. You've never gone to bed hungry. You've never had to work out in the rain on a freezing cold day until your hands are numb and your shoulders ache. Your clothing is washed for you. Even your bed is made for you. How can you understand what my family has to endure? I have no regrets for loving you. You are the most beautiful woman I have ever known. Yes, I accepted your love, but it was in return for mine. I truly love you, Concetta, but like you, I must do as my parents see fit for me."

Concetta responds angrily. "I have not done what my father demands…I have defied him because I love you. And, I have resisted his demands that I marry one of the men he chooses for me."

"But ultimately you will give in to him and I'll be forgotten."

Concetta begins to cry.

"No, no, I won't forget you and I won't marry anyone else. I swear it, Antonio. Please don't leave me."

"I must, Concetta. Don't think about me any more. You must forget me."

As he begins to leave, he looks back and sees that Concetta has fallen to the ground heaving and sobbing into her hands. His eyes well with tears as he thinks of how he has devastated her. And for what? Loyalty to his family? An enormous guilt overtakes him, and for a moment he hesitates, but he does not return to her. He is committed to marrying Anita.

Chapter 11

Reality

The searing hot weather of July descends on Gagliano. Burning, humid air is transported on the wings of a Sirocco, the fierce summer wind blowing north from the Sahara, bringing with it a virtual plague of large, sandy-colored Egyptian flies. For those living in the depths of Gagliano, there is no escape. Doors and windows are shut against the flying malady, but the terrible sound of buzzing can be heard from inside. To open a portal for air or entry is to invite a swarm of unwelcome flies. There is no vision of green fields and mountains or the sparkling sea a few miles away. The image is only of walls blackened by masses of flies and animals rolling in the mud to shake them off.

Until the Sirocco spends its rage, it is a slow, steady hell for the peasant working in the fields. He is tied for life to the earth that barely allows him to subsist. He prays for the sweltering wind and venomous flies to vanish so that he may better tolerate the work that feeds his family.

Inside the home occupied by Caterina and Raffaele, the air is stifling and the covered doors and windows darken the room. The young couple is occupied with spotting unwelcome entrants and swatting them. Caterina is noticeably disturbed.

"Raf, I don't think we ever had this many flies at the villa. Can't we do something?"

"We can only wait out the wind. The flies are attracted to this end of town because it is the lowest point in the valley and is most humid; and because of the animal odors and our dirt floors. There is nothing else we can do."

Raffaele is disheartened. Again, he feels the anguish of having brought Caterina to this lowly place away from the comfortable life she had been living at *La Stella*. How can he ever expect to provide anything close to what she had? He is a field hand and will always be that and no more. Caterina sees the anguished disappointment on his face.

"Don't worry, Raf, I'll be fine…as long as I'm here with you."

Raffaele's face lights up amid the sweat running down his forehead and his sweat-drenched shirt.

After four wretched days, the wind dies and Caterina opens the front door, desperate for a breath of fresh, cool air. The temperature has fallen and the sky has become blue. She brushes off flies that immediately attach themselves to her, and strides up the street to the fountain in the square. She must have some water, some cool water to wash her face from the captivity of the last four days. She carries a large jar so she can bring water home to Raffaele. At the fountain, she competes with fifty men and women, all with the same impulse as hers, some of them stripped down to the bare essentials of modesty. They have arrived at the fountain before her, and though she must wait for them to finish enjoying their respite from the menacing heat, she is grateful that they have cleaned the layer of dead flies that floated on the water and clung to the sides of the large basin. One swallow of contaminated water can condemn the innocent slaker to a lifetime of struggle with disease or even endanger his life. After an hour's wait, Caterina finally is able to wash her face, hands and arms and to fill the jar with fresh water that she will boil and use for cooking and drinking.

When she arrives home, she finds that Raffaele has left. Her nearby neighbor explains his absence.

"He has gone with the others to see if the halt on work is over. They are all anxious to get back to work."

But Caterina is disappointed. She would have kissed him and waved as he walked off with the others. She feels his absence and is determined to somehow remedy this dread feeling of loss each time he leaves her.

It is an hour before the men arrive back home, pleased that they have been ordered back to work the following morning. Raffaele is smiling and, as he enters the house, Caterina places her arms around him and engages him in conversation.

"Do you miss me when you are at work?"

"Of course I do. Why would you ask a question like that?"

"Because I think I know how we can avoid missing one another."

"And how is that?"

"I could take a job working alongside you."

"Don't be silly. A woman can't do that hard work."

"They could pay me less and assign me some of the easier tasks."

"I don't like it, Caterina. I've never seen a woman on the job and I don't want you to labor like a man. I'll earn our living, don't worry."

"That's not my worry. I just don't want to be away from you all of the time, waiting for you to come home at the end of the day. And, the extra money will be welcome."

Raffaele sees that it is useless to try to convince Caterina otherwise. He would like to politely imply that perhaps she would rather start a family, but he is wise in avoiding the topic. She has thus far been unable to conceive. He grudgingly agrees to her seeking employment as a field hand, but offers no assistance with approaching the foreman.

"Very well, but you'll have to figure out how to get hired."

A cool, dry dawn arrives and the men make their first appearance at work since the Sirocco descended on them. They wear long sleeves to keep the still menacing flies away from their arms and are careful not to be bitten. It is the growing season and grapes, olives and citrus fruits, the pride of Calabria, are everywhere on the trees and vines. They show the debilitating effects of the heat and the marauding flies. It is important to renew the vigor of everything growing. Their roots must be irrigated. The men are organized to bring water to Count Leone's trees and vines from a stream that runs close to the edge of the grove in which they labor. Buckets are handed out and the men begin their laborious trudge from creekside to tree. As they begin the day, they are spry and willing, but after laboring for hours they will be sore and tired. *Siesta* will be a welcome respite if the mosquitoes are gone or at least fewer.

Raffaele hauls his bucket to the next tree to be irrigated and dumps the water on its roots. As he turns to make the trip back to the creek, he is confronted by the sight of Caterina carrying a water bucket.

"What are you doing here?"

"Working alongside you!"

"You can't handle that bucket. Hand it over to me."

"Like hell, I will. I can do any work a man can do."

"Caterina, didn't you ask for work that is more suitable for a woman?"

"Yes, but that would have taken me two miles from here. What good is that? I want to work where we can be together."

"Does the foreman know that you're a Zinzi?"

"Yes. He didn't want to hire me until I mentioned my father. Even then, he insisted that I take a job where I could sit, sorting chestnuts. I finally convinced him to try me out on the job I want."

Raffaele is angered. They had agreed that she would not take on the hard work of the field hand, yet she is shouldering the same work load as he and the other men.

"Caterina, I want you to give this up and go home."

"No, I won't do that. I don't like being alone at home. I like being here where you are."

Raffaele has no choice. He must allow Caterina to work beside him. She is strong willed and determined...and the daughter of a powerful man.

For several months, Caterina and Raffaele work side by side on Count Leone's properties. The uncomplicated irrigating of summer yields to a frenzied autumn harvest, with its more demanding rigor of climbing into the trees to pick fruit, swiftly cutting grape clusters from vines and delivering the bounty to the collection point for sorting and tallying. Crop quotas are assigned according to expectation, and Caterina receives the smallest quota of all. Still, she struggles to keep up with the others, all of them men. Raffaele pities her inwardly, but he will not allow himself to show his feelings. Caterina has defied him by insisting on working along with him and must now perform her duties. It is uncommon for a Calabrian woman to demonstrate the celebrated hard-headedness of the Calabrese when it comes to her husband, but Caterina is unable to suppress her temperament. The men in the work crew resent her presence at first, but are loath to show it because she is Raffaele's wife and because they know that she is Vitaliano's daughter. Eventually, they accept and even admire her for her resolve. They avoid speaking the usual male profanities and walk well out of sight to relieve themselves.

Caterina is worn and tired, but she is content to be where she can see Raffaele with the turn of her head. She has mastered the skills necessary to function adequately and works along, bravely enduring the heat and work load. When they arrive home at night, she willingly extends her day to prepare their evening meal. By nightfall, she is exhausted and falls fast asleep. Her nearness to her man during the daytime has substituted for their time together at night. Raffaele is alone, though his wife lies beside him in bed, asleep and too exhausted to acknowledge his presence. He wonders if this is what is meant by marital discord. Once before, in the year they have been married, have they had a disagreement and that was over where they would house a goat they were given when they moved in to their tiny home. Caterina wanted the goat to stay with them in the house and Raffaele was repulsed by the idea. He prevailed, and the goat was kept outdoors. He thinks about the advice his mother gave him on the eve of his wedding: *She is a strong woman. You must expect to have disagreements. They are to be taken seriously and talked out between you. Disagreement is present in every marriage.* Is this what she was talking about? He had to let Caterina know how he was feeling about his life. She would understand.

The early light on the horizon brings with it another bright, sun-filled autumn day, with yet another grove to harvest. Caterina has already risen and has brewed chicory and toasted bread. She calls out for Raffaele.

"Wake up; we need to get to work."

Raffaele does not answer. He walks into the main room of the house and looks at Caterina with a somber face. She notices it immediately.

"What is it, Raf? What's wrong?"

Raffaele sits in a chair, ignoring the cup of steaming chicory that Caterina has placed on the table for him. He breathes in a long breath and sighs.

"I am not the man I want to be, Caterina. I have wanted to work hard and provide for you, and have you stay here to care for our home. But you've chosen to work in the fields and do the work that I do. I am losing my dignity as the man of the house. I feel I am failing you and will never be able to give you a satisfactory life."

She is stunned by his statement.

"You know very well that I am working alongside you because I love you and can't bear to be without you during the long work day. My working has nothing to do with your ability to provide for me. We have talked about this before."

"Yes, we have, but I have never been able to accept your working in the fields. You are from a family of means and have been schooled and nurtured. I cannot adequately provide for you so long as I work in the fields for a land owner. I must change my life if I am to satisfy myself that I have done my best."

"Raffaele, what are you saying?"

"Caterina, I have been hearing from some of the field hands whose relatives have gone to America and found great opportunity there. I have decided to go to America to make my fortune. I'll return after a short while, and we'll be able to purchase a property. I'll be working for myself then, and able to give you a better life. Then I will have the self-respect that I now lack."

Caterina is baffled by Raffaele's sudden revelation to her of his feelings. She could not have imagined that he would feel this way.

"Can we go together to America?"

"No. I will be better able to skimp and save if I'm there alone, and shorten the time it takes to earn enough money to bring back with me.

"No, Raf, please don't do that. I couldn't bear it if I didn't see you every day. I'll stop working if that changes your mind."

"My mind is made up. I'm going to America as soon as I can arrange for the passage."

Chapter 12

Reprise

The warm Calabrian sun makes a weak appearance at the horizon, looking small and pale as an unripe melon. It is a welcome sight after early winter rains that have kept the skies dark and overcast. Harvest is over and the bounty is being tallied and parceled between landowner and tenant. The sharecropper's meager share will prevent his family from starving, but it allows the landlord to fill his pockets. Winter will require still more of the worker. He must prepare his owner's properties for the coming season. Channels must be dug to direct the harsh rains away from the trunks of trees and to protect homes from flooding. Long canes and tree limbs need pruning and sealing against the elements to give the trees and vines potency in the next season. Cisterns must be filled with rainwater while there is rain cascading down the hills from winter storms. The sheep and goats must be fed and protected from the elements. Goats' milk must be processed into cheese, nuts must be roasted for market and olives must be cured. For some, the work is a blessing, keeping them busy and away from thoughts of the subjugation they endure. For others, it is a time of resentment of the system and for flights of fantasy about opportunity in a foreign land.

Antonio awakens in his luxurious bed alongside his sleeping bride. It is a luxury only recently attained, contrasting with the stark life he led in his young life. He feels revulsion for having wed a woman older than his own mother, but he is fascinated by his lavish surroundings and his new promi-

nence as a landowner of considerable means. He has escaped the bleak life
of the southern Italian peasant and brought providence to his aging parents.
Antonio, his father, is now supervisor of Anita's vineyard. And Maria, his
mother, has new clothing and a full cupboard. Still, Antonio faces life with a
heavy heart. On the one hand he has broken the spirit of the one woman who
has ever captured his heart; and on the other hand he has no desire to be with
the woman who lies in the bed beside him. She has in fact been very understanding these few weeks since they have become man and wife, of his utter
lack of desire to consummate their marriage. Anita Ruggiero is nevertheless
thrilled with her circumstance. She has landed one of the handsomest young
men in Gagliano and garnered considerable admiration among the towns-
women for having perfected her revenge against Giovanni, the husband who
slighted her in marriage by his faithlessness. And, since she has no offspring
from that marriage, she has little to be concerned about from a young husband
who will claim her complete fortune upon her death. Nor is she concerned
about the absence thus far of intimacy with Antonio. That will come in time,
she thinks. After all, he is human and will eventually yield to the carnal ener-
gies coursing through his young body.

It was a quiet, modestly elegant wedding. Father Alfarone of St. Rosalia's
church accommodated the couple and their guests by going to the Ruggiero
home to perform the ceremony in a house chapel maintained by Anita. The
small group of less than a dozen attendants included Antonio's parents, his
siblings and their spouses. Only one dignitary attended from Anita's side, her
spinster companion of forty years, Gina Lamporella, who could not take her
eyes off of Antonio. The bride wore a peach, ankle length brocaded dress that
hugged her body and made it awkward to walk. Her headpiece was a tiara
speckled with diamonds. A short necklace around the bride's neck gleamed
with a dozen dark rubies, giving Antonio's brothers and sisters pause in their
questioning of the motives for the union. Looking almost out of place, Antonio wore a black suit made for the occasion, and looked older and more
handsome than ever. He beamed his toothy smile, feigning his anticipation
of the moment.

Anita had arranged the reception, a five course dinner served at a large oblong table in her prodigious garden. The diversity of the flowers seemed to provide all of the color and aroma that had attracted Antonio the first time that he entered her home. A string quartet played several Puccini and Brahms favorites, adding the element of sound to the otherwise generously overflowing ambience. The traditional foods and gifts of kind were dispensed with, highlighting the stark difference of this event from peasant proceedings and further filling the groom's parents with pride and confidence in having done the right thing.

The honeymoon was arranged entirely by Anita. The couple boarded a private craft in the Catanzaro marina that swept them to Capo Rizzuto, a small island off the Ionian coast, where they lounged for a pleasant but loveless week, sightseeing and tasting the local foods and drink. Several times Anita made overtures of *amore* to the distant Antonio, but to no avail. He slept the entire time he was in bed despite Anita's caresses. Once, while they were on the island, she asked him if he was happy with their marriage and he gave her an unconvincing assurance.

"Why would you ask me that?"

"Because we have not made love. Don't you want to take me in your arms and make love to me?"

"Yes, but right now I'm feeling a little sick from overeating. We need to eat less and be more active."

But, the only activity that appealed to Antonio was diving to the bottom of the sea to find starfish and other curiosities that amused Anita and kept her hoping that Antonio would soon turn his attention to his conjugal obligations.

▸┼▸❋◂┼◂

It is their fourth week of marriage, and Antonio finally makes an attempt at sexual relations with Anita. They are back from their peculiar honeymoon and the nervous Antonio paces the Ruggiero property like a rooster chick waiting to be gelded. He realizes that he must perform his duty as Anita's husband. He had promised his parents that he would marry *La Signora* for the good of the family and everything has worked as imagined, except for his mating with Anita. Now he will follow through on his vows.

As they approach their bed for the night, Antonio changes his tactic. He does not turn away and feign sleep so as not to be confronted. Nor does he dress himself in the long nightshirt that has protected him from being seen naked. Instead, he removes all of his clothing and stands naked, facing Anita from his side of the bed. Anita excitedly accepts the lure, quickly removing her nightgown and slithering under the sheets excitedly. Then, as Antonio slides into bed, they come together in a firm embrace. Anita has so contemplated the moment that she wraps her arms and legs around Antonio, as though she is laying claim to him. As Antonio enters her, she becomes uncontrollably energized, copulating furiously and groaning as though she were finally liberated from her years of forced celibacy.

Anita climaxes repeatedly, calling out over and over, "Antonio, my love, *mi amore...*I love you...*te amo.*" After a lengthy ecstasy, she falls back on the bed in exhaustion and complete sexual fulfillment. She had been right. He does make a good bed companion, his tight young skin and his unending energy, copulating continuously until it was clear that her passion was spent. She had never experienced such satisfaction in all of her days with Giovanni. Antonio was worth everything she had to give to land him. His father is now in charge of an important part of her estate, and she is obliged to ensure that Maria wants for nothing, but what does that matter? She has found a man who can satisfy her untamed sensuality and help her to perfect her hatred of Giovanni.

In her eager euphoria, Anita has not noticed that Antonio does not experience the same frenzied sexual pleasure that she has. He does not feel the sensual rapture and sweet physical exhaustion. His thoughts are of another ecstasy, that with Concetta Zinzi. He cannot avoid comparing her silky fresh skin, her sleek fragrant body and her youthful face to that of Anita, whose skin is stretched and wrinkled and whose fragrance is derived from a perfume bottle. Even her words are that of another, older generation, lacking the buoyancy and sparkle of youth.

In the days that follow, Antonio tries to keep from thinking about Concetta. His place is with Anita. He has given his oath...for better or worse, until death do they part. There is no quarter here for ending marriages. He and Anita are locked permanently in marriage until one or the other dies. His mood is dragged down by thoughts of spending his life with Anita and inevitably hearing that Concetta has married and is lost to him for all time. Why did he agree to his parents bidding? Their greed has cost him his happiness and there is nothing he can do about it.

※

It has been three weeks since rain has fallen on Calabria and the coarse, dry ground is cause for great concern. Rain must fall soon or the crews will have to carry the cold winter water from streams to the roots of the trees and winter vegetables. Some make invocations to the Deity, asking for rain, while others curse the devil for causing the unnatural weather. Only Antonio is content with the circumstance that has others alarmed. He has long waited for this opportunity to visit the lemon grove that he and Concetta used as their meeting place. The grove will be dry and thus accessible. Though Concetta will not be there, Antonio's dark mood might be mollified by standing on the spot where she fell to the ground with grief when she learned of his intent to leave her for Anita.

Antonio rides out to the grove on a mare that has been saddled for him by a field hand. The ride takes twenty minutes, ample time for him to recollect those happy days when he held Concetta in his arms and she looked up into his eyes. The enchanting aroma of the lemon grove fills Antonio's senses within moments of arriving. The still air reminds him of how the ambience of this magical place added to Concetta's vulnerability as he took her in his arms and caused her to defy her father's wishes. He feels her presence as he dismounts and walks to the spot where he last faced her and sent a salvo through her heart. He takes in a deep breath of regret and suddenly feels tears rolling down his face. He sobs as he thinks to himself of the stupidity of what he has done. Now he is married to Anita and can never again hope to share his life with Concetta.

"Oh, Conce,' what have I done," he says softly to himself.

He hears a rustle in the distance and quickly crouches behind a tree, hoping not to be seen. Thankfully, he has left his horse hitched to a distant tree, out of sight. He is very still as his eyes scour the direction of the sound. As the rustling grows louder, he is able to make out the form of a woman. Her dark hair is tied back in a bun and she wears a dark sweater and skirt. His body quivers as he sees the features of the woman's face. It is Concetta and he can see her face clearly enough to notice dark lines around her eyes and a body slouch he had not seen before. She is deplorably depressed, as though she is in mourning of a close relative.

"Conce' is it you?" he calls. Startled, she looks up and recognizes him. She immediately turns and runs.

Antonio calls out "Conce'! Don't run away. Come back!"

It is of no avail. She does not stop. He knows that he could reach his mount and easily snare her in a chase, but to what purpose? What could he say to her if they were face to face? What would he do?

In the weeks that follow, Antonio rides to the lemon grove each day, hoping to catch a glimpse of Concetta and ignoring the rain that has returned and drenched the landscape. He returns home muddied and tired, but unrelenting in his determination to see Concetta again. In his heart of hearts he fears that he will find the courage to take her in his arms again. This time he would not only be defying Vitaliano Zinzi, he would also be ignoring the commands of his God and betraying the woman he vowed to honor forever.

Anita sees the condition of her young husband, who rides out each day, disregarding the inclemency of the weather and returning home drenched and looking despondent. She wonders why, but does not want to confront him. Patience has worked for her before. It will work again. She is satisfied that whatever is going on in his life will pass and that she will eventually be his focus.

The early spring buds create the illusion of a bountiful fairyland in which all is good and that all will share evenly the abundance that will soon appear on the trees and vines. The ground is no longer saturated and the tall grasses are green and velvety. White and pink blossoms flourish everywhere. It is the season of growth and inspiration. Peasants breathe deeply as free men and landowners are secure of another year in which to add to their prosperity. It is a moment when all seems right in a world that has been painted anew by

Mother Nature.

But, not so for Antonio. He has braved the winter in his quest to meet again by happenstance, the woman with whom he is still obsessed. Spring has eased the burden of travel to the familiar spot in which they stumbled across one another, increasing the chance that they will meet again. With the coming of Spring, the lemon grove has become a welcoming destination. White petals line the ground under the trees. There is an intense scent of fresh blossoms and, as the sun leaks through the trees' limbs, there is a surreal sense of walking into the midst of a hushed white cloud. It is a stark contrast to the cold muck that Antonio had experienced in his daily trek during winter. Worn from the inclement weather and disappointed with Concetta's persistent absence, he had reduced his visits to once a week. Now he resumes his daily ordeal.

It is the first warm day of the new year when Antonio dons riding boots and journeys once more to the lemon grove. His effort is at last rewarded. There, to the side of the grove in a grassy knoll, Concetta sits in a thick green carpet of grass picking wildflowers that have sprung up in the new season. She wears a long, thick garb of ashen color that has been fashioned to wear well in the field. A white ribbon holds her hair back, and the red and gold flowers give her the look of a young maiden in a Renoir painting. She looks up as Antonio trudges through the grass to her side. He can see that the black circles around her eyes are gone and her back and neck are straight again. It appears that she has recovered from the heartbreak that Antonio caused her.

"What are you doing here?" She is harsh in her first words to the now troubled Antonio. He perceives her anger.

"I have come to find you. I have made countless trips here over the past three months, hoping to find you."

"Why is that? Haven't you hurt me enough? Are you here to add to the desolation I feel from being rejected by you?"

"No, that's not why I'm here."

"Then why are you here?"

Antonio looks down at the face he has been dreaming of and searching for, fearing that he might never see it again. It is angelic, as he remembered it a year ago when he first met her at the grocery store in Gagliano. Her youthful form, sitting in the matted grass amidst the flowers she has picked, stirs him. He must tell her how he feels and risk her rejection. He has put her through the most tortuous time of her life and she is likely to mistrust anything he says to her. But, he must tell her how he feels. He lowers his head as he speaks.

"I am here to beg your forgiveness for what I have done to hurt you. My actions were not entirely my own and I regret having not asserted myself with my parents. I have not stopped loving you for a moment since the day that I left you in this very spot to endure the hurt I caused you. Can you ever forgive me?"

Concetta is oblivious by the look on her face. He has told her that he still loves her. Her mind fills with the words she has just heard. It is a reprieve from a past disaster, a momentary escape from the torment of rejection. Her heart beats faster than it has for a long time. She would like to spring into his arms, but her reply is guarded.

"I forgive you. If that's what you want, you may leave now."

"It is not all that I want."

"What do you want?"

Antonio is silent. He is overrun with thoughts of his overwhelming desire for Concetta and the consequences of perfecting that love. He has been mulling that over in his head since the day he abandoned her and has tortured over the decision to give up all that he has added to his life from marrying Anita. But, if anything is going to change, he must act now.

"I want you in my life, Conce.' I can't eat or sleep. I think of you constantly. I know that my actions thus far have belied my love for you, and I know there would be enormous consequences were I to leave Anita for you. But I am willing to do that if you will have me."

It is what Concetta has wanted to hear and has dreamed of repeatedly, but now that she has heard it from Antonio she is confused and fearful of the consequences.

"How do you propose to leave that woman for me? She is your wife and she is entitled to you."

"No, she is not entitled to me. Our union is one of convenience that was imposed on me during a moment of greed. It was wrong of me to have allowed our love to be put aside so that I could marry for wealth."

"What are you proposing to do?"

"I want to leave Anita right away. I can rent us a house in town near your sister and we can live there as man and wife."

"How can we do that? Everyone will know that we're living in sin and that we have defied my father and your wife so that we could be together."

"I am willing to confront anyone or anything that stands in the way of our being together...and I know you feel the same way."

"I do, Antonio, but I'm afraid."

"Don't be afraid. Say that you'll do it and I'll find us a place to live right away."

Concetta is speechless. Never has this possibility crossed her mind.

"I need to talk with my sister first. Then, I'll give you my answer."

He reaches out for her hand so that he could convey the desperation he feels about the possibility of losing her. She pulls away from him, collects her flowers in a basket and walks off. As he watches her leave, he is certain that he must have her at all cost. He has never desired her more.

⊷━◦━⊷

The sisters Zinzi are at the same time very different and very much alike. One is tall, the other short. One is quiet, the other vociferous. One has soft, gentle eyes and the other, round piercing orbs. One is the oldest of the four Zinzi siblings, the other the youngest. But their similarities are striking. They both have the cupid-like face and heart-shaped lips. Both are rebellious, determined women who will not easily submit to convention. Now they meet in the lowly hut that Caterina lives in with Raffaele. It is evening and Caterina has come in from the fields to wash away the day's toil and prepare the evening meal. Concetta is at her door waiting for her arrival. Caterina can tell that her sister is in crisis and needs help. As Raffaele will soon be home, Caterina washes quickly and hastily begins the preparation of the meal while the two converse. Caterina speaks first.

"What is it, Conce', you look troubled."

Concetta is wide-eyed as she tells her tale.

"Caterina, you are my older sister and the one person whom I can confide in. I need your help to decide on an act that will define the rest of my life. I have never before taken anyone into my confidence about the love that I have shared with a man. No one is aware of it to this day. But I must have your advice about what to do.

"Who is the man?"

"It's Antonio Russo."

Caterina nervously places a handful of pasta into the boiling water. She swallows hard and steadies herself against the table as she asks the next question.

"Didn't he marry Anita Ruggiero a few months ago?"

"Yes, and he abandoned me so he could marry her. Now he realizes that it was a terrible mistake and that he was pressed into the marriage by his selfish parents."

"What does he want now?"

"He has told me that he still loves me and wants me to leave home and live with him."

"Where?"

"Here in Gagliano."

Caterina's head is spinning. She imagined that her rebellion over marrying the man of her choice would be the height of controversy in the Zinzi family, but this is a much more serious matter.

"What do you want me to do?"

"Tell me what you think I should do."

"I don't know what to advise you. Living with a married man would mark you both for life so long as you live anywhere near Gagliano. You'd be snubbed and ridiculed by everyone. Yet, I know what it means to sacrifice to be with the man you love."

Concetta is unhappy with Caterina's response.

"Answer me one question. What would you do if you were me?"

Caterina draws in a long breath. She is reluctant to give an opinion in such a serious matter, but since Concetta has acknowledged her as her ultimate counsel, she feels obliged to reveal her inner thoughts.

"Conce', you are my dear little sister whom I have protected and helped through difficult times, especially after our mother died. I have not always been a good example, though I have tried to be. I truly don't know what is best for you and I would not want to be wrong in giving you this advice. But, if it were me, I would go with the man I love in spite of any hardship that I would have to endure."

Concetta is elated! She throws her arms around her sister.

"You're wonderful! I knew you'd understand."

At that moment, Raffaele walks into the house and sees the sisters embracing.

"What's going on?" he asks good-naturedly.

"Concetta has decided on who the man in her life will be, and she is expressing her joy."

"That's wonderful news. Who's the man?"

Caterina does not respond. Concetta calls out, "It's Antonio Russo."

Raffaele frowns and turns away. He says nothing, but his silence makes his feelings clear. It will not be the last of many such reactions that Concetta and Antonio will encounter.

⊱•⊰

Chapter 13

Desertion

The Paschal season has arrived in Gagliano and preparations are being made for processions and religious rites for this most sacred and respected of the holy days. It is Palm Sunday and images of the death and resurrection of the Savior are replicated everywhere. Palm leaves, some twisted in the form of crosses, some simply folded and tied, are displayed in every house. The Ruggiero house, likewise, is adorned with ornaments commemorating Christ's resurrection. Colorful Easter eggs, deep fried crullers and wheat pies with crosses on top fill the tabletop in the kitchen. They will be given to friends and family as tokens of Christian kinship and generosity.

It is midday, and Antonio awaits Anita's return home from church, having earlier declined her invitation to join her at the mid-morning Mass. In the two hours that he would be alone, he has packed his belongings and carefully included several valuable pieces of jewelry, all gifts from Anita. Earlier, his friend, Umberto, wheeled from across town in a donkey cart and transported Antonio's belongings to the tiny hut that Antonio has rented for Concetta and himself. He will move to a far lesser domicile in order to share his life with the woman he loves. Concetta has told him that she will move in with him and willingly suffer the consequences of a shameful existence, living an openly adulterous life and giving up the material comfort she enjoyed in her father's home. Now, as Antonio awaits Anita's arrival, he contemplates what he will say to her. He has decided that he must confront her and not merely flee. That will give him the greatest chance of assuaging her fury and reducing the possibility of retaliation. He chooses to be direct, with no acrimony for her misdeed of arranging their marriage behind his back. She arrives holding palms she received upon leaving the church. As she approaches him, Antonio girds himself for the hostility he is likely to arouse.

"Antonio, you look so tense. What is it, dear? Are you all right?"

His eyes stare blindly as he faces his moment of truth with Anita, fearing the outcome. He can barely speak.

"Anita, I have something to tell you."

"Can it wait for a while? I want to change out of these church clothes and get more comfortable."

"No, I'm sorry, but it can't wait."

"What is it, Antonio, why do you seem so strange?"

The moment has arrived. He must tell her now.

"I…I'm leaving you, Anita."

She looks at him, more curious than alarmed.

"You're what?"

"I'm leaving you. My clothes and other belongings are packed and gone, awaiting my arrival at my new home."

Anita's face contorts. She is beginning to understand what he is trying to tell her, and she at once feels fear, embarrassment and rage. What will she do without this man in her life? How will she face others knowing that they will ridicule her behind her back for having married a man so much younger than she? Why is Antonio doing this terrible thing to her?

"How can you leave? You're married to me and you must live here in our home."

"I'm sorry, Anita, but I'm leaving."

"Where are you going?"

"I will be living in the center of town, near the square."

"Why would you want to do that? Those tiny houses are horrible. Our home is beautiful."

"Please understand. I am going to live with the woman I love. We love each other."

"What woman are you talking about?"

"She is Concetta Zinzi, and I love her more than life itself."

The picture is at last clear for Anita. Antonio has fallen for another woman who is younger and prettier than she, and he is deserting his marriage in order to be with her. Moreover, the woman is the daughter of Vitaliano Zinzi, giving the gossipy women of Gagliano an additional bit of grist to chew as they perform their daily routine of washing their clothing in the town square. She feels a deep and overwhelming anger as she thinks about how she will be the butt of jokes all over Gagliano. She seethes as the thought crosses her mind that Antonio is the second man in her life to betray her. He is no better than that *bastardo* Giovanni, the husband whose infidelity was revealed after his death. She becomes uncontrollably hostile as the reality sets in on her: she is being betrayed for the second time in her life. Her face twists into a fearsome mask, eyes protruding, skin reddening and mouth twisting at the edges. Her speech is hardly discernable as she loses control and screeches.

"You son-of-a-bitch! Who do you think you are? Do you think you can treat me like a sack of potatoes? I'm Anita Ruggiero! You can't do this to me. I'll have your head removed and embalmed."

Antonio pleads with her.

"Anita, please calm down. Surely you must know that I don't love you and that I married you for the position it would provide for me and my family."

"You will never again receive anything from me as long as I live!"

"I know that, and it's not important to me to have wealth."

"That goes for your parents as well. They will go back to the miserable life they had before we married…and, as for you, I'll see to it that you never find employment anywhere."

Anita is beginning to cry, tears forming and her body heaving. She drops the palms to the ground and staggers into the house, her hand over her heart. Her motion allows Antonio to slip by her, and as he leaves, he looks back for one last glance at the life he is leaving to be with Concetta. He feels no remorse over what he has done. As he turns away and walks off, he hears Anita screaming at the top of her voice.

"Leave, you rotten bastard! You'll never work again so long as you live anywhere near here. And your parents are through receiving any help from me. You stinking peasant! I should have known better than to fall for you.

You're all alike, taking whatever you can get your hands on and giving nothing. Get out of my sight and don't ever come back asking for anything from me."

She dashes into her bedroom and throws herself face down on the bed, sobbing uncontrollably. She will never see Antonio again.

⊶──◦──⊷

Vitaliano Zinzi spends the early moments of the day reading his business journal. All is well, he thinks. The citrus crop is especially profitable, due to a dearth of competition from imported produce, and the increased demand for olive oil throughout the world has increased its value. Even his wine grapes have grown in importance since the northerners discovered that Vitaliano's fruit makes remarkable wine.

Perhaps more important than his monetary accomplishments, however, he has been able to set aside his grief for his late wife and to take up with a number of eligible women, any one of whom would be delighted to be the next *Signora* Zinzi. He has become a changed man since his life has refocused on long absent pleasures, smiling often and walking with a youthful gait. As he contemplates his liaison with a countess from Reggio, his mind strays from the business affairs that have dominated most of his life.

The Zinzi villa is unusually still this Palm Sunday morning. Since Caterina left to marry Raffaele, her exuberance has been lost to her family and a dreary quiet is prevalent. But this morning it is especially quiet. Vitaliano puts aside his journal and searches the first floor of the house. There is no one there. He climbs to the second floor. Vincenzo, his younger son, is fast asleep in bed. So, too, is Saverio, home on leave from the seminary. He notices that the door to Concetta's room is open and walks in. The bed is unmade and there is no sign of her. Where could she be? He spots a note on her pillow, and reads it:

Dear Papa:

By the time you read this note, I will be gone from this house and will be living with Antonio Russo in a house he has rented in the center of town. I do not expect you to understand my leaving in this way, and I know that you will be unalterably opposed to what I am doing, as will everyone else. I cannot help myself, as I am deeply in love with Antonio and have been since before he was dragged into a contrived marriage to Anita Ruggiero. I realize the implications of what I am doing, and I am willing to take the consequences in order to be with Antonio. I hope that you are able to forgive me. I love you.

    Conce'

Vitaliano is numb with shock. He is unable to react. It is beyond belief that yet another of his children, his only other daughter, has chosen to defy him. At least Caterina left to marry her lover. Concetta will live with her man without benefit of marriage. Nor can she hope to marry Antonio so long as Anita is alive. What could possibly cause her to be so reckless with her life? Vitaliano himself knew true love but would not have created such a horrible state of affairs for that or any other reason. Why should his children be any different? The thought of word circulating around Gagliano about his daughter leaving his house to live in a hovel with a married man burns into his brain. He shouts out his fury.

"No! Goddammit! I will not accept this deception. From this day forward, I will consider Concetta dead. I want no part of her illicit life and I will not assist her in any way or ever allow her back into my life."

His head hangs low as he leaves Concetta's room, her farewell letter crumpled in the palm of his hand, feeling as though his life has been shattered. Vincenzo and Saverio are awakened by his outburst. Vincenzo comes to the door of his room, rubbing the sleep from his eyes.

"What's wrong, Pa?"

Maria Russo walks hurriedly down the street from the church towards her home, following an evening prayer service. She is dressed in a navy blue silk dress that she received from Anita the week after she wed Antonio. There are small cobalt-colored beads around her neck and her black shoes complement her dress. She feels eyes on her from passersby on the street and thinks as how they are envious of her newly begotten wealth. She can remember envying others and now, with a measure of this newly found wealth, she believes she is receiving the same envy. She is wrong in her assumption. Word had begun to spread about Antonio as the first of his possessions were moved from Anita's house, and the onlookers are staring at one who is sure to fall victim to his indiscretion. It is not long before Maria is confronted. Her neighbor, Irma Morgano, braves the possibility that Maria does not yet know that her son has left Anita Ruggiero and is living with the daughter of Baron Zinzi. She is cautious in her approach.

"Good morning, Maria. You're looking well."

"*Bon Giorno*, Irma. Thank you for the compliment."

Irma's eyes are as wide as a barn owl's and she breathes heavily as she continues, coyly avoiding the words she would like to speak.

"Is Antonio furnishing that house in town for his brother?"

"What do you mean? Antonio is at home with Anita. There are no plans for one of his brothers to move. Why do you ask?"

"Maria, forgive me for prying, but do you know that Antonio has moved into a house in the center of town?"

"No. Why would he do that? He and Anita have a beautiful home."

Irma has lit the fuse of fear and curiosity in Maria. She will find out what Maria knows for sure, now that she has lured her into conversation. Irma is bolder now that she sees an anxious doubt form on Maria's brow.

"It's just that I saw Umberto in the square transporting Antonio's clothes into a house there. And later, I saw Concetta Zinzi arrive with what looked like her clothes and some other belongings."

"Are you sure it was Antonio?"

"I'm sure."

Maria is mortified at having bared her ignorance about a scandal involving her son. She turns to Irma. Her manner is curt.

"Don't be hasty in drawing conclusions about my son. I'll call on him and see for myself what's going on. When I find out, I'll let you know, since you seem to be interested in what our son is doing."

Irma is apologetic. She can see that Maria is upset.

"I'm sorry, Maria, I didn't mean to pry."

Maria walks quickly in the direction of the house that has allegedly been rented by her son. As she reaches the street, she can see the name *Russo*, freshly painted over the entrance to the house. She walks up to the door and knocks. Concetta appears wearing a simple peasant dress, her presence disquieting the older woman. Maria speaks first.

"Is this…Antonio's home?"

Concetta recognizes Antonio's mother though she has rarely seen her before. She has expected the inevitable visit from her.

"Yes, Antonio lives here. Are you his mother?"

"Yes, I am."

Maria peers inside, but does not see Antonio. Concetta decides to be welcoming.

"Won't you come in?"

As she enters the tiny front room, Maria speaks up.

"Why has Antonio moved here? And what are you doing here? Aren't you Baron Zinzi's daughter? Where is Antonio?"

In the next instant, Antonio steps into the room from the rear of the house, clothed in simpler garments than he had been wearing during his marriage to Anita. He was hoping that his mother would not have accepted Concetta's invitation to come into their home.

"Here I am, Ma. When did you hear about Conce' and me?"

"I heard it out on the street…just now!" Maria displays her irritation with him for surprising her with such weighty news.

"I'm sorry, Ma, but I knew what your reaction would be, and I'm not going to allow you to interfere in my life as you did when you arranged my marriage to Anita."

"I did that for your own good."

"No, you didn't! You did it for your good. Look at that dress you're wearing. It was part of what you received for marrying me off to Anita. And that jacket that Pa wears is new. He could not have afforded that without the inducement he received from Anita when he agreed to become her father-in-law."

Maria draws in a fast breath.

"What do you mean? You're very wrong to feel that we arranged your marriage for self gain. You're married to one of the finest women in Gagliano.

Stop this nonsense, whatever it is, and go home to Anita at once!"

Antonio's face reddens as his temper flares and he assumes control of the conversation.

"I'm never going to do that or anything else that you tell me to do. I'm in love with Conce' and we're going to live here as man and wife. Perhaps it's difficult for you to understand, but we don't care about what you think, what others think or even what the priests think. We are going to spend our lives together and nothing anyone thinks or says will change that."

Maria's face stiffens as she receives reproach from her son, but she persists in trying to reason with him.

"How will you support the two of you without working?"

"I will have a job before long."

"Who will hire you?"

"I don't know that right now, but I'll soon have work somewhere."

Maria has confirmed her worst fears and has exhausted her anger. There is no point in arguing further with Antonio. As she turns to leave, she looks back.

"Don't count on finding work. You've angered two very powerful people and they are not likely to forgive you for what you've done to them."

The door shuts on Maria as she leaves. For Antonio and Concetta, being together in their own home is all they want. Each looks at the other and grins in disbelief. They have audaciously defied convention and the people most connected to them. They have wanted to be together more than anything in the world and now they will spend the rest of their lives together, forsaking a past of profusion for a future of uncertainty. It does not seem to matter to them. They lie in bed holding one another, impervious to the reality that lies ahead.

⊢•⦁•⊣

For the past week, Vitaliano's agony over Concetta's actions has crowded his mind. What has he done to deserve this enormous smear? How can he have been so ignorant of the peculiar desires of both of his daughters? How can he be seen in the streets of Gagliano ever again, his family having been tarred with the brush of adultery of the brashest form? Agonizing turns to hatred and anger for Concetta and Antonio. He grits his teeth and once more swears to himself that he will never again allow Concetta to cross his path.

There is a knock on the door. It is Guglielmo Arcata, Vitaliano's supervisor for the Martino ranch.

"Baron, may I speak with you for a moment?"

"Yes, come in, what is it that brings you here this late in the day?"

"Antonio Russo has applied for work at the Capurro estate. As Antonio is now out of favor with you, Count Leone's foreman seeks your approval before considering his hire."

Vitaliano feels rage consuming him, but realizes that he must not lose his composure. He musters all of the control he is capable of and replies very coolly.

"Of course anything Count Leone wants to do is up to him, but since Concetta is involved with Antonio Russo to my complete discontent and disapproval, I have strong feelings about this matter. To the extent that the Count wants my approval to employ Antonio, the answer is unalterably no."

"I understand, Baron, I will see to it that the word gets back to them."

As Guglielmo leaves, the agony that Vitaliano feels seems oddly to subside. There is a satisfaction that has replaced some of the anger, by avenging the wrong done to him and his good name. He has struck a blow that will soon reverberate throughout the countryside. Antonio will not be able to work in the fields of Gagliano, and he and Concetta will soon know why. Vitaliano returns to his work, this time with less anger alive in his mind.

⊷⊶⊙⊷⊶

Anita is approached in her home by Vito and Rosa Altamonte, an unusual visit for a local merchant. They are Antonio's former employers who, as a barren couple, once treated him as their adopted son. They view his separation from Anita as an opportunity to win him back into their lives and want desperately to have him return to their *drogheria*, the principal grocery of Gagliano. It would provide him a means of support and at the same time, sway him into sharing his life with them. Because of Anita's prominence in the community, they do not want to lose her as a customer and fear her influence on their best and most moneyed customers. Vito takes the initiative with

Anita, complimenting her generously.

"Signora, we are always so pleased when you come to our store. Your presence there adds a measure of dignity."

Anita is inwardly suspicious of their purpose in coming to call on her, but she shows no distrust. She gets straight to the point.

"Thank you, Vito, but to what do I owe the pleasure of this visit?"

"Signora, as you know, we employed Antonio Russo for a time previous to his marriage to you. He now is seeking employment and we would like to have him back in our employ."

Anita is quiet. She is fighting the urge to shout out her feelings. Take him back, indeed! Do they have any idea of how she is grieving the loss of Antonio? Can they possibly comprehend the hatred she feels for him and his new mistress? Anita's eyes narrow, as though she is experiencing pain, and her throat is choked. Her eyes become glossy as they fill with tears, betraying her outward calm. Finally, she hisses and with considerably less self control than she would like, blurts out a response.

"So that's it. No! You may not have my consent to giving that lout back his job. He is a wicked deceiver of women and will do the same thing to that harlot he is living with as he did to me. If you employ him, I will not be seen in your store again and I will announce my feelings to anyone who will listen to me."

It is the expected reply. Vito and Rosa quickly react with a compliant response. They are unable to chance that Anita will indeed injure their business if they do not honor her wish. There is urgency in Vito's voice.

"Say no more, signora, we understand how you feel and will not consider taking Antonio back."

It is what Anita wants to hear. Her cool demeanor returns. She is triumphant in her defeat of Antonio and feels a wave of satisfaction surge through her body. As the disappointed couple leaves, they display complete understanding and submission. Inwardly, they are depressed and resentful. Their feelings are concealed in their parting nod.

"Don't worry, Signora, Antonio will never again work for us."

<hr/>

Reality closes in on Antonio and Concetta, who up to now have confidently enjoyed their leisurely cohabitation in the belief that Antonio will eventually find employment. But, as summer arrives, they look back on three months of refusal after refusal. Antonio's most likely employers, the Altamontes, are unable to help, lest they awaken Anita's wrath. And no one will risk Baron Zinzi's fury by the mention of Antonio. It becomes clear that Antonio has been black-balled by Anita and Vitaliano and that he and Concetta must act soon, before their money runs out. Their predicament is cause for the first stern words between the amorous couple. Concetta's concern for their welfare triggers a question.

"Have you heard whether that job at the Beccio ranch has been filled?"

Antonio flushes. He feels pressured and resentful. He fires back a response.

"No, dammit, they don't even have the decency to tell me that your father won't allow me to work anywhere in his orchards."

Concetta continues her questioning.

"Why don't you force an answer?"

"What's the use? That father of yours won't hire me and he won't let anyone else hire me, either."

"Well, you had better decide on what we're going to do before we're put out on the street for not paying our rent."

"Concetta, don't you think I know that? I'm trying to find work."

Concetta is disappointed that Antonio has not found a solution. She decides to let Caterina know of her plight, reckoning that this is what sisters are for, to help one another in times of need. She leaves her house and walks down the street to where Caterina and Raffaele live, careful to avoid Raffaele's presence. In a few moments she has disclosed her crisis to Caterina.

"What do we do? We have enough money for the moment, but it won't be long before we'll be destitute."

The older, more mature Caterina measures her words carefully as she responds.

"There is no hope here in Gagliano for sure, and Pa's reach is farther than you might think. It's doubtful that Antonio will be out from under Pa's grasp even in other parts of Calabria. You'll need to go a long distance to get away from him."

"What do you mean?" Concetta senses that Caterina is offering up a solution.

"I haven't told you this, but Raffaele has decided to go to America to earn enough money to return and buy a farm. Friends have told him that it will be easy to find a high-paying job with the railroad there and he believes that he'll be back within a year. He wants me to remain here and wait for his return."

"Are you thinking that perhaps Antonio should do the same?"

"Yes, and you should go with him."

"I wish he were more like Raffaele. He knows we have an insurmountable problem here, but hasn't thought about leaving."

"Then you need to assert yourself. Tell him that if he hurries, the two of you can leave on the same ship with Raffaele and he can help you locate a *padrone* when you arrive in New York."

Concetta expresses a concern.

"Do you think that Raffaele can accept us? He seems upset that we are living as we are, with no prospects of ever being married."

"Don't worry about Raffaele. He'll do this for me. And don't worry about not being married; in America everyone will assume you're both single and you can be married there."

Anita is thrilled with Caterina's advice. Her lips press together and her eyebrows arch in a facial gesture of gratitude. She startles Caterina with her next words.

"Thanks for your counsel, Sis. I'm going to do just as you say. And, since I'm here and you've been so helpful, I want you to be the first to know. I'm going to have a child."

Caterina looks lovingly at her young sister. How lucky she is. She and her man have been together only a few months and already she is pregnant. She must have conceived within the first week of their union. And now, she will be going to a new land, the America that everyone talks about, its greatness and its promises of prosperity for the common man. She thinks of the everyday lament among the immigrants who are forced to leave Italy to seek their destiny in America. *Oh Italy, Italy why must we leave you to find the good life? Why must we leave the land of our fathers, where we grew up and in whom we invested our youth?*

Chapter 14

Immigration

The summer of 1900 wreaks havoc in Italy. King Umberto is assassinated on July 29th, throwing the country into hysteria and causing disruption for travelers. Many are forced to cancel their trips altogether, and others must stay overnight in unexpected places while they wait for the panic to pass. Such is the case for three weary travelers from Gagliano, who have arrived in the teeming port of Naples, expecting to clear customs and board a ship bound for New York. They are disappointed to learn that the ship on which they have booked passage, the S.S. Dante Alighieri, will not leave harbor until it is certain that the conspirators against the king have been captured. Only first class passengers are permitted to board the ship for comfort and safety. Steerage travelers like Antonio, Concetta and Raffaele, are stranded ashore. They will live on the dangerous streets of Naples while the Alighieri awaits clearance. Antonio's quavering voice belies his effort to appear unruffled as he appeals to Raffaele.

"What can we do? We can't afford a hotel room in Naples for the next several days."

The older, more experienced Raffaele is relaxed.

"Don't worry, Antonio, we'll be all right."

Concetta is concerned. She has never experienced a predicament like this. For an instant, she wishes that her father were here to reckon with the crisis.

Raffaele, with his keen sense of survival, perceives an opportunity. He spots a scruffy British passenger ship of the White Star Line that has fired up its boilers and boarded its passengers. It has somehow received permission to sail. He races to the boarding ramp and engages the duty officer in conversation. The two men glance from side to side, assuring themselves that they are not being overheard or observed, and an exchange is made. Raffaele waves his arm anxiously at Antonio and Concetta, beckoning them to gather their belongings and follow him onto the British ship. Within a few hours, they are aboard the S.S. Lord Nelson, steaming out to sea. They are on their way to America.

As they look back on the lush coast of Italy, Antonio and Concetta are torn between their complete familiarity with this land of their birth and the sheer uncertainty of the bountiful America that they have heard so much about. They have little regret for having torn themselves away from their estranged families who remain behind, and the staid society that refused to accept their unconventional way of life. In America, they will be out of the grip of Anita and Vitaliano and have hope for marrying, despite the fact that Antonio cannot divorce.

For Raffaele, it is a far more emotional moment. The absence of Caterina's womanly presence heightens his love and desire for her. He feels more vulnerable and lonelier than he has ever felt as the distance between them grows. He is suddenly uncertain of his decision to emigrate without her. He vows to make his time away short, but the uncertainty of the days ahead gnaws at his confidence. He gazes longingly at the vanishing coastline from the deck of the speeding ship and feels the tug of sentiment felt by the millions of emigrants that have left their loved ones and the land of their birth in just the same way. His eyes fill with tears as he murmurs.

"*Ciao, Italia, ci vediamo!* Farewell for now. I will be back soon."

The high-funneled steamship was born of the need to transport huge numbers of emigrants from overpopulated Europe to the labor-poor Americas. The practiced S.S. Lord Nelson has wound its way through European ports for a quarter of a century, boarding masses of humble humanity and delivering them to the Americas. Few of its passengers see much daylight or enjoy the luxury of the open deck or private cabin. They peer through portholes from the cramped lower levels of the ship, separated by nationality, men apart from women. They sleep on mattressed bunks hinged to steel bulkheads, lowered each evening before nightfall and lifted in the morning to allow space for passengers to more easily tramp their way to toilet facilities and seating areas. Food is dispensed in a common area where anxious families try to come together at crowded tables. The food is, frequently, a monotonous repetition of the previous day, mostly green vegetables boiled flaccid, and gray mutton seasoned only with a heavy dose of salt.

Many of the passengers will be seasick for the entire voyage and unable to eat very much. The air is hot and stagnant and has a lingering aroma of bleach left behind by the crew that swabbed the living area prior to leaving port in Liverpool. It will not be cleaned again until the ship reaches Rio de Janeiro, its final destination before returning to England with a huge consignment of Brazilian coffee.

By hand gesture, a ship's petty officer is able to make Raffaele understand that he needs to see passports for the three Italians that were boarded at the last moment in Naples. Raffaele wonders how this stranger has come to know that he is holding the passports for all three of them, but he complies. In the next minute, the crewman asks that a large sum be paid for the return of the documents with the appropriate stamp that will get them through customs at Ellis Island. Raffaele hesitates, sensing that he is being subjected to a ruse; but in the end, he has little choice but to dig into his reserves and produce the money. For the remainder of the trip, he avoids coming into contact with any of the ship's company. Nor does anyone approach him. They have depleted his resources to the point where he is of no further interest to them. As Antonio and Concetta entrusted a portion of their money to him, he must let them know of the swindle. The dinner hour has arrived, giving him the opportunity to be together with them. He speaks quietly so as not to be overheard.

"My friends, we were cheated out of half of our money today. I was aware of what was being done, but helpless to do anything about it. Our passports were at stake."

Antonio is angry.

"Who was it? We can report him to the captain."

"I'm sorry it happened, but there is little we can do without risking retaliation of some sort. Forget it, Antonio; we'll make up for it when we're in America."

The hot summer weather heats the hold of the ship and adds to the misery of life for the emigrants, but it becomes possible for the sleek vessel to steam full throttle to its destination. There are no gales to redirect the ship or cause it to slow to a crawl. There are no steep swells to navigate. Nor is there heavy winter rain to cloud the captain's vision. In twenty six days from departure in Naples, the S.S. Lord Nelson reaches the entrance to the New York Bay.

It is morning and, to their enormous delight, the sea-weary passengers are instructed to pack their belongings and climb to the open deck. They will reach port within a few hours and will transfer to Ellis Island in time for some to clear immigration. A frenzied bustle overtakes the hold, as though the last breath of air will be consumed in the next desperate moment. Luggage is nervously brought out and hastily filled with whatever scattered belongings are not being worn. Some search the shallow crevasses of the mattresses for anything left behind. Some primp as though they will be met by royals. The three-foot wide ladder-like staircases leading to the deck are packed with those who would be first to reach the fresh air and see at last, the elusive America they have painted in their minds. Men seem not to notice women struggling up the stairs. Elderly men and women are bumped aside by younger, stronger passengers. In the next hour, the deck is teeming with a convergence of nationalities. There is huge relief as Poles, Slavs, Greeks, Russians and Italians breathe in the fresh summer air. A morning breeze courses down the Hudson River and into their nostrils. The scourge of the past twenty six days is soon forgotten as the anxious moment arrives to look out onto the American shore.

⌐⊶⊸⊷⊶⌐

The monstrous room is the largest undivided space they have ever seen, its forty-foot high ceiling and its cavernous interior a wonder to three Italians from Calabria. They stand in awe of the Great Hall on Ellis Island, where they are channeled through a long line of fellow immigrants awaiting

physical examination. While they wait, ladies of the Salvation Army, looking much like proper Quakers in their ribboned bonnets and aproned dresses,
wend their way through the crowd handing out thick sandwiches of soft white
bread generously filled with boiled ham and store cheese. The immigrants
marvel at this strange food wrapped in a waxy paper, the first nourishment
they have had since leaving the ship. They have never before seen a sandwich
or tasted American bread; but it is a welcome gesture in this alien place. And,
it reminds them of how hungry they have become.

Raffaele, Antonio and Concetta are declared to be in good health and free
of vermin, sparing them a delousing experience; but the women's examining
physician chalks "Pg" on Concetta's dark linen blouse. He has noticed her
pregnancy and she will have to be examined further to ensure that she is not
in immediate need of medical attention. Should that be the case, she will
be immediately deported back to Italy. Directed to climb a staircase to an
enclosed examining room, Concetta looks nervously about for Antonio and
Raffaele. They are not there. They have been moved forward to the last phase
of examination, an interrogation about their contacts in the U.S. and their
financial wherewithal. The few words of Italian muttered by the inspector are
barely enough for Concetta to get the gist of what he is telling her, but she
understands that she must climb the stairs to where she will be examined. She
is fearful of having lost contact with her traveling companions.

"This way, *signora*." The inspector leads Concetta into the examining
room. It is a small, white-tiled room with shiny medical instruments in wall
cabinets behind glass-paned doors. Other implements sit ominously in trays
on steel tables. It is very cold despite a large, intense light glaring down from
the ceiling and unintentionally heating the area immediately below. To Concetta's amazement, the inspector is able to speak Italian, though his appearance is more that of a northern European. He closes the door and drops the
latch in place as they enter the room.

"Remove your outer clothing," he says authoritatively.

Concetta obliges, revealing her slender nakedness beneath her threadbare
underwear. She thinks that she would not be so obliging were she not so eager
to end the process and rejoin the others.

"Sit up on the table." The inspector gestures toward the examining table in the center of the room. She complies. He places his hand on her thigh and begins to rub it gently back and forth.

"I can make this examination very easy for you. Just lie back and I'll be done in a moment."

Concetta is at once aware that she is being defiled, that he is not the examining physician and that he can prevent her immigration with a flick of his pen. She is sickened by the thought of giving in and screams.

"Antonio! Raffaele! *Aiuto!*"

The unexpected shouting galvanizes the depraved inspector and he flees in panic. As he makes his way quickly down the stairs from the examining room, he bumps aside a woman wearing a stethoscope around her neck, on her way up to examine Concetta. She looks back at him for an instant and then turns to the task of examining Concetta. With five months left to go, Concetta's pregnancy is ruled not to be a hazard and she is directed to dress and proceed to the Registry Room for interrogation. As she makes her way across the gargantuan room, she is elated as she catches a glimpse of Antonio and Raffaele across the packed room. Dismayed and depleted, she calls to Antonio, her voice noticeably pained.

"*Cara!*" Antonio recognizes her voice and perceives her anxious tone. He rushes across the room to her side and embraces her.

"What is it, my dear?" She is unable to tell him of her experience, afraid that he will create a disturbance and prevent their passing through immigration.

"It's nothing…just nerves. I can't wait for this to be over."

⊱⋅•⋅⊰

Located at the windy southern tip of Manhattan, South Ferry is a crowded landing point for commuter transports plying their way across the blustery bay from Brooklyn and Staten Island. It is also the port for Ellis Island's launch, the only unscheduled vessel. It will leave the island when its hulk is filled with passengers. Most of the anxious immigrants will be met by a relative or close friend who will assist them in starting their life in America. Those not being met must produce evidence of resource in the form of currency. Raffaele, Antonio and Concetta are each able to produce the minimum twenty-five dollar reserve required for those who will not be met. From what Raffaele has heard, they will be offered employment as they leave the dock, from several *padrones* competing for strong, young men from Italy. Raffaele has heard correctly. As they disembark, the trio does not have to look far. Several recruiters, obvious by their capacity to recognize their quarry, are there to greet them.

"Hey, paisani!" The stout man in a flowered short sleeve shirt is first to call out to the hapless threesome. He has the short, thick build and dark skin of a Mediterranean. Luigi Castiglione is wearing a shabby, straw fedora sporting a tiny Italian tricolor in the band. He speaks the southern Italian dialect that his prospects are likely to understand. He holds a pencil and paper that appears to be a roster of recruits that he has managed to enlist. He approaches Antonio, the youngest and more muscular of the two men.

"Are you ready to take a job paying two dollars a day?"

Antonio is astonished. His eyes widen and light up. He could not receive that much money working for a month anywhere in Calabria.

"What would I have to do?"

"Work on the railroad. I'll take you to where you can join a work crew. If you sign up today, we can get you started within a few days time."

"What about my woman?"

"No women allowed. She'll have to stay here."

Concetta interrupts the conversation.

"No! Antonio and I came here to be together and I don't want him leaving me for a place neither of us knows anything about."

"Lady, your husband is not going to get paid that kind of money anywhere. Do you realize how much money he can save in a year? He'll earn over seven hundred dollars."

Concetta looks at Antonio, a dull, expressionless gaze on her face. She is against accepting the offer. Antonio reluctantly turns to Luigi.

"As you can see, my wife is not in favor of this, so my answer is no. Is there any work where we can live nearby?"

"Yes, but it pays less money. For a little commission, I can get you work north of the city, at the Croton Dam, for a dollar thirty-five a day, general labor. Are you interested?"

"Yes, but how much will I have to pay you?"

"I'll charge you only a month's pay, and I'll let you pay me over a year. You'll hardly notice that it's missing out of your pay."

Antonio looks at Concetta. She seems amenable. Then, he turns to Raffaele, who has been quietly listening in on the conversation.

"What do you think, Raf?"

"If Caterina were here with me, I would choose to work where we could be together."

Antonio hesitates no further.

"Ok, I'll accept the work on the dam."

Luigi turns to Raffaele.

"And what of you? Are you interested in going to work?"

Raffaele's eyes gaze unseeingly. He misses Caterina more than he imagined he would. He thinks about what he has set out to do and how he can speed his return to Caterina.

"Must I pay a commission for the railroad job?"

"No. No commission."

"I'll take it."

Concetta and Antonio say their sad farewells to Raffaele, their constant companion of the last harrowing month, as they made their way to America. Their parting expression is a promise to some day meet again. Now they turn their attention to settling down in their new country, like robins migrating north for the summer and looking for a place to roost. The half-day trip from New York to Croton-on-Hudson is an excursion that allows them a first look at the fabled land they had heard so much about in their primitive Calabrian village. They walk to Grand Central Station, a gleaming edifice of marble and steel, recently constructed to house trains navigating to and from the north. There, along with a group of other Italians who have likewise been recruited for work on the dam, they board a steam-driven train with cars that each allow one hundred passengers to board with all of their belongings. It takes them north through the cluttered city and into the spacious hollows of the fragrant countryside. The enormous size and number of buildings they see from their train window is mind-boggling. Six story tenements and office buildings are everywhere, a continuum of structures for the length of the city. Occasionally, they see large homes on spacious lots in the Victorian style with which they are unfamiliar. They are the homes of the rich bankers, politicians and professionals of society. As they continue northward and emerge from the great New York metropolis, they are awed by the convergence of large, steely rivers winding down from the north to form the placid waters surrounding a majestic Manhattan Island. Now there are trees in full summer bloom, thousands upon thousands of them, Pin Oaks, Tamarack pines and Dutch Elms. There are mountains, not as high as the Appenines that divide Calabria's east and west, but lush and plentiful for as far as the eye can see. It is true, Antonio thinks, this is a vast land of plenty.

Less exhilarating is the mammoth site of the dam, contiguous to the area where they will live and work. It is no longer Nature's landscape. Dull and artificial, it is as though a human giant hacked an enormous black gulch with a large clever through the surrounding jade-colored hills, denuding the land and generating huge mounds of dark gray mud. Cranes and booms are planted everywhere, collecting the wet, pulverized earth for removal to a distant place.

The building of the massive Croton Dam begins in 1892 for the second time, having failed fifty years earlier when heavy rains and snowfall caused the earthen dam to slide and collapse, silting the Croton River and dashing hopes for providing precious water to the burgeoning metropolis to the south. By 1900, it is clear that the project will succeed, albeit at higher cost and with many more years of work than were imagined at the outset. Thousands of southern Italian stonemasons are recruited to provide cheap labor. Some bring their families from Italy. Others come alone and send for their families after they are established. Many simply vanish from sight and will remain in the area following completion of the project.

It is evening and the Italian migrants are led to the area set aside for them to live. They gasp as they gaze at flimsy, aged shacks propped high on stilts that appear to be worn and leaning. Below in a dreary mud flat, there is a horde of rats in such great number that the ground seems to pulsate as they scuffle about in search of sustenance. Only the high poles that hold the buildings aloft prevent them from invading the workers' shacks. To be sure, thinks

Antonio, Gagliano has its share of rats, but not the huge number that crowd the ground below. And, they seem unperturbed by water around them that threatens to rise and drown them. The shacks are old, built perhaps fifty years earlier as vacation dwellings in a time when fishing on the Croton River was a popular pastime. They were built hastily and without benefit of exterior paint. Two hundred seasons of heat, wet and cold have shrunk and split the now blackened planks that constitute walls and floors, creating gaping holes that allow Nature's elements to creep indoors. There are scant furnishings in the shacks left behind by the previous occupants from the failed attempt to build the dam. Rent for the dilapidated shacks is set at one dollar per week, the tenant being required to provide maintenance. There are no stores where one might purchase their food and other necessities. The workers are required to make their purchases at the lone general store within miles, a small, window-less storeroom owned by the project manager and euphemistically referred to as the "plucking store."

Tired and hungry, the Italians do not complain. It is not what they would have expected in America, but it is not any worse than the hovels they left be-hind in the poor towns of southern Italy. After the long trip to Croton, they are happy to have any bed on which to rest. For Antonio and Concetta, it is the first time in almost three weeks that they have been alone. Once inside their hut, they bolt their door and climb into one another's arms in a union of their limbs and torsos. It is a reaffirmation of the magnetism that has drawn them together in the time they have shared their bodies.

Antonio rises at dawn on the morning following their arrival. He dashes out to the work area to meet the gang boss for the first time. Large and ruddy-faced, he is a man of middle age dressed in the American style, overalls and checked shirt. Only the beret he wears tells of his recent European origin. He looks intently at Antonio, as if to assess his derivation. His voice is gruff and his dialect of Italian is difficult for Antonio to comprehend.

"Are you from southern Italy?"

"Yes, from Calabria."

The older man sneers.

"What have they told you about the job?"

"Only that I will be paid a dollar thirty five a day for general labor."

"Did you bring tools with you?"

"I don't own any tools."

"Aren't you a stone mason?"

"No, sir, I'm not."

"Then what are you doing here?"

"I was brought here with the promise of a job. Please, sir, my wife is pregnant and we've come a long way. I need work."

"Well, you're lucky that we have something for you to do, but you won't be paid full wage. We'll pay you a dollar twenty-five a day, take it or leave it."

Antonio is angry, but manages to curb his temper.

"That's fine. When do I start?"

├─►─○─◄─┤

Chapter 15

Jeopardy in the New Land

The dusty, shadowed streets of Manhattan's West Side are littered with malodorous horse manure, abandoned wagons and an occasional tattered drunk who has found his refuge in a doorway or at the base of a lamppost. Nightfall adds the danger of mugging by desperate vagrants or ferocious gangs that walk the streets looking for pickings from a lone traveler. It is clear that the impressions of the new world given to the immigrants by predecessors were greatly exaggerated. There are no gold-lined streets or handouts from compassionate humanitarians with bulging pockets. It is a stark and unwelcoming landscape and, despite its urbanized atmosphere of buildings, burnished and faceless, looming above its grimy sidewalks, New York is evocative of harsh conditions left behind in a more familiar rural Calabria.

Raffaele and seven other immigrant Calabrians are walked up the West Side of Manhattan by their padrone, Luigi, intending to board the next ferry for Hoboken. There, they will find the train for Ohio and the promised employment with the railroad. As they round Five Points, the notorious point of separation between Greenwich Village and the Chelsea district of lower Manhattan, they are suddenly confronted by a bizarre gang of leathered hooligans wielding bats and waving ominous chains. They are disheveled, their clothing tattered and dirty as chimney sweeps, their faces showing the stained ravages of recent street fighting. They are missing teeth, wear eye patches, have bloody bandages on arms and legs and bear signs of knife wounds on their grimy torsos. One of the men calls out with a guttural accent that complements his repulsive appearance.

"Hey, look at dis, we found us a bunch of Dagoes. Where ya goin' you pieces of shit? To steal jobs from us decent folks? Well, we're not gonna allow it. We're gonna beat your brains out right here and now."

Though the men do not understand English, they are able to comprehend that their lives are in danger. Their faces show fear as they look to Luigi, their padrone and mentor in this sudden tangle of life and death. The band is so large that it causes Raffaele to flash back in his memory to a story of the 1896 battle of Adowa, which his father's friend, Cristiano, had told him from personal experience. There, an Italian expeditionary force faced odds so enormous against a fierce and well armed adversary of Abyssinians, that their defeat was inevitable despite their bravery. They were slaughtered by the overwhelming force of the opposition. Cristiano's survival with only the loss of one eye was miraculous. Raffaele feels his body trembling as he and the others in the small group of immigrants now face this tremendous force of attackers.

A hoodlum near the front of the group heaves a large wooden bat hewn from oak, directly at Salvatore, one of the Italians. It darts through the air like a lance and strikes him squarely in the forehead. He drops instantly to the ground in a single movement, laying motionless and bleeding at the spot where he was struck. He does not appear to be breathing. The other men are terrified and, in spite of the odds, drop their belongings to the ground, stiffening their arms and preparing to defend themselves with fists and knives they have brought with them from their days of pruning the vineyards of Calabria. A tall, lean tough in a torn top-hat pushes his way to the front of the ruffian crowd. He holds up his hand as though commanding a halt to the assault. His cronies back off. He looks at the frightened Italians and calls out in an affected Cockney accent.

"Who's in charge here, anyhow?"

"I am." Luigi steps forward, clutching his chest in a motion that reveals his intense dread. He is the only one who can speak and understand English, and he is the only one who has any chance of saving the Italians and himself from certain death.

"Well, what'll you give us to get us on our way without killin' ya?"

"Please, sir, these men are newly arrived immigrants from southern Italy and have nothing. They are on their way out of the state to work, so they aren't going to take any of the local jobs or cause any trouble."

"What about you? What can you give us?"

"I will give you anything I have on my person, but please don't harm us."

"What have ya got?"

"Here, look, I have thirty dollars in my pocket and a fine pocket watch worth another thirty dollars at least."

"Are you kidding? You expect me to allow you all to live for a mere sixty dollars?"

"That's all I have. Please, sir, don't harm us. Take what I have and let us go."

There is a sudden disturbance, a clanging sound from a city block away that intrudes on the commotion. Someone has summoned the police and three of their patrol wagons filled with a score of policemen speed their way towards the tumult. They are anxious to put their billies, and perhaps even their revolvers, to use in restoring order to the dark, scruffy streets for which they are responsible.

The stern, confident look on the gang leader's face turns to fear and panic as he looks up the street and realizes that he has only moments to make an escape. He reaches out and clutches the money from Luigi's hands, not taking time to seize his watch. With one simple gesture, he commands his followers to return to the shadows from which they appeared. The threat is gone and the Italians are enormously relieved as a flood of blue-coated lawmen stream out of their vehicles and race after the thugs. Raffaele rushes to the unconscious Salvatore, but it is too late. He had indeed stopped breathing shortly after he was struck on the head.

It is midnight before the police complete their investigation of the lurid events. One of the policemen that can speak a few words of Italian is able to corroborate Luigi's report of the confrontation with the immigrant men. They are allowed to get on their way, resuming what has become a grim journey. They head warily for the ferry building a few blocks away, taking only moments to look back as Salvatore's body is wrapped in a blanket and carried to a police wagon. One of Salvatore's hands is visible, as it dangles inertly from under the blanket. Raffaele's head is spinning with thoughts of all that has happened. He wonders if Salvatore's family will ever learn of how he met his end in the new world.

It has been a long day for Raffaele. What had started with the endurance of Ellis Island's cold indifference ended in his almost losing his life. He had said his farewells to Antonio and Concetta, and was confident that they would meet again. Now he is uncertain as he ferries across the Hudson River to Hoboken and boards a small, steam-driven train of the Erie Lackawanna Railroad. A bare and foul-smelling cattle car will be the men's quarters for most of the next two days. The conductor who boards them is irritated because they have arrived hours after they were due. Never mind that they encountered the worst experience of their relatively short lives in this strange new land. They shouldn't have inconvenienced him. Thanks to him, they can now begin their westward trek to a place called Ohio, to work for wages that are seductively attractive. Not once do any of the humble recruits question the unlikely generosity of the railroad for work that does not require any special knowledge or skill. In spite of everything that has happened, they cling to an expectation that all will eventually be made right. This is America, where fortunes are earned and ordinary Calabrians return home with riches. No matter that they now are made to sit on filthy wooden planks that become their roost for the long trip; nor does the absence of any form of nourishment trouble them. They can take care of themselves as they did in the old country where their needs were largely ignored by the landowners.

The night travel does not afford the Italians the opportunity to see the land that speeds by as the train makes its way toward Ohio. Exhaustedly, Raffaele lays his head down on the roll of cloth that sheaths his belongings, trying to ignore the stench of dried cow manure on the floor of the car. In the sparse moonlight, he spots a column of russet-colored cockroaches making its way from one side of the car to the other, heading for a pod of dung that has not yet completely dried out. He snuffs them out with one slam of his boot, the noise momentarily waking the others. It is a small bother when added to the sounds of the train's wheels grinding against the rails, screeching occasionally, emitting their strangely metallic odor and resonating an endless clicking and clacking. Each turn of the wheels reminds Raffaele of the growing distance between him and Caterina. Cold and hungry, he lies there silently imploring the patience of the woman he has left behind in Calabria.

"Caterina, I am here in America. It won't be long. I'll soon earn money enough to return to Italy and to you. I will never leave you again."

Chapter 16

Agony

The crisp morning sun streams in through fractures in the sides of the aged cattle car, beckoning the Italians to awaken from their crude sleep on their way to Ohio and the promise of work on the railroad. Raffaele is second to arise, joining the first at a circular opening between two boards that may have been made by a powerful kick from a discontented steer. The view is of an endless horizon of emerald, jade, and olive, a forest of trees crowding each other in a quest for survival. It is unlike the America the new immigrants have seen up to now. In an occasional clearing, the inexorable decrepit shack appears, the familiar dwelling of a poor, adventurous family out on the land fending for themselves.

Immediately upon rising, the men find a shovel in a corner of the car and clear the filthy floor though an opening in the boards. The shit is gone and the smell of the air improves immediately. There is a bucket of fresh water that has been left for them, the only thought given to their welfare. They fill containers they have instinctively kept for themselves to hold drinking water, a custom of Calabrian farm laborers. The empty pail has no further use except as a latrine from which they can conveniently dump their waste into the untamed outdoors. They pool their meager resource of food from their belongings and are able to provide two sparse meals for the group, a breakfast of stale provolone cheese and crusty bread, and lunch of hard, dry soppressata salami and flaccid green olives. Their hunger is not satisfied, nor are they starving.

The train slows noticeably as they pass a more populated area, the rhythmic clicking and clacking slowing and giving notice that there is something unusual ahead. A dense gray city appears in the distance, its smoke-filled skies adding darkness to its gloomy silhouette. Alongside the railroad right-of-way, littered gullies releasing the ugly odor of decomposing refuse are reminiscent of the dung the men expelled from the filthy rail car. Raffaele strains to glimpse a lettered sign as they glide past a train station. It reads *Canton, O. population 34,563.* He reasons that the O means Ohio and that the Italians have reached their destination, or are at least close to it. He is wrong. The train continues on for the balance of the day, maintaining an unhurried pace. It journeys through increasingly dense forests that separate faded towns and dreary cities, the few visible inhabitants dressed in drab work clothing and engaged in physical labor.

⊢◦⊢⊙⊣◦⊣

The train has been stopped now for the last hour with no indication of whether it will start up again or if the weary, hungry men have at last reached their destination. The trainman has never been visible to the men inside the car and now seems to have vanished into emptiness, ignoring the cargo of life he has delivered to this distant place. As the Italians peer between the slats in the car, they can see large piles of crushed stone and tidy stacks of steel track and wooden ties. A small timber shack sits idly in the distance beyond the building supplies, a hint of smoke rising from its cylindrical, blackened steel chimney. They can see nothing else other than the natural terrain, a thick forest of green climbing a hill that ascends to the south. There are no signs of life and the overcast skies add to a somber ambience. The men remain still, listening for a sign that their presence is known and that they will soon be released from the miserable confinement of the last two days. At last, they hear a rustle of feet outside, and suddenly, the door to the rail car glides open and slams back against a block at the end of the slide. The long and wearying journey is over.

Three powerfully built men appear outside the rail car, two at the rear dressed in khaki shirts and trousers and clutching Springfield rifles, the muzzles pointed upward toward the murky sky. They are both white-faced, with pale blue eyes, their northern European features distinguishing them from the Italians. The third, a stern-looking man, the archetypical gang boss, faces the Italians in front, his thick arms folded and legs apart. Mario DeGennaro is middle-aged and mustachioed and wears the uniform of the railroad gang supervisor: a short-sleeved, red checked shirt, blue overalls and a peaked cap stained at the brow with the sweat of many seasons. His olive complexion and aquiline features confirm his Mediterranean heritage. He is tall, though, almost six feet, with muscular arms and torso. Hailing from the northern Italian city of LaSpezia, his disdain for the southern Italians under his supervision is at once evident in his swagger; and his bitter facial expression betrays his ardent wish to be back in Italy with his family. He wears a side-arm, a 38 caliber revolver strapped to his waist, and a small, leather-encased club in his back pocket, the loop of its grip dangling from its roost. He scowls the few words that he mutters in a dialect that is difficult for his minions to comprehend.

"You men are at camp 15 of the Baltimore and Ohio Railroad. You are part of a work crew installing tracks to the west. Do your part and you will be properly rewarded. Cause us trouble and you will regret ever signing up for this work."

He brusquely removes the club from his back pocket and carefully strikes the palm of his other hand several times, a menacing look distorting his face. The men understand his meaning, troubled that this will be the tenor of their existence during their first work encounter in the new country.

"Now, get to your bunks and drop off your belongings. You will eat before being issued your work assignments and tools."

It is the best news that the Italians have heard. They have not had a full meal for two days. They are so hungry that they will agree to anything to receive a meal, including putting aside the fear imposed on them by the harsh reception they have just experienced. They are led to a rail car sitting nearby on the tracks where they are assigned cots in a space large enough to sleep twenty men. The sleeping surface of the cots is made of canvas and only an unencased pillow and a folded blanket sit on the end of each bed. All personal possessions are simply placed at the foot of one's bunk in whatever satchel they have been contained. Several of the cots are already taken, indicating that there are others whom they have yet to meet. Outside, there is a latrine that, from its trampled look and rancid odor, seems frequently used. There is a wellhead not far from the shack where a dozen upturned wooden buckets wet from recent use are stacked beside a cast iron water pump with a curved handle.

It is a warm, dry evening and the smell of pine trees permeates the air, the gray shadows stretching out across the breadth of the camp. The men are led to a coarse wooden table in the outdoors. A cook wearing a bright red undershirt and a dirt-stained apron appears from behind the shack in the distance. He is carrying a large, steaming pot of white rice sparsely fortified with overcooked chicken. To the seven Italians, it is an unfamiliar smell of steam and bland, unseasoned meat. They are hungry and do not comment, taking their plateful of the ration and ravenously spooning the food into their mouths. A blue marbleized steel coffee pot containing water and six steel cups are brought to the table by the cook so that the meal can be washed down into their bellies. Their first meal is not much like the peasant food of Calabria. There, they would have enjoyed a simple, meatless meal of *pasta fagioli*, but it would have been rich in texture with the creamy-like feel against their palates. A liter of red wine would have titillated their taste buds and assisted them in sleeping the night. But they are grateful for the food that now lies in their bellies and gives them comfort after too long a time.

As the men finish their meal, a large handcar emerges on the new rails coming from the west. There are twelve occupants crowding the open surface of the car, two of them pumping the levers that drive the car. Beneath the smudges of grit and sweat on their faces are the features of Italians, most probably from the south, the railroad's most common harvest ground of laborers hungry for work and ravenous for the wages they are told to expect. They are back from the feral end of the track they have just laid, their day's work done with the disappearance of daylight. Tired and dirty, they hastily wash their hands and faces in cold water, snatch a plate of food from the pot that sits on a bench near the shack, and flop down at tables alongside the one occupied by the new recruits. There is an air about these men that is disturbing. They seem not to notice the new arrivals, focusing only on the food in front of them as though they must eat quickly and as much as possible before it is taken away from them. Their table manners are coarse and repulsive, some eating with their hands despite having access to flatware. Food particles cling to unshaven whiskers, belches are released unabashedly and a flatulent odor is prevalent. It is as though they have been dehumanized by this life of constant work without relief. A fight breaks out between two men who have returned to the pot seeking a second plate of food. The quarrel is over who should be first to dip into the sparse remainder of rice and chicken. As they push and tug at one another and raise their voices, a guard with a rifle appears. He has been out of sight until now. The men are frightened by his presence, stiffen and become docile, gathering their food quietly and returning to the table to devour their pickings.

The gang boss arrives and shouts an order to the new recruits.

"You six new men, follow me."

They leave the table and scramble to keep up with their gangly new boss. He takes them to the main shack, where a small pile of rough-hewn tools is kept. There are large two-sided picks and long, heavy hammers. He points at three of the men closest to him.

"You three, each take a hammer."

He gestures to the other three men by craning his neck and glaring.

"You three take a pick."

Then he barks his brief orders in his almost indiscernible dialect.

"We'll show you how to use these tools in the morning. Be outside and ready to work as soon as it's daylight. And take care of those tools. If you damage or lose one, you'll have to replace it."

The sight of the large and clumsy steel implements is an omen of the hard labor that will be required of them. Names of the men who preceded them are carved into the handles of the implements. Quickly, the Italians carve in their own identity, removing the previous name.

⊳⋅◇⋅⊴

The boxcar that is home to almost twenty men is confining, like a narrow dungeon that deprives them of air. There are no windows, no more than twelve inches between the cots and barely a yard of space separating the two rows of cots. A narrow door at the end of the car is opened for access and to admit fresh air. The large sliding doors on either side of the car are sealed shut. During the summer, daytime temperatures inside the car will soar above 100 degrees. No matter, since the crew will not be inside during daylight hours. In winter, the space is heated by a small stove with a tin smokestack at one end of the car. It leads the smoke outside, but it smolders and allows smoke to creep into the car, creating a sense of suffocation.

As the new recruits enter their lodging for the first time, having personalized and stacked their tools outside the door, there is a defensive air in the room. The dozen occupants have finished their meal and lie on their cots, seething at the prospect of sharing their cramped space with yet another six occupants. They are exhausted from their day's work and are edgy from the heat and staleness of the air in the room in which they must sleep. An older man of the group with a white gauze patch over one eye sits up on his cot and addresses the new occupants loudly, in Sicilian dialect.

"You men had better be quiet and respectful of those of us who have been living here. We don't want any more of you in here cramping us and smelling up the place."

Raffaele is angered and decides to respond.

"We don't want to be in this stinking hole any more than you want us here. We don't have a choice or we wouldn't be here. But, we have a right to be here and we expect to be treated fairly."

"Hah! You want to be treated fairly, do you? Wait until you start work. You'll see how fairly people are treated around here."

Raffaele presses on. "What do you mean?"

"You will be awakened before dawn tomorrow by a clanging on the doors of this car. There will be little time to rush to the latrine, wash up and eat something before you are herded to the end of the track. There, you'll work without relief except for a midday meal hardly worth eating, and then you'll immediately be back at work until nighttime. You won't be permitted to talk. You can't even bring your own water. And don't complain about anything or you'll be severely punished."

While Raffaele and the other man talk, the others drop exhaustedly onto their bunks and fall fast asleep. Finally, Raffaele lies on his cot. He places the crucifix that dangles from his neck between his teeth in a gesture of anxiety, and prays as his body yields to fatigue and he falls into a deep sleep.

The morning sun is hot on the weathered backs of the Italians as they quietly perform their mind-numbing work of extending the railroad tracks to the west. Only the clanging of tools can be heard, sound made by humans that interrupts the tranquil resonance of birds chirping their morning call and the roar of hillside streams descending on the creeks below. Picks smack the earth and meet with hard stone. Rakes pull stacks of crushed gray stone into evened paths. Lengths of hardened steel clank into place and hammers spike them into wooden ties. There is an urgent pace that responds to the wild determination to join east to west, and to the need of a driven people to fulfill their destiny.

Raffaele swings his heavy hammer at a spike, delighted that he is able in one blow to drive its head half way into the tie below. His second blow places the spike head firmly against the rail, demonstrating that he can indeed do what is required of him. Thoughts of the generous sum he will receive for his work enter his mind and he is again confident of his decision to sidestep the life he has built with Caterina while he amasses sufficient capital to return to her flush with newfound wealth. There are no further thoughts of the indignity of his journey to this place, nor of the threat to his life from the dregs of humanity left behind on the streets of New York. He can feel his strength returning after a long respite from manual work, though there will be ache-filled nights following his first days of work. He glances fleetingly at a fellow laborer who appears to be greatly experienced. A single heavy blow from his hammer falls squarely on the spike and drives it in place. He is lanky and works at a slower pace than the others, but places the highest number of spikes. Raffaele notices scars on his weather-beaten bare back, as though he had been clawed by a bear. They are wounds that have whitened with time, marks that are no longer able to receive the sun's darkening rays. Raffaele decides to ask the man about his injuries, but he must wait until the midday break before he is allowed to speak.

A whistle blasts a welcome shrill. It is at last time for the men to cease their odious work and enjoy their midday rest and meal. Raffaele turns quickly to the man he had been observing and calls out, wondering what he will hear in return.

"Friend, can I have a word with you?"

The man's eyes squint as though he has difficulty seeing in the bright midday light. His face is a mask of abhorrence and disgust.

"I am not your friend. And, no, you may not have a word with me."

Raffaele is both wounded and elated. He is distressed by the words spoken; but he is euphoric at the sound of the man's voice, clearly speaking in the Calabrian dialect. He must somehow persuade the man to speak to him. As they take their meal of boiled potatoes and kale, Raffaele sits next to him on the bare earth.

"Please, *signore*, I am from the town of Gagliano in the province of Catanzaro. I seek only friendly discussion with a fellow countryman."

The man's face seems to soften. His voice is less gruff.

"Do you know Antonio Russo?"

Raffaele is elated. He has struck the chord of commonality.

"Yes, he is betrothed to my wife's sister…and he and his woman came to America on the same boat with me. Do you know him?"

"He is my cousin's closest friend and I've heard all about him and his mischief with Baron Zinzi's daughter. Where are they now?"

"They are in Croton-on-Hudson in New York. Antonio has signed up to work on a dam they're building there. They hope to soon be married. *Signore*, may I ask you a question?"

A brief smile appears on the man's face. He has been won over with reminiscences of the old country. Raffaele continues.

"What are the marks on your back? Did you have an accident?"

The man's expression turns to fear. He does not reply for a few moments.

"I will answer your question tonight when we are not pressured to return to work and when we won't be overheard."

The second shrill of the steam whistle is not a welcome sound. It summons the men back to work for the balance of the long day.

━┅━○━┅━

Michele Barilla hails from Maida, a small village not 40 miles from Gagliano. There, his cousin Umberto's closest friend, Antonio Russo, had bedded the lovely Concetta Zinzi, a baron's daughter; and, in utter disregard for the enormous scandal he would create, abandoned his arranged marriage to an older woman to be with his true love. To Michele, this act of defiance towards the Establishment was the ultimate expression of hatred for a system that squelches opportunity for the ordinary man in favor of the rich. Having decided two years earlier that life in Calabria would never be more than daily survival, Michele ground out money enough from his meager pay for passage to the United States. Upon his arrival in New York, he was met by a certain Luigi Castiglione, a padrone with contacts that bred opportunity for the newly arrived. Michele was excited by the lure of high pay and was signed into service for the railroad. Now, two years later, he is a broken man. He walks with a slight limp and coughs dryly from a nameless, unidentified malady. He thinks about how to respond to the questions that now come from this man from Gagliano who has suddenly appeared and whom he has newly befriended.

The truth will be difficult for him to disclose. Two years earlier, Michele had discovered that, while the daily pay was an astounding two dollars, there were many expenses that he would incur that were paid back to his employer. Costs for lodging and meals were very high and were deducted from his pay with no consent or previous notice. The company vendor rode to the camp in a wagon filled with items that could be purchased. A bottle of wine was available for a half dollar, whiskey for a dollar. The cost would be deducted from their pay, making it easier for the purchaser to indulge himself. As it was the only available recreation, most of the men found themselves squandering their hard earned pay for high priced articles sold to them by their employer. At month end, pay envelopes were very thin. In Michele's case, there were months when his pay envelope was simply a statement of how much he owed the company. At the end of his first year, he found that he owed the company forty five dollars. He decided to leave and return to Italy, but was told that he had signed himself into a labor contract that could not be revoked. He would have to stay on for a minimum of another nine months. Appalled, Michele decided to leave without permission.

As nightfall arrives and the crew takes their evening meal, Michele is cornered by the ravenously curious Raffaele. He has little choice but to tell the story to his newly befriended Calabrian, of his attempt to flee the yoke of his strange and debilitating employment that had no reward and no end. He is careful not to be overheard.

"When I realized I would end up with nothing, working for the railroad, and that I would not be released, I tried to escape. I gathered my few belongings, those that I owned from the time I arrived, and slipped out into the black night. I carefully avoided awakening the other Italians, lest they insist on coming with me. I was terribly frightened that the least sound would awaken one of the guards and I would be found out. Thankfully, I managed to slip away under a moonlit sky that assisted me in finding my way eastward along the tracks. I ran as far as I could that night. As daylight arrived, I believed that I would be stalked, so I walked in the woods along the tracks, to avoid being seen. I encountered snakes and felt vermin clinging to my skin, sucking blood out of me and itching my skin. When the sun was up in the sky, I could hear dogs barking in the direction from which I had come. Then I heard the muffled sound of an engine from a truck driving along in the ditch we had dug the month before on one side of the tracks. It was obvious they were after me. I heard my name being called. It was Mario DeGennaro, our foreman, riding in a truck with four men in the open back, all with rifles and billy bats. He called out in his freakish Italian, demanding that I stop running and return to the camp. When I didn't come forward, they released a team of dogs from the back of the truck. They easily found my hiding place in the woods and charged at me with their teeth showing and growling ferociously. I was never so frightened. I wet my pants as I frantically tried to climb a tree to get away from the dogs. When they reached me, they first snapped at my ankles and then managed to grip my legs until I could no longer cling to the tree. I fell to the ground. They would have torn me apart, except that two of the men arrived and placed leashes on their collars and dragged them off. I was bleeding from dog bites on my legs. Two other men arrived and grabbed at me, pushing me to the ground on my face and tying my hands behind my back. Then, they marched me back to the truck and hoisted me onto the rear."

At this point, Michele stops talking. He draws in a breath, his brow descends, his lips purse and his eyes well. Raffaele acknowledges his friend's agony and silently places his hand on the man's shoulder. Michele takes several deep breaths and continues.

"The bed of the truck was a nightmare of commotion with dogs straining at their leashes and snarling at me from one end of the truck, Mario admonishing me from the ground below the truck bed and the men pulling at my restraints and striking me at will with their fists and bats. By now I was also bleeding from a broken nose and one eye was completely closed."

The two men walk away from the table to a shadowed corner of the clearing, where Michele's sobs could not be seen or overheard. Raffaele urges Michele to continue.

"Mario called out to me. 'When we get you back to camp, you tell the others about how we captured you and that you'll never try it again.' I told him that what he was doing wasn't legal and that I would never stop trying to escape. That was when he directed his men to beat me. They stretched my arms out and tied me to the side of the truck with my face buried. I could barely see what was happening because my neck was pressed to the side of the truck, but I caught a glimpse of a belt with steel studs reaching from the buckle to its tip. Then, they tore the back of my shirt from me, exposing my entire back, and they took turns lashing my back with that belt. The pain was terrible as the skin peeled off of me and the blood ran down and saturated my trousers. I blacked out. When I came to, I was face down on my bunk and a large cloth drenched in water had been placed on my back. It took a week before I could stand and do some menial tasks until my strength would come back and they could put me back to work."

Tears stream down Michele's face and he can no longer talk. Raffaele is quiet, acknowledging his friend's pain only by a tug on his shoulder. Now he knows the origin of the scars on Michele's back and what he himself would face should he decide to escape from this penitentiary of torture and misery. He recalls from his youth in Italy, the talk of America's slavery and how it had ended after the terrible war between the North and South. It happened at the same time that Italy won its independence from its captors and became a nation. How was it possible that, in this new century of peace and liberty, that the freedom that men had fought for and won could be so blatantly ignored? He will not accept this outcome for himself. He must escape from this terrible place.

Chapter 17

Escape

The fall night is lighted by a huge harvest moon, a bright lamp that Nature has provided to light the way amid the blinding shadows of tall trees and the hazards of running streams. There are no poets here to savor the beauty, nor those who would share the sight with their mates. This is the place where men are warily alone, and where desperation has overtaken pleasure and delight, where men long for the gentleness of the land they left and will never see again, where thoughts of mothers, lovers and little children wilt into the reality that they are in confinement with no end.

It is clear to Raffaele that the bargain he struck with the padrone in New York was a sham. There is no opportunity here to fill his pockets with the reward of honest labor. He is here against his will and will never succeed at returning to Italy to take his place among the proprietors of the land. He is utterly frustrated as he thinks of his home in *La Bella Calabria*, and of his love, Caterina, who had acquiesced and allowed that they would live apart for a year until he would return to her. It mattered not to her that they would live as peasants. It was his overwhelming need to change his status in life that has brought him to this wretched place. He would now gladly give up what has become a false hope and return to her in humility, except that he is a prisoner of depraved men with rifles and dogs, who would delight at hunting him down and pounding obedience into his core.

Raffaele has decided that he must escape. But first, he must learn from

Michele's failed attempt, of the dangers he must avoid. He levels a barrage of questions at Michelle. To his amazement, Michele appeals to Raffaele not to attempt to escape.

"Don't do it, Raf, you'll get caught and it will give them pleasure to beat you to a pulp...or worse."

"I don't care. I'm not staying. I'm going back to Italy."

Raffaele's confidence batters Michele. He looks longingly toward the gray sky, as though he can see his serene village of Maida, the merriment of the *passeggiata*, the sensual food, the invigorating wine and the engaging *signorine* dressed in their traditional patterned dresses of sea green, down to the ankle, with stark white aprons and matching bonnets. He breathes in as though he can smell the salt from the Ionian Sea that is reputed to bestow longevity. When he finally looks down and regains his senses, he surprises Raffaele with his pronouncement, a turnaround from just moments ago.

"I will help you to make your escape...but only if you take me with you."

It is not what Raffaele had expected or wanted. To have another man along, especially one so infirm, could become a serious hindrance. Michele is older than Raffaele and more likely to falter. His first attempt at freedom failed, why should he succeed now? If he fails this time, it means that Raffaele will likely fail with him. In the end, Raffaele knows he must have Michele's insights and agrees to take him along. He begins plotting their escape.

"What was it that led to your capture?" he asks.

"I ran through the woods the whole time. I should have known I couldn't outrun the dogs and the men on trucks."

"What should we do differently?"

"We need to find a hiding place in advance of our escape and stock it with a change of clothing and some extra food and water. Then, we need to hide in that spot until they stop searching for us."

"What about the dogs? Won't they sniff us out?"

"Their smell needs to be confused. The change of clothing will help and scattering pepper along the trail behind us will confuse them."

Raffaele is satisfied that he has heard enough. He has confidence in Michele and in their ability to escape. The glow in his browned face and the smile on his lips project confidence.

"We'll wait until the next full moon to make our escape. And, on Sunday, we'll find a hiding place out there to store food and a change of clothing."

⊢·+·0·+·⊣

For two weeks, Raffaele has tracked the nightly marvel of the moon rising in the sky, a barely visible mass evolving mysteriously with each new appearance, looking sometimes like a crescent on a Muslim flag and then, in time, a lighted orb with flecks that imitate the face of man. Raffaele has toiled away the days and dreamt away the nights waiting for this moment. He will be free in just a few hours, free to find his way back to Caterina, to face his fate in Calabria, to be an Italian again. The thought of being back with Caterina and holding her once more overtakes his fear of failure. Capture would mean enduring grinding torment for the balance of his youth, perhaps even for as long as it takes to die and be buried. He must think positively. He turns to Michele, who waits obediently for his nod. There is no need for words. They have rehearsed the details of their escape since the night that Michele asked to be taken along. They have since gone into the field and found their hiding place, a cradle of limbs high in a tall oak. At its roots, under a pile of brush, they have buried the supplies that will assist their escape. All that remains is to leave this living hell.

The two men quietly collect their belongings and rise from their beds. The silence in the room is broken only by the snore of one man, enough sound to cover the least creak in the splintered floor of the rail car as Raffaele and Michele make their exit. They have worked that day and feel the exhaustion from heavy toil. But, this night there is cause to ignore their limits. There is spring in their walk, joy in their anticipation. Within moments, they are in the outdoors beyond the reaches of the camp, and on their way to freedom. Both men breathe in as though they are gulping in the naked breath of liberty. They may not speak, nor cause the snap of a twig beneath their feet. In this hushed forest, the least sound travels far and could reach the ears of the dreaded guards. Michele exhibits enormous strength and endurance as he makes his way through the punishing underbrush, mile after mile. By midnight, they have reached their stash. They have heard no stir of pursuit by the guards. They pause for a momentary smile at each other as they remove the cover of leaves and bushes and find that there has been no tampering by some curious creature. They collect their belongings and climb high into the lap of the old oak. Its thick branches are like strong arms held out to them, wishing for them to be free. The ground is far below, their food and clothing tethered to a nearby limb.

For the last two miles, Raffaele has scattered red pepper that he requisitioned from the company store and now remains as an unpaid item to be charged against his earned wages. He smiles as he imagines the purser's pain when he learns of the escape. From the treetop, Raffaele scatters the pepper remaining in the small bag, so that it drifts to the ground below like tiny red snowflakes. The two change into clean clothing and propel the old clothes high into the tree with a crudely made sling, far from detection. Then, they lie back and sleep as they wait for dawn to arrive.

There is an indescribable fear that grips a fugitive as his trackers are first heard and then come into view. It is a strange combination of panic and indecision blended with resolve. Sweat appears on the brow regardless of the ambient temperature, and hands tremble. Often the objective is questioned. There is sometimes regret for having undertaken the escape. Such is not the case with Raffaele and Michele. They have rested for two hours in the earliest part of the dark morning and are more resolute than panicked. They do not question the depth of their motives. They lie very still and await the approach of the railroad guards. At first, they hear the distant howling of hounds. It is followed by the sound of engines and the creaking of trucks rocking on their chassis. Sound turns to sight as the pursuers come into view, first the dogs and then the men and trucks looking like tiny specs that increase in size with every lapsing moment. Raffaele places his hand on the back of Michele's neck in a gesture of confidence. His motion tells Michele that they need not worry, that they will not be found.

The first sign of victory is the chaos created as the dogs breathe in the pepper. They wheeze and sneeze and then whelp as they scatter aimlessly trying to expel the pepper from their nostrils and pick up a trail. The men stalk in every direction, swearing heatedly.

"Goddamn those fucking Dagoes. They managed to confuse the dogs. Well, it won't work. We'll just stay out here until we find them."

One of the guards produces camping gear from a truck and soon an encampment is evolved, complete with small canvas tents and woolen sleeping bags. The eight guards pair off and search in four different directions, looking for the least sign of a footprint. As night falls, they have found no trace of the Italians. When morning arrives, the hungry guards make their last attempt to find their prey's tracks, to no avail. They angrily scoop up their belongings and leave. The search for Raffaele and Michele is over.

The successful fugitives do not gloat. Rather, they are very still, not trusting that the guards will not make another appearance. They are still in strange terrain and have many miles to travel to get back to a civility they can partially trust. They take advantage of having brought food enough to last another day high above the ground and out of sight in the tree. They eat and rest while they reflect on their escape and contemplate freedom.

"God has intervened in our favor. May he remain with us while we make our way from this point forward." Raffaele is quick to hand over the credit for his success to the Deity, a common custom of the pious Calabrians who have won in a clash with an enemy.

Michele beams from ear to ear. "Take some credit for yourself, Raf, no one has ever succeeded in escaping from that camp. In a few days, that place will be but a memory."

The landscape of western Ohio is provident in fall. There are farms with apple and peach orchards filled with ripe fruit ready for harvest, and everywhere in the wild there is blackberry and elderberry for the taking. Raffaele and Michele will not go hungry. As they head eastward, they remain under cover of forest, but stay within sight of the path that the railroad has furrowed, occasionally stopping to enjoy the wild fruit. Once, they snare an unsuspecting rabbit in a trap which Michele fashions from thin branches taken from a pine tree. The meat is a welcome delicacy, tasting like the *coniglio* of Italy, except that it is not steeped in spicy tomato sauce and consumed with pasta and beans. Once, they are invited to help harvest a crop of apples by a farmer who spots them in one of the rare moments that they are out of the forest. They are wary about employment, having experienced the horrors of the rail gang, but harvest has a special appeal for these men of the land. For two weeks, they work on the farm and are housed and fed on the orchard. No question is asked about their limitations in speaking English, nor are their meager belongings a cause to doubt them. It is a time of economic depression, when many men are adrift in America, some seeking work and some seeking refuge from a former life. All that is important is that they toil to bare the trees of their fruit and live harmoniously with the others.

For the Italians, the harvest is reminiscent of their days in Calabria, when all hands are busily collecting Mother Nature's bounty. Raffaele calls excitedly to Michele, "Next year we will harvest citrus and olives…in Italy!" They savor the prospect of returning to their homeland. They are energized and more briskly climb the ladders to the tops of the heavily laden apple trees and energetically gather the fallen fruit into baskets. When finally the harvest is done, they are well fed and rested from the ordeal of their escape. Their pockets sport the pay that they receive for their work. The farmer is so impressed with their efforts that he asks them to stay and work on preparing his farmhouse and barn for winter. But such is not the concern of these two men. There is little joy in the work they have done. Their enthusiasm has been born of the reality that freedom has returned to them and by the prospect of returning home. Raffaele politely refuses, and the farmer makes one last attempt.

"I'll pay you well. A dollar a day for each of you including board."

It is an appealing offer, but it fails. The two men refuse to stay. Raffaele thinks to himself that this was how working in America was meant to be from the beginning. But fate placed him into the wrong hands, a world where brute force ruled and thrust its will on the vulnerable and naive. As they leave the apple farm, they wave gratefully at the ruddy-faced farmer as he smiles broadly and waves a fond farewell to his Italian helpers.

It is a warm, dry fall that produces little rain or frost to impede their journey eastward. They are now more confident of their freedom and look for a passing freight car that they can board and ride free across the land that lies between them and New York. Raffaele tells Michele of what they might expect when they arrive in New York.

"Our friend Antonio is somewhere in upstate New York, and won't be easy to find, but there are many Italians in New York City and perhaps we can find help."

Michele smiles, his stained, broken teeth showing the harsh treatment and neglect that he has endured his three years on the railroad gang. He is confident of Raffaele's direction. They will find friends in New York among other Italians and get help in finding their way back to Italy.

They hide in high brush free of thorns near a great turn in the rail track, where trains are obliged to slow to a crawl to navigate safely, an opportunity for wayfarers to climb aboard. It is late afternoon before a large train carting a heavy load of hogs slows almost to a halt, its engine grinding its huge steel wheels in reverse, causing the train to slow and creating an ear- piercing screech. Twenty-six cars back, near the end of the train, there is a partially open door in a car that has been emptied from deliveries made along the way. It is an easy task for the Italians to hoist themselves into the car unseen. Once inside, they scramble to the end of the car and plop down in the darkness on recently mucked straw. The rancid manure odor reminds Raffaele of the trip to Ohio almost a year ago, and of how they shoveled animal droppings out of the car in order to breathe easily. This car seems sturdier, and its slats do not allow daylight to stream in. Except for the doorway, it is very dark. Before they are able to settle in to their new surroundings, a rustling noise emerges from the other end of the car sounding much like game scurrying along in the pine forest they have just left. It is followed by muffled chatter that is undoubtedly human. Raffaele and Michele are not alone in the car.

A voice calls out, "What the fuck are you two doing here? Who asked you to come aboard and disturb us? Get up and get out of here before we come over there and kick your ass."

The two Italians are wary, barely comprehending what they have heard. Raffaele speaks for them, his broken speech revealing that he is not an American.

"Sir, we are two Italians on our way home. We want only to be left alone and promise that we will not disturb you again or cause you any harm."

The speed of the train has by now picked up and the swaying from side to side makes it difficult to stand and walk, but an overweight man steps forward into the light of the car's center. He is shabbily dressed in weathered gray trousers that are held up by a rope fed through the loops at the waist. He wears a long sleeve cotton shirt that is torn in several places. His shoes are limp from having recently been drenched. He is unshaven and his dirt-caked body emits a foul odor that fills the space between Raffaele and him. In his hand, he holds what appears to be a much worn policeman's billy bat that he strikes carefully against the side of his leg as though he is making a threat.

"Why should we allow you to stay here and interrupt our quiet?"

Raffaele thinks hard and fast. He must have an incentive for this burly man and his compatriots who are surely lurking in the pitch black of the rail car's end, to allow him and Michele to stay aboard and ride the rails to New York. Before he can speak, a second voice rings out, sounding like that of a southern woman slurring her words.

"For Chrissakes, Norman, what the hell are you doing? Leave those two bums alone and get back here with that bottle of Lightnin.' I'm gettin' very thirsty."

"They aren't bums, Vera, they're Dagoes and they can't be trusted. They'd as soon put a knife in your ribs as talk to you."

Raffaele senses that the man is alone except for the woman. He shouts back, "We're not Dagoes, we're Italians and we don't attack anyone who is decent towards us. Now put that bat down and change your attitude. Who are you and why are you here?"

There is silence, and then a complete change in demeanor as the man's bluff is challenged by Raffaele. The heretofore tough drops the bat and looks sheepishly at his possible assailant, hoping to wipe away the words that he has just spoken.

"We're two people who are out of work and have no families to care about us. We've chosen a hobo life rather than be pushed around by big money bosses and their henchmen. We're on our way to find a hobo camp where we can get some shelter for the coming winter."

"What's a hobo camp?" Raffaele is curious.

"It's a group of people like us who travel around and have no homes or jobs. Most of the time we live out in the open, but in winter that gets pretty difficult and we can't always get to the warmer weather down south. There's a large camp along the way in Pennsylvania, where we might be able to live indoors in a shack through the cold months."

"What if you don't find it or if they don't allow you to live there?"

"I can find it and any bum who brings a woman there is sure of getting shelter. They like having women around as long as you don't claim them."

"Does that mean you share your woman?"

"Of course. Everything the bums have is shared. Their food, their shelter and their women."

At that moment, the woman whose garbled voice was heard earlier, steps into the light from the diffused shadows of the car. She is barely able to stand, both from the motion of the train and because she is drunk. Like her companion, she is shabbily dressed. She wears threadbare men's pants and shirt and a large spherical cap that engulfs her blonde hair entirely, leaving only a slight sign of golden tress around her ears. Her ruddy face is drawn, her eyelids are barely open and her lips are a maze of thick red color, as though someone has intentionally pressed a tube of lipstick against her mouth. It is difficult to tell her age, but Raffaele guesses that she is hardly thirty years old. Her clothes appear to have been put on hastily in the last few moments. Her voice is still slurry.

"Do you guys have any money?"

"A few dollars," Raffaele warily responds.

"You can have a roll in the hay with me for four bits."

Raffaele looks at Norman, who smiles, "Go ahead; it's OK with me if that's what you're thinking."

Raffaele has not been with a woman since he left Caterina behind in Italy, and his body feels the pull of his sexuality, but his loyalty to his spouse and the smell of alcohol and filth drifting from the woman's body are reasons enough to decline her offer. He directs his response toward Norman.

"It's not what I'm thinking. I have a beautiful wife back in Italy and I won't betray her trust in me."

The woman frowns her disappointment. She smiles at Michele, "What about you? Would you like to fuck me for only a couple of quarters?"

Michele has been confined long enough to have gained complete control of his urges. He smiles back at her, "I wouldn't mind, but this isn't the place and you're too drunk."

She can barely understand Michele's highly accented speech, but she knows that neither man will take her up on her proposition. She returns dolefully to her berth and falls into a deep sleep on straw wet with the scant remains of pig droppings. Norman also returns quietly to the refuge of the darkened car and stays silently out of sight.

For two days, the train slowly makes its way eastward through the mostly rural farmlands of Ohio and the coal and steel country of Pennsylvania. The Italians generously share the food and drink they have brought along with the Americans. At times, the train slows to a crawl long enough to allow the men to disembark and appropriate produce from fields awaiting harvest. Inside the car, they are able to safely start a small fire on top of a steel plate so that they can cook ears of white corn in a stolen kettle filled with water from a stream that runs not far from the tracks. Once, it appears that Raffaele has waited too long to re-board the train before it resumes its speed. Michele is frantic, watching helplessly from inside the car while Raffaele struggles to clutch a steel ladder on the side of a distant car that will allow him to lift himself to safety within the train. He notices a trainman in the caboose and has the feeling that they have been spotted.

As nighttime falls, the train brakes suddenly and unexpectedly and comes to a stop for no obvious reason in what appears to be the train yard of a small city. Inside the car, it is so dark that the four interlopers are unable to see their hands and feet. An eerie feeling engulfs them as they sit motionless in the shadowy yard, their car seeming to be an execution chamber and they the condemned prisoners. The stillness is broken as the loud voices of several men are heard in the distance. Raffaele peers cautiously out one side of the car and sees a group of railroad policemen carrying torches and stalking across the yard in the direction of the train. Though their conversation is not discernable, they appear to be an angry mob looking for lawbreakers. Raffaele tries not to panic the others.

"We must leave immediately. There is a band of men heading this way with torches and clubs. If we leave now, we can get away from them."

Michele and Norman are ready to leave, but Vera has been awake long enough to have swigged from the bottle of moonshine that Norman has in his possession. She becomes difficult to reason with.

"I'm not going anywhere. Just close the door and they won't even know we're here."

There is not a moment to lose. Raffaele knows that Michele is with him. He looks at Norman. Fear and uncertainty are apparent in Norm's facial expression. He responds before Raffaele can ask a question.

"I can't do it, Raffaele. If I leave her behind in her condition, there's no telling what they'll do to her. I need to stay and protect her as best I can."

Raffaele is astonished. A moment ago, he held this cuckolded excuse-for-a-man in disdain for his readiness to share his woman with anyone she wishes to pander. Contempt for him turns to esteem as her champion now proclaims that he will not abandon her even in the face of extreme danger to himself. He looks into Norman's frightened face and extends his hand.

"Good luck, my friend. You are a brave man."

The Italians leap down from the train and, as quietly as possible, slide the car door shut and drop the latch over the door handle as though there is no one inside. Norman and Vera are locked inside and as invisible as they can be made. The two then race away in the long shadows of the night, making their way along the crushed stone track bed. They can hear a ruckus back at the train. They look back and see the mob sliding open the door to the empty car housing Norman and Vera. They observe in horror as the couple is herded forcefully out of the car. Norman is thrust to the ground by one of the men who maliciously clubs him in the forehead with a hardwood bat. Two men each take one of Vera's arms and lead her away as Norman's limp body is thrown into a wagon and carted away. The Italians hear words shouted in the distance by the railroad police that they can decipher.

"There were more than two hoboes. There are at least two more. Let's find them before they get away."

Raffaele and Michele recover from the frightful scene and continue their dash for freedom from the mob. The voices continue.

"There they go off in the distance. I knew there were more than two."

Raffaele spies the look of fear and abandon on Michele's face. It is not a good sign. He must act quickly.

"Come on, Michele, we need to run."

Michele begins to run, but he cannot keep up with Raffaele. As they turn to get out of the line of sight, a shot rings out. Michele falls to the ground.

"Raf, I'm hit. Run and save yourself."

But Raffaele will not leave his companion behind. He stops to examine Michele's gunshot wound and pulls him into bramble brush alongside the tracks. Michele is bleeding heavily from the chest and barely able to move or speak. He is pulling something from his pocket. He strains to talk.

"Here, Raf, take this money I've been saving. You'll need it to get you to New York. There's nothing you can do for me. Now, get going, the mob will be here any moment."

They are Michele's last words. His body becomes suddenly limp in Raffaele's arms, his eyes still and open, his lifeless lips apart, a thin stream of blood oozing from his mouth. Raffaele is shocked and bewildered. The man whom he unintentionally inspired to make a second attempt to flee the railroad work camp lies dead in his arms within a few weeks of their escape. How can this be? Where was *Dio nostra* to keep this from happening? Raffaele's head slumps down and he sobs into Michele's motionless chest. It is one more tragedy in his life since he came to America.

"I think we got one of them. But, I could swear I saw two of them."

The railroad police continue their pursuit, now within a few hundred feet of Raffaele's hiding place. He must make his move if he is to avoid capture. He places Michele's still body gently on the ground and covers it with foliage from the surrounding brush. He makes the sign of the cross and whispers, "God rest your soul." Then, he rises and runs as fast as his legs will take him away from this dreadful place.

There are limits to man's endurance and ability to persevere in the face of unmitigated odds. His body weakens and his mind begins to vacillate and to consider the benefits of submission. Sleep comes easier than before and the pace of his sprint slows and permits his adversaries to gain ground. It is a day later and Raffaele sees in the distant field through which he has just trudged, a mounted duo that has been following steadily in his wake. They have food and water in their saddle bags and can choose to sleep during the unaccommodating black of the night. Raffaele's tracks allow them to follow at their own pace until he drops from exhaustion. He wonders why they are so persistent in tracking him and begins to question his ability to escape. Perhaps if he surrenders they would allow him to sate his urgent thirst. They might even have an extra bit of food in those saddle bags. And sleep, precious sleep, surely they will allow him to rest. He feels himself drifting to sleep and begins hallucinating. He thinks he sees Caterina, her face surrounded by a glowing white light, as though she is a Madonna that has come to save him. He calls to her, "Caterina, my love, it's Raffaele. I'm so sorry for my failure. Take me back with you and I will never again yearn for riches."

Her form disappears and is replaced by a man's face, obviously a farmer with bib overalls. Raffaele reaches out to touch the image, and collapses face down to the ground. When he awakens, he has the feeling that he has been asleep for a long time. He finds himself on a couch in a farmhouse. The farmer looks down at him from a standing position. Raffaele speaks just above a whisper, the loudest voice that he can offer.

"Where am I?"

"You're on a farm. We found you near the railroad tracks on our way home from town. You were being stalked by two men on horseback. You were well hidden, so they couldn't find you. We barely saw you there in that brush. Are you on the run?"

"Yes, I am, but I am not a criminal. I was riding an empty rail car, trying to get to New York so that I can find passage back to Italy."

The woman arrives with a large glass of water. Raffaele snares it from her clutch and drinks it down in a huge gulp. Then, he sits up on the couch coughing up a drop that has found its way into his wind pipe. She brings him a glass of warm soup, which he consumes at a more moderate pace than the water. He begins to gain civility as his hunger and thirst are beginning to feel satisfied. The woman questions him, "Are you the Italian that escaped from the railroad policemen?"

"I was never in their custody. They shot my companion dead, and one of two people they captured was beaten. The other, a woman, was led away by two policemen."

"The railroad people have said that you're a criminal and have offered a reward for your arrest."

"Why am I so valuable to them? I'm just a poor farm worker that they enslaved for a time laying track for them."

"We don't see many Dagoes around here. They just don't want you on the loose."

"Are you going to turn me in and claim your reward?"

"No, we don't want the railroad's blood money. You can rest here for a few days until you're feeling better and until they've stopped looking for you. Then, we'll get you on your way back to New York."

Chapter 18

Caterina's Decision

Fall weather sweeps the Calabrian countryside, and around the village of Gagliano, the vegetation has begun its glorious transition. Grape leaves turn bright with color and light up the landscape, shifting from a homogenous green to a glory of reds, yellows and browns. An early rain douses the land, darkening the soil and producing glimmers of fresh green growth. The grass is the first sign of the broad verdant canvas that will emerge below the barren trees and vines of winter, the haunting dream of those who have left this lush land for vistas with greater promise.

Caterina runs a long-toothed comb through her dark, silky hair. She looks for the occasional gray strand to pluck. She worries that she will grow old and disappoint Raffaele when he returns from his mission to America. In the year since Raffaele's departure, she has remained slim and shapely, and her youthful, cupid-like face still bears no sign of ageing. She has not heard from him and consoles herself with the thought that communication from America is elusive for everyone. She tries not to think about him so that the time will pass quickly, but as the year ends, she finds herself indulging her memory of him more and more. Her memories are of the sensuous moments they have spent together in the short span of their marriage. She longs for his touch, the feel of his naked body against hers and his presence in the middle of the night when she awakens and needs to entwine her limbs with his. Her solitary life has been like an empty jug floating in an endless sea longing to be united with the owner who cast it away.

She has been under Vitaliano's watchful eye and at his table frequently since Raffaele left for America. He has surreptitiously arranged for her to work as a clerk so as to preclude her need to work as a field hand, and been fatherly in many ways; but he has not eased the stricture he placed on her when she married Raffaele against his wishes. He has not gifted her with part of his riches. In the private recesses of his mind, Vitaliano has a niggling doubt about the Egyptian's assurance that Raffaele is not of his blood and therefore not half-brother to Caterina; but the fact that Michela was Vitaliano's lover within less than a year of Raffaele's birth still worries him. There is pain in thinking that perhaps Caterina's inability to become pregnant after her early months of conjugal life is evidence of a blood relationship to Raffaele. He frustrates over her obstinate determination to marry Raffaele in defiance of him. All of this worry could have been avoided if she allowed Vitaliano to arrange her marriage.

Following the death of his wife, Rosaria, Vitaliano followed a chaste, widowed life for a time; then briefly consorted with a lone woman at Maria's *bordello*. Finally, he took as his bride the youthful Elisabetta Spadaro, a single woman of determinate means ten years his junior. Nowhere in his second marriage did he follow his own parameters of equal status. Elisabetta, while not a peasant woman, is by no means the equivalent or even comparable to Vitaliano's fortune. Fair skinned with ebony hair and azure eyes, her appeal to him is based solely on the fact that she was very lovely with no former marriages or children to lay claim to the Zinzi fortune. She is not educated and sophisticated as was Rosaria, but she is a dutiful wife who is proud of having become Donna Zinzi. She is willing and able to perform household tasks when that need arises and does not condescend in the relationship with the many people who work in their fields and in their home. She is viewed by all to be yet another of Vitaliano's intelligent choices. Still, she is not accepted by Caterina as being worthy of her impressive father. Her mother was every bit his equal, the foundation for many of his successes and the inspiration driving him on to the heights of his attainment. Elisabetta can never hope to match her predecessor on that score. Nor does she have to. Vitaliano no longer needs that trait in his woman. He needs her youthful sensuousness to keep him young, and her genuineness to help him preserve his image of the mustang-like young peasant who rose to fortune in his own time, unassisted by familial connection.

Vitaliano frequently touches on the subject with Caterina of her refusal to acknowledge Elisabetta as her stepmother.

"What makes you feel so cold towards her?"

Caterina returns a biting response.

"That woman has none of the qualities that my mother had. She is incapable of assisting you as Ma did. And, she doesn't have any of Ma's social graces."

Caterina's criticisms of the woman he married are stinging, but Vitaliano listens patiently, hoping that something will come about to endear Elisabetta to her stepdaughter.

⊢·•⋄·•·⊣

It has been a year and a half since Nunzio Laguzza was deeply disappointed by Vitaliano's refusal to allow him to marry his eldest daughter. Time has proven that Nunzio is incapable of driving her from his thoughts, perhaps because of her enormous physical attractiveness or possibly because she has become forbidden fruit since marrying another man. In his most reflective moments, he admits to himself that he has remained unwed in the hope that Caterina's marriage to that peasant-of-a-man will fail and that Raffaele will disappear into the bowels of America like so many of his contemporaries. Don Vitaliano would have to change his disapproving attitude toward Nunzio if he were willing to accept Caterina following a proper annulment. And, of course, he would relinquish his claim to receive as dowry, Vitaliano's most prized possession, the Star property. It does not cross Nunzio's mind that he is homely by virtue of his corporeal proportions. In reality, his attractiveness is derived from his wealth, as evidenced by the offers of marriage that are thrust at him by the gluttonous fathers of certain of the local *signorine*.

Nunzio has followed the account of Caterina's exploits in heartbreaking detail: her father's disapproval of the man she loves; the horrible scandal of surrendering her virginity out of wedlock; the strange involvement of the Egyptian, who drew blood from the veins of Vitaliano, Caterina and Raffaele to perform his bizarre experiment; and Raffaele's well-intended departure for America. Nunzio's frequent inquisitions have resulted in these findings and other conclusive reports that Raffaele has dropped out of sight in America and that Caterina has not had a single communication with him since he left. Then, there is speculation that the blood tests performed by the Egyptian were done to prove whether or not a sibling relationship exists between Raffaele and Caterina. He is emboldened with the information he has obtained and decides that it is time to sound out Caterina.

⊢•+•0•+•⊣

It is late on a balmy fall evening and Caterina is at home in the tiny dwelling that she and Raffaele shared until a year ago. She is pensive as she toils quietly to prepare her evening meal, a leftover risotto that she has taken home with her from a meal at her father's house. She complements what is already there with fresh basil and sauce made from plum tomatoes that she has grown in her garden. She and Raffaele would have enjoyed this evening fare and then joined the townspeople for the *passeggiata* in the nearby town square. Now her meals here are eaten alone and she does not join with the others as they walk briskly and banter incessantly in the shadows of ancient structures. Instead, she dreams of being with her beloved Raffaele as she cooks her meal. She imagines that he places his muscular arms around her waist from behind and draws her to him. His hands are cupped on her breasts and he kisses her on the neck, creating a sensuous stirring in her groin.

"Caterina! Are you there?"

It is an unfamiliar voice that carries across the threshold and jolts Caterina out of her momentary reverie.

"Who is it?"

"It's Nunzio Laguzza. Surely you remember me?"

Caterina is appalled. What is this man doing here? She recollects his beady eyes fixed on her in the town square and she recalls his approach to her father for permission to court her, anticipating the Star as part of her dowry.

She never thought she would see him again. Now he is at her door calling her name.

"Of course I remember you. What brings you to this part of town?"

"May I come in? I want a word with you."

"All right, but don't close the door. We don't want to start tongues wagging."

Nunzio is surprisingly pleased, despite Caterina's cool response. He has been allowed to enter her home, the opportunity he was hoping for. He tries not to appear snobbish by peering at the meager furnishings inside, but he is bolstered by the obvious lack of comfort that he knows Caterina was accustomed to before leaving her father's home. It is a simple peasant home and every object is roughly hewn. There are no divans or sofas or any soft surfaces to give comfort. No object has been purchased to indulge the occupants. To Nunzio, it is lowly and not in any way worthy of the lady who lives here. Considering Raffaele's long absence, perhaps she will be happy to leave this lonely place that is devoid of frill and place herself in his care. He boldly takes a seat a few feet away from her and accepts her offer of a glass of mild red wine. He begins his pursuit of her in a very frank manner.

"I was very disappointed when your father refused to allow me to court you. I was perhaps too aggressive in asking for a dowry that would include his favorite property, and I don't blame him for rejecting me. Afterwards, it was distressing for me to watch from afar while you became involved with a man who is perhaps not worthy of you."

Caterina quickly interrupts and responds confidently, "Raffaele is very worthy of me. He is this very moment in America working to earn money to purchase land in Gagliano."

"My dear, it is almost a year and a half since you married Raffaele. I admire your courage in leaving the life you had for this more simple life, but do you think matters will ever change?"

Caterina patiently responds.

"I found the trappings of my father's home boring compared to the life I have with Raffaele."

"Is it true that your husband has been in America for more than a year?"

"Yes, it's true, but I expect him to return home any time now."

Nunzio moves closer to her and looks into her eyes, his sullen glower reminding her of his repugnance. His voice hardens.

"How do you know? Has he written to tell you where he is and when he will be returning?"

Caterina remains composed. She breaks off eye contact with him.

"It is not easy to send messages or letters from America to Calabria. There are lots of others who have not heard from their husbands."

"Does that mean that you haven't heard from him?"

"No, I haven't, but he'll be home soon."

Nunzio becomes more aggressive. He must plant the seed of doubt in her.

"Many of the men who go to America don't ever write and some don't ever come home. They just disappear and aren't heard from again."

Caterina shows some anger with Nunzio's words.

"Are you saying that Raffaele isn't coming home?"

"I doubt that he is. He can't be found any where in America."

"How do you know that?"

"Because I took the trouble to find out." Nunzio looks smugly at Caterina. Her confidence dissolves as she purses her lips and glances away. Her response betrays her fear that Nunzio might be right.

"I don't care what you think you know; Raffaele loves me and he knows that I love him."

Nunzio cannot chance that he has not created doubt in Caterina's mind. He had hoped not to divulge all of what he has learned, but he cannot allow himself to leave this place without causing Caterina to consider the distinct possibility that she will never again see Raffaele. He decides to risk her wrath from perhaps hearing too much of what he knows.

"Raffaele may know more than you think. He may know of the outcome of the Egyptian's blood tests and be repulsed by what was learned."

Caterina's head is spinning. Surely this man can't know more than she already knows. The blood tests were done to accommodate her father's wishes and were never discussed thereafter. Was there something she should know? Her mood towards Nunzio further hardens.

"What is it? What do you know about those blood tests?"

"I dare not tell you." Nunzio heightens her curiosity.

"You came here to tell me what's on your mind. Now, tell what you know."

Her anger has finally surfaced. Nunzio's pretense of holding back what he knows has been exposed. He is now free to tell her what he desperately wants her to know. He draws in a breath and lets the words pour forth.

"Raffaele is your half brother. His mother, Michela Brutto, was your father's mistress before she was married. She gave birth to Raffaele only a few months after marrying another man."

Caterina is stunned. She stares blindly ahead of her and wells. Tears roll down her face. Now she understands her father's dictum that she not marry Raffaele. Why wasn't it he telling her this? Does Raffaele know about this? Did he know when they first made love? She is angry and unable to hold back her fury.

"How dare you come into my home and tell me a story like that about my husband?"

"It's true, Caterina, it's true," Nunzio sees that he is losing Caterina and becomes desperate, "as much as I want you for myself, I would not deceive you about something so profound as this. Come with me now. I can make you a fitting husband and take you away from all of this scandal and misery."

Caterina's face is hard. She grits her teeth and again purses her lips, this time to reveal her hostility.

"Get away from me. There was never anything between us and there never will be. Don't ever approach me again."

For the second time in his life Nunzio is repudiated in his unremitting desire to have Caterina as his wife. She is refusing his offer to make all things right for her despite the collapse of her entire world. He stares longingly at her for one long moment, knowing that he will never have her. For an instant, his eyes look askance and show the disappointment. He turns and leaves. She will never see or hear from him again.

⊱──⊱⊰──⊰

It is late and Vitaliano sits reading and smoking a rope cigar in an arm chair in his office. He is disturbed by sounds breaking the silence of the night as a visitor reaches the front door. There is quick acknowledgement by a maid and an unexpected visitor enters the house. It is Caterina, who has come to demand the truth from her father about the shocking words she has heard from Nunzio. Her face is taut and her eyes are red and swollen, revealing her devastation and rage. Vitaliano immediately perceives her troubled demeanor.

"What is it Caterina, what's wrong?"

Her fury is at once released on her father.

"Why didn't you tell me the reason you had my blood, Raffaele's blood and your own blood tested? Why did I have to learn it from someone else? Did you think you could hide it from me forever?"

Vitaliano is horrified. His most deceitful act towards any of his children has been suddenly exposed. His first thought is to ask for forgiveness. He does not. Instead, his words impose the responsibility on Caterina to judge his act in the light of facts she does not know.

"What is it that you've been told?"

"You had an affair with Raffaele's mother and, after she married, Raffaele was born in just a few months. Your concern was such that you had our blood tested to find out whether or not Raffaele is your bastard son."

Vitaliano is in his element. He must defend himself yet again against societal conventions, and he must call on his natural ability to reason and convince.

"My affair with Michela Brutto took place before I knew your mother. Because I didn't marry her, she found someone else. A child was born to them a few months later. When you announced your feelings about the man who grew from that child, I needed to find out if he was my child. Should I have simply allowed you to marry him? I think not. Should I have upset your life by telling you about that? Of what use would that have been except to create doubt in your mind about Raffaele? What should I have done differently?"

The tenseness clears away as the logic of Vitaliano's words sinks in. Caterina is no longer the tigress clawing her prey. Her father has explained the circumstances with unshakable judgment. She no longer blames him for keeping the secret. She looks tearfully up to him.

"Pa, what should I do? Raffaele has been away a year now and I have not heard from him. He seems to have vanished."

Vitaliano breaths easily. He is no longer under attack. Caterina's anger has turned into calm and she is seeking his advice. It is the best outcome he could have wished for. He struggles to give her the most sensible advice that flashes into his mind.

"You must ask yourself if this new knowledge about Raffaele changes the feelings you have for him. If it causes you to doubt him and if you believe that he has abandoned you, then you should begin annulment proceedings. But, if your feelings are as they were before you learned of the purpose of the blood tests, then you must find him and bring him home."

Caterina is pensive. She is considering Vitaliano's advice.

"Does Raffaele know about the blood tests?"

"No, I don't think so, though it is possible that he learned about them from the same person who revealed them to you."

"Pa, as soon as I get some money, I'm going to America to find him."

It is an opportune moment for Vitaliano to further ease the tension with Caterina over her marriage to Raffaele. He seizes the opportunity.

"I will finance your trip with as much money as it takes."

Caterina surprises him.

"I won't take money from you, Pa. I've managed without you all of this time and I'm not going to compromise now. I'll get the money somehow."

There is a stirring in the room. Elisabetta has been eavesdropping. She steps into the room from the corridor and addresses Caterina.

"Please forgive me for listening in on your conversation. I was coming to tell my husband that it's late and that he should come to bed."

Her face forms a mask of sympathy as she continues.

"But since I've heard what was said, I want to offer you the money for your trip to America. I have not been involved in the entanglements of your marriage to Raffaele and I want to see you reunited with him."

It is the moment that Elisabetta has hoped for, the opportunity to demonstrate a kindness to Caterina that might win her over. Vitaliano's facial expression loses its usual self-control. He smiles broadly, hoping that Caterina will accept the offer.

Caterina is overwhelmed. She would be foolish to cast away this opportunity to have her search for Raffaele financed. She could immediately set out for America without concern about money. If she were lucky, she could find Raffaele in a matter of weeks. Her view of Elisabetta is suddenly changed. Enmity and distaste dissolve into the joy of knowing that she will soon be united with Raffaele. Her response is almost a shriek.

"Thank you, Elisabetta, I will accept your offer if you will allow me to repay you when I return."

"That isn't necessary, but if that's what you want, so be it."

In an astonishingly bold gesture, Caterina approaches Elisabetta and throws her arms around her in a hug of gratitude. It is the end of the aversion that Caterina feels for Elisabetta. Vitaliano looks pridefully at two of the three women alive who mean most to him. They are finally in harmony with one another.

Joy returns to the residents of La Stella as Caterina moves back into the villa with her family while she plans her search for finding Raffaele in America. Elisabetta arranges for cablegrams to be sent ahead to New York to friends Caterina has made among field hands and share-croppers who, like Raffaele, have gone to *America* to seek their fortunes. They are made aware of Caterina's plight and given her approximate arrival date in New York. A cablegram is also sent to Concetta in Croton-On-Hudson, suggesting that she and Antonio meet Caterina at the pier in New York. In a few days, Caterina will begin her journey to Naples to board the steamer that will take her across the Atlantic.

⊷─◦─⊶

The young courier slides perilously on ice forming on the walk leading to the front door of the villa, the first discernable frost of the early winter. He holds an envelope in his hand as he announces his presence on the front door, and is greeted by a maid.

"May I speak with Caterina Brutto?"

"Who is calling?"

"I am Alfredo, servant to Nunzio Laguzza, with an important message for *La Signora*."

"Just give me the message and I'll see that she gets it."

"I can't do that. I have specific orders to speak with *La Signora* and to leave a letter only with her."

"Very well, then, have a seat and I'll see if I can find her."

Caterina arrives at the front foyer, a look of exasperation on her face. That Nunzio hasn't yet stopped irritating her with his advances. What could it possibly be now? She peers sternly at the courier.

"Yes, what is it? What does he want now?"

Alfredo looks haltingly at Caterina. His face turns pink enamel and his eyes are bulging globes. He hesitates to speak.

"Come on, what is it?"

Alfredo stammers.

"Signora, I am Don Nunzio's valet."

He seems unable to continue. Caterina is becoming restless with this man who is unable to speak.

"Yes, yes, why are you here? What do you want?"

"This morning…I…I found Don Nunzio dead on the floor of his bedroom. He killed himself with a bullet to his head."

Caterina is shocked and momentarily speechless. She feels the rush of blood to her head. Her speech is breathless.

"Why have you come to tell me this?"

"Because he left a letter for you, his final act in life. It is my duty to see that you get it."

Caterina's hand is trembling as she accepts the small envelope containing Nunzio's suicide letter. She turns and heads for the privacy of her bedroom as the front door closes on the dispirited Alfredo. Caterina shuts her bedroom door and falls into a soft chair, a look of confused despondency on her face. She stares at the envelope in her hand, wondering what possible reason Nunzio had to take his life. His religious belief would have been that this last act he performed in life would condemn him to an eternity in Hell. And why would he presume to write his last words to her? Finally, she slides a letter opener across the fold of the envelope. A one page, quill-penned letter falls out into her still trembling hand. It is difficult to fathom that this message is from a dead man whose last thoughts were of her.

My dearest Caterina:

I have thought over and over since leaving your home the other day about how I will never know the ecstasy of your embrace in this life. The agony of that truth is too much for me to bear and I cannot go on living. For that reason, I have decided to end my earthly existence and wait for you in the hereafter. I hope sincerely that you will be able to mourn my death and that you will one day anticipate our union in Heaven. Please do not blame yourself for my demise, but rather, think of me and look forward to the day that we will be together.

Your ardent companion,
Nunzio

Caterina is puzzled. Nunzio was never her companion and she gave him no encouragement at all. There is surely more to the abrupt suicide of this forlorn man than his amorous feelings for her. She has thought about it long enough and must resume making arrangements for her trip to America. She hopes that some truth will emerge about Nunzio's death other than his unrequited love for her, but that will have to wait until she returns from America with Raffaele.

Chapter 19

Raffaele in New York

It is a different New York that Raffaele sees as he alights from the Hoboken Ferry onto the city streets. As an early winter has set in, temperatures plummet to record lows and trees are suddenly adorned with frost that glistens in slanted light. Icy snow fills the sky like tiny crystals sent to cleanse the acrid air, the fresh aroma an escape from the choking smolder of the city. White fluff coats the streets and is soon stained with the black soot of chimneys and the footprints of those who venture outdoors. Collars are turned up on heavy overcoats and vapor pours out from the nostrils of draught horses. The season is suddenly different, and Raffaele wishes that he were wearing a winter overcoat and not the thin jacket given him by the farmer in Ohio. He has ridden the empty rail car to the cliffs above the Hudson River and used the spare pennies in his pockets as fare to cross the river to the city.

As he looks across the broad, cobblestone avenue along the river's edge, Raffaele's focus is drawn to a massive red brick building sporting a huge sign reading WHOLESALE MEATS. There is a group of visibly grubby men transporting sides of beef on their backs into the building and placing them on tables where others dismember the carcasses into fractions that can be sold. Raffaele can smell what lies ahead, an odor so raw and crude that he places his hand over his face to filter the sour air. He hears a constant sound like the buzzing of bees in summer, and realizes that it is the sound of a hundred hacksaws raking forward and back across bone. There is clacking of hand trucks and thumping of cleavers. Men work at tables wearing white smocks smeared with the blood of the meat they are processing, their shoes slipping in the muck of blood and meat fragments that have fallen to the floor beneath them, the fragments rotting and sending up their stench to human nostrils. For Raffaele, it is a far cry from the uncomplicated process he recalls in Calabria, where meat is rare and seldom a part of the peasant diet. In those infrequent instances, the farmer slaughters the animal himself, butchers the meat and smokes it over his hearth to preserve it. The remains are buried deep in the earth, there to make a timeless return to nature.

Raffaele is impressed with the process he now observes. Each man at the long bench has a precise task he performs on each beef side, so that the whole side placed on the table at the entry point is packaged in sections by the time it reaches the far end. As he stands there gaping, a large man with a round, red face shouts at him,

"Don't just stand there, pick up a beef side from the truck and take it to that table over there. And hurry, they're waiting for something to do."

Astonished by the fortuitous offer, but grateful for the opportunity to work, Raffaele walks quickly to the foul-smelling truck, where an empty grain sack brown with dried blood is placed on his shoulder and a huge side of beef is lowered onto him by two gargantuan truckmen. Barely able to walk with the weight he now holds on his shoulder, Raffaele walks as fast as he can to the table of butchers awaiting the arrival of the next carcass. His legs bow and his back twinges, but he continues for the balance of the day to transport meat from the truck to the table he was assigned. He has no knowledge of when the day will end or what pay he will receive, nor does he know where he will spend the night. But, he senses that luck has somehow happened his way and will bring stability to his otherwise volatile existence. He is wrong.

As daylight ends and the work tables no longer require their labor, the men huddle in the cold as they await their day's wages from the plant's supervisor. When he arrives, he hands each of them a fifty-cent piece. Raffaele is given a quarter, signifying that he has worked half as long as the others. Then, the huge doors to the meat plant close and the trucks drive off, leaving the scruffy group of six men alone in the cold and dark. They are hungry and thirsty and shiver in the icy night.

"Let's go over to Barton's," the oldest of the five men suggests. The others do not speak, but show their assent by moving in the direction of the dim, smoky saloon adjacent to the plant. It is Raffaele's first exposure to these men, all of whom are nomadic vagrants who have spent the day lifting to earn their day's keep. They are all Americans, two from New England, one from Virginia and two from upper New York State. The youngest is 24 and the oldest is 43. Their clothing is shabby and hasn't been laundered for too long a time. Their faces are dirty and unshaven. They are part of an army of tramps roaming the economically beleaguered, turn-of–the-century nation, in search of an elusive permanence, much the same as the hoboes Raffaele encountered in the Midwest. As Raffaele speaks his first words, it is obvious that he is not American.

"Where can we get food and shelter for the night?"

They are indifferent to his accented speech and easily accept him as part of the group. The older man has assumed leadership and speaks for the others.

"Barton's has some food at the bar that's free to customers who can pay for drinks. We can hole up for the night at the camp on the docks."

Barton's Bar and Grill is a large, smoke-filled room crammed with drifters whose principal activity is consuming alcohol in every form. Many of the patrons are visibly intoxicated, some sleeping soundly in sitting positions, others asleep where they staggered and fell to the grimy floor. There are brass cuspidors every few feet, one of them overflowing with urine. Every lip holds a lit cigarette and there are smoldering butts everywhere on the plank floor. A medley of punchy songs of the flapper era emerges from a lone piano being played by a bearded black man at one end of the room. Four bartenders serve the throng of customers three deep at a bar one hundred feet long. At each end, there are bowls of hard-boiled eggs and plates of roast beef cooked gray and sliced thin. There are cups of dry brown mustard and piles of sliced white bread. Half sober men stumble to the bar and clutch at the food. They pile meat onto bread, hoping to construct a sandwich. The grimy floor beneath them is littered with food that has slipped through hands and fallen, where it is mashed into the floor by passersby. A lone cockroach, mostly unnoticed, navigates the food on one end of the bar.

Raffaele and his new companions are hungry and do not perceive the filthy condition of the food they consume. They grasp the food and consume as much as they can before the bartender arrives and calls out to them.

"OK, you guys, what'll it be?"

━━◦━━

Pre-prohibition America affords the poor ample opportunity to imbibe. The cost of liquor, some of it questionable as to its origin and toxicity, is cheap enough that the six men consume more than their constitutions can absorb. They sway like a flotilla of sailboats in crosswinds as they make their way across the wide avenue to the edge of the gray river where a provisional camp exists that will afford them survival of the freezing night. There are huge blankets of oiled cloth used by day to shelter cargoes from exposure to the elements. They have been appropriated by homeless day workers and propped up at the center to create tents. A single candle in each tent heats the interior and there are blankets scattered about the dirt floor with scores of occupants, mostly men, warming their frozen bodies. Outside, there are pots of steaming gumbo that one can dip his spoon into, so long as he has contributed to the concoction. One of Raffaele's new companions produces a hunk of meat that he had hidden in his pocket and releases it into a simmering pot over an open wood fire. Then, he removes a large spoon from another pocket and dips it into the pot repeatedly and sips until he fills his stomach. When he is done, the spoon is passed to one of the others. Eventually, it comes to Raffaele. He does not hesitate to fill his stomach with the strange stew. The taste of tomato on his palette propels his mind to Gagliano where every yard grows the juicy fruit abundantly and every dinner table includes it in one dish or another. In his mind's eye, he can smell steaming tomato sauce cooking over the hearth. He envisions long strands of thin pasta crowding his plate with a thick coating of tomato sauce seeping through the open spaces. He imagines the aroma of a single leaf of basil and the feel of rich olive oil in his mouth. He looks to the dark sky above and a loud voice inside him cries out, "*Italia, Italia, dove sei?*"

"What's the matter, buddy? Don't you like our stew?" A large, ragged man confronts an otherwise preoccupied Raffaele.

"Yes, of course I like the stew. The tomato reminds me of home."

"Well, if you're gonna sleep here tonight, you'd better pick your spot.

There'll be few left before long."

Raffaele looks around the smoky, dark tent and spies an unclaimed corner. As he heads for it, a lone woman pops her head out from under a blanket and stares unashamedly and deliberately at him, beckoning him to join her in the vacant place beside her. She wears gold earrings, but she is disheveled and shabby, her white face smeared with black streaks. She is clearly a woman wanting the company of a man and her intentions are obvious. Her arm is out from under the blanket, revealing the allure of the smooth white skin of woman. It has been a year since Raffaele has felt the comfort and warmth of a naked woman, his tender wife Caterina. The lust that now surges through his body overwhelms his reasoning. Fidelity to Caterina cannot restrain his need for human contact, if only with a specious harlot. Her hair is black and matted and her large, silvery eyes are surrounded by dark circles. She is thin and lies on a red, checked flannel shirt. As he climbs below the blanket that warms her, he slowly fondles her body, touching her thighs and buttocks. Her mouth and breasts are so inviting that there is no turning back. He quickly removes his clothing and is immediately erect. His thoughts of penetrating her consume him despite her flatulence and wretched appearance. Lovemaking with Caterina was never like this. Theirs was tender and enraptured. This is rampant lust. As their lower bodies entwine, he throws his arms around her torso and their lips come together in a fiery kiss. He enters her and they copulate for only moments before they climax. They do not perceive the stares of several unnoticed voyeurs who share the tent. Privacy is a luxury none of these vagrants can afford. Here there is pleasure in the outrageous amusement that one occasionally stumbles upon.

The exhausted couple is satisfied and relaxed. They fall into a deep sleep that will last for several hours. Raffaele is awakened in the early dawn by the enormous guilt he feels for having betrayed his marital trust. He thinks of Caterina and how she came to him as an innocent woman, seeking his love and committing herself to him. He has cast aside her faith in the most trivial manner and with a most unlikely partner. The woman lies alongside him, sleeping through the night, her lust appeased by the interlude. Raffaele imagines that he is perhaps one of hundreds who has shared this woman of indigence and depravity. He is sickened by the thought that he has added to her degradation as he climbs out from under the swathe of blankets and dresses himself. He cannot avoid thinking that he has become like her. What has happened to his life? He leaves the camp and walks southward along the river. He finds a heavy jacket that has been cast away in a garbage can. He dusts it off and climbs into its warming interior. He is protected from the morning cold. The dawn is coming and he must collect himself.

⊶─◦─⊷

Luigi Castiglione arrives at the pier at South Ferry as he does most week-day mornings, bundled to fight off the winter cold, and wearing his shabby fedora sporting a tiny Italian tricolor in its band. His gloved hands are planted firmly in the pockets of his heavy jacket and a scarf is draped around his frosty ears and tied in a great knot underneath his fedora. He is here to recruit unsuspecting Italian immigrant men for work on the railroad with promises of lucrative pay, just as he enlisted Raffaele fifteen months ago. His eyes are fixed on the Ellis Island launch as it reaches its berth in South Ferry and disembarks its passengers, a fresh harvest of strong, young men mostly from southern Italy. They are here alone, having left wives and children behind to seek fortune in the New World. He will speak to them in their dialect and make them feel as though they have stumbled onto the very opportunity for which they left their homes. This is America. Everyone works for high pay and all can become wealthy if they harness their appetites for consumption of the myriad temptations that surround them. He is called *padrone di lavore*, boss, and his recruits pay keen attention to his advice. Mostly, it is to sign a labor agreement with the railroad for a year's employment at high wages. He does not elaborate on the details of the agreement that requires them to pay the company for room and board at rates that will ensure that very little will actually end up in their pockets at the finish of the year. Nor does he mention that they will be incarcerated in the wilds of the American plains during their term and that there is a likelihood that they will be enslaved for as long as it takes to finish the transcontinental railroad. He is permitted to function in this manner because of the absence of laws to protect unsuspecting immigrants and because he has bribed the law to ignore his presence at the South Ferry dock. After all, who are these opportunist interlopers who stream into

America looking for an easy way to fill their pockets with American currency so they can send it off to another country. Whatever happens to them is their own business, so long as they don't cause him any trouble.

Luigi's latest prey is a huge, bald man from Reggio, an anomaly to the short, thickset Calabrian. He is eunuch-like, tall and muscular, and in another world, would be guarding his Caliph's harem. He is entranced by Luigi's description of the work he would be expected to do and by the pay he would receive in the year ahead. From the corner of his eye, Luigi sees the figure of a man approaching him, potentially invading the privacy of the conversation he is currently conducting. His prospect is tall and very thin, with circles under his blue eyes and dark facial hair long enough to form the start of a beard. His clothes are threadbare and the jacket he wears is mud-spattered and torn. His deliberate pace is disturbing as Luigi concludes that the man is there to barge in on the conversation with his prospect. As the man reaches Luigi, he calls his name.

"Luigi, you bastard, you sent me to Purgatory for more than a year. Did you enjoy the profit you made from the sale of my soul to those terrible men?"

Luigi is frozen in his spot. His eyes are opened wide and he is fearful. He has worried that one day a victimized immigrant would seek retribution or perhaps even revenge for the torture imposed on him as a result of Luigi's recruitment. Would this be his day of reckoning?

"Who are you? What do you want from me?"

"I am Raffaele Brutto, and I want to break you in two for what you have done to me."

The recruit by now has surmised that Luigi is not what he had thought him to be. He turns and leaves. Luigi tries to mollify Raffaele.

"What have I done? Have I arranged your employment?"

"No! You turned me over to a gang of thieves who held me prisoner and from whom I had to escape at the risk of my life."

Raffaele lunges at Luigi and knocks him to the ground.

"Help!" Luigi shouts directly at a policeman standing a few yards away. The policeman rushes to his aid, pulling Raffaele off him and pushing him against the side of a nearby delivery truck. He quickly pulls Raffaele's arms behind him and places manacles on his wrists. The scuffle with Luigi is over. Luigi gets up from the ground holding his hand over a bleeding bruise on his forehead. A crowd has assembled to watch the activity.

"This man attacked me for no reason at all. I insist that he be arrested."

The policeman asks Raffaele, "What have you got to say for yourself?"

"Only that he arranged for me to be employed by a gang of criminals who enslaved me and kept me prisoner for a year."

The officer does not seem impressed.

"Come with me. You can tell your story to the judge."

As they leave, Luigi dusts himself off and resumes his position on the dock. The crowd will soon disperse and he will be back in business.

The dreary precinct house on Water Street is in the southeast corner of Manhattan. It has but one cell to contain prisoners awaiting transfer to a facility in midtown where they can be held while they await trial. The cell is a mere twenty feet long and twelve feet wide and holds twenty-two prisoners. Most of them are standing for lack of a place to sit. A few are on small wooden benches along two sides of the room. A white ceramic sink sporting a single spigot doubles as a urinal. The air smells of alcohol, vomit and stale body odor. There are inmates sound asleep on the floor, smelling of alcohol and the grime of the alley in which they were found. Some stare blankly into the space in front of them, contemplating their fate. There is a large, brutish man, looking angry, as though he were daring the others to brush against him so that he could slake his hostility on them. There is a groan from some of the prisoners as the cell door is opened and Raffaele is placed in the crowd, another body to breathe in the sparse air and crowd them further. Raffaele looks around and feels the discomfort of having been brought to this foul place and charged with assaulting Luigi. What now? His life has been a series of disappointments for the last year and a half. Can it get any worse? What must he do to succeed in this promising country that has offered him nothing but disappointment? He thinks of Caterina. He has not made contact with her since they parted in Calabria. She was to wait patiently for him to earn his stake and return to her. It was expected that it would take just a year. What will she think of him when she hears that he has been convicted of assault and sent to prison? *Oh Lord,* he thinks, *what will become of me?*

It is as though Providence has decided that this will be the moment for Raffaele to break through his cloud of frustration and regret. In a fortuitous incident, he is accidentally pushed up against another detainee in this terrible place. Like Raffaele, he is obviously Italian, his English broken, his skin the color of olives, and his movements lively and distracting. It is Pietro Stopolla, a recent immigrant from Calabria, who has run afoul of the law and has serendipitously found his way in the path of this fellow countryman with a huge streak of bad luck. Pietro left his impoverished family struggling to survive in the farmland surrounding Cosenza, not fifty miles from where Raffaele labored in the orchards of Count Leone. The Stopolla family found themselves compromised when they hastily signed an agreement with a large land owner to grow fruits and vegetables on a rocky hillside that was later found to be deficient in minerals and lacking a sufficient water supply. They would be slaves to the barren land for the contract period of fifteen years. Pietro chose the escape of many such damaged young men and immigrated to America. He was met in New York by a relative who had preceded him to the New World, and given room and board in a tenement house in the Mulberry Bend. He was also given a coveted job stevedoring imported Italian products delivered to the port of New York from ships in the nearby Hudson River. He was later asked by the owner of a local coffee house to collect bets for a lottery popular with Italians in lower Manhattan, and to deliver them to a central office in Greenwich Village. It added several dollars weekly to his already sufficient income and brought affluence into his life for the first time. He learned too late that the activity was illegal. Before long, he was apprehended while making his collection rounds and faced with a prison sentence for his misdeed. He was assured that his job on the docks would be secure and would await his return, but someone was needed to fill the void during his absence. There was also the matter of who would take his place in the boarding house.

Raffaele listens with great envy as Pietro relates his story, and breathes a sigh of understanding when the story ends with the impending prison sentence that is certain to be levied on Pietro at a trial to be held the following week. He tells Pietro of his horrid experience of facing imminent death on the West Side of Manhattan the year before, the hideous encounter with the railroad gang, and his homeless existence since his escape. The two men are interrupted by a guard who unlocks the cell door and, with a meeting of eyes and a nod of the head, summons Raffaele to come out of the cell. Raffaele is startled and apprehensive.

"What's this about?"

"Never mind, just come to the front desk and take your things. You're free to leave."

There is a sudden elation in Raffaele that he has not felt since Caterina expressed her love for him in the vacant Beccio ranch house in Calabria. It is almost too good to be true. He has known freedom of the open spaces in two countries. Now he would be free again. Life would hold promise. But what would he do? As he leaves the cell, he hears Pietro's voice calling, his hand reaching out to hand him a slip of paper.

"Raffaele! Here, take this. It's my address on Mulberry Street. Go there and talk to the landlord, Domenico Pascale. He will arrange for you to have a place to stay and perhaps even help you find a job."

As he reaches the front desk of the station house, a policeman hands him his belongings.

"You're free to go."

"Why am I being set free?"

"Your padrone, Luigi, dropped the charges against you."

⊢·✦·○·◆·⊣

The boarding house at 1306 Mulberry Street is the largest residential building that Raffaele has ever seen. It is six stories high and eighty feed wide. The bottom floor contains two storefronts, one on either side of the entrance door to the building. One is a restaurant, the other a butcher shop. There are no less than 24 apartments in the floors above with a total of 96 rooms, many of them partitioned to provide private living space for small families starting out in the New World. There are two toilets in the hallways of each floor that are shared by as many as twenty people. The odors of stale garbage placed outside the tenants' doors awaiting collection, the layers of congealing paint that have been hastily applied over the decades, and the smoke finding its way in from the gas street lamp just outside the front door are mostly overtaken by the smells of cooking seeping into the hallways from the apartments surrounding them. The unmistakable aroma of pots of steaming tomato sauce laced heavily with garlic and spices combine to overwhelm the senses. It is a heavenly combination of smells ordained to overcome the otherwise malodorous interior of the building. To Raffaele, it is a high-rise Gagliano that oozes the same aromas and sounds. He is at ease as he enters the house that is soon to become his first home in the U.S. He is immediately drawn to an elderly man with a crop of white hair and a mouthful of empty spaces bracketing a few yellowed teeth.

"Are you Domenico Pascale?"

"Yes, and who might you be?"

"My name is Raffaele Brutto and I've been given your name by Pietro Stopolla."

"Where did you see him?"

"At the precinct jail."

"Well, Pietro has gotten himself into a heap of trouble. These Americans consider the lottery a serious crime. He'll be sent to prison for a year or more."

Raffaele changes the subject.

"Can you give me board? And do you know of any work I can do to earn a living?"

"You can have Pietro's bunk and we can get you in to take his place at the docks, but only until he returns."

Raffaele is elated. He has obtained the foothold he will need to rebuild his health and gather the money he will need for his passage back to Calabria. He decides that he must be honest with Domenico and state his intentions up front.

"Once I have saved enough money to buy passage, I must find my way back to Italy. I have been away for over a year and haven't corresponded with my wife. She must be wondering where I am."

"Where are you from?"

"Gagliano."

The old man's face drops. He is obviously more than the mere householder of the boarding house.

"Is your wife Caterina Zinzi?"

Startled, Raffaele is confused by Domenico's question.

"Do you know her?"

"No, but she has written letters asking everyone here to send her information about how to contact you."

"Can we send her a telegram?"

"It's too late. She has already left Italy and will be arriving here in America very soon."

Chapter 20

Bigamy

In the year that has passed since Antonio and Concetta took residence in a near derelict shack on stilts at the Croton Dam, their lives have changed. For one, Antonio has proven his worth with hard labor on the project and has won the right to be paid the same as the cherished stone masons. Steady work and careful spending has brought a measure of affluence to the fortunate couple. The home that was lacking all but the furnishings left behind by previous tenants is now filled with trappings purchased second hand by Concetta. Then, there is the birth of the daughter that was conceived in their final days in Gagliano. It is an event that forever transforms the relationship between Antonio and Concetta from irreverent young lovers to mature, caring parents of a vulnerable new being. Such was their joy that they named her Maria in gratitude to the Blessed Virgin. As she presses the dark-haired infant to her breast, Concetta engages Antonio in discussion.

"We must not forget that we are yet unmarried. It is unfair to our child to grow up as the offspring of parents who live as man and wife without the benefit of marriage. If anyone finds out, she will be labeled a bastard before she is even old enough to understand. We must go to the priest and ask him to marry us."

Antonio is incensed by Concetta's dampening of his otherwise satisfying life.

"How can we do that? I'm already married to Anita. Just because we live together doesn't mean that I am free to marry you. I would be breaking the law."

Concetta reasons with him.

"We are thousands of miles away from Anita and that whole town of gossips. No one knows us here. The priest would marry us if we asked him to and no one would be the wiser."

Antonio considers the possibility that distance may make a difference in their ability to remain anonymous. What's more, Maria's birth has been recorded with Antonio and Concetta as her wedded parents. He decides to take the chance.

"All right, if that'll make you happy. But, you'll have to talk to the priest alone. I'm too busy earning a living to think about such things."

⊱────•◦❖◦•────⊰

In the village of Croton-on-Hudson, a Catholic church is an anomaly. Founded in the 17th century by Dutch settlers escaping religious persecution and economic adversity, Croton-on-Hudson was entirely a Protestant community for over two hundred years. Then, the dreadful potato famine caused the Catholic Irish to cross the sea in great numbers to North America. With the breaking of ground for the original Croton Dam Project, the need for laborers was huge, coinciding with the arrival of an army of Irish farmers in need of work. Before long, Croton-on-Hudson had a Catholic population large enough to warrant the building of a church. Now, fifty years later, the make-up of the population in Croton-on-Hudson changes again with the advent of the great Italian migration and the reactivation of the Croton Dam Project. Hordes of skilled artisans and unskilled laborers pour into the area from Italy, willing to work for wages that suit the project's needs. Eventually, the numbers of Italians seeking God's redemption in Croton-on-Hudson are such that it justifies the presence of a priest who is himself Italian and can understand the language and culture of Italy.

Father Umberto Romano first opened his eyes to the world in the hamlet of Citta' Sant Angelo, not far from the coastline on the Adriatic Sea, in the region of Abruzzi. As he was the only child of the town's prefect, he was afforded a middle school education as part of his father's compensation from the tiny village. Tragically, as Umberto was completing his studies, his parents were killed on a dangerous trek in the mountains above Citta' Sant Angelo, when the earth in the road beneath their feet gave way and they plunged help-lessly and finally over a cliff's edge to the bottom of a ravine. The shaken town council, in a moment of great compassion, graced the devastated boy with the opportunity to continue his education. He was enrolled in a monastic order of higher learning and, a year later, transferred to a seminary in Rome. After he was ordained, he opted to immigrate to America and was assigned to the parish of St. Ann's in Croton-on-Hudson, there to bring the word of God to hapless Italians who found themselves among Protestants who distrusted them instinctively and Irish Catholics who feared that they themselves would be replaced by new immigrants willing to work for lower wages. It is under-standable, then, that Concetta Russo would ask for Father Romano at the rectory of St. Ann's Church. She will not have to explain herself in broken English, nor will she face the lack of empathy of an Irish priest.

The young, freckle-faced housekeeper answering the door is undoubtedly Irish, her red hair tied back in a bun and white apron fixed neatly over her dark green uniform. She is annoyed that her routine has been interrupted by this foreigner holding an infant, but she does her duty.

"Come in and have a seat. I'll let Father know you're here."

Thirty minutes later, a stern-looking priest in his middle thirties, wearing a long, black cassock, enters the foyer. He speaks to Concetta in Italian.

"I am Father Romano. Come into my office."

When they are seated across the cleric's desk from one another, he surveys the mother and child with an indifferent look and coolly asks, "What brings you to St. Ann's?"

Concetta is apprehensive of what she must say to this aloof man who is barely older than she. Perhaps he already knows about her situation. In her most pensive moments, she has hoped for understanding and assistance, de-spite her irreligious life of the past few years. Judging from Father Romano's stern appearance and cool manner, she is not certain that her plea to be mar-ried in The Catholic Church will be received with openness. Her response is guarded.

"Father, I have not been a good Catholic for the past two years. I followed my heart and joined my life to a man to whom I am not married. We now have a child and want desperately to be married. Will you do that for us?"

Father Romano sits up in his chair and glares at Concetta. His response shows little compassion.

"So, now that you have a child, you want us to marry you to bring legitimacy to the child's life. Is that it?"

Concetta's response surprises him. She holds her head high and answers crisply.

"Not entirely. There is also the matter that my husband and I regret our past diversions from The Church and will confess our sins to you in the confessional. We would like to receive the sacraments here in our new country."

The priest seems to have received the response he wanted. He is less stiff as he continues.

"Why did you simply decide to become partners and not seek a proper church marriage in Italy?"

Concetta girds herself for the half-truth she must tell.

"My father is a large land-holder in Calabria with much influence in the community. He was opposed to my marriage to a man of poor means. Leaving my father's home to be with Antonio was the only way that I could prevail over my father's will."

"And do you think it was a good thing to flout your father's wishes?"

"I did not wish to hurt my father. I wanted only to be happy in my marriage to the man of my own choice."

"And, so now you wish for me to marry you in spite of your father's disapproval?"

"I want to be married regardless of the opinions of anyone. I love Antonio and want to be married to him and only him."

Father Romano is impressed by this spirited woman who has, uncharacteristically of her peers, taken matters entirely into her own hands and directed her life away from family and church. Aside from the defiance of Holy Mother Church, there is an odd quality in what she has said and done that makes him want to assist her.

"I'll see what can be done. In the meantime, you are not to sleep in the same bed with the man you call your husband until you are properly joined in

Holy Matrimony."

Concetta is thrilled. She has heard the words, "until you are joined in Holy Matrimony" and assumes that the priest expects to succeed in his quest. There is hope that she and Antonio can be married after all. Her little Maria can grow up in legitimacy. And, who will know whether she sleeps with Antonio or not? She returns home with the good news.

In the humble community of shacks that line the perimeter of the Croton Dam Project, amusement for the Italian inhabitants takes the form of the strumming of a mandolin, the singing of old provincial songs and the reminiscences of the great landscape they left behind. It is infrequent that an unknown visitor comes to this place of homes on stilts looming above lurching waters and rats that congregate below. It is a shock, then, when a well groomed woman climbs the several wooden steps up to their home and calls to Concetta.

"Conce' are you there? It's Caterina. I thought I'd never find you."

Concetta is ecstatic. It is the voice of her dear, older sister, whom she has not seen in more than a year. She places Maria in her crib and races to the door. The two women throw their arms around one another and hug for a long moment, tears in their eyes. Then, Concetta excitedly releases a flurry of talk so quickly that she is difficult to understand.

"Caterina, come in. You must be tired from your trip. When did you arrive? Are you hungry? Can you stay?"

Caterina is speechless. She looks across the room and sees the five month old Maria. She walks to the side of the crib and takes her up into her arms. Her emotions are mixed as she feels the warmth of the child's body against hers and looks into her chocolaty brown eyes. She is the next generation of the Zinzi family and Caterina is full of pride. But she is now mindful that she herself is bare and is unlikely to ever hold her own child. She is unable to take her eyes off Maria. Finally, she expresses her thoughts.

"Mamma. She looks like Mamma."

Concetta is beaming from ear to ear.

"Yes, I think so, too. She was born last fall. The midwife registered her as the daughter of Antonio and Concetta Russo. Everyone here assumes we're married."

Is there anything to say you're not?"

The two women sit and talk for an hour. Concetta tells of the trip to Naples that coincided with the assassination of the king, the boarding of a British ship and how they were fleeced by a member of the crew, the landing at Ellis Island, the experience with an official who tried to rape her in an examining room and, finally, the parting of company with Raffaele in New York.

Concetta innocently asks Caterina, "How is Raffaele? We've lost all contact with him."

Caterina snaps her reply to Concetta.

"What makes you think I know any more than you do? I haven't heard from him since he left me behind in Gagliano."

"Oh my God, Caterina, I hope nothing has happened to him."

Caterina, strangely, does not show concern about Raffaele's well being. Her face is tense and her eyes narrow.

"I am, of course, worried that some harm has come to him, but I am also prudent enough to understand that more likely he has chosen not to contact me for reasons that are unthinkable."

Concetta is silent. She understands Caterina's concern and ends the discussion. Caterina updates Concetta on the news from home, including Nunzio Laguzza's visit in which he inferred that Raffaele had deliberately dropped out of sight in America. She also tells of Laguzza's suicide and the preposterous note left behind claiming that he killed himself because of Caterina's refusal to take up with him. She then tells of the Egyptian, and how he was engaged by their father to determine that Raffaele is not somehow a sibling to Caterina. At this, Concetta draws in a hard breath. Until now, she was unaware of her father's liaison with Raffaele's mother and what that implies.

Caterina looks sternly at Concetta, "Conce' I'm going to find Raffaele and determine the truth as to why he hasn't contacted me in a whole year. I also want to find out what he knows about his lineage."

In the three days that Caterina has crowded Antonio and Concetta in their tiny house, she has met everyone in the community and slyly inquired about Raffaele and his whereabouts without raising suspicion about her fears. Finally, she meets an elderly man who has recently moved to the Croton Dam Project from New York. Antonio Fundaro has made many trips between Sicily and New York. He has had more than his share of successes in finding lucrative employment in America, and has been able to save a good portion of his earnings; but he has not been able to face the relocation of his wife and children to America as a final act of permanence in the new country. As a consequence, he has made several expensive trips to visit his family in Catania, refusing to take them back with him to America. Thus, he has relatively little to show for the efforts of his last twenty three years of life. Now, at age 60, he labors with men half his age in the construction of the great dam and dreams of his next voyage home. He is intrigued by Caterina's plight to find Raffaele. She is different from the other women he has seen either in Italy or America. Her suave, confident stride and her ability to converse in the many dialects of Italian are unlike any of the others. When she inquires about the husband she is trying to find, he is eager to assist her.

"I was living on Mulberry Street until just a few weeks ago. There was a young Calabrian there who meets your description. He was living in a boarding house run by Domenico Pascale, my friend of many years. I'll give you the address if you want to go down there and find out if it's your husband."

Caterina is cautiously optimistic, but she feels the anticipation of perhaps having located Raffaele. Somehow, she thinks, Antonio's lead will bring her to Raffaele's door. She must get to New York immediately.

━━◦━━

It is a month since Father Romano declared his intention to pursue Concetta's wish to marry Antonio and return to the church. It has been a long and tortuous time for Concetta, who dreams nightmares that include the groundless notion of her child being taken away by the authorities for want of legitimacy. There is not a day when she does not peer in the direction of the village, looking for the messenger that will bring her news from her priest. Even Antonio has been seized by the anticipation, hoping and praying that his beloved Concetta will have peace of mind by formally joining their lives in marriage. His apprehension towards committing a bigamous act has not completely left him, but he is now confident that the distance between him and Anita is sufficient to submerge the duplicity.

As the winter sun rises in the sky and lights the ice below, the lone figure of a heavily clothed man is silhouetted against the white of snow and ice as he walks slowly toward the Russo house. He calls in a loud voice from the ground below.

"Concetta Russo, are you there?"

Concetta rushes to the door and immediately recognizes the sexton of St. Ann's church. She is breathless with anticipation.

"Yes, I'm here."

"Father Romano has asked that you come to the church rectory to meet with him at two O'clock tomorrow afternoon."

"I'll be there."

Concetta is beside herself with joy. At last, she and Antonio will be married. Father Romano must have finally received the pastor's blessing to proceed with the marriage. She must borrow the wedding dress owned by a young friend recently married at the Dam site, and fit it to her body. And, Antonio will have to find a respectable suit to wear for the occasion.

Antonio finds a jubilant wife when he returns home at the end of the day. She has lit every candle in the house to provide the greatest amount of light for the moment when she tells Antonio of their impending marriage. He is overwhelmed by her joy.

"Conce' what exactly did the sexton say?"

"He said that Father Romano wants to see me tomorrow."

"What makes you think that the news is good?"

Concetta is livid. She shouts her response.

"What's wrong with you? Don't you see that Father Romano wants to marry us and bring us back into the church?"

⊱•◦❀◦•⊰

There is a certain quality to the rectory of St. Ann's that speaks of authority and attachment to the supernatural in a way that differs from the other Christian churches of Croton-on-Hudson. There is an ambience of faith and of religious opulence. Its entrance corridor sports a huge crucifix, a three foot long oaken cross with a luminous casting of the dead Christ in solid brass. Below it is a marble font with holy water for those wishing to bless themselves upon entering. Except for an occasional certificate of merit, the walls are mostly bare, but there are polished marble slabs four feet high that beam their dark reflection throughout the passageway. There is the faint aroma of incense as one enters, and a shattering silence implying that there are no people living here. Concetta is relieved that she has left Maria behind with a friend, so that there is no chance that her cries will disturb this tranquil space.

The young woman who had previously answered the door for Concetta now greets her again and gives a curt command, "Come with me." She is led to a small chapel sometimes used for the hearing of face to face confessions. It is a small room, dimly lit except for a small gothic altar which is bathed in light by gaslights on either side. There are two chairs with a side table alongside one of them. A confessional stole lies diagonally across the seat of one chair, obviously reserved for the priest. Concetta is barely seated when Father Romano enters the room. He proceeds directly to the chair containing the stole, places it on the table adjacent to his chair, takes his seat, and acknowledges Concetta's presence in his usual cool manner.

"I am pleased that you're here. There is news that I must share with you."

Concetta gushes as she utters her first words since entering the rectory.

"Father Romano, I'm so happy. When can Antonio and I be married?"

The priest does not appear to share the enthusiasm shown by Concetta. His face is austere, his eyes downcast, his arms folded and his hand held pensively to his face. Something has gone wrong. He speaks in an understanding tone for the first time since Concetta has met him.

"Are you the daughter of Vitaliano Zinzi of Gagliano?"

Concetta is restrained. Father Romano has obviously probed into her past and determined facts that she wished not to reveal to him. She thinks, *Oh, God, where will this lead? Are our chances at marriage now over?*

"Yes, I am. I believe I told you that last time we met."

It is as though Father Romano has not heard her response.

"And is Antonio Russo also from Gagliano?"

"Yes, Father, he is. Why do you ask?"

"My dear, are you aware that your Antonio is currently married to a woman in Gagliano?"

So that was it. He has discovered the truth about Antonio, but does not appear to know that Concetta was involved in the scandalous separation of Antonio and Anita from the start. Concetta decides to be completely truthful and responds in a blunt tone.

"Yes, I knew it. Why do you think we had to leave Italy? Because of the laws there that did not permit Antonio to undo the marriage that his parents arranged for him, we had to live in sin. We were scorned and shunned. Antonio was unable to find work that would pay him enough to support us. But our love for one another has been strong and we have not allowed the ridicule to dampen our union. Now we are here in America and Antonio is appreciated for his work. We live among people who assume we are married. We want only to be married in the church and to raise our daughter as a respectable Catholic."

Father Romano holds up his hand. He has heard enough. His tone of detachment returns as he addresses Concetta.

"How do you expect me to marry you to man who is already married in the eyes of the church? Surely, as a Catholic woman you know that what you have done breaks the sixth commandment. You are living an adulterous life with another woman's husband!"

Concetta is shattered. She had come to this place with great hopes and now confronts the worst of her fears. She and Antonio have been found out. She collects herself and stands up. There is a reckless quality about her as she admonishes her priest.

"So that's your answer. I might have known that there is no room here for understanding and compassion. To hell with your precious church and its foolish dogma. I'll find a way for us to be married and a church that will understand the problems that people sometimes face."

She turns and stomps out of the rectory, creating a disturbing commotion and leaving behind a shocked and shaken Father Romano.

꘡◦꘡

The city hall of Croton-on-Hudson is a Federal style mansion, appropriated by the Colonial government as restitution from a wealthy Tory family that supported the King in America's War of Independence. Its swags, garlands and elliptical windows make it the most impressive structure in the town, and bespeak of its authority. One such authority is the right to grant marriage licenses to those rightfully entitled according to the laws of the land. Once obtained, the license would entitle the holders to a municipal ceremony joining them as man and wife.

It is a Monday, and Antonio has taken the day off from work and traveled to town with Concetta and Maria. They stand at a window of the office of the town recorder as Concetta conducts her business across the counter from the clerk.

"We are here to seek a civil marriage."

"Did you bring your birth certificates?"

Concetta hands the documents across the counter to the clerk.

"I'm sorry, Madam, but these certificates show that you are aliens. Do you have naturalization papers?"

Concetta is confused. She had not expected this.

"We are not yet citizens, but we are planning to apply for citizenship when we are qualified."

"You'll have to come back when you have proof of citizenship."

Concetta feels tears welling in her eyes, but she will not give up.

"That could be years from now. What about my little girl? Does she have to be in this situation for all of the time it takes for us to become citizens?"

The clerk looks over at Maria.

"How old is she?"

"Five months."

"Do you have her birth certificate?"

Concetta excitedly produces a birth certificate from her purse. The clerk studies it and notices that the child was born at the Croton Dam area by a midwife. Antonio and Concetta are her parents of record and the birth was registered in the very office in which they now stand.

"Well, this makes a difference. Your baby is an American citizen by birth and, as her parents, you are entitled to residence here. So, we'll overlook the fact that you're foreigners and grant you a marriage license."

Jubilantly, Concetta asks, "Is the judge able to marry us today?"

"Wait over there in the wedding room. He'll be out in a moment to perform the marriage. Do you have witnesses with you?"

Concetta's quest is almost over. She beams at Antonio and he stares lovingly back at her. They will at last be formally joined as husband and wife. No matter that he is still wed to the elderly Anita, that their marriage will not be sanctified by Holy Mother Church, nor that their witnesses are people whom they've never met. The certificate will show that they have committed their lives to one another. Most importantly, Maria's parents will indeed be married.

Chapter 21

Reunion

The blustery winter paints the landscape white with new snow that falls through the night. A fresh white cover appears in the morning that shows no sign of melt or stain. The pine trees are dressed once again, their boughs filled with masses of white, their cones protruding upward through the snow. There is a sense of profound quiet and the scent of sparkling air that steals one's breath. The morning sun places its glow on the landscape and promises to ease the sharp chill. It is an exhilarating new experience for Caterina as she turns up the collar on her woolen coat and makes her way from the Croton Dam to The City in an icy cold car of the New York Central Railroad. As the heavy vapor forms outside her mouth, her mind flashes back to Gagliano. For sure, it has its wintry cold, but its icy frost vanishes each day as the sun rises in the sky. She experiences a flash of longing for the sunny warmth of southern Italy.

As the countryside whizzes by the speeding train, its wintry beauty is diminished by the frequency of man's invasion of the landscape. At first, wide swaths of land reach across the horizon, but soon the exurb is left behind and the great city makes its imposing appearance. There are a few large homes, each occupying ground of several acres, the rolling hills and heaps of snow framing them; but shortly the size of home and lot are greatly reduced until the buildings stand side by side, filling their tiny allotment of land, the snow muddied by man's commotion and pushed aside to make way for his bustle.

There is a sudden jolt from the train and it comes to complete halt, the un-expected movement shaking the passengers and scattering their belongings. The locomotive has struck a cow that has somehow wandered onto the track and found itself inexplicably and fatally in the path of the behemoth. What would have been a three hour journey takes the most of the day. In the dusky evening, the train is free to resume its trip. It is not long before the speed of the train slows to a crawl as it approaches its terminus at Grand Central Station. It is a confusing if not overwhelming sight for Caterina. A corridor of smoke extends north from the station along a rail yard that is a mile long. To the west, there are rows of factories and a single brewery. To the east, there are brick tenements, warehouses, a slaughter house, remnants of squatter shacks and even a herd of goats.

The train descends into the dark, wide mouth of the railroad terminal. From three stories deep in the bowels of the earth, a horde of passengers alights onto a swarm of steps leading upward to a great hall, dimly lit and bustling with travelers rushing to reach their trains. The vaulted ceilings of the huge chamber are frescoed, adding majesty to its vast size. Long, thick chains descend from the high ceiling that end in lighted fixtures above ticket booths and retail stands. The main floor stretches out for two acres, its floors and walls lavishly veneered with marble.

There is paradox in the appearance of the occupants of this enchanting place. A few of the men and women are more formally dressed than Caterina has ever seen. The women wear colorful wool dresses that sweep down from their necks to their ankles. Matching shawls surround their shoulders, adding warmth and encasing the frill of plackets on their blouses. Their hair is worn upturned and held in place by combs and pins poked generously through their ornate hats. The men wear dark, heavy overcoats over vested woolen suits and white shirts with lively bow ties that seem to hold their stiff collars in place. Bowler hats provide the final touch to this stern look of wanton affluence. They are followed by red-capped porters transporting their luggage to trains or to carriages that wait outside.

But, by far the preponderance of persons bustling through the terminal reflects the hardship of the times. They are mostly men who wend their way home after a long day of work in the city. Their dress is scruffy, corduroy pants that are inches above their shoes, jackets that barely reach their waists and large tweed caps pulled tightly around their heads. Their clothes are barely adequate for protection from the cold, and often threadbare and crumpled. The faces of these men reveal the insecurity they feel, their anxious eyes encircled by dark rings of doubt and uncertainty about their livelihood. It is a time of economic depression coupled with social indifference. It has led to a society of stark contrasts between those few who are comfortably prosperous and the masses that live from day to day.

It is an awakening for Caterina. Like so many immigrants who presume this pinnacle of opportunity to be devoid of hardship and poverty, she is awed by the sight of the demoralized poor. She first supposes that she has stumbled onto the extraordinary but, as she walks the street to her lodging in mid Manhattan, she observes large numbers of beggars and street harlots. It reprises the brief time she spent in Naples on her way to America. There, beggars and tarts were everywhere and it did not seem to matter. Here, it is difficult to face the reality that New York is not the pristine colossus that she imagined. She thinks of Raffaele and his mission to earn a large sum of money and return to Italy within a year. How was it possible in this sea of distress and anxiety? Perhaps his apparent disregard for communicating with her was caused by his sense of failure. Perhaps he has fallen on hard times. Whatever dissonant suspicions she may have had of him now turn to concern and apprehension. What has become of her man? She must get herself to the Mulberry District and find him.

⊶○⊷

It is a bright and mildly cold day that a concerned Caterina chooses to leave her hotel in midtown and walk the four miles to the intersection of Canal and Mulberry streets in lower Manhattan. Along the way, the spectacle of the poor and unemployed persists, but there are also the sights and sounds of a busy society that is surviving the hard times. Caterina marvels as she passes bustling shops displaying their wares: clothing, books, foodstuffs, furniture and more. Stables are crowded with draught horses being shod and fed, their owners trading merchandise in nearby markets. There are garment factories employing large numbers of sturdy women and street peddlers selling pots, pans and fresh farm produce from open wagons. Caterina perceives this as the real America, not the land of storied wealth waiting to be claimed, not even the spurious realm of impermanent boom created by the building of the Croton Dam. The City now seems less fearsome to her than her first disillusioning look from the floor of Grand Central Station. Surely in a place this large, there is room for a crafty person to prosper. She mulls the thought until she reaches the Mulberry district and her mind is suddenly filled with the perception of having gone back in time to the land she left.

The Mulberry of 1901 is unlike the gang quarter it had been for most of the previous century. Gone are the Daybreak Boys, the Swamp Angels, the Patsy Conroys and other such rival gangs, quarry to intense pressure by church groups and focused law enforcement. In their wake came the Italians, seeking refuge from the pitiless country they left and hoping to join this new society. They are driven instead to huddle in what has become their place, the Mulberry District. Further lawlessness here is dealt with by a dubious, monolingual and uncaring police force that has lost its drive to keep Mulberry free of crime and violence, now that it has become an enclave for Italians. It is a far cry from the notion of the *easy road to prosperity* that is proffered to the Italians who come to America seeking fortune. It is a callous-looking place, redeemed only by familiar faces and the opportunity to function in the language and customs of the old country. Caterina is both amused and puzzled. Everywhere there are signs of an unchanging culture that she thought was left behind. Only the street signs are written in English. All else is in dialect Italian. There are the stores: the Salumeria with its unique delicatessen of Italian cheeses, salami, olives, and exotic dark coffees; the Pasticceria offering the canoli, almond candies and other pastries and confections so familiar to Caterina; and the Macelleria with their fresh meats hanging from gleaming hooks waiting to be reduced to family size proportions. Caterina had expected that these foods would be available, but here in Mulberry it is preponderantly the food of the immigrant Italian. Only the sense that these foods are being purchased and consumed by ordinary Italians, not merely the rich, impresses Caterina as a vast departure from the old country.

The buildings in which the people live and work are rather different from Italy. There are hundreds of them, side to side, and their construction of brick and height of four stories is dissimilar to the separated one story masonry buildings of Calabria. The brick buildings show signs of decay. They are stained dark by fumes from gas lamps and street fires, despite being barely a century old. The Calabrian building of only a hundred years is considered new and is likely to be in near perfect condition; though its rooms are small and its interior walls are of smooth masonry.

The bearing of the man who walks the streets of the Mulberry seems oddly different from the humble Italian peasant. Still respectful and willing, he is somehow elevated in his manner. There is optimism in his gait and confidence that did not seem to exist in Italy, where the system was stacked against him. The usual scorn that is felt for the newcomer is not evident in this sheltered place, where everyone is a recent immigrant. The women seem to have abandoned the obligation to wear plain, black clothing. They wear colorful print dresses and their manner is less inhibited. The young women walk hand in hand with young men, decrying the need for chaperones. Their chatter is peculiar as they speak in different dialects to people who have come from various regions of Italy speaking their distinct form of Italian.

Caterina is taken with the revealing experience of the culture of this tiny corner of America. She spots the house in which the man who is likely to be her Raffaele is living and walks into the vestibule seeking Domenico Pascale, the building's owner.

⊢·✦◦·◦✦·◦·⊣

"Are you Signor Pascale?" The plump, middle-aged man who answers the door looks into Caterina's bright and hopeful face and responds in a dialect that identifies him as a *paisano* from Calabria.

"Yes, Signora, and who might you be?"

"I am Caterina Brutto, wife of Raffaele Brutto, who I am told lives here. I've come to be reunited with him. Is he here?"

Domenico can see the expectant anxiety on Caterina's face. It is an almost painful wait for his response. Domenico is guarded.

"There is a man with that name rooming here, but who can say if this is the man you are looking for? He is tall and blue-eyed and is from Gagliano..."

"That's him! That's my husband!" Caterina's eyes fill and her contorted smile expresses joy as a tear rolls down her cheek. Domenico can see that the woman is weak with emotion stemming from the long absence of her husband. He is filled with pity.

"Come in, Signora. Sit down and rest. I'll ask my wife to bring some coffee."

For the next hour, Caterina talks about her journey to America to find the man she must be with. She takes the sympathetic Domenico into her confidence, revealing her background as the daughter of Baron Zinzi and disclosing Raffaele's desire to earn a stake in America large enough to purchase land in Calabria. Domenico perceives the eager anticipation building in Caterina that she will soon come face to face with Raffaele. At first, he has qualms about having unwittingly placed himself in the midst of marital discord, but those fears are dismissed as the facts of the separation are made clear. Finally, Caterina can no longer stand the strain of waiting to see Raffaele. She is abrupt with Domenico.

"Signor, where is my husband? When can I see him?"

His response is agonizing for Caterina.

"Unfortunately, it will not be for several days. This morning, a gang of stevedores was called to sail out to a ship that has been wrecked five miles off the coast. It will take them a week to salvage the cargo in the hold of the ship. Raffaele is out there with the others."

Caterina feels defeated. Another week of waiting to see Raffaele is more than she can bear. What will she do in the meantime? How does she even know that someone will inform her when he returns? She turns to an uneasy Domenico and asks for help and understanding.

"It has been well over a year since I last saw or heard from my husband. I have come across the ocean to find him and determine why he has not contacted me and to assess his state of well being. Now I learn that I may not see him for yet another week. Have you ever been separated from your wife, Signore? Do you know what it means to lie alone in bed wondering what has happened to the person you love? Has the thought of losing your mate ever crossed your mind? These things have tortured me from the moment that Raffaele left to come to this unfamiliar place, requiring me to stay behind so that I would not slow his progress. Now I am told I must wait. I am tired of waiting. I want to see my husband. I don't care if he's at sea. I must see him now."

Domenico takes pity as Caterina stiffens her back and wells, her hands clenched together and her pained expression showing signs that her enormous patience has run out. A thought flashes in his mind. He cautiously suggests a course of action.

"Signora, my wife and I will be going uptown for the next two weeks to stay in a rooming house that we are considering buying. It would help us to have someone we can rely on to be here to deal with the daily emergencies that are always coming up. If my wife agrees, would you consider staying here and representing us?"

Caterina is flattered.

"You don't even know me. How do you know I can be trusted? How do you know I am competent? I can barely speak English."

"My dear, any daughter of an Italian baron who has the courage to pursue her man across the ocean easily has the ability to handle a rooming house. As for your integrity, let's just say that I can tell that you are honest from your face and by what you have said to me today."

It takes Domenico only moments to discuss the matter with his wife. She returns with him from the kitchen to view this lady who has so impressed her husband with her nobility and integrity in such a brief encounter.

"We agree that you should stay here and represent us while we're uptown. You can use our apartment as your own, and deal with the problems that come up. If you need us in an emergency, here is the address of the house that we'll be staying at."

Domenico hands her a small piece of paper bearing the address *302 E.11th Street*. She wonders how far that is from the Mulberry and what emergency she might encounter that would require her to contact Domenico. That evening, she checks out of her hotel in midtown and moves her belongings into Domenico's apartment in the rooming house.

It has been a long week for Caterina. A surprising number of incidents require her intervention. There is a marital dispute resulting in shouting and disturbance, an attempted burglary of the apartments by a gypsy band, a gas lamp whose flame would not remain lit, a faucet that would not turn off and a drunk who believes he lives in the rooming house and cannot be convinced to leave. Caterina is amazed at her agility in coping with urgency by arbitrating, involving police, enlisting tenants' assistance and sometimes making repairs herself. For the roomers who require meals, she supervises Domenico's provisional cook to see that meals are adequately prepared. At night, she sleeps as soundly as if it were her own home. Were it not for the misery she feels over having to wait for Raffaele's return from the salvage mission, operating the rooming house would be almost pleasurable.

When she is not otherwise engaged, Caterina walks to the sitting room facing the street just above the street level. There are scores of people walking by, pushcarts teeming with merchandise being propelled by their weary owners, and shopkeepers busily sweeping and washing their sidewalks. Gloomily, she prays and invokes God's intervention in ending the separation from her beloved. Once, she sees a tall, slim passerby walking along the street outside, dressed as she would expect Raffaele to be dressed. She ecstatically sprints to the front door, only to have her hope dashed away by a look-alike. She is pursued romantically by roomers and others who believe that she might be single and looking for a man to marry. It is a repulsive thought for her, and she wishes in those moments that she were less attractive. Then, she thinks of Raffaele's return to her and thanks Providence for her good looks.

On the last day of the week, the boarders must state their intention to remain in the rooming house for another week by delivering their rent, two dollars, for the next week's board. When they do not arrive at the landlord's door by evening, it is assumed that they have either found a better accommodation or that they have moved up to living in a private apartment. Their bed is quickly rented to a newcomer who may have been sleeping on the street or in a cellar while waiting for space to become available in a rooming house. Caterina is impressed with the boarders' promptness. It was different in Calabria, where payment for goods and services often lagged, and where shopkeepers and landlords sometimes were required to pursue payment. Here, the population growth of young immigrant men needing lodging creates a keen and biting competition for accommodations in the boarding houses of the Mulberry. By evening, all of the rents have been collected save those of the three men who were part of the stevedoring gang out on the ocean. It is assumed that they will be returning and will pay for the absent days. Raffaele being one of the three, Caterina wonders when she will hear his knock on the door to Domenico's apartment and how he will react when she opens the door. Will he take her into his arms? Will he kiss her deeply and hold her body against his as he did so many times in Calabria? Raffaele's return from the sea is a romantic thought that keeps her from descending into the depths of despair.

At 10 O'clock in the evening, Caterina decides to shut the lights and go to bed. As she reaches for the first gaslight control, there is a knock on the door. She brings her arm down quickly from the lamp and holds it across her chest. Is it Raffaele at the door? Is her hair combed? Did her dress wrinkle from the long day? What will she say when she sees him? A second knock brings her to the door. She flings it open to the sight of Angelo Catena, a familiar face from Gagliano, and one of the men on the special assignment to salvage the damaged ship off the coast. He recognizes Caterina at once and announces his surprise.

"Caterina, what are you doing here?"

"I've come to America to be reunited with Raffaele. I'm running the rooming house for Domenico while he's away. Where is Raffaele?"

"Here. Here is my board and here is Raffaele's as well. He asked me to pay it for him."

"Why, for heaven's sake! Where is he?"

"I'm sorry to tell you this, Caterina, but he's on his way to Croton Dam. His intention is to make contact with you in Italy through your sister, now that he has work that provides him a good living."

Caterina slumps into a chair and holds her head. Her mind is a mass of confusion. How can this be? The misery she has felt until now is magnified. The irony is too much to bear. She decides that she will do nothing further to find Raffaele. He will have to find her.

Sunday Mass in the Mulberry is conducted at the Church of the Transfiguration at the north end of Mott St. Built of castaway stone at the turn of the 18th century, it began its existence as a protestant church with congregants from Germany, England and Scandinavia. It became Catholic as the flood of Irish immigrants arrived in the Mulberry and supplanted the Protestants. Later, as the Italians ensued, the church began offering sermons in Italian.

For Caterina, attending Mass at the Church of the Transfiguration means refuge from the disappointments she endures. Its vaulted ceilings, frescoed walls and sculpted Stations of the Cross speak to her of a higher order than that of mere man. There are images of adoring angels everywhere, their cherubic arms and faces lifted to the heavens, vowing their fidelity to Him and awaiting His commands. How can one think of the materiality of the world when in the presence of such supernatural images? Caterina is at peace in this holy and captivating place, her pain of despondency at rest. She prays her silent prayers after receiving the Host at the altar rail, and pleads for Raffaele to be given the grace to find her soon.

She is totally absorbed as she leaves the church on a sun-filled but cold midday to walk the three blocks to her rooming house. Her strides are leisurely, as though there is no urgency in her life. Yet, she wears her Sunday finest, an azure bodice and gray wool skirt reaching to her ankles, enclosed in a thick, warm cape and capped with a wide-brimmed, plumed hat. It is as though her elegance and splendor are wasted for want of Raffaele's eyes to take notice and adore. She is but two hundred steps away when she peers down the street to examine the condition of the front walk of the house. Her thoughts are scattered. Does she need to sweep? Is there an itinerant lying across the steps? Has someone left a message for her on the doorstep?

There is a man sitting on the steps, his waist length jacket turned up at the collar, breathing vapor into the cold air and holding the ends of his lapels together, as if to add protection from the cold. He looks her way and stands. He is six feet tall and slim. Could it be? No, she will not be tricked again by desire and anticipation. Her heart cannot stand another false hope, another flutter for no cause. Besides, he is too thin and seems too bent over. Yet, as she draws closer, it seems more and more like him...her Raffaele. The tall man stands frozen in her path, and when she is close enough, she sees the unmistakable crook of his neck and the cerulean eyes that so often pierced her heart.

It is Raffaele indeed, home from the sea, home from the ravages of the past year, home at last to tell and explain and to place his arms around her vacant being. The world around her fades into nothingness as she races towards him, arms reaching out and feeling faint.

She screams, "Raffaele!" and is immediately engulfed in his arms. They stand there for a long moment, reprising the feeling of their bodies pressed together, their faces touching and their breaths hot against one another's necks. The steeple bell at The Church of the Configuration rings out, announcing the last Mass of the day, but to Caterina it is her God applauding the triumph. She is in Raffaele's arms at last. Slowly, their bodies part and they have the first opportunity to look deeply into one another's eyes and silently express the love that they have held within themselves this past year and a half. The silence is finally broken by Raffaele.

"Is it true that you are staying in Domenico's apartment and running the boarding house for him?"

"Yes, but they will be home in a few days and I will have to decide where I'll...where *we'll* live."

It is all that Raffaele needs to hear. He reaches down and sweeps the petite Caterina up into his arms, cradling her across his chest with both arms. He carries her up the steps of the boarding house and through the vestibule to the first apartment door on the left. He has been there many times before to pay his rent and chatter with Domenico, but now he enters with thankfulness that there is no one there besides him and Caterina. They are united at last and are completely alone in this opportune place. As the door slams shut, they both unleash their passions and embrace in a profound kiss, tearing at one another's clothes and breathing thickly. They are almost completely unclothed when they fall into bed, their limbs entwining under the heavy winter bedclothes, their hands clutching the flesh that has inadvertently eluded them these past months. Within moments, Raffaele has entered her and begins to copulate heatedly, the act that he has craved and thought of so often for more than a year. He hears Caterina call his name tenderly and repeats her name over and over. Finally, they are both fatigued and fall into an exhausted sleep, still holding one another in a bodily embrace. It is the early afternoon before they awaken. It is time for them to talk. Caterina is unable to hold back her questions.

"What happened to you? You didn't write to me or contact me at all. Didn't you realize that I'd be worried about you?"

"Yes, of course I knew that, but I was held prisoner in a work camp in western Ohio and wasn't allowed to write or send messages."

She ogles him with understanding and compassion. She understands better his thinness and pallor. Her tone is caring.

"Is that why you look so thin? Didn't they feed you?"

"Yes, we were fed, but we also worked hard and long. And, to get away from them, I had to escape and come back across half the country without any money, always fearing that I'd be captured and sent back to the railroad gang."

For the next hour they talk and brief one another on the events of the past year and a half. Raffaele tells about his failure to achieve his undertaking to save money enough to buy land in Calabria. He tells of how he journeyed the day before to Croton Dam to see Concetta and get her help in contacting her, only to learn of her presence in his very rooming house in the Mulberry. He tells of how he raced back to the train station and caught a train back to New York at the last moment. Caterina tells him about the suicide of Nunzio Laguzza and the note he left behind blaming her rejection for his death. Raffaele is amused.

"Ah, that Ndranghetta; they're worse than the Mafia. When they're finished with you, they make up stories about how you killed yourself for some foolish reason. That's so no one will think to blame them."

"Was he associated with them?"

"Yes. His father kept watch on the Carabiniere in Catanzaro for them and saved their asses more than once. He had to leave and settle in Gagliano so he wouldn't be suspected of being one of them. When Nunzio came of age, they took him in as full member, so long as he could maintain his allegiance to them and furnish them with information. He must have done something to irritate them, and of course their solution to every problem is to murder someone."

Caterina is surprised at Raffaele's certainty of Nunzio's fate. There is no room for doubt in his mind. He is certain of his belief and there is no reason for her to create doubt in his mind.

For the next two days, the couple lives in Domenico's apartment, appearing to others as though their moments of intensity have receded, but spending every private moment in one another's arms. Caterina operates the rooming house and Raffaele departs to his stevedoring work during the day. But, both are vibrant as they have not been since their parting a year and a half ago. At nighttime, they are content to light their gas lamps and feed their wood fire, holding one another and listening to familiar love songs played on a mandolin by a distant boarder. Their lovemaking is like the fervent mating of newlyweds, as though they are naked together for the first time, exploring one another and reveling in their discovery.

Chapter 22

The Lower East Side

The dawning sun awakens man and creature in the gray hodgepodge of immigrant neighborhoods on the Lower East Side of Manhattan. There is an eerie sense of quiet in the stillness of the cold winter morning, a hiatus before the commotion of the day begins. Rows of weathered brick structures create a barrier to sunlight as the winter sun lifts above the horizon, casting long shadows across the narrow streets and sheathing the buildings just beyond. The structures are frayed tenements of assorted shades of brick, housing recent arrivals from Europe: Poles, Irish, Jews, Germans, Italians and others, all seeking the mysterious and legendary gold-lined existence of the New World.

In the early morning, Domenico and Assunta Pascale look wearily onto the barren, icy street from their window. For two weeks, they have operated the boarding house on 11th Street, an Italian enclave among the predominance of Irish gradually giving way to a new order. The couple's intent has been to purchase the rooming house from Giuseppe Savonaro, a disillusioned landlord who would use the funds from the sale of his building to take his young family back to Sicily. For the past ten years, Giuseppe has labored at hacking ice from the frozen Hudson River during the winter months and tending the gardens of the nearby Tompkins Square Park during the other months of the year. Though the pay has been small, he has been able to support his family and save enough to purchase a dilapidated boarding house. It is tended during the day by his wife, Angelina, who cleans the halls and front steps, cooks for boarders, washes clothes and handles a steady stream of crises, all the while rearing their six young children. At the end of his work day and on Sundays, Giuseppe tends to the repairs and renovation of the rooming house, collecting his rents and paying his bills.

It would seem that Giuseppe's token success in the New World would create a sense of belonging and permanency, but the unfailing memories of his seaside village of Avola on the Mediterranean Sea, and the easy lifestyle there, are all too alluring to permit contentment with the frenetic pace of life in America. The skies above Avola are intensely blue, the temperatures warming and the air totally free of smoke and dust. Living in Avola is communal, a camaraderie among the peasants that transforms the scant life into an almost festive existence. In Avola, Angelina's life would be devoted to raising her children, and Giuseppe's new wealth could afford him a fleet of three fishing boats with nets to angle the anchovies that fill the sea around the village. If only the Pascales would purchase the rooming house and free them to leave, Giuseppe's dream could be realized.

The experience that Domenico and Assunta face has been grim compared to their rooming house in the Mulberry. Here on 11th Street, scores of sewer rats have found their way into the culverts connecting the drainpipes of the rooming house to the city's sewer system. They roam freely through the cellar, depositing their feces and claiming domain over the lower reaches of the house. There are so many of them that efforts to rid the house of them have been futile. As an alternative, the cellar is sealed off from the rest of the house and ceded to the rodents. A second decided problem is the steady stream of vagrants that occupy the front steps of the house, occasionally entering the vestibule to seek refuge from street gangs. At the very least these sad specimens of humanity are intoxicated beyond the limits of their consciousness, and at worst they have been broken by a callous rabble and lose their will to live. Often enough, the lifeless body of one of them is found on the front steps and taken by the police to a potter's field.

If rats and vagrants were not enough, the plight of some of their boarders unnerves the Pascales. In Mulberry, there seems always to be honest work for the willing and strong. Here, there are numerous incidents of immigrants being bilked by dishonest employers. Guglielmo Contrario worked for weeks in a meatpacking plant on Sixth Avenue with the promise of top wages, using the meager funds he brought with him from Italy to pay for his keep in the meantime. Eventually, he learned that the company had no funds to pay him. He was unable to continue paying for his board and gave up his bed, sleeping on the wintry street and often begging for handouts of food. Angelo Polito, a stone mason from Calabria, returned home to the boarding house with bruises on his face from an altercation with a gang of locals, fashioning themselves as vigilantes and unlawfully barring immigrants from working at a brick factory on the Bowery. Angelo eventually found other employment, but returned to Italy when he was again beaten by the same mob and could no longer stand the torment that seemed to follow him. The blatant and unrestricted lawlessness toward immigrants was the final straw. It so affected the Pascales that they decided to return to the Mulberry, satisfied to restrict themselves to the sole enterprise of their one comparatively docile rooming house.

It is Wednesday morning when Domenico Pascale and his wife return to their home, agonizing over the condition they will find it in. As he glimpses the house from the far end of the street, a broad smile crosses his face. It is what he had hoped for: the stoop is swept clean and there are no neighborhood vagrants lying on the steps. As he enters the house, the vestibule looks and smells clean. The house is quiet, with no disturbances to quell. He knocks at his apartment door, then unlocks it and swings it open. His judgment of Caterina is further validated. The apartment is clean and orderly. Raffaele has left for work and Caterina has straightened up. She is sewing in a back room when he calls out.

"Caterina! We're back. It looks as though you've done a good job. The house looks clean and everything seems to be in order."

Caterina is not entirely pleased to hear Domenico's booming compliment. For her own reasons, she is curious about how their real estate purchase has progressed; but she must now face moving out to allow Domenico to return to the apartment. But where? She has been so pre-occupied with Raffaele and the boarding house that she hasn't thought about where they will live when the Pascales return. She excitedly recounts her reunion with Raffaele to Domenico.

"Can you imagine, I was on my way home from Sunday Mass and there he was, sitting on the front steps waiting for me. After all these months of waiting, I'm glad he first saw me dressed in my Sunday clothing."

Domenico grasps at a moment of self-praise.

"It seems that my thought to have you stay here and manage the building was a good idea."

Caterina brushes aside Domenico's comment and changes the subject with a blunt question.

"Did you purchase the house on 11th Street?"

Domenico is impressed with Caterina's interest, but his cheerful manner suddenly dims as he responds.

"I wish I could tell you that it was a good experience. It was not. For two weeks, we managed the building for the owners. There were constant repairs, squabbles between tenants, rats occupying the basement and tenants out of work and needing to borrow money to pay for their board. Giuseppe is away at his regular job and Angelina is busy with six children. I thought matters would improve in the time we were there, but they didn't. We've decided not to purchase the building."

Caterina's mind is racing. Her eyes light up.

"Have they sold it to anyone else?"

"No. They were very disappointed with our decision, but we can't handle that place. They're very anxious to return to Italy, so I don't know what they'll do."

Domenico is taken aback by her next question.

"Do you mind if I go there to see it?"

His somber voice masks the hilarity he feels inside toward the prospect of Caterina becoming involved in that unruly house. His response bares his feelings towards the interest in enterprise by Italian women.

"Caterina, your husband wants nothing more than to return to Italy. Now that you've found each other, why would you consider looking at a rooming house to run or buy?"

Caterina is intense. Her mind is a flurry of confusion followed by crisp reasoning.

"Buying it is out of the question for me, but perhaps I could manage it.

Raffaele and I need a place to live, and we still haven't earned the money we'll need to buy land when we get back to Italy."

In her last remark, she amazes herself. It is as though she has become sated with the same desire that Raffaele expressed in Italy as he left for America full of hope and determination. Until now, she has been able to accept a scant life in the bilges of Gagliano, so long as she lived it with Raffaele. But her short experience in *America* has fed her ambition. Why settle for crumbs when the cake is there for the taking? She suddenly wants more and can clearly see the path to affluence. Now, she too is in America and she has decided to do what must be done to derive the wealth they must have.

<hr />

It is late afternoon by the time Caterina reaches the unkempt boarding house at 302 E.11th Street. It is just as the Pascales described. She must push her way through vagrants to reach the front door. As she enters the littered vestibule, fetid with the smell of stale vomit, she hears the raucous shouts of a man and woman hotly disagreeing and flashing kitchen knives at one another. Giuseppe stands in the hallway, quarrelling with a boarder over his unpaid rent and inadvertently breathing in gas from a lamp that has flamed out and left the narrow hall beside the staircase in unsafe darkness. He gestures politely with an uplifted hand to Caterina, asking that she wait until he is able to talk with her. It is an opportune moment of reflection for Caterina. Though she has not seen the basement and experienced sight of the horde of rats, she is impressed by the obvious similarity of the problems she faced in her two weeks in the Mulberry. Perhaps the problem with this house is the Savonaros. Were it not for their six children, Angelina would be better able to cope with the challenges that arise during the day, leaving Giuseppe to deal with the structural problems of the building. It would take time to redirect the vagrants, and to find a solution for the rat problem, but Caterina senses that she and Raffaele could succeed at operating the boarding house. She shivers with excitement at the prospect.

Eventually, Giuseppe settles the issues that confront him with amazing facility. He collects his rent money, separates the combative couple and reignites the errant gas lamp. He turns his attention to Caterina at last.

"What can I do for you, signora?"

The worldliness of her early youth emerges in Caterina. She has contrived a circumstance that will secure the desired result from Giuseppe.

"I am interested in taking over the operation of this house and have a sponsor who will purchase it from you, but only if I say so. Is it true that you wish to sell it?"

"Yes, yes signora. I want only to return to my home land."

"Then, I will make it possible for you to sell your property at once, but you must pay me a commission of fifteen percent of the purchase price and you may never speak of it to anyone."

Giuseppe thinks hard and long. Is it worth the price he must pay to get out from under the burden of this house? Perhaps he can add the commission to the price he had been asking.

"Signora, what price did you have in mind for the house?"

"The price has already been negotiated with my sponsor."

"And who might that be?"

"His name is Domenico Pascale."

By evening, the excited Caterina has convinced Raffaele of the merit of her grand design to remain in America and earn the riches that he intended to acquire on his own. She will persuade the doleful Domenico to finance the purchase of the 11th Street rooming house by offering him a lower price than he had negotiated and guaranteeing that the insufferable conditions existing at present would become a scant memory under her management. She would entice his interest by ceding her commission to him in return for a stake in the property; and she would correct the horrific problems of 302 E.11th Street by enlisting the support of neighbors and others whom Giuseppe shunned because they could not converse with him in Italian.

An adoring Raffaele is enraptured by his enterprising young wife. It is a side of her that he knows exists but has rarely seen. He had almost forgotten how her coffee-brown eyes narrow and her cherubic lips purse when she wears her serious face. It is those times when she seems not to know him as her lover, but rather as a combination of mentor and confidant. It is difficult for him to deliberate with her, so great is his admiring love, but the merit of her proposal breaks through the fog of desire and he acquiesces to redirect his life back to the quest for fortune in America.

It is nighttime before Caterina can corner Domenico. As she approaches him, he seems irritable. It is late and he is fatigued from the last two weeks of attempting to operate the 11th street house. He has arranged for Caterina and Raffaele to occupy a dreary, windowless one-room apartment in the building that has conveniently become vacant between tenants. His mood is evident in his tone.

"Caterina, it's late and I want to go to bed. Can this wait until morning?"

She baits his attention with a provoking comment.

"Well, of course it can wait. There isn't anyone else interested in that house, is there?"

"Wh…what do you mean? What's happening with that house?"

Her ruse works. Though Domenico has proffered that he is no longer interested in the property, the mention of it brings his nodding mind to life and awakens his interest. It is Caterina's opening to convince him to invest in the property.

"You are being hasty in refusing the purchase of the 11th Street house, Domenico. I believe the problems can be worked out and make the property more valuable."

Domenico's eyes roll. What must he do to end this conversation so that he can go to bed?

"I don't want to invest in a property with such problems. Giuseppe has his hands full with that place and I don't want any part of it."

Caterina's eyes gleam. She is about to play her trump card.

"What if I told you that I could get a lower price for it?"

Domenico shows interest.

"How much lower?"

"By fifteen percent. If I succeed, you would give me a ten percent share in the property. If I fail, you owe me nothing."

Domenico raises his hand to cover his mustachioed lip in a contemplative stance. How can this little woman deal with the mammoth problems facing the Savonaros? Does she even know what a rat looks like? And what of the drunken hooligans on the front stoop? How will she ever get rid of them? Moments pass. Finally, he responds simply, "No."

Caterina is crushed. Her hopes have gone awry. What can she say now that will get Domenico to change his decision?

From a corner of an adjacent room, Assunta listens in on Caterina's appeal to Domenico, and is far more fascinated than Domenico with the prospects that Caterina has laid out. It would be for Caterina to deal with the problems that beset the 11th Street house, and with a fifteen percent price reduction, they could easily resell the property should Caterina fail to unravel the difficulties. She politely enters the discussion.

"Domenico, perhaps we are being too hasty."

Tired and angered by the dissidence he perceives, Domenico is curt.

"My dear, perhaps you should get back to your household duties and leave this matter to me."

Incensed by her husband's condescendence, Assunta hardens her stand and is less polite.

"I'm sorry, Domenico, but you are giving up an opportunity because you don't see what Caterina is trying to tell you. I say we give her a chance to prove herself. I would like to purchase the property."

Domenico is inwardly enraged, but does not want the disagreement to persist. After all, he and Assunta did originally consider the investment a good one, and Caterina will somehow eliminate the problems they encountered or end up working for nothing but the pittance she will receive for managing the property.

"Very well, Assunta, but this investment had better work out."

Once again, Caterina finds herself aided by a woman when all other prospects appear bleak. Her mind flashes momentarily to Elisabetta, her father's wife, whose improbable largess has enabled Caterina to come to America in search of Raffaele.

The crowded apartment once crammed by the Savonaro family with their six young children is far too spacious for Caterina and Raffaele. Now that the

Savonaros have the proceeds of the sale of their house and are joyously wending their way back to Sicily, the young couple quickly rents the apartment to a large family for a handsome rent. The apartment they will now occupy is much less appealing. Dark and gloomy with angled light only from a narrow airshaft rising through the center of the building, the two-room apartment does not give them a view of the busy street outside, nor does it allow them to breathe the fresh outside air. Only an occasional gust entering the front hall from outside trickles through their open apartment door and replaces the stale air that drops down the airshaft. Still, they are ecstatic about their prospects for the future and a present in which they are back together under the same roof, sharing their meals and their bed.

Raffaele pursues his livelihood as a longshoreman, and is surprised that he is no longer required to show up at the morning *shape-up* to determine whether he will work or not each day. His job becomes less insecure with Pietro Stopolla's return from prison. It is now based on the fact that he is proven to be strong and willing. His duties soon include supervision of a small gang of Italian longshoremen who are assigned the more difficult tasks of retrieving cargo from the narrow holds of foreign ships. Occasionally, they foray into the harbor on a small boat, mounting a ship that is anchored for lack of docking space, and carting its goods back to the wharf. He is paid well and works steadily, but it is for Caterina to plan ahead for amassing the fortune they must have for their eventual return to Calabria. She operates the rooming house with a creative flair that Giuseppe Savonaro and Domenico Pascale could not have understood. There are bright-colored potted flowers growing from boxes fastened below the front windows of the house and brought in at night to prevent their exposure to the severe weather. The interior of the malodorous building quickly takes on a citrusy aroma from quince that she has found growing obscurely in the neglected back yard and placed into the halls in small baskets. She engages the glances of neighbors who have been reluctant to associate with her by virtue of her predecessor's reputation for wishing to be distant. They are surprised by the amount of English Caterina is able to speak after so short a time in America.

Eileen McGinty and her husband have been superintendents of two apartment houses adjacent to 302 E.11th Street for the last nine years, having moved to the Lower East Side from Boston. It was to seize opportunity when Eileen's brother Dennis, an enterprising New York City policeman, unearthed the opportunity for them to operate the apartment houses for the absentee owner. By now, there is little that Eileen doesn't know about the operation of a building. She has noticed with keen interest, the change in the dilapidated house that Caterina now operates and has been eager to meet her. Caterina's warm glance encourages Eileen to speak the first words.

"What's yer name, dearie?"

"I am Caterina Brutto. My husband and I operate this house."

"Yes, and it's a sight better since you got here. What are those flowers you're growin'?"

"They're geraniums. They are grown in Italy on my father's ranch."

"Ranch? I thought you Italians was all poor."

"We are very poor, but my father is not. He's a land owner in Italy."

"Then why in hell did you come to this country? Weren't you happy there?"

"No, I wasn't happy to be under my father's authority all of the time, doing as he directed and following the stubborn traditions of the old country."

"You seem to be doing well here with this property. It was a mess until you got here."

"I wish that I could agree, but the truth is that it's still a mess."

"What do you mean?"

"We've got rats in the basement and drunks crowding our front entrance. And, there's a gang of hoodlums threatening some of our roomers who work in the brick factory."

"Would you like some help with those problems?"

Caterina draws in a deep breath. She is guardedly elated. Improving the ambience of the house was the easy part. Now she needs to face thornier obstacles if the house is going to be worth anything and if she is to earn her share of ownership. She looks hopefully at Eileen.

"Oh, yes, madam, I need help."

"Well, you can start by calling me Eileen. What did you say your name is?"

"I'm Caterina and my husband is Raffaele."

"What kind of names are them? What does Caterina mean?"

"I think it's Catherine in English."

"Oh, yes…Catherine…we'll call you Katie. That's the translation from Irish. From now on, you're Katie."

The women laugh and continue to explore one another's backgrounds. There is a connection in their voices, a shared status that transcends the bother of overcoming language and cultural impediments. They are women thrown together at a time and place that offers them the opportunity to cultivate friendships outside of their immediate ethos. With assistance from this more established woman, Caterina feels more confident in her ability to perform on her promise to Domenico; and Eileen derives an inner satisfaction by providing assistance to a woman of lesser means, who but for time and descent, is reminiscent of her own life in America.

The very next day, Caterina is surprised to see a ruddy-faced policeman, one she has not seen before, walk up to the grubby vagrants milling in front of her building to inform them in very decisive language that they are breaking the law and are not welcome there.

"OK, get yer asses outta this place," he bellows. As they proceed to leave and look back despondently over their shoulders, he adds, "and don't come back or you'll have me to deal with."

Ridding the house of the constant intrusion of this loathsome horde is a triumph of some consequence for Caterina, but it is a severe blow to the brow-beaten tramps, who have become accustomed to the unprotected stoop as a haven in which to congregate. Even when weather precluded their inhabiting the stoop, they were able to find refuge inside the tiny vestibule and smelly halls of the old building. Now they must find a new refuge where they are not likely to be dispossessed.

Caterina's joy spills over as she visits her benefactor to express her thanks. She throws her arms around Eileen and hugs her as she would have in her native Gagliano to express her appreciation.

"Thank you, Eileen, and don't try to pretend that you didn't get that big Irish cop to come to my rescue."

Eileen flushes with the enormous sense of gratitude being expressed far more demonstratively than in her own culture.

"He's my brother Dennis, and it didn't take much effort at all. I doubt those bums will be back. I've also asked Denny if he would give the word to those ruffians who think they're saving America, to leave your boarders alone. They won't risk Denny's ire, so don't be surprised if that nasty business is over."

Caterina is overwhelmed. Eileen has ostensibly solved two of her three most debilitating problems within a day, without mentioning a word of what she was doing. Now Caterina can focus on the conundrum with rats, one of huge numbers of large, dangerous brown rodents living their nocturnal existence within her basement; and breeding and feeding there, despite the revulsion of the humans who wish desperately for their exodus.

The great migration of the Northern Europeans to America in the eighteenth century, and the trade it generated with Europe, brought with it the repugnant brown Norwegian rat that historically infested the European waterfronts. The rodents instinctively climbed aboard European transports and hid on board, where they were unknowingly fed and housed until they could reach the next shore. They found that New York City was the ideal milieu of wharfs, rivers and garbage left behind by careless humans, and they propagated as never before. By the early twentieth century, New York City had unwittingly become home to millions of the nocturnal creatures.

As they lay in bed, Caterina and Raffaele can hear faint sounds of the fearsome rodents one floor below them in the abandoned basement. They have come alive for the night as they churn endlessly and wrangle among themselves for the last scrap of food seized from garbage left unprotected. Their claws make distinct scratching sounds as they move about, like a branch blowing against a glass window in a storm. Their voices are simultaneously shrill and faint and their movements cause a muffled thumping. An unmistakable sickening odor seeps through the floorboards, of fresh feces deposited on a bed of decomposing carcasses and excrement that has been collecting since the Savonaros sealed off the basement. Considering the danger of a confrontation, Caterina and Raffaele would perhaps be more tolerant of the situation except that it is now the last major hurdle they must face before they can claim victory and ask Domenico for their share of the ownership. They decide to get to the root of the problem by confronting the rats. They rise from bed and dress. Raffaele takes a poker from their belly stove for protection and they both proceed to the door leading to the basement. Raffaele brings his longshoreman's hook to pry open the sealed door.

It is very dark as the pair warily reaches the boarded entrance door to the basement. They are petrified as they contemplate baring access to an abyss of swarming rats. The muffled sounds heard in their bedroom are now magnified by the proximity of the rats to the door, frightening them all the more. They light a gas lamp in the hallway that had earlier been extinguished for the night. Still, the stairway down to the basement is certain to be pitch black and covered with rodents champing to invade the upper floors of the house. The possibility of finding a solution keeps them from withdrawing and surrendering for the night. Raffaele swings his long, steel hook firmly into a board that rivets the door steadfastly to the frame. There is an eerie quiet. The sounds they had heard inside the cellar stop suddenly with the thud from Raffaele's hook. The rats are instinctively aware that someone is at the barrier that has restricted one end of their domain. It is a door that they long hoped would open.

In the next instant, Raffaele pulls on his hook and the nails in the board give way. He then places his hook in the other end of the board and pulls back with all of the weight of his body, forcing the board to the floor at their feet. All that remains is to turn the door knob and open the door. Raffaele looks at Caterina. She is white with fear, but her face shows resolve. Raffaele takes the timeworn doorknob in his hand and turns it. He swings the door open. In an instant, a swarm of large, furry rats flocks into the building, racing around his and Caterina's feet, like pounding surf flooding their ankles. The sight of hundreds of wide-eyed rats on the wooden staircase, all screeching and grappling to climb the stairway on one another's backs is terrifying. They are near enough now for a fleeting glimpse of their large translucent eyes, coffee-brown orbs looking chillingly human and projecting hostility and malice. Caterina and Raffaele have opened the most frightening of Pandora's boxes, and the result is pandemonium.

Without a moment of thought, Raffaele swings the door shut, snaring a number of the creatures in the doorway, causing them to squeal loudly and show their long, pointed teeth in anger. Caterina is behind Raffaele savagely clubbing the escaping rodents at the door and around their feet as they attempt to flee into the upper floors of the house. The floor beneath their feet soon becomes slick with the blood and entrails of the repulsive creatures. It is evident that opening the door was a mistake. Now all they can hope for is to seal off the opening again and prevent the rats that have escaped from remaining in the house. Caterina races to the front door and opens it, giving scores of the frightened rats an escape to the street. Then, she holds the board in place over the closed door as Raffaele nails it shut with the spikes that he had yanked out only moments earlier. The sounds now emanating from behind the basement door are louder than ever. Certain that they have secured the opening, Caterina and Raffaele have only to clean up the horrific mess that they have unwittingly caused. The boarders and neighbors will have to cope with the rodents that have escaped Caterina's fury and fled into the building and onto their street.

⊷⊶◦⊷⊶

Popeye O'Reilly got his name from a war injury received during the Spanish-American War. As brigades of American cavalrymen rode down the rolling slopes of the Cuban terrain into battle with Spanish lancers, many of them fell to the skillful enemy. The lancers were instructed to thrust their weapons directly into the faces of the oncoming American attackers, inflicting terror and frightening wounds. Such was the case with Sean O'Reilly, who received a near-fatal blow to the left side of his face, closing his eye for good and scarring him for life with an alarming appearance. As his remaining eye looked out on the world, it seemed to protrude from his face in an effort to compensate for its absent twin. He was soon dubbed Popeye and the name stuck to the point that his given name was forgotten. After seventeen months of healing in a military hospital, Popeye was released from the army and returned home to the Lower East Side, a war hero whose Quasimodo-like face frightened on-lookers and reminded them of his great sacrifice for his country. He was given an enviable post on the Hudson River docks, that of inventorying cargo as it was placed on the dock. The longshoremen, whose daily earnings depended upon showing up at the *shape-up* ahead of dawn and being selected for the day's work, waited patiently for the start of their work day until Popeye arrived, pencil and pad in hand.

Despite the cachet of his job, Popeye soon became bored, hoping to liven up his life with a diversion from his dull routine. Digression from a boring job was unlikely to come from those of the opposite sex, since his face was so maimed that it frightened off women and caused them to piteously avoid him. He was acquainted with the colossal problems caused by New York rats by an enigmatic friend whose strange occupation involved dealing with the swarms of filthy vermin and unwelcome creatures for much of the Lower East Side. Popeye was fascinated by the prospect of ridding his own house of the armies of roaches and rats that tenaciously avoided all efforts to exterminate them. In particular, he took note of the use of Strychnine, a lethal poison that was becoming known as a dangerous but effective weapon against the creatures of the night. He began experimentation inside his own apartment and found that his new hobby stirred an odd passion within him. He took an eerie delight at removing the dead carcasses of the huge rats who would no longer roam his apartment at night, leaping onto his kitchen table and making off with the least crumb left uneaten. As his work cleansed his apartment of the pests that had endangered his health, he offered to do likewise for all eleven of the grateful families living in his building. His complete success at dealing with the elusive rats so delighted the others that he soon was being summoned by a growing network of victims tired of being plagued by rats inside their own homes. Soon, the very sight of rats conjured up the catchy name and the horrendous image of Popeye O'Reilly.

As morning arrives on East 11ᵗʰ St and Eileen McGinty clears her head of the night's sleep, she is reminded of the ruckus created by the inadvertent release of the cellar rats by Caterina and Raffaele the night before. She is incensed by the sight of an emboldened rat sitting on the sill outside her open bedroom window, sniffing at the terrain and seeming to want entry. She quickly picks up a broom and rushes to shut the window. The rodent squeals from fright and leaps into the street. Eileen's temper flares as she throws on a heavy robe over her nightshirt and pulls back her long dark hair. She carefully opens the front door to be sure there are no more rats lurking in her path and races next door to Caterina's house.

"Katie! Katie! What the hell was goin' on here last night?"

A drawn and woeful Caterina comes to her front door. There are deep lines under her eyes from a sleepless night. She is obviously concerned about the harm she has caused.

"Oh, Eileen, what will I ever do? We stupidly opened the door to the cellar and found ourselves overwhelmed by the rats. I'm so sorry."

"Well, there's no time for pity. We need to take action right away."

"What can we do? We don't have enough money to hire an exterminator for the house and even that wouldn't help with the rats that escaped to the street."

"We need to contact Popeye. He lives just two blocks away. Tomorrow is Sunday and he'll have time to come over and see what can be done."

Caterina is humbled. She has spent the most bewildering night of her life in confusion over how to deal with the damage that she and Raffaele have done. Though unintended, the result was to cause a harm great enough to turn the entire neighborhood against her. Now her new-found friend will come to her assistance yet again. The next day, she is shocked by the unexpected appearance of the man whose terrifying face and uncanny skill with Strychnine is legendary. His strong, deep voice belies the visual impression that precedes him.

"Are you Katie?"

"Yes, I am."

"Tell me what happened."

Caterina proceeds to explain how the presence of huge numbers of rats so confused and confounded her predecessor that he sealed off the basement and ceded it to the rats. She feels the need to admit the existence of the incentive she has to correct the problem, and how she and Raffaele foolishly attempted to confront the problem by opening the entrance door to the cellar.

Popeye's reaction is both welcome and reassuring.

"No one should give in to the rat population. They need to be eradicated.

You just didn't go about it in the right way. I want you to get me as many scraps of hard cheese as you can find. Hurry, we want to do our work before the daylight is gone."

It is noon by the time Caterina returns laden with two large burlap sacks filled with bits and pieces of cheese. She has been able to convince two of the local Italian grocery store owners to contribute their cheese scraps to her venture with the prospect that the solution to her problem might also apply to them. Popeye has been busily drilling two small holes in her apartment floor and has taken a large earthen pot from the back yard and placed his lethal solution in the bottom half. Using a wooden ladle, he places the cheese bits in small batches into the solution and then onto empty burlap sacks to dry. After an hour, he drops the small pieces of cheese through the openings in the floor-boards to the basement. There is a surprising lack of stirring or sound from the rodents as he covers the holes over. Several pieces of the toxic cheese are placed in the hallways after warning the tenants to keep themselves and es-pecially their children and household pets, away from the poison. That after-noon, he deposits his lethal cheese along the curb for the length of the block. The neighborhood curiosity-seekers need little coaching to keep their distance from the potion that has made Popeye their champion. They are keenly aware of Caterina's blunder and are relieved that Popeye has taken charge.

The early morning shows promise of success. Dead rats line the street along E. 11th Street, and several of the creatures are carried out in coal shovels from the hallways of Caterina's building. There are no further sounds from the basement and the odors rising from the cellar are now mixed with a faint chemical scent. A week later, Raffaele and his longshoreman crew open the basement door, this time in broad daylight, and discover an enormous heap of dead rats. They shovel and fill pails with the corpses, and soon there is a huge pile of the rodents in the street in front of the house. They douse the pile with kerosene and burn it. The walls and floors of the basement are scrubbed clean and the openings that allowed entry by the rats are filled with concrete. No longer will a rodent army inhabit the basement of 302 E. 11th St., thanks to the man with the terrible face and peculiar name.

Chapter 23

Good Times

The hiatus of good times between the Gay Nineties and Roaring Twenties has not stilled the spirit of New Yorkers for merriment. Despite the gloom of corporate losses and the despair of the unemployed, taverns and cabarets serve up record amounts of highly alcoholic beverages, and theaters are packed with spectators enjoying flapper music and long-legged chorus dancers. Among the poor immigrants, levity is found at festivals and minstrel shows performed along the city streets. Summer has arrived, with its elevated temperatures, its intense humidity and the leafy growth of trees and shrubs that stubbornly subsist in the city's streets and parks. What had been the cold gray pallor of winter skies and barren trees is now a flood of green swamped with the warmth of a butterscotch sun. It is a time for diversion from the stern reality of hard times.

There is an overwhelming satisfaction that Caterina feels, having spent her first six months in America reuniting with Raffaele and in humanizing the E. 11th St. house. Now she hears of a huge street festival taking place in Italian East Harlem and is besieged with a need to celebrate the new life she has fashioned. The feast is in honor of Our Lady of Mount Carmel, the largest of the festivals in her own village of Gagliano. She wonders what Americans know of street festivals, even those who experienced them back in the old country, where centuries of tradition are knotted into the sacred processions, and there is an *abbondanza of* unpretentious music and time-honored foods.

The Italian immigrants arriving in the late nineteenth century who are not inclined to the Lower East Side are likely to gravitate to East Harlem, the northeast end of Manhattan, where employment is sometimes plentiful for those willing to accept a static low wage. There are also more of the low-rent boarding houses available and less of the dense air of lower Manhattan. As the number of Italians occupying the northeast end of the city grows to a majority, the area becomes known as Italian East Harlem. Their beautifully gilded and frescoed shrine is named The Church of Our Lady of Mount Carmel. The appreciative flock is quick to express its gratitude for the building of the church by spawning an annual festival in the Madonna's honor. Now in its fourth decade, the festival accommodates a large congregation and a smattering of non-Italians who come to observe and enjoy merriment in the Italian tradition. On the final day of the feast, a procession will tread piously through the crowded streets of the neighborhood, ignoring the intense heat of the day and pulling a huge float with a gigantic statue of the Madonna

It is the last day of the festival when an excited Caterina attempts to galvanize an otherwise apathetic Raffaele with the prospect of riding the First Avenue trolley uptown to the festival.

"Raf, we must get to *La Festa*. It's the final day and we can get to see the procession."

Raffaele has been dressing for work and does not acquiesce.

"I need to get to work or I'll lose the day's pay."

"Forget that. Take the day off and come with me. I want to thank the Madonna for all the good luck we've had these last six months. And, where better to do that than at the feast?"

Raffaele looks at her thoughtfully, his adoring face close to hers. His arm slides effortlessly around her waist and he smiles sheepishly.

"You can't fool me, *cara*, you just want to have a good time."

"Well, what's wrong with that?"

In the next moment, Raffaele takes her into his arms. Her charm has not diminished with time. Her sparkling chocolate-brown eyes, her flowing black hair and her alluring smile are as seductive as ever. He must hold her close to him. He speaks softly.

"*La Festa* is not until this afternoon. What can we do in the meantime?" Caterina smiles and leads him back to their warm bed.

The aroma of the customary foods of southern Italy, the plaintive sounds of band music and the sporadic eruptions of fireworks reach their senses several blocks before the couple arrives on the festival streets. There are rows of bright-colored circus lights strung across three avenues and along the intersecting streets from E.112th to E.116th streets. Hundreds of tricolor flags, unmoving for want of wind, their red, white and green colors reflecting the blaring sun and generating emotions that are more of camaraderie than of patriotism to the old country. The lilting music of the *Tarantella* clashes with the melody of *Vicino Mare*, competing for the ears of the crowd. Aromas of spicy sausage and meatballs, succulent veal and pepper drowning in steaming tomato sauce fill the air; and the sweet taste of *canoli* and candied almonds is on everyone's palate. Children dart about, chasing one another recklessly and triggering anxious admonishments from parents. From the end of the long street, a colorful float carrying the statue of the venerated Madonna emerges and makes its way in their direction. The sculpted features of The Lady's tinctured face are fixed in sympathetic gaze, her eyes staring piously at her reverent flock. There are three adolescent girls, dressed as heavenly angels, suspended perilously from high wires and encircling the Saint, their feathery wings flailing as if to keep them aloft. Ten burly men in black pants and white shirts open at the neck, tug at the heavy ropes to give mobility to the enormous float. They wear the scapular of Mount Carmel, the brown badge of confraternity that proffers protection and redemption to the wearer. The craft inches slowly down the street, providing eager patrons with their precious moments to pin dollar bills to the Madonna's dress, seeking her indulgent grace. Occasionally, a five dollar bill appears on her garment, setting off an approving bellow from the crowd. A procession of believers precedes the float, carrying effigies of human limbs whose owners have ostensibly been mystically healed by the supernatural powers of the Madonna. A phallic symbol of enormous proportion, the largest among the artificial limbs, reaches high above the ground, either begging for potency or giving thanks for a successful intercession. Behind the float, a cadre of repentant sinners walks barefoot on the steaming pavement as a penance for their transgressions. Some even crawl behind the float on bare hands and knees, sensationalizing their plea for the blessed Saint's intercession. The float draws to a complete halt as a middle-aged woman dressed entirely in black throws herself in front of the Madonna, reviling her own past promiscuity and entreating forgiveness. She is removed from the path of the Madonna by two of the men who then rejoin the others in pulling the float along. It is a throwback to medieval times when such effusiveness was relished.

Caterina's senses are inundated by the sights and sounds surrounding her as she and Raffaele make their way through the congested streets, savoring the foods and absorbing lyrics and music they have not heard since leaving the old country. There is no further doubt for her that this specimen of Italian culture has been transported to the New World in its genuine form and, despite their lowly status in the New World, the *immigranti* have added a flare of affluence from what existed in their humble villages. It is the first diversion that Caterina and Raffaele have allowed themselves in America and they are completely exhausted and satiated at the end of the night. As they fall into bed consumed by their fatigue, Caterina mumbles her last words of their fun-filled night of nostalgia.

"It was almost like being at home in Gagliano."

As she drifts off to sleep, she savors the thought that she and Raffaele have found their niche in America. They will continue to save assiduously for their future in Calabria, but they will also treat themselves to occasional delights such as the one they just enjoyed. The Columbus Day celebration just ahead is the ideal gathering for their agenda.

⊢⊶⊙⊷⊣

Francesca Ciarelli is peculiarly different from other women. She peers into the future and predicts events that seem always to occur. She knows the intimate secrets of her clients by studying the palms of their hands or by viewing their futures in a glass ball on her table. She has flawlessly predicted pregnancies, births, divorces and deaths. Among her best successes is the once warned undertaker Benito Scarpullo, who refused to take on the burial of an old Neapolitan who had purportedly died from emphysema. It was later discovered that the man had been surreptitiously murdered, causing untold grief for another unwitting undertaker who had handled the funeral. Then there was Connie Amico, warned by Francesca not to marry Tommaso Bianchi, a recently arrived immigrant. She was brokenhearted but nevertheless obedient to Francesca's presage. To his great embarrassment, Tommaso was later summoned to Ellis Island by immigration authorities to greet the wife and five children he had left behind in Naples. Francesca's ability to augur the future is so evident that many of her patrons refuse to make weighty decisions until they have received her advice.

Born in Romania, Francesca is the daughter of a gypsy mother and a Calabrian father who, through a minor association with the Ndranghetta, learned of a work opportunity in a labor camp on the edge of Bucharest. There, he met the stunning gypsy girl, Belia, when her tribe, roaming the area in search of wagons and machinery left unattended, came upon Franco's work gang. Belia's classic facial features, cobalt blue eyes and alluring figure so captivated Franco that he deserted his employer and joined her troupe with promises of devoting himself to the manual work that the gypsy men abhorred. Franco won the affections of the voluptuous Belia, fighting off would-be suitors, and eventually marrying her in a heretical Gypsy ceremony. Within a few months, Francesca was born. For almost two decades thereafter, she was schooled in the mystical life of the gypsy. Fortune telling occupied much of her time. When Francesca was 19 years old, her father contracted consumption. Against Belia's wishes, Franco left the band and returned to the healing warmth of Calabria with only Francesca, who by this time was bored with the itinerant existence.

Life in her adopted country was strangely satisfying. The enormously superstitious Calabrians swarmed Francesca with requests to unearth their destiny and seek her advice. She had offers of marriage from young men who were greatly attracted to her, but she chose to remain unattached, living alone in relative squalor. Though she continued to dress in the peculiar gypsy robes of her tribe, she effortlessly acclimated to the Calabrian culture and swore never to return to the nomadism of her early life. As the fate of many of her patrons languished with the times, the huge majority left for America. Curious about the New World and needing a more pecuniary place to offer her unconventional services, Francesca said her goodbyes to Franco and left for America. In New York, she found the familiar faces of those who had abandoned her for the New World. She was able to establish a small following among people she had known and those who were told of her mystical powers. She rented a dilapidated storefront on Mulberry Street, equipped it with stolen draperies and rugs that projected her magnetism and mystique, and brandished a printed sign over her door in dialect Italian, *"Advice on all matters of life, love, health, marriage and business dealings."* Her bed was a long pillow in the rear of the room and her toilet was located in the hallway of the adjacent building. She attended all of the Italian street festivals and many private celebrations so as to mingle and be noticed. Such is the evening of Columbus Day in 1907, at a party marking the discovery by the celebrated navigator.

‖—•‖—○—‖•—‖

The years on E. 11ᵗʰ Street have been kind to Caterina and Raffaele, who act like two mustangs loping in the high grass, their manes trailing in the wind. Any focus on returning to Italy has been virtually supplanted by the lively existence they have adopted. Rooted by their enormous love for one another and the minor affluence they have found in their occupations, they take pleasure in a succession of outings to the opera, minstrel shows, vaudeville and the Italian theater. They are constantly beckoned to join friends on the Lower East Side for revelry at one of countless parties. Twelve saints' days, Unification Day, the King's birthday, Thanksgiving, Christmas and New Year's Day are all pretexts for celebration, and there is also a growing interest in observing a day in honor of Christopher Columbus.

Caterina is almost childlike as she anticipates the Columbus Day party at the Giavanoni house in the Mulberry, like a kitten frolicking with a spool of yarn or a puppy begging to be chased. Raffaele is less enthusiastic, but it is worth his effort to venture out from his snug home if he can be cloaked in her vitality. He feels pride in sharing her excitement, and pleasure in watching her facial expressions change with each new discovery. She is immersed in her youthful anticipation of the party she and Raffaele will attend this evening of

October 12th, deciding on what she will wear and what item of food she will contribute to the host's table. She waits eagerly for Raffaele's return from the docks, hoping that he won't have a new scrape or bruise to show for his day's work, and that he is in an agreeable mood. She often reminds him of his reluctance to leave the house and of how he later experiences the most enjoyment of all, once he's involved in the activity. She is on the front steps when he arrives, his walk lively and his head erect. It is a good sign. She greets him with an immediate reminder of her intention for the evening.

"I'm glad you're on time, Raf, you need to get ready so we can get downtown to the Columbus Day party."

An acquiescent Raffaele does not like the prospect of leaving his home this night, but responds with a simple assent.

The "Italian horn" on Alessandro Giavanoni's front door has kept the dreaded *Malocchio* from plaguing his life with maladies. The envy and petty jealousies of his admirers would otherwise induce the *Malocchio* and cause headaches, fever, nausea and gout. He might even have a run of bad luck. The peculiar-looking horn is a replica of an imaginary devil's tooth, a twisted thin red pepper carved in hardwood. It is painted crimson red with an emerald green stem, its imaginary pungency expected to ward off malevolent influences, much like the evil-busting of garlic. Its antidotal mission is to combat the effects of the "evil eye," a momentary glimpse of envy that is often made with innocent intentions by close friends and relatives lavishing compliments on another's good fortune. Once contracted, the *Malocchio* can be removed by a *strega*, one Serafina Piccolo, an elderly immigrant woman-witch recognized for her diabolical faculty to purge curses. In the case of *Malocchio,* she applies the celebrated oil and water test to assess the severity of the spell, imparts dietary and life-style advice, and uses the exorcising powers of an amethyst ring. Only once has Alessandro had to seek Serafina's assistance, and her invocations quickly overcame the spell. As Caterina enters the apartment, she is quick to notice the crimson horn and her thoughts flash back to a time in her youth when her father's chief foreman glowed with pride over his association with Gagliano's foremost landowner, Vitaliano Zinzi. Caterina had overheard him crowing to others about Vitaliano's rise from privation to a position of wealth, touting Vitaliano and Rosaria as a handsome couple and noting the attractiveness of their children, like a brood of Affen Spaniels. Having heard of the *Malocchio* and witnessed its effect on others, Caterina sounded out her fears to the man and implored him to end his extravagant praise of her father immediately.

"Nicco, you must not tempt fate with such praise of my father. You'll invoke the *Malocchio*."

Nicco laughed, "Don't be so superstitious, little girl. I'm merely praising your father, not showing envy."

"Please, Nicco, please don't say any more." It was too late. Two days later, Vitaliano fell from his horse and broke his right arm. Later in the same week, Rosaria became ill with what was believed to be Malaria. Their little son Vincenzo suddenly began wheezing as though he had contracted emphysema. Fortunately, the wise Vitaliano quickly concluded that his family was being assailed by the *Malocchio* and knew of the psychic who could expel it. At substantial cost to Vitaliano, the victims received constant intercession for a week by the mystical Maria Fortunato. The oil and water diagnosis showed that a substantial spell had been cast. The use of an amethyst stone passed over the chests of the victims, a constant diet of tiny specks of pasta in garlic and olive oil and the chanting of ancient verses brought results. Vitaliano's arm showed astonishing improvement, Rosaria rose from her bed with only a trace of a cold and Vincenzo's breathing became normal. The *Malocchio* was gone.

⊱•––◦––•⊰

Caterina makes the sign of defense against the evil eye, her right hand pointed to the horn, the forefinger and pinky extended, the other fingers folded tightly to her palm. It is all she can do on her own to ward off the possibility of contamination by the *Malocchio*. As she enters the room, a crowd of ten huddles around a small woman in a far corner of the room. Her name is Francesca Ciarelli, the well-known gypsy from Calabria. She is clad in a flowing chestnut-colored robe, her head bathed in a beige kerchief tied behind her head as if to hide her auburn hair. Beside her is a disheveled young boy in a weathered shirt and knickers, his bare feet sullied from the dusty streets. His bright red hair and freckled skin are an anomaly to this mostly swarthy assembly and his presence at this adult party is curious. She is also accompanied by a scruffy canine that is likely the combination of setter and collie. She is engaged in negotiating for her services as soothsayer, assuring her prospects that her predictions will be precise and that her interventions can change the outcomes of their lives. She has agreed with Alessandro, who wishes to add excitement to his party, that she will meet with each of his friends to provide a capsule of their fortunes.

Caterina recognizes Francesca as the legendary gypsy girl from Gagliano, but has never spoken to her. She and Raffaele take seats across the table from her and are mildly apprehensive of her strange presence and that of a small boy and dog. As the evening progresses, Francesca begins her fortune-telling with each of the people seated around the table. She begins with Teresa Morrone, a recent widow at the party alone, dressed very conservatively in a dark, flowered dress.

"Show me your palm. Ah, yes you have a long life ahead. You can see that by the long line in the center of your hand. And here, this line shows that good fortune will soon come your way. There is a tall, dark-haired man in your future of whom you will become very fond and who will secure your future."

The widow is beaming, but does so cautiously so as not to show the excitement she feels over Francesca's predictions so soon after her husband's death. The tradition of wearing black and mourning continually for many years following the death of one's husband has not been entirely left behind in the old country. Widows are not expected to smile and show much enthusiasm for life, out of respect for their dead husbands. The fortune-teller moves on from person to person before reaching Caterina and Raffaele. By now, the wine and the gaiety have put the festive couple in the party spirit and their earlier apprehension of Francesca is gone. They are both glowing with acceptance as Francesca approaches and sizes them up. She immediately senses that there had been some uneasiness in accepting her unsolicited presence. She is aware that Caterina is from the family of Vitaliano Zinzi. Though they have never met, she is nevertheless ready to plunge into forecasting the destiny of the happy couple. She approaches Caterina first.

"Signora, may I see your hand, please?"

Caterina holds out her right hand, palm up, a broad smile on her face. Surely, this fraud of a fortune-teller will divulge something that will fill her with hilarity. She will have to suppress her laughter, however, so as to not offend the poor girl. After all, even poor gypsies need to earn a living. Moments pass and Francesca has not spoken. She stares quietly at Caterina's hand with a solemn look on her face. Finally she looks up and speaks.

"I'm sorry to tell you this, madam, but I can see here in the palm of your hand that you will lose your fortune and never find it again."

Caterina is unable to contain her laughter. She laughs aloud.

"Fortune? What fortune is that? Between us we don't have enough money to even visit our parents in Italy."

Francesca is silent. Her mood remains somber. She does not appear to be offended by Caterina's nervous burst of laughter. She moves on to Raffaele, who is already holding out the palm of his hand for her to read. Once again, Francesca does not speak. She is motionless as she stares into Raffaele's palm, her eyes seeming to bulge at the sight she discerns. There is a tense moment in the room as those who have heard the depressing results of Caterina's fortune are painfully silent. Several agonizing moments pass before she finally speaks.

"Signore, I have never before seen kismet in the palm of a hand with such dire portent."

Raffaele draws in a swift breath. He is familiar with the forecasts of Gypsy fortune tellers from his youth in Gagliano. They can be deadly accurate. He must know what she has seen in the palm of his hand.

"Gypsy, tell me what you see. What is your prediction? I must know."

Francesca's face is filled with fear, her lips quivering as she mutters Raffaele's fate.

"Signore, you will die at a table surrounded by friends."

Silence fills the room. They have all heard the dire prediction. Francesca stands and summons the young boy accompanying her with a glance. They head for the door, Francesca's face grimacing with fear. Her dog silently follows her as she departs, leaving behind a grateful few whose fortunes she did not tell.

It is up to Alessandro, as host of the party, to restore gaiety now that Francesca is gone. He regrets having agreed to her joining the party, considering the shock that permeates the assembly of superstitious believers. But he will not restore the gaiety in Caterina and Raffaele. As he looks around, Alessandro sees that they, too, have left the party.

⌐┼═◊═┼┐

Domenico Pascale is both delighted and humbled. His building on E.11th St. has become worth more than he could have hoped for. The vagrant loiterers are gone, the local hoodlums no longer harass his tenants working in local factories, and the enormous horde of rats is gone from the basement. While he is most appreciative to Caterina and has kept his promise of granting her a ten percent ownership in the property, he is also troubled with himself for not having sensed the opportunity. Aside from costing him a share of the property, he must now acknowledge the woman he ridiculed when she first showed interest in managing the property, arrogantly advising her to return to Italy with her defeated husband. Now to the contrary, as further expansion enters his mind, he realizes that Caterina is the key to increasing his ownership of boarding houses. He is coy as he approaches Caterina to talk about an imminent prospect about which he has received information.

"You were great in your handling of our building. I would not have imagined such enormous improvements in just a few months."

Caterina is suspicious of Domenico's flattery. What could he be up to now? Her response is obsequious.

"It was just good luck."

Domenico can see that he must get to the point if he wishes to keep Caterina's attention.

"Caterina, I am considering buying a boarding house and want you to be my partner."

"What do you mean? Tell me about it."

"If you agree to operate the new property, I can get someone to take over our E. 11th St. house and you can earn a fifty percent ownership of the new house just for making it successful."

Caterina is stunned by the proposition. A half ownership could be a great deal of money. And, she would still have her share of the E. 11th St. house. Partnering with Domenico might be the opportunity of a lifetime. Her mind is open to the possibility.

"Where is it located?"

"In Sharon, Pennsylvania."

Chapter 24

Lost Fortune

It is a particularly dreary day in Sharon, a lifeless gray landscape of rain and wind intruding on huge puffs of sooty black smoke emerging from smokestacks atop the steel mill. There is a pungent chemical aroma descending on the surrounding community, the white hot fusing of iron and carbon. A legion of sweaty men, their faces blackened and looking like minstrels from the Broadway Theater, feed furnaces with coke, iron ore and scrap metal, the lifeblood of the new industrialized world. Some of the Italians in the group will end their day at Caterina's boarding house, where they have a clean bed, familiar food and washed clothing to wear. It is a drab existence of intense heat and grime with only Sunday to intervene to give them respite, but they hold hope in their hearts for returning to Italy with enough cash to become land owners.

Caterina stands inside her rooming house, peering through a front window to the bleak day, hoping to see a trace of Raffaele. He is due back from New York this day and she feels the excitement of his presence even before he arrives. She thinks of the men working at the mill who await the final whistle signaling the end of the day. Those who live in her boarding house depend on her to have their meals cooked, their clothes washed and a place to wash their stained bodies when they arrive after dark. Thankfully, she has been able to engage the services of Olivia, a strong young woman recently immigrated to Sharon from Italy with her parents. She has taken over most of the work and

needs very little direction. It allows Caterina time for respite, when she and
Raffaele will walk over to see flicks at a movie theater that recently opened
in town, or perhaps listen to a Verdi opera on a Gramophone owned by the
manager of the steel mill and shared in his living room with opera aficionados
living in Sharon. If only Raffaele would get home today, there is an invitation
to listen to Puccini's *Madama Butterfly* that evening.

The rain seems to be easing a bit. Caterina spots a lone Western Union
delivery boy on a bicycle, his brown uniform covered by a rain poncho. *Bad
news*, she thinks, *it's the only time anyone receives a telegram. It must be important
for him to come out in all this rain.* The boy comes closer. *Who is he looking for,*
she wonders? Her heart begins to pound as he comes closer and closer still.
She feels her head fill with blood as she watches the cold, wet boy come to her
door. Her senses are blunted by fear and shock. The telegram is indeed for
her. She signs the manifest with trembling hands and takes the small yellow
envelope containing the message into the house. As the boy leaves, she sits
on the floor inside the front door, not able to move her legs. She opens the
envelope and reads the telegram.

> Caterina. Stop. Regret I must tell you shocking news. Stop.
> Raffaele has had a heart attack and is dead. Stop.
> Please come at once. Stop. Enzo.

No! It isn't true. It can't be. It's a mistake. Caterina's thoughts are of denial.
*It is a cruel joke to get me to leave Sharon for New York, where all of our friends are
and where there is enormous merriment. Who would do such a malicious thing?...
Is it possible that it's true?* As reality begins to set in, an enormous flood of
anxiety and frustration overtakes her and she lets out a cry.

"No! Raffaele, Raffaele, I love you! I need you! Please come home to me!
You're everything to me, my very life."

Her cries are wrenching, her body heaving with each sob. From her seated
position, she falls forward on the floor, unconscious. When she awakens, she is
in the same place, unnoticed by anyone. She stands, goes to her bedroom and
packs her clothing. She will go to New York and find out what has happened.

Giuseppe Rossi answers the feeble knock on his front door and finds Caterina on the other side. Her face is drawn and dark circles surround her reddened eyes. She is barely able to stand.

"Come in, Caterina, I'm so sorry for what happened."

A stooped and frail Caterina enters the house and immediately takes a seat in a chair.

"What happened? Is it true that my Raffaele is gone?" She sobs uncontrollably into a handkerchief for a few moments.

"Yes, it's true. I'm very sorry. It was at the dinner welcoming Enzo to America. He wasn't eating or drinking. Suddenly, he stood up and, in front of all of our friends, fell onto the table dead. It was an enormous heart attack. We were all shocked."

Caterina has heard him, but does not seem to be listening. She stares into space and thinks to herself. *So...that gypsy was right. He died among his friends...and I lost my treasure and will never find it again.* She tries to hold back her tears, but there is no use. He is gone from the world and she will never see him again, his gentle, adoring face before her in her mind. *Why did he have to come to America? Perhaps the terrible struggle of his first year caused this to happen to him. His heart was strong in Italy.* The memory of their first meeting, their outlandish encounter in the old Beccio ranch house that declared to her father, and the world for that matter, that they wished to be together for as long as they both lived. What did anything else matter? Did her father think that her mind could be changed by a dowry? Perhaps he had forgotten what love means to a woman and man who have found their soul mate and acted on instinct. How lucky she was to have had him for the twelve years of their marriage. And who was it that suggested that they may have been siblings of the same father? Oh, yes, it was Nunzio Laguzza. Was it his jealousy of her relationship with another man that prompted that story? Could there have been anything to it? Her eyes seem to instantly dry, her face less callused by the image of the kind, adoring lover she married.

"Caterina, what will you do? Where will you go?"

Giuseppe's voice jolts her back to reality. She has determined what happened to Raffaele and has no further interest in this place. She must find out the truth about Raffaele.

"I'm going back to Calabria, Giuseppe, to Gagliano."

>—+—+>—0—+—+—<

The horse-drawn hearse makes its way up the slight incline to the striking Victorian gatehouse of Greenwood cemetery, followed by a second carriage containing Caterina, Concetta, Antonio, Enzo and Father DeCicco from the Church of the Transfiguration. They are dressed in mourning clothes, the black that pervades the country they all left. It is a crisp autumn day and the rolling green hills, shimmering lakes and shade-dappled ground add a mystical sense to Raffaele's burial. A winding path meanders by the spot where the earth has been opened to receive the coffin containing the love of Caterina's life. As she sits in the coach awaiting the start of the religious service, she again reflects on the life she and Raffaele had together and how it had been so brief a time. *He was so handsome when I saw him for the first time in that vineyard that I simply had to respond to his advances. I couldn't get him out my mind after that, his wonderful blue eyes that contrasted with his dark hair, and his mild manner that was so captivating. We might never have developed our interest in one another if he hadn't accidentally cut his wrist harvesting my father's vineyard. Who would have imagined that he wouldn't live to see his 40th birthday? That gypsy fortune-teller knew. She was afraid to tell us, afraid of what our reaction might be. I have indeed lost my treasure and he is irreplaceable.* Tears stream down her cheeks and her stupor prevents her from deciphering words that the others around her are speaking. She is helped down from the coach by Antonio and approaches the grave site, suppressing her emotion and walking stiffly, arm in arm with Concetta. She has never felt so alone. It is almost impossible for her to imagine her life from this time forward.

Father DeCicco's words return Caterina's focus to their purpose for being in this strangely beautiful place, with green carpeted hills and sculptured mausoleums and tombs. They are sheltered beneath huge century-old oak trees, and surrounded by small carved headstones perfectly aligned and generously spaced below a ridge overlooking the skyline of Manhattan across the bay.

"...requiem eternam dona eis, Domine et lux perpetua luceat eis...."

As the coffin is lowered into the open ground, Caterina wells with emotion. She feels herself stagger and holds onto Concetta, but still she contains her emotion. *Why am I here, Lord, why do I have to live on? There is nothing left for me. He is gone forever and I will never see him again, never again be in his arms, and never again share my life on earth with him. I am better off to die and join him in the hereafter.* She is led back to the carriage and is no longer able to control herself when the finality of her walk occurs to her. She turns and scurries back to the grave site, where two diggers are busily shoveling dirt into the abyss in the ground containing Raffaele's coffin.

"Stop that! My husband is down there. Bring him back up. I can't leave him behind."

She is sobbing uncontrollably as she falls to the ground at the edge of the open grave. Antonio is by now beside her and takes her in his arms. He carries her back to the carriage, only half conscious. As the carriage leaves the cemetery, she falls into a deep sleep. It is a grim chapter of her life that is over, but she will come to visit this place often for the rest of her life.

—•—

Chapter 25

Home to Calabria

Gagliano is no longer a place of happiness and joy for Caterina. Every corner produces a reason to think of Raffaele, a reason to want to cry or scream. It is still a haven from the cold weather of the north and a place where people are friendly and amiable, always wont to help one another. There is her family homestead at La Stella, an escape from the often harsh life of the peasants. The sun still rises over the lemon trees, lighting the fruit like candles in the early dawn. The sunsets redden the sky and create a blood orange backdrop to the spectacle of birds settling in for the night. But there is no escape, even here, from the memories. If New York is a difficult place for mending her heartache, then Gagliano is impossible.

Caterina has settled her accounts in New York with Domenico, taking her share of the properties in cash, and sailing for Calabria unfettered by the need to think about the boarding houses and their link to Raffaele. She had hoped that her time in America would have cleansed her mind of recollections in Italy. It has not. Now in her father's home, she sleeps in a comfortable and familiar bed from her youth; but sleep does not come easy. She lies awake at night with memories that persist and will not allow her the peace she is by now yearning for. She has learned that reciting the customary prayers and invoking God's will on behalf of Raffaele's soul can calm her so that eventually sleep takes over. She has walked the streets of Gagliano, past the house that she once occupied with Raffaele, past Concetta's house a few doors away where she and Antonio set up their first home together. At first, it was difficult to look in the direction of her home. Then, she saw a small boy playing in the street and discovered that it was her home that the boy lived in. She eventually was able to talk to the boy's mother, and to accept an invitation to enter the tiny home. She wept as she stood before the hearth where they had cooked their meals and warmed themselves. She walked past the house that Raffaele's parents occupy, and knew that she must confront Michela to confirm Raffaele's lineage. But she was only able to commiserate over his death without mention of other matters. That would come in good time, but not now.

Michela Brutto finds breathing difficult these days. As she deals with the ravages of age and a bout with consumption, she thinks of the two sons she has lost: her youngest, Enzo, who lives in America and is unlikely to ever return home; and the other, Raffaele, who died suddenly from a malady unknown in her family. She believes he was driven to the pursuit of wealth by his ardent desire to restore his wife to a life of plenty. When he was not heard from for many months, Michela feared for his welfare and prayed daily to the Blessed Virgin for his safety and his eventual return to Gagliano. *Now his widow has returned, flush with the money that she and Raffaele earned in their final years together, seeking comfort from the pain of having lost him. She could have brought his body back to be buried in his home village, but instead she chose to bury him in a place called Brooklyn in a cemetery that isn't even Catholic. Didn't she think that his mother might have wanted to visit his grave frequently and pray for the repose of his soul? Now Caterina is here in Gagliano and he is buried in America away from his family and his culture.* Michela is not comfortable with Caterina's request to meet with her privately at their next meeting. *What could she possibly want from me that Lorenzo can't be present to hear? I don't like it, but I can't refuse her. After all, she is my son's widow and she is from the Vitaliano Zinzi family. It would be an insult to refuse her request.*

It is mid-morning when Caterina knocks on Michela's door, a time when it is likely that she will be home alone. Lorenzo works in the fields alongside much younger men and earns a pay equivalent to the others. Only her daughters are apt to be present to blunt Caterina's conversation, but they are not there. At last, Caterina has cornered Michela and can dig out the truth about Raffaele's true father from the only person in the world who would know for certain. She is careful to put Michela at ease.

"Good morning, Ma, I brought you some peaches from my father's garden. May I come in?"

"Of course, please come in. The peaches are beautiful. How did they ever escape that frost we had last week?"

Both women are aware that Caterina has a specific purpose for visiting Michela and that she will eventually reveal what is on her mind. After several moments of idle talk, Caterina is less subtle with Michela.

"Michela, may I ask you a frank question?"

"Certainly."

"I must preface my question by telling you that I am aware of your bond to my father many years ago. It has pained my father that the possibility exists that Raffaele was conceived of that association and that he is in fact my half brother. Only you would know that for sure, Ma. Is it true? Is Raffaele my father's son?"

Caterina looks into Michela's face to observe her reaction and determine if Michela's response is truthful. Her question has hit a nerve. Michela has a dazed look on her face, like a burglar who is suddenly discovered by a light turned on in his face. Her first words are muttered.

"Wh...where did you hear about that? Who told you that?"

"That's not important. Just tell me if it's true."

Michela does not respond as directly as Caterina would wish.

"It is true that your father and I had a friendship that led to a man, woman liaison. It was before I met Lorenzo and before your father married your mother. Your father was a very easy man to love. He is not merely successful, he is warm and affectionate. He showered me with gifts and even sent a crew to repair my roof. At first, he visited me almost daily. I believed that I had found the man of my life and that he would overlook my past and marry me. But, in the end, he spurned me in favor of his business and eventually married Rosaria. When Lorenzo appeared in my life, he asked no questions and made it clear that he was committed to me. He is a humble man of very modest means, but his love is true and our family is the focus of his life. In just a few weeks, we announced our bans and were married. I delivered him a son a few months thereafter. That was the man you married, my son Raffaele."

Caterina can see the emotion build in Michela, her face showing embarrassment, her eyes welling and releasing a tear to descend one cheek. Her question still unanswered, Caterina presses Michela to narrow her discussion.

"Please, Ma, was Raffaele my father's son?"

Michela feels nakedness in revealing the fact that her liaison with Lorenzo had begun so soon after she concluded that Vitaliano no longer had an interest in her. But the importance to Caterina of knowing the truth about her dead husband is overwhelming. Michela looks directly into Caterina's face and exclaims, "Raffaele is Lorenzo Brutto's son. I am certain of it. He was conceived before we were married, but he is of Brutto blood."

Michela seems suddenly to turn hard and angry. Her voice is elevated as she shouts at Caterina, "All of that agony that your father endured could have been avoided if he had come to me and asked about my pregnancy. His false pride prevented that, so he deserved the agony of having his daughter enter into matrimony with a man who might have been her brother."

Michela's enmity is revealed by her sudden outburst. All along, she has been discontent with Vitaliano's callous manner in ending their intimate relationship and has never forgiven him for not reacting to notice of her intent to marry Lorenzo Brutto. The irony in the marriage of Vitaliano's daughter to her son assuages her anger, but forgiveness is another matter. She is not trash to be discarded in such a manner as Vitaliano did, despite the fact that she was forced by the circumstances of her life to compromise her purity. It is all that she can do to remain civil toward Caterina, but she must explain her behavior.

"Forgive my outburst, Caterina, it is not with you that I have an issue. I know that you did not want or encourage my son to leave Italy for America. It was his own doing. And, I have admired yours and Raffaele's courage in defying Vitaliano and proving your love for one another."

As Caterina leaves, she looks back at Michela. The loss of her sons has taken a huge toll on the old woman. She wonders what had really happened between her father and Michela. She also wonders if Michela has told her the truth about Raffaele's conception.

—◦—

Elisabetta Zinzi rises from her bed in the early morning and quietly descends to the first floor of the villa. She will stoke the fire in the huge fireplace that heats much of the ground floor and serves as smokehouse to the meats hung from the mantle above the reach of the intense heat. She will draw two cups of coffee from a large porcelain pot that hangs directly over the fire, placed there by a servant an hour earlier. Vitaliano will soon awaken and she will please him by bringing coffee to him as his eyes open on the day. She must step up onto the long, wide stone hearth to keep her balance as she reaches for the heavy pot with her toweled hands. Suddenly, her equilibrium is gone as her smooth-bottom slippers slide out from under her and her body crashes down on the fire, like a log being flung onto embers to liven them. The coffee pot overturns, drenching Elisabetta's body with intensely hot coffee and soaking her nightgown and robe. Her arms are helplessly entrapped in the flames, two logs that induce the fire to rage uncontrollably. Sparks are hurled onto the hearth and into the room.

"Aiuto! Aiuto!" Her cries for help are unheard at first, but the smoke from the fire awakens the household and Vitaliano, Caterina and two servants rush to the kitchen. They are in time to extinguish the fire but, as they remove the battered Elisabetta from her pyrrhic roost, it is evident that she is gravely injured. Her body has been burned by the steaming coffee, but the drenching has saved it from the fire. Likewise, her face has been badly singed, but her features and eyesight have escaped intact. Not so with her arms, both of which are burned beyond hope. As the limp body is removed from the burning heap of rubble and rushed to a clinic in Catanzaro, it is evident that Elisabetta will never be the same.

It is up to Caterina to take over the running of the household, choosing the meals and directing the servants. She comforts her father as much as she can. Vitaliano walks aimlessly, bumping into furniture and walls, oblivious to the world around him. For the second time in his life he has been confronted with the sudden turn of events affecting his treasured spouses, first the abrupt and unexpected death of Rosaria and now the tragic accident that will disable Elisabetta for the rest of her life. It is more than he can fathom. He is despondent to the point of being unable to act in his familiar calm and unassuming manner. He rages at Caterina when he disagrees with her choices for the food he eats or the wine he drinks. And, he frequently countermands her direction to the servants, leaving them confused. Caterina has become captive to an irrational father who imagines that his life is being orchestrated by his daughter. She can no longer reason with him.

It is four weeks before Elisabetta is returned home from the hospital, her burned arms hideously removed from above the elbow in order to save her life. They might have kept her in a hospital bed longer, but the demand for beds is such that she is discharged to make room for others in the tiny clinic. She will be bedridden at home for several months and require assistance for the rest of her life to move about and take her meals. It will be all for two housemaids to do to perform their normal duties and care for Elisabetta. Vitaliano's equilibrium has almost entirely returned, but his attitude toward Caterina has not mellowed. He demands that Caterina take charge of caring for her stepmother.

"Pa, you can't be serious. I can't devote my life to your wife. I've come to accept her, but she isn't my mother. I just can't do it."

"You must, Caterina, she is your stepmother and needs your help."

The impasse between father and daughter again raises its familiar specter. Caterina is back under the oppressive influence of her father. It is déjà vu from her fight to declare her right to marry the man of her choice. The indecision that has beleaguered Caterina as to how to direct her life now that Raffaele is gone is suddenly over. It has never been clearer. She was inspired by the events in her life in America: an atmosphere of hope and opportunity, the challenge of learning the operation of the boarding house, meeting people of dissimilar backgrounds, dealing with itinerant drunks, ridding the house of the rat infestation, and taking on a new boarding house in faraway Sharon. There was nothing at which she failed. Here in Calabria, she is smothering in her own home, once again under the thumb of her domineering father, and feeling incomplete by the fact that she is a woman in a man's world that is mired in tradition. She must leave and return to America.

Chapter 26

A New Life

It has been four years since the Croton Dam has been completed and heralded as a triumph in dam construction. Along with celebration comes displacement of thousands of immigrant workers who must find other employment to support their families. Jobs are hard to come by for those who participated in a series of strikes that undermined the project and delayed its completion. Many leave and take jobs in the New England textile mills, the Midwestern meat-packing plants and the orchards of California. But for Antonio Russo, who has become a journeyman stone mason and who kept a low profile during the strikes, there are offers of employment in Croton-on-Hudson. A housing boom has begun along with the return of prosperity, requiring scores of trade craftsmen, and he is quickly employed. The secret of his bigamous marriage to Concetta has become sealed in the passage of time, and their home in the rickety shack standing on stilts above the dam site has been replaced by a more stable but unassuming home inside the city limits of Croton-On-Hudson.

By now, Concetta has delivered three more children, two boys and a girl. Samuel, Vincent and Josephine are siblings to Maria, all spaced little more than a year apart. The moderate affluence that the couple has achieved makes for a far better life than their existence in the bilges of Gagliano or anywhere in their region of Calabria. It allows for a more generous diet and the possibility of education for the children as they come of age. Antonio and Concetta unwittingly speak Italian among themselves and to their children, and because their English is broken, they inadvertently open themselves to wanton discrimination by a predominantly Anglo-Saxon community. Italians must live in the end of town that is least pleasant and accept a low wage that is unmistakably reserved for the immigrant worker. They are shunned socially and often feared for the reputation they are handed for fighting with knives and for ostensibly belonging to the *Mano Nero*, a netherworld organization that terrorizes the immigrants. *Mano Nero's* frequent demands for money and favors are accompanied by threats of death, their written communiqués stamped with the form of a black hand. But, despite the looming intimidation by criminals and the condescendence of a conformist establishment, Antonio and Concetta are content to live in a freer society. In the end, it is America that allows them to live a better life with hope for the future.

⊱⊰

It has been months since Concetta joined Caterina at Raffaele's burial. Now she receives word from their brother, Vincenzo, of Elisabetta's debilitating accident and of Caterina's imminent return to America to escape her father's suffocating demands. Concetta and Antonio journey to the city to surprise Caterina as she disembarks from the S.S. Dante Alighieri. They intend for Caterina to return to Croton-On-Hudson with them and locate herself there permanently. It will be comforting to her to have a sister living nearby, Concetta thinks, who has helped them all of their lives and who she can now assist. With her skills in operating boarding houses, Caterina would perhaps even be interested in a property in nearby Peekskill that they have learned is being sold by a Neapolitan bent on returning to his village in Italy. Perhaps after a respectable time passes, she might even be interested in finding a husband among the several bachelors and widowers that quarter in the rooming house on the south end of Croton-On-Hudson. At age 37, Caterina is still young enough to find bliss in a second marriage, they reason, and there are certainly enough eligibles from whom to choose. Though considerate and well meaning, Antonio and Concetta will soon learn that Caterina has her own thoughts about the life she will live.

Caterina is astonished to see Antonio and Concetta waiting for her arrival as she disembarks amongst a throng of passengers calling to friends on shore and filling the dock like a gaggle of honking geese. Within moments, she is in the embrace of her sister and bursting with news of Gagliano.

"Concetta, you wouldn't believe how horrible Elisabetta looks. She has no arms. They had to remove them to save her life."

Concetta grimaces, as though she could intercept the words emerging from Caterina's mouth. She can no longer listen to Caterina's sordid report of their stepmother's condition.

"Tell me some good news, Caterina; I can't listen to that gruesome report about Elisabetta."

"The good news is that I've escaped Pa's grip for the second time in my life. I'm here in America and I'm going to live on the Lower East Side somewhere, where I'll be around the places that Raffaele and I patronized for more than ten years. I've reached the point that I want to be around his memory, and the remembrances are here in New York."

Concetta is disappointed. Obviously, her sister is not coming to live nearby in Croton-On-Hudson. But, merely having her here in America, in New York City, is comforting. It will allow them to communicate easily and see one another without the long, expensive journey across the ocean that so many Italians experience when they visit with their families. At the end of the day, Concetta and Antonio board the train for Croton-On-Hudson alone, disappointed that Caterina is not with them.

<hr />

It is not an unexpected call when Domenico appears at the front desk of the ascetic and unadorned Excelsior Hotel in midtown Manhattan. He asks for Caterina Brutto, trying to look more like an uncle than a paramour. She has been anticipating his visit, having notified him of her decision to return to America, hoping that she might fit into his plans to expand his ownership of boarding houses in the Lower East Side. To be sure, their previous connection was gainful for both. The property on E. 11th street, replete with Caterina's amazing transformation, provides a handsome income to Domenico, despite his putting forth very little effort. And, the now thriving rooming house in Sharon has continued to flourish notwithstanding Caterina's sudden departure. There, her assistant, Olivia Gigante, took control of the property that Caterina titivated to the point of it being the most attractive boarding house in Sharon. It was another success for Domenico at the hands of Caterina. Now, as he waits for her to descend from her third story room, he thinks about the opportunities that proliferate for one with the talent to transform unproductive properties into profitable rooming houses. As Caterina descends from the stairway, he jumps to his feet.

"Caterina! How nice to see you. How was your trip?"

He has something on his mind, Caterina thinks, *he isn't usually so polite.*

"My trip was fine, and I'm really happy to be back in America. I was very happy living here in New York."

Domenico's eyes flash, sensing a moment of prospect. Caterina has provided segue to the subject he would like to discuss.

"How about New Jersey? Wouldn't you like to live there?

"What are you talking about?"

"There's an old four-story apartment house in Secaucus that would make an ideal boarding house in a place where there isn't one for miles. It's alongside a huge pig farm that is tended by Italians who are just arrived and don't have a nearby place to live. We could fill that house with boarders overnight."

Caterina interrupts him, though he would like to continue.

"I will live only in New York. It is important to me to live among the places and people that Raffaele and I enjoyed so much. I don't have him any more, but I can hold on to his memory by being here in New York on the Lower East Side."

Domenico does not give up.

"But Secaucus is just across the Hudson River. You could come to New York as often as you wished."

"Don't you understand? I'm going to live in New York, not in Secaucus or anywhere else."

A look of disgust and hopelessness forms on Domenico's face. His chance at establishing yet another boarding house is gone. He will not attempt it without Caterina's involvement for fear of failure. He is not through with Caterina, however, and he renews the conversation in a voice that lowers to a whisper.

"How would you like to take over the E.11th St. property again?"

Caterina's face lights up. It is the very place where she and Raffaele first lived after being reunited. And, they worked together to make that property a viable boarding house. Why is he offering this to her? And why is he whispering?

"Yes, I'd like that, but don't you already have someone there? And, why are you whispering?"

Domenico's voice remains at just above a whisper.

"When you moved to Pennsylvania, I hired a woman named Lena Mattera to operate the property for me. Unlike you, she doesn't talk to the American neighbors and has lost the connections you had for keeping drunks and beggars off of the property and for keeping the house properly fumigated. The property has lost much of its charm. The halls smell of garbage and the flowers are gone from the sills on the front windows. Lately, Lena doesn't want me near the property, saying that the boarders shouldn't know that the building is owned by an absentee landlord. She has given me enough rent money to satisfy my needs, but I suspect that she's keeping a portion of the rents for herself. I've thought of replacing her, but it's too risky. A woman like that is likely to cause damage before she leaves. And, I don't have a replacement for her."

It incenses Caterina to think that her work has been unraveled in part by this heavy-handed woman. She and Raffaele toiled endlessly to clear up the building's shortcomings and re-establish it from its crisis condition. To be sure, she was paid for her efforts, but there is an overriding emotional attachment to this building. She questions Domenico.

"What would you like me to do?"

"Caterina, if you could get her out and take over, I'd make you a ten percent owner again."

A smirk appears on Caterina's face. Once again, Domenico is unable to do his own dirty work and needs her to do it for him. She drives a hard bargain.

"Make it fifteen percent and you have a deal."

⊱────◈────⊰

Eileen McGinty is having a bad day. Her husband has been laid off from his trucking job, one of her tenants has notified her that he is moving his family to the fashionable Grand Concourse in the Bronx; and her policeman brother has been reassigned to patrol the streets in the dangerous Five Points precinct. The sound of a knock on her door brings her to her feet. What could possibly add to the misery of the day? She opens the door to the smiling face of her old friend, Caterina Brutto.

"Katie! You're back!"

Caterina extends her arms and engulfs Eileen in an affectionate embrace that reminds Eileen of the friendship they formed combating the difficult problems that Caterina faced when she first took charge of the house next door. The two women have not seen one another for two years, the year that Caterina and Raffaele lived in Pennsylvania, and the year that Caterina spent in Italy following Raffaele's death. It occurs to Caterina that Eileen may not even know of Raffaele's demise.

"I want to hear everything about the last two years here on E. 11th St, but first I need ask if you…heard about Raffaele's death."

The hesitation in Caterina's words reveals the emotion that is pent up in her, even now a year later.

"Yes, Caterina, Domenico let me know last year when it first happened. I just couldn't believe that a strong, healthy man like Raffaele could die suddenly from a heart condition he didn't know he had."

Eileen does not mention that Domenico shared with her the uncanny prediction of Raffaele's death by a gypsy fortune teller.

Caterina must change the subject. She is not here to mourn and her eyes have started filling from the sentiment just expressed. She breathes in a long breath and directs the conversation toward her purpose for visiting.

"What do you know about this woman, Lena Mattera? Domenico suspects that she's dishonest in operating the house for him and is being discouraged from direct contact with tenants."

Eileen's response is a burst of ill will that she has been stifling for the past two years.

"Just look at that place. Since you left, it's been declining by the day. We don't need the flowers that dressed it up so prettily, but the place doesn't smell the same with all the garbage that's strewn around. She's inviting the rats to return, if you ask me. And there are bums on the stoop now that she's insulted my brother and doesn't have him looking after the house any more. She asked him if he was looking for a handout for protecting the house. And, she ignores me whenever we cross paths, which I hope doesn't happen too often."

It is an earful for Caterina.

"Help me get her out," she says, "and we'll be neighbors again."

"It won't be easy. She won't go willingly. She keeps a constant vigil on the place, and has this big dog inside her apartment, ready to pounce on anyone who comes close to her door."

Caterina smiles mischievously at Eileen.

"We've faced tougher problems than this one."

>——•——◦——•——<

Lena Corigliano was born in the Calabrian seaside village of Crotone, to a family of poor fishermen. When she was sixteen, her parents promised her in marriage to a man twice her age whom she had never met and who, after observing the attractive young Lena from a distance, offered to pay her father the equivalent of a year's wages for her hand in marriage. She was not told of the arrangement until her father collected the money. Then, she was ordered to marry in order to provide financial assistance to her family. It would not be long, she was told, until she would fall in love with the prosperous husband she had not yet seen. When she met Antonio Mattera, she felt repulsed. He was overweight by at least 80 pounds, was afflicted with allergies that caused his nose to run constantly and had a body odor that smelled of the Caciocavallo goat cheese that he produced for his livelihood in a small workroom of his home. Despite the revulsion she felt towards him, her primal sense of duty to her family and the great embarrassment they would undergo should she decline the marriage, impelled her assent. The wedding was followed quickly by a connubial life in which Antonio justified his investment by forcing himself sexually on his young bride several times daily. And, if his repugnance were not enough, his lovemaking took the form of self indulgence with total disregard to Lena's desires.

In her third month of marriage, Lena discovered that she was pregnant. Despite what was by now a hatred for her husband, she felt a sense of fulfillment in that she would soon have a child on whom to focus her life. When Antonio learned of Lena's pregnancy, he became furious, vowing to disown any progeny that she allowed to come to term. Implicit in his manner was his wish for her to illicitly abort the fetus and return to being his vassal. As the weeks passed, Antonio became increasingly abusive, using coarse language and forcing her to stand for hours at a time to work with him in forming curds from goats' milk. She frequently felt faint and on two occasions lost consciousness and fell to the floor. It was not long before she surmised that her body could not bear the physical stress of standing for hours at a time and that she would eventually miscarry.

For Antonio, Lena's pregnancy signaled a revolt from his advances and he ceased to have sexual intercourse with her. Instead, he began to beat her. For two months, she bore the bruises he inflicted on her arms, legs and face, and stayed out of sight of anyone who might carry the word back to her parents. Only the danger to the baby she was carrying frightened her, but he had not struck her torso. She had traded the abhorrent sexual intimacy with the boorish and sickening Antonio for the pain of his thrashings.

Eventually, Antonio could no longer stand the self-imposed abstention and lashed out directly at the unborn baby by striking Lena in the stomach with a large wooden ladle. She had begun to feel movements inside her, but now the baby suddenly went limp. As Antonio approached her again, his face a twisted mass of rage and resentment, she produced a large butcher's knife that she had carefully concealed in her dress. He had done enough harm to her and the baby inside her and she would now defend her baby and herself to the death. Tears streamed down her face and her eyes became huge orbs bursting out of her bewildered face. As he reached out to snatch the knife from her hand, she plunged it directly into his heart. His fury turned suddenly benign and, finally, startled and disbelieving. As he looked impishly down the front of his shirt at the handle of the knife marking the spot in which the blade was imbedded, he dropped to the ground and bellowed like a cow begging to be milked. A torrent of blood spilled out, forming a dark pool below him on the floor. Within moments, he twitched convulsively and stopped breathing. A swarm of relief and despair came over Lena, a young girl who had taken matters into her own desperate hands in the hope of saving her baby from further abuse. It was too late. As she limped to her bed, her body bent in two, she could feel her insides quaking and releasing a flow of blood and clots from between her legs. Within moments, her tiny baby was born dead.

The inquest into her murder of Antonio concluded in short order. The overwhelming evidence of abuse gave credence to her account of the incident and she was quickly acquitted. She was free to go on with her life, but the tragic loss of her baby and the violence she experienced in the several months of marriage to Antonio transformed her into a bitter, hardened shrew. She promptly liquidated her deceased husband's estate and used the funds to flee from the family that had wantonly handed her off for their own purpose to a man they hardly knew. Having been captivated by the stories of gold-lined streets in America, she booked passage for New York, bribing officials with money and sexual favors wherever necessary to overcome the absence of official documents and her underage status. After working first in a laundry and later in a meat-packing plant, she settled down to operating the boarding house on E.11ᵗʰ St. for Domenico.

In almost two years of managing the boarding house at 302 E.11ᵗʰ Street, Lena has not earned Domenico's trust or approbation. He has concluded that she skims rents. This he learned from receiving protests from boarders whose rent had been increased but not reported to him. Perhaps less disturbing, the ambience of the building has changed for the worse. Caterina's custom of placing flowers on front-facing window sills has been discontinued; tenants are permitted to store their garbage in the hallways; and the aromatic quince that Caterina had nurtured and brought into the building from the back yard is no longer cultivated. Boarders seem less pleased with the food and the cleanliness of their accommodations. Vagrants have found their way back to the stoop of the building and Eileen's policeman brother, Dennis, is no longer overseeing security of the property, having been alienated by Lena. It is no wonder that Domenico is anxious to replace her.

Caterina decides to be forward with Lena. As Lena exits the building carrying garbage to an outside receptacle, Caterina approaches the younger woman directly, using her Calabrian dialect and origin to her advantage.

"Good morning, *signorina di Calabria*, may I have a word with you?"

Lena is startled by Caterina's tactic and is thrown off guard, less defensive than her normal self. Who can this woman be who is obviously a *paesana* and a very chic and attractive one at that?

"Do I know you?"

"We have never met. I am Caterina Brutto, your predecessor here on E.11th Street. May we talk?"

So that's it, Lena thinks, *Domenico has sent an emissary to wrest the property back into his control. I've heard about this woman so often, about how great she was in her time of running the boarding house and how tragic the death of her husband was. I'm tired of listening to it. Talking to her can only lead to one thing…losing my job and maybe even being deported if they find out that I'm an illegal resident.* Her antagonistic persona suddenly returns and she is back in control of her emotions. She shrieks at Caterina.

"No, I don't want to talk to you! And you can tell Domenico for me that he needn't send anyone here to fight his battles for him."

Lena turns and stomps inside the vestibule of the building, slamming the door behind her and locking it. Caterina is stunned by the depth of this young woman's anger. *It must be monstrous to lose your only child,* she thinks. *But, since she is now on notice of Domenico's intentions, I must act quickly.* She looks up at the house in the direction that Lena left.

"Very well, we'll have it your way."

►━►◉◃━◃

It is a dank morning and a light, cold rain is falling on the city. Lena is up in the early dawn, darning socks and stitching torn clothing. Her boarders will soon be awake and will want their breakfast of coffee and toasted, crusty bread. She thinks of the day a week ago when Caterina approached her, and it still bothers her to think about it. *Such nerve. Who does that bitch think she is? She was prepared to demand that I turn the house over to her. Fat chance. Domenico will have to move a derrick in here to get me out.*

There is a knock on the front door. She puts down her sewing and scurries down the dark hall. It could only be the bread delivery at this early hour. She is surprised as she looks out through the two sets of glass-paned doors in the entry hall to the faint dawning outdoors. There is the silhouette of a tall boy in a messenger uniform waiting patiently in the rain for her to open the door.

"Here's a message for you ma'am. You are Lena Mattera, are you not?"

"Yes, I am. What's this all about?"

"I've just come from the Immigration authorities and they are holding your brother, Pietro Corigliano, until you can claim him and take responsibility for him."

Lena is angry. She snatches the message from the boy and returns to her apartment. *Why is Pietro here, and what does he expect of me? I don't want to be near that family of mine ever again.* When she has had time to think calmly, her thoughts turn uncharacteristically tender. She imagines her brother, two years older than she, as a victim of the same parental indifference that she experienced. She deciphers that she must help him. She studies the message, an official communication of the Bureau of Immigration with an address on Ellis Island, and decides she will go to her brother's side.

It is mid morning by the time Lena arrives at Ellis Island, having completed her early morning chores and found a ride on a covered merchandise cart that had dropped off its wares and was returning to Mott Street. The driver had made a wide swing through the West Side so as to leave her off near her destination at South Ferry. She had sprinted the last two blocks in the drizzling rain to catch the launch to Ellis Island, and was the last to board.

Now on the island, she quickly determines the whereabouts of the issuer of the directive and is escorted to a room containing a table with four chairs. There is nothing else in the room except a lamp that hangs directly over the table lighting only the center of the room. A feeling of apprehension comes over her. It is not the atmosphere for one who has been asked to come at her own volition to give assistance to an arriving immigrant. Fifteen minutes pass before a uniformed immigration official enters the room and takes a seat across the table from her.

"Good morning, madam. My name is James Evans and I would like to ask you a few questions."

"I am here to assist my brother, Pietro Corigliano, as you requested I do."

"Yes, well, let's talk about you first. Can you identify yourself as Lena Mattera?"

Lena can feel her body tense. He is the man who wrote to her asking her to come to claim Pietro, but his stiff formality worries her.

"Yes, of course, here is the letter you sent me. It has my name and address on it."

"How about a more positive identification? Do you have a passport?"

Lena is feeling pressure. *Why is he asking that? This is about my brother, not about me. Have I made a mistake coming here?*

"No, I don't."

"How about a birth certificate or naturalization papers?"

"No, I'm sorry but I don't carry those on me. Why are you asking me that? I'm not the person needing help; I'm here to provide assistance."

"We first need to prove your identity before asking you to take on the responsibility for a new arrival."

Lena is very uncomfortable. She feels the heat thrown off by the lamp hanging over her head and begins to sweat. Breathing comes harder than it has for a long time. She regrets having decided to come to this place in the first place and decides to leave. She stands and walks toward the door.

"Mr. Evans, I'm sorry I took up your time. I'll have to go home to get my identification papers and come back."

The officer is silent. Lena reaches the door and turns the handle. The door is locked from the outside. A feeling of panic comes over her.

"Why is this door locked? I've done nothing wrong. Open this door and let me out."

"Lena Mattera, you are under arrest for falsifying documents that permitted you to enter the United States illegally. You will be held here on Ellis Island for a period of ten days pending proof that you are a legal resident of this country. Failing that, you will be deported to your country of origin."

The door is unlocked by a buxom matron who enters the room and asks Lena to follow her to a detention area. Lena is stunned. *So that was it. Caterina has turned me in to the authorities so she can take over the house.* Her anger is overwhelming. She looks at the expressionless matron and then at the somber immigration officer. There is no alternative but to do as they say. Blood rushes to her head and the room begins to spin. She blacks out and falls to floor.

Eileen McGinty and Caterina Brutto stand approvingly in the front hall of the boarding house at 302 E.11th Street. They are pleased with what has been accomplished in just a few days following notice that Lena Mattera would not be returning to the house, that she has been deported to Italy. The halls are free of stinking garbage, the aroma of quince fills the air and, most importantly, the vagrants are gone from the front steps. The bond of friendship between Eileen and Caterina has fueled the transformation of the house a second time, and the two women once more live as neighbors. To Domenico's great delight, Caterina has moved back into the house on E. 11th Street and has begun to operate it in the fashion that she and Raffaele did for a decade. Eileen's brother had cheerfully become the catalyst in bringing swift action by the Federal Immigration Bureau to deport Lena and in convincing the itinerants not to camp on Caterina's front stoop. In her usual fashion, Eileen is very complimentary of Caterina.

"Katie, you've done it again. The place is beautiful. Just don't leave us again and let that place get into the wrong hands."

Caterina gives Eileen a long, affectionate glance.

"You know that I could not have accomplished much without your help… and especially your brother's help, too."

In her most private moments, Caterina wonders about the woman she has, for her own purposes, delivered to the authorities in a cold manner not befitting her persona. She is aware of Lena's lurid background, but she feels the pangs of guilt nonetheless for having condemned this woman to deportation back to the Land that offered her very little.

⊱━━━◦━◦◦━━━⊰

Caterina wants never to receive another telegram. If there is one consistency in her life, it is the belief that telegrams are used to tell people very bad news. In a way, as the delivery boy approaches, he prepares the addressee to receive a shock simply by showing up with the small yellow envelope in his hand. But in the end, result for the reader is the same: telegrams breed shock, grief and often, bereavement. Caterina has had enough of that with the loss of Raffaele. Now that she's back on E. 11th Street, rain or shine, she has a full life; not the same as before, but with enough happiness to sustain her. Still, there are certain reckonings that will not be denied. When a telegram arrives, it must be opened immediately so that its message can be read and absorbed, its abbreviated sentences scrutinized over and over to ascertain that its meaning has been properly deciphered and understood. It is in this context that Caterina looks out onto the stoop as the Western Union delivery boy arrives seeking Caterina Brutto, a small yellow envelope in his hand. It is a cablegram from Italy.

Blessed Mother, what can this be? Maybe it's a mistake. It's happened to others before. Do I have to accept it? What if I don't? Terror fills Caterina's heart as she contemplates the message, then reaches out and signs for the small envelope that has her name typed clearly on the front, except that her surname is spelled with only one *t*. She walks slowly to her apartment and drops into a chair. She tears open the flap and reads the message:

> Dearest sister. Stop. Sorry to inform you that our
> Stepmother has died. Stop. Father deeply affected.
> Stop. Visit if you can. Stop. Saverio

Caterina leans back in her seat. Thank God. To her surprise, she is relieved more than shocked. It is not like the disaster that she was handed a year ago when she thought she herself would die of heartbreak. She is regretful for sure, but not shocked out of her senses. Not emotional. Not lost to the world. Her Stepmother, Elisabetta, came into her life as resentment, filling her mother's place in her father's heart. For a time she was hated. Acceptance took time and was aided by the accident of chance that Elisabetta was able to greatly assist Caterina in her time of need, providing the funds to get her to New York in search of Raffaele. Caterina thinks of how it is best that Elisabetta suffers no more from the terrible burns and the amputation of both arms. She mutters a prayer of devotion for Elisabetta's repose. There is a flash of regret that she did not rise to the occasion of caring for Elisabetta in her final days as her father had wished. How short a time it would have been and how huge an impact it would have made.

Visit Italy? No, Saverio, not likely. I have just returned to America and my focus is on restoring my life in New York, where I lived happily for so many years. Saverio and father will simply have to understand. It is not selfishness when one has been through the ravages of life such as I have. Perhaps next year. She moves from the chair to the bed, where she lies down and feels a tear stream from the corner of one eye and drop to the bed, evidence that there is emotion, after all. She becomes very pensive as she thinks of the new life that has evolved for her and the others in her life. There is pride in the fact that she is furtively pursued by many of the males who cross her path. They are mostly immigrants who are attracted by her beauty and know full well that she is a resourceful woman from an impressive Calabrian family. There is also Eileen's nephew, an Irishman who is less subtle in his approach to Caterina. He cares not about the connection to the Zinzi family in Gagliano. He is simply attracted by this handsome woman of 38 years who is very appealing and also available. His advances are obvious and frequent. They are tolerated by an uninterested Caterina only because of her fondness for Eileen. In her heart, she knows that no man can ever take Raffaele's place. There was too much chemistry, too much love and devotion to one another, too much hurdle to surmount for a new love to blossom. Their love flew in the face of Italian custom and convention and her father's strong will. No one could ever replace Raffaele, not those eyes that looked into her soul, not his strong arms that gave her gentle security, not his mind that was so totally engulfed in her. Nor does she need a man in her life to feel fulfilled. Her building, her boarders, her neighbors. They all need her and she needs them. Life is good. She has the independence she sought all of her youth and first achieved when she defied her father successfully and married Raffaele. Now she has the hope and reliance on others that is so necessary for her to feel alive. All that is left for her to wish for is the warm, clean air of Calabria, the sea breezes that blow gently across the land and refresh it every day, the glorious sun that never disappoints, its warm rays kissing rows of orchards every day and spawning their abundance. *Ah, bel Italia,* she thinks, *how is it possible that I can live happily here in this cold, hard place devoid of nature and alien in so many ways to your warmth, your people and your spirit? Still, I envy not your splendor. I am here where my Love is buried and I will live with his memory to the end of my days.*

Epilogue

The affluent young Calabrian woman whose deep infatuation with a field hand resulted in a breech in familial harmony had ended up in America. She had buried the love of her life there and found her calling in a new country operating a boarding house for immigrating Italians. Taking on the manual labor of housekeeping and cooking had proved not to be an obstacle for one who had grown up in comfort. At one point, her cleric brother, Saverio, demanded that she return to her family in Italy, as she was no longer a married woman. America was no place for a single Italian woman, he asserted. So strong was his sentiment that Caterina found it necessary to marry a second time in order to quell Saverio's criticism. For a moment in time, she yielded her fierce independence, in the most humbling manner, to the mores of a male dominated society that held great esteem for the clergy. Her union with Giuseppe Scozzafava was, at most, a marriage of convenience, the constant comparison to Raffaele a grating obstacle. Eventually, her brother Vincenzo's daughter, Catherine, whose mother had died in childbirth, would come to live with her in New York. It was Caterina's only experience at motherhood. She became known as Aunt Katie to her contemporaries in New York, the name dubbed by her friend, Eileen McGinty. In 1960, at age 85, Caterina passed away, her life of independence and resourcefulness over. She had known true love and given up much for the experience of living twelve years of her life with her *amore*.

Likewise, her sister, Concetta, found happiness in the life she and her true love had made in the reaches north of New York City. To her great joy, she and Antonio were finally able to marry in the Catholic Church following the death of Anita Ruggiero, Antonio's wife from his ill-fated first marriage. As

xii   ◈   Out of Calabria

they prospered in the New World, Antonio and Concetta provided guidance and connection for a gathering clan of immigrants of the Zinzi and Russo families and many of their Calabrian *paisani,* who were able to immigrate to America without the uncertainty that faced Concetta, Antonio and Raffaele.

Vitaliano Zinzi married yet again following the death of Elisabetta, and lost connection to the family as old age engulfed him. He lived to be 105. The young family priest, Saverio, was appointed as pastor of Our Lady of Mount Carmel church in Gagliano, where he resided for the rest of his life. The widowed Vincenzo eventually re-married and spawned a second family with wife Giovanna Marino. He eventually found his way to America as well, settling first in Minnesota and later in New Jersey.

Immigration to America did not come easy for the majority of Calabrians. Mostly, they were illiterate and had few possessions when they arrived. They either had no one to greet them or didn't know how to contact those persons who had preceded them. They were viewed by many Americans as parasites from the bowels of Southern Europe, interloping in a land that was largely developed by Northern Europeans; and despoiling the relationship of established locals with employers opting to retain the lower-paid immigrants. Calabrians were often viewed as criminals despite their individual leanings, simply because they were victims of the *Mana Nero,* an association of criminals who preyed on vulnerable immigrants struggling to find their way in a society disposed towards ignoring their plight. Still they came, an estimated one million immigrants, to settle in the land of promise. It was a journey that would eventually lead to achievement and integration into the fabric of America.

About The Author

Peter Chiarella started life in the Bedford-Stuyvesant section of Brooklyn in 1932. He was educated in the public school system and at St. John's University. Retired from the corporate world, Peter lives in Napa, California and enjoys the life of a gentleman farmer as a wine grape grower and vintner. He is married and has four children and two grandchildren.

The author's mother was born in Calabria, but was brought to America as a toddler when her mother died from an illness brought on by childbirth. She became the ward of her Aunt Katie, the principal character in Out of Calabria, and grew up in the Lower East Side of Manhattan. Just as Peter's previous book, Calabrian Tales, recounts unforgettable stories about his paternal roots, Out of Calabria recounts his maternal roots with powerful stories revealed by his mother and other family elders. Unwittingly, the two books reflect a very early feminist daring that impacted future generations of the family.

For as long as they can remember, the author and his brothers heard these stories at family gatherings and soaked them up like the gravy of a Sunday meal. Knowing Peter's love of history and of all things Italian, the family encouraged him to take on the task of writing two historical novels, reflecting on the struggle and compromises that past generations of his family endured in turn-of-the-century southern Italy and America. At times you will have to remind yourself that these are true stories with real people.

Family Relationships
And Character Descriptions

<u>Family Members</u>

<u>Other Characters</u>

Anita Ruggiero – Antonio's elderly first wife.
Dr. D'Angelo – Zinzi family physician in Gagliano.
Domenico Pascale – Owner of boarding houses.
The Egyptian – Nineteenth century embalmer and scientist.
Eileen McGinty – Next door neighbor on E.11th Street in Lower Manhattan.
Elisabetta Spadaro – Vitaliano's second wife.
Enzo Brutto – Raffaele's youngest brother.
Francesca Ciarelli – Gypsy fortune teller.
Giuseppe Rossi – Raffaele's first contact in America.
Lena Mattera – Ousted manager of E.11th Street house.
Luigi Castiglione – Recruiter of Italian immigrant workers.
Michele Barilla – Railroad gang companion to Raffaele.
Michela Brutto – Vitaliano's old flame, Raffaele's mother.
Nunzio Laguzza – Caterina's unsuccessful suitor.
Vito and Rosa Altamonte – Antonio's employers.

ISBN 142514218-4

9 781425 142186